The
House
on
Sun
Street

✴

The House on Sun Street

A NOVEL

Mojgan Ghazirad

Mojgan

— BLAIR —

Printed in the United States of America
Cover design by Laura Williams
Interior design by April Leidig

Blair is an imprint of Carolina Wren Press.

*The mission of Blair/Carolina Wren Press is to seek out, nurture,
and promote literary work by new and underrepresented writers.*

We gratefully acknowledge the ongoing support of general operations by the
Durham Arts Council's United Arts Fund and the North Carolina Arts Council.

Library of Congress Cataloging-in-Publication Data
Names: Qāzi'rād, Muzhgān, author.
Title: The house on Sun Street : a novel / Mojgan Ghazirad.
Description: [Durham] : Blair, [2023]
Identifiers: LCCN 2023017692 (print) | LCCN 2023017693 (ebook) |
ISBN 9781958888100 (hardcover) | ISBN 9781958888148 (ebook)
Subjects: LCSH: Qāzi'rād, Muzhgān—Fiction. | Iran—History—Revolution,
1979—Fiction. | LCGFT: Autobiographical fiction. | Novels.
Classification: LCC PS3617.A95 H68 2023 (print) | LCC PS3617.A95 (ebook) |
DDC 813/.6—dc23/eng/20230414
LC record available at https://lccn.loc.gov/2023017692
LC ebook record available at https://lccn.loc.gov/2023017693

To my parents,
Nasser and Shahin,
who endured the terror of
the Iranian Revolution

Author's Note

All the epigraphs set at the beginning of
each chapter are from the stories of *The Book
of a Thousand Nights and a Night,* an English
translation of *Alf Layla Wa Layla*
by Richard F. Burton.

Part One

✴ ✴ ✴

Grapes on the Kufi

Now he had two daughters, Shahrazad and Dunyazad
hight of whom the elder had perused the books, annals
and legends of preceding Kings, and the stories,
examples and instances of by-gone men and things.

"The Story of King Shahryar and His Brother"

Every time my grandfather Agha Joon turned his head, the silvery threads glittered on his kufi. A fine filigree of a vine tree was embroidered on that hat. I followed the twinkles that climbed the grapes and slid down the curly stems, fascinated by the flash dance of light on his head. I wished he would finish the conversation and pay attention to me. I was six years old then, and I had tried all day to be a good girl, not stamping on Agha Joon's beloved flowers when I ran after my younger sister Mar Mar while playing hide-and-seek. It was hard to be patient when he had promised us a magical gift.

We had gathered in my grandparents' house on Sun Street that night in August 1978. The house was surrounded by a vast garden in central Tehran, neighboring the mansion of Prince Shapour, the younger brother of Mohammad Reza Shah Pahlavi. We were sitting on a wooden divan in the garden, Mar Mar beside me playing with her bangs, listening to Agha Joon, Baba, and my uncle Reza as they talked about the Shah of Iran and the turmoil brewing in the country. Reza had brought the three wooden divans from the basement and had spread the paisley-patterned Kashan rugs on them after washing the scorching terrazzo tiles with cold water to cool down the terrace. The lanterns gleamed golden light over the intertwined carpet flowers and brought life to the parched garden. My grandmother Azra had placed her globe-shaped samovar on a birch table between the divans and brewed tea in a giant teapot on top of the samovar. Narrow-waisted istikans glistened in china saucers as she poured tea and placed the istikans on the tray. Maman and my aunts Leila and Saba were listening to the conversation and passing the tea tray among the family. Water burbled in the golden samovar, and the rich aroma of cardamom black tea wafted in the air as they drank and talked about the events happening in the country.

Reza, tall and slender, in his late twenties, was reading aloud from the *Kayhan* newspaper. He worked in Agha Joon's glaziery, and every day, on his way back home, he brought the afternoon newspaper. He had rough stubble on his jaw and had buttoned his sky-blue shirt up to his neck. His Adam's apple bobbed up and down in rage as he read in an irritated voice, the newspaper trembling in his hands. "Six hundred people burned alive in Cinema Rex Theater in Abadan. Three hundred and seventy-seven are dead, and the rest are in critical condition." Reza turned the page and continued to read: "Charred carcasses were found inside the ruins of the theater building. 'We smelled the smoke while we were watching the movie,' one of the survivors of the fire told our reporter in the hospital. 'People started talking to each other, wondering where the smoke was coming from. A few individuals rushed to the exit doors, but they were closed from outside. People swarmed toward the doors, yelling, screaming, and pushing each other to escape. We were locked in. Someone wanted to burn us alive!' The theater building collapsed into ashes. Half-burned doors had scratches over them from unfortunate victims pleading for their lives."

"La elah ella Allah! Who could've done this to the people?" Agha Joon said, tapping his forehead. His smooth, shiny skin extended from his bushy eyebrows all the way to the back of his scalp, where he'd pinned the kufi to his sparse gray hair. He wore that white kufi—the small round cotton hat some Muslim men wear—after his Hajj pilgrimage.

"This tyrannical dynasty would do whatever it can to halt the people's revolution, bloody murderers!" Reza said. He folded the newspaper and threw it at the center of the rug.

Baba listened to the news while he whirled the spoon in his istikan of tea. He had been staring at Reza with his steely eyes while he read. The hair above his ears was growing gray, but the rest of the short, kinky coils were still black. He shaved with double blades, his face always sleek and smooth. "It's too soon to say who has done this crime," Baba said.

"I've heard many were killed in the stampede beside the doors. Who orchestrated such an atrocious crime?" Agha Joon said.

"It might be the ones who want to make the whole situation muddy—Fedais, Marxists, Mujahedin, or Hezbeh Toodeh. No one knows," Baba said.

"No one belonging to the uprising would commit such a heinous crime. The revolution is already winning. We're winning! The Shah is living his last days," Reza said, directing his talk to Baba.

Baba bit his lips in silence and didn't reply. He scratched the scar he had under his left ear, a nervous habit of his when he found himself disagreeing. The smooth, pale scar was a mark he carried from a skin infection he contracted during the years he'd lived in army barracks close to the Iran-Iraq border. Years of service in the army as a high-ranking officer had forged in him a devout belief in Mohammad Reza Shah's military power.

I stood up on the divan and leaned forward on the carpet to see the newspaper up close. I gaped at the picture of a charred woman that occupied the front page. She had nail polish on the fingers that remained of her burned hand. She must have broken her nails as she'd desperately scratched and pushed the exit door. No one at that moment paid attention to me. My heart pounded as I pictured her banging, shouting, pleading for help as the blazing fire consumed her body.

As the conversation dwindled among the family, Azra emptied the water that had dribbled in the bowl underneath the globe-shaped samovar and blew the blue flame inside its chimney through the gridded opening. White smoke funneled up the samovar's chimney and vanished in the air. Maman helped Azra take the samovar and the tea set back to the kitchen. Leila and Saba brought mattresses and pillows from the guest bedroom, unfolded the mattresses on the divans, and covered them with white starched sheets. Reza erected the mosquito nets on the divans and made sure all the hems of the canopies were tucked under the mattresses.

Mar Mar and I slept on the middle divan, next to Agha Joon and Azra's mattress. The ivory canopy swayed with the cool night breeze, and its lacy knitted flowers quivered with the gentle wind. We placed our heads on down pillows, tucked our small bodies under a thin blanket, and waited impatiently for Agha Joon to come back. He'd gone to his room to bring the gift. What was he going to give us from his deep, shadowy closet? A talking doll he'd bought in Mecca during his pilgrimage? A sewing machine that worked without a hand wheel? A world map that would speak and give information if we touched a country? The night seemed too long for the anxious little girls who had been waiting since early morning. I watched the stars shining in the clear night sky of Tehran, hoping the serenity of the night would calm me. Even though I tried to think about Agha Joon's gift, I couldn't wipe the picture of the charred woman from my mind, how she'd screamed and scratched the door until the last minute before dying.

Finally, after what felt like a year, I heard Agha Joon's leather mules shuffling on the terrazzo tiles. He returned with a termeh—a special embroidered cloth he used to wrap important things—under his arm, lifted the net, and squatted to slide under the canopy. He placed the termeh beside his bolster and retucked the canopy's hem under the mattress so that no mosquito could sneak in after him. He took off the pin attached to his kufi and shoved the kufi under the bolster. He glanced at Azra, who was sound asleep.

"Do you want to hear a story?" he asked in a hushed voice.

"Yes," we said.

He placed the termeh on his lap and unfolded the sides, revealing an old bulky book. Was that his magical gift? The edges of the book's brown leather cover appeared jagged, but the spine looked sturdy and stable. There was a three-quarter profile of a young lady on the front cover. She had large, beautiful up-slanting eyes and straight black hair cascading down her shoulders.

"Who is this lady?" I asked.

"This is Shahrazad. Moji, if you're patient, you will hear her story." He cleared his throat and, with a voice that captured my heart he told the tale of Shahryar, the powerful king of Baghdad. On a trip to visit his brother in the neighboring country, the king finds out that his beautiful queen has betrayed him and slept with their slaves. Hapless and enraged, upon returning to his palace, he kills the queen in her sleep and vows in revenge to marry a girl every night, only to kill her the morning after the wedding.

At first, when Agha Joon started the story, I thought the profile on the front cover belonged to the queen. But as he spun the yarn, I became certain the image on the front cover had nothing to do with the queen. Scared and confused, Mar Mar and I squatted on the mattress and huddled together while we listened to his story. "Day after day," Agha Joon said, "a girl was killed until there was no unmarried girl left in town. King Shahryar had a vazir who had two daughters by the name of Shahrazad and Dunyazad. It was time for the vazir to offer his daughters to the king."

"Oh no," I said. "Are they going to get killed?"

"When the vazir told the story to his daughters, Shahrazad, the older daughter, who was very smart and knowledgeable, assured her father that she would marry the king and trick him out of killing her and her sister."

"What trick?" Mar Mar asked, her big black eyes wide open in the lantern light.

"Shahrazad told a story so fascinating that King Shahryar wanted to hear the rest the following night. He let her live for one more night—"

"What was the story, Agha Joon?"

"The rest, I'll tell tomorrow night. You need to go to sleep." He placed a folded paper between the pages to mark his place and wrapped the book back in the termeh.

We jumped out of our mattress, sat on his lap, and begged him to read a little more for us. He caressed both of us, kissed our hair, and tucked us under the blanket. He lay down and pulled the white linen over his feet. Soon I could hear him snoring. Mar Mar and I gazed at Tehran's night sky from underneath the mosquito canopy, enchanted by Agha Joon's story. We had no idea a revolution would ignite soon under those same glittering stars.

To me, Agha Joon became a completely different person when he took off his kufi, the wayfarer of long journeys transforming into an old man whose voice captivated my childhood dreams.

Every Thursday and Friday night, we would visit the house on Sun Street, and he would read from *One Thousand and One Nights* for me and Mar Mar. I often forgot he was the storyteller and let his voice carry me to faraway cities like Baghdad, Damascus, Basra, and ports I imagined sailing toward on a giant ship. I would envision my down pillow to be the vessel that floated on the teal blue seas. I plucked the feathers that stuck out of the cover, hoping I could call for an ifrit. In Agha Joon's stories, those ghostly creatures appeared when someone spoke a spell and burned a feather in a dark night. They became servants for the one who had conjured them and granted the master's wish. Ifrits frightened and fascinated me at the same time. They could take me to mysterious places and show me unimaginable things. They also possessed evil powers and could commit horrible crimes. Agha Joon reminded me not to pull the feathers out of the pillow as he read. He thought it was a bad habit to pluck one's dearest night companion. But what child could stand the temptation of feathers when she thought an ifrit might appear? Agha Joon never censored the stories for us children. Young beautiful women cheated on their husbands and sacrificed their lives for their loved ones. They were caught, tortured, and killed, their remains wrapped in rugs, placed inside chests, and thrown into deep blue seas, only to be found years later when a lonely sailor longed for a giant fish.

At dawn, I woke up shivering from cold. Mar Mar had wrapped the whole blanket around her legs, and there was nothing left to cover me. The cool breeze of early morning whistled through the Corsican pines in the garden. Agha Joon was gone, but everyone else was still asleep. The pigeons walked gently on the edge of the garden's russet brick wall, cooing to each other. In my childish imagination, I thought they were speaking in code.

Maybe they harbored an important message to me from Shahrazad. But ravens were hiding in the pines, and they crowed to break the encryption. The pigeons became silent and aborted their dispatch. I crept toward the edge of the divan, stretched out my legs, and slithered my feet into my wooden sandals. The slapping sound of the sandals on terrazzo tiles echoed in the stillness of the morning.

Agha Joon's kufi was moving between the branches of the vine tree near the garden's front gate. I dashed between the fig trees he had watered earlier in the morning and slipped into the slimy mud that covered the ground. A thick layer of muck stuck to my sandals and soiled the hem of my nightgown. He was trying to wrap the rambling branches of the vine tree that had toppled around the trellis.

"Salam, Agha Joon!" I shouted.

He was standing on the second rung of his narrow ladder, facing away from me. He peeked at me from under his armpit and noticed my dirty nightgown.

"What are you doing in the mud? If your mother finds out, you'll be in trouble."

I hesitated to answer, but I couldn't stand the urge to ask about last night's story. "Agha Joon, will Shahrazad survive at the end?"

He stopped doing what he was doing and stared at me for a few seconds. He pointed at a thin rope coiled beside the ladder with his chin and said, "Now that you're all muddy, why don't you help?"

I didn't budge. He stood still on the ladder, waiting for me to fetch the rope.

"Don't stand there staring! Pick up the rope and hand it to me!"

I fumbled with the ball of rope and stretched out my hands so that he could grab it. He uncoiled the rope and furled the vine around the main beam of the trellis. A bunch of champagne grapes touched the dome of his kufi. The golden gleam of dawn shimmered through the crossing beams. Tiny round grapes glistened everywhere, on the vine branches and on the silver threads of his kufi.

"Agha Joon, what story did Shahrazad tell the following night?"

He was a man of one task at a time. He could never stand children messing around in his garden, nor did he have the patience to answer a nosy six-year-old so early in the morning. He shouted from beneath the vine tree, "Tonight! The rest I will tell you tonight!"

Ifrit of the Crooked Vase

*But presently there came forth from the jar a smoke
which spired heavenward into ether (whereat he again
marveled with mighty marvel), and which trailed along
earth's surface till presently, having reached its full height,
the thick vapor condensed, and became an Ifrit, huge of
bulk, whose crest touched the clouds while his feet
were on the ground.*

"The Fisherman and the Jinni"

Maman claimed she had seen Prince Shapour from the rooftop of the house while he was strolling in his vibrant garden. I believed her, but every time I looked from the second-floor windows, I couldn't see anyone. The prince's beautiful mansion neighbored my grandfather's house, and the windows facing the backyard had a view to his garden. He was the younger brother of Mohammad Reza Shah, and he stood in for the Shah on many ceremonial occasions, especially the national sports events. Many people believed the prince was responsible for the mysterious death of the beloved Iranian wrestling champion Gholamreza Takhti. Rumor had it that he was outraged when he noticed the crowd didn't applaud for him as he entered the arena for the wrestling championships but cheered and hailed Takhti as soon as he stepped on the wrestling mat. His dark, dodgy reputation of being the murderer of the champion floated everywhere among the people of Iran.

Hidden between the crowded Corsican pines, we could only see Prince Shapour's mansion at night, like a constellation of glowing stars seen from afar. A giant shallow pool decorated the center of the courtyard. Water trickled from a circle of fountains in the pool, creating a mesmerizing scene with its harmonious cadence. Clean-cut boxwood shrubs snaked through the green grass and hedged a narrow cobblestoned path that vanished into the pines. If it weren't for the occasional view of the old, stooped gardener carrying his wheelbarrow around, planting white-purple violas and yellow daffodils in rows around the pool, I would have thought an ifrit had cast a spell onto the courtyard. No one walked in that luxurious garden. I conjured up the charming Prince Shapour treading the cobblestone path, bending over and sniffing the aroma of the blooming flowers. But I was never lucky enough to spot him.

The house on Sun Street was located in the royal neighborhood of central Tehran, and Marble Palace was a couple blocks away from it. Reza Shah, the founder of the Pahlavi Dynasty, lived in that palace, and after his death, from 1970 on, it became a museum of his heritage. The house was a two-story structure with spacious rooms. The lower rooms had French doors that opened to the terrace in the front garden, and the upper rooms had tall lattice windows decorated with stained glass. It usually took us about an hour to get to Agha Joon's house from our apartment, which was located on the northeastern side of Tehran. I loved my grandparents' house more than our apartment. Except for the guest room and Agha Joon's room, I could play in any corner of that giant house. Once a week we visited my grandparents and stayed with them for the weekend. Some days even during the week, Maman took us there so that Azra could take care of us while she attended after-school meetings at the middle school where she taught mathematics.

Agha Joon's room was on the first floor, overlooking the back garden. Golden-straw shades rolled over the stained-glass windows, giving a misty look to the objects in his room. There was a floor-to-ceiling closet embedded in the wall opposite the window. A tall mirror was hung on the closet door, reflecting the colorful light that combed through the blinds. Agha Joon didn't let anyone enter his room, let alone allow a curious girl like me to peek into his closet. A couple of weeks after he'd started reading *One Thousand and One Nights*, I snuck into his room when he was busy with the fig trees in the front garden. Mar Mar was helping Agha Joon outside, and Azra was cooking her favorite aash in the kitchen. I left the garden to go to the bathroom. When I came out of the bathroom, I noticed the door to his room ajar. All the magical gifts were coming out of the closet in that room. How could I resist the temptation to get a closer look?

I crept into his room. The closet door squeaked as I slid in the space between the door and the shelves. I could perfectly fit in that space even when the door was shut. The closet was full of mysterious things, as if an ifrit had cluttered his treasures in it. I spotted Agha Joon's book on the middle shelf. I unwrapped the termeh and peeked through its rose-water-scented pages. I loved the touch of the old, yellow papers on my fingertips. In the dim light that seeped from the room, I saw drawings of beautiful ladies dancing with long patterned skirts, naked girls with upright breasts swimming in a large pool, a young lad peeking at them from behind the trees. I was fascinated by their nakedness and the playful poses they struck in the pool. They were the ravishing women of *One Thousand and One Nights*, whose stories Agha Joon had only begun to tell us.

In the dark, I noticed a narrow, crooked-neck vase with a mouth resembling a big eye. Its opening was clogged with a cork. No flower stem could be placed in that glass vase, nor could it be used as a pitcher with its strange crooked neck. I put the book back on the shelf and carefully took the vase. I unscrewed the cork and sniffed the inside. It didn't smell of any particular scent. I thought it could be a perfect place to ensnare an evil ifrit—like the winged creature Agha Joon had described the night before. King Solomon had detained that ifrit in a jar, sealed and placed it in a chest, and thrown the chest into the Mediterranean Sea. One thousand years later a poor fisherman had pulled the chest in his trawler's net and broken Solomon's seal. Out of bad luck he'd freed the ifrit. Suddenly, I heard a high-pitched screech. Was it the ifrit wailing in the vase, trying to get out? Terrified to death, I realized the grave mistake I'd made. What if an ifrit was trapped in that crooked vase? I wished I could utter the spell that could instantly take me to the garden. I didn't want the ifrit to appear in front of me. My heart raced like the poor fisherman's when he first saw the body of smoke spiraling into the sky from the jar. I was sure it could take my life at any moment. I shoved the cork into the vase, placed it back on the shelf, and dashed across Agha Joon's room into the garden.

Agha Joon was trimming the withered leaves from the fig tree. Mar Mar followed him, picking up the fallen ripe figs in a small straw basket. She had on her cotton trapeze dress and wooden sandals—just like the ones I had. Her straight black hair caressed her plump cheeks when she bent down to fetch the figs. Maman always gave her a bob haircut that fell just below her ears with bangs covering her arched black eyebrows.

She simpered with surprise when she saw me. "Why did it take you so long to come back?"

I clung to the fig tree, panting and all sweaty.

Agha Joon stopped cutting a dry branch and said, "Where have you been? Why are you so pale?"

"I am fine, Agha Joon."

When he turned his face back to the fig tree, I whispered into Mar Mar's ear, "I saw a real ifrit in Agha Joon's closet."

"No way!" She knitted her eyebrows. "Didn't Agha Joon say not to go near his closet?"

She tried to be serious, looking hilarious in her five-year-old stern gesture. Her deep dimples appeared even with the slightest upward movement of her lips. I liked her honeyed voice, even when she reprimanded me. She always reminded me about the things Maman and Baba had told us not to do. The feeling of the ifrit's presence was so real that I was convinced it lived in that vase. I never got close to the closet again, knowing there was a reason Agha Joon didn't like anyone to go to his room in his absence.

I spent the afternoon with Mar Mar sliding down the railing of the stony staircase at the center of the house. We played a game and raced up the stairs, stepping on specific flowers woven in the carpet that covered the stairsteps. I stepped on the navy blues, and Mar Mar on the crimson reds. The winner got extra turns sliding down the railing. That afternoon I lost every time we played. I suspected my mind was distracted by the ifrit who'd escaped the crooked vase and was haunting me while we played.

I could not sleep that night. My feet hurt from stamping the rug flowers on the stairs. I whimpered under the thin blanket, feeling petrified and powerless in the hands of Solomon's ifrit. It could be sneaking under the divans, waiting for everyone to go to sleep to set the terrace on fire.

"What's the matter, Moji?" Agha Joon tossed in his mattress and stretched his hand to reach for the book.

I sniffed. I didn't answer.

"Are you scared of something?"

"No, no, I am not scared of no ifrit." I wiped my nose with the edge of the blanket.

He smiled and nodded, as if he knew where the ifrit was hiding. He opened his book and said, "Where was I last night?"

"Where the ifrit flew into the sky," I said.

"Oh, I remember . . . the ifrit looked down at the fisherman and told him he can choose how he'd like to die. The fisherman said, 'What have I done to you but to free you from the jar? Why do you want to kill me?' 'For one thousand years,' the ifrit said, 'I lived in the jar. The first hundred years, I promised I would grant the wishes of the man who frees me. But no one came. Four hundred more years passed, and I got enraged. I vowed to myself I would kill anyone who releases me at last.' But the fisherman thought to himself, 'I have the intelligence and wisdom of a human being. I can outwit this evil creature.' He looked up at the ifrit and said, 'I only have one question before you take my life. How did you fit in this little jar?' 'You question my power?' 'Nay. I just wonder.' 'I'll show you.' The ifrit turned into smoke and swirled back into the bottle. The fisherman immediately capped the jar and said to the ifrit, 'I'll throw you back into the sea and I'll build a lodge in the beach, telling every fisherman there is an evil ifrit in a jar in this sea. Don't you ever release him from the jar.'"

Agha Joon glanced at me and Mar Mar, wondering if we'd fallen asleep. As he finished the story, I knew he had ensnared the ifrit back in its crooked vase. He who owned the beautiful house on Sun Street and cared for the vines and fig trees had the wisdom to trap my childish fears and anxieties. Finally, I could sleep. The full moon winked at me through the knitted flowers of the ivory canopy. I could smell the honeysuckles that saturated the night with the sweet aroma of their nectaries.

✳ ✳ ✳

Badr-al-Budur

*This thou must traverse by a path thou wilt see in front
of thee measuring some fifty cubits long, beyond which
thou wilt come upon an open saloon and therein a ladder
of some thirty rungs. Thou shalt there find a
Lamp hanging from its ceiling.*

———

"Aladdin; Or, the Wonderful Lamp"

On a wintery night in 1978, Agha Joon told us the story of
"Aladdin and the Magic Lamp." Azra had erected a korsi in the
living room—a traditional, mother-made piece of furniture Iranians use to keep warm in winter nights. She'd spread a gigantic
square quilt over a low-lying table and placed a round brazier
full of burning charcoal under the table. We gathered around
the korsi, covered our legs with the quilt, and let the charcoals
warm us through the night.

I hid my head under the quilt when Agha Joon mentioned
the Moorman in the Aladdin story. I imagined those glowing
pieces of charcoal were the jewels Aladdin saw deep in the
cave. Agha Joon said the princess that Aladdin fell in love with
was named Badr-al-Budur. Mar Mar and I both laughed at her
odd name and wondered why the storyteller had chosen such
a funny name for the princess. "She was a beautiful Chinese
princess with a pale round face like a moon." Agha Joon told us
that names in the East have meanings and Badr-al-Budur meant
full moon of the full moons in Arabic.

As he described the virtues of the princess, I fell in love with her just like Aladdin. It was the first time I heard about love. He painted the immaculate, pallid face of love in front of my eyes, and the unblemished tableau of Badr-al-Budur enchanted me for years. Never did he elucidate how a person can fall in love at first sight, nor did he enlighten me about the blinding consequences of love. Badr-al-Budur had soft black hair circling her attractive, almond-shaped eyes—the measure of beauty in Persian literature. Serene and reposed, she was a perfect pitch for a little girl's fantasy. I was obsessed with her during my childhood, and she became the model of feminine beauty in my mind. Years later, when I saw the Disney production of Aladdin, I noticed the huge difference between what I imagined in my childhood and what was portrayed in that animated movie. Princess Jasmine was never like the pale, moonfaced Badr-al-Budur I adored. How could a girl with bull-sized eyes and a triangular face resemble a full moon? I felt lucky that nobody painted the image of beautiful ladies in front of my eyes. I was left alone with my own imagination of heroes and heroines as I heard their stories. It was me, the silence of the mystifying nights of Tehran, and the sorcery of Agha Joon's suspenseful stories that captivated my dreams.

A few nights later, Mar Mar and I were brushing our teeth and getting ready to go to bed when the retro-style rotary phone rang in the hall. The only phone in my grandparents' house was placed on a round table near the staircase. I peeked through the bathroom door to see what was going on in the hall. Mar Mar tried to squeeze her head between mine and the bathroom door, her toothpaste-filled mouth touching my ear.

Uncle Reza answered the call. Most of the phone calls were for him anyway. He climbed a flight of stairs while he listened and cocked his head toward the staircase window. The phone's coiled cord stretched all the way, almost lifting the phone from the table. "Sobhan Allah!" he shouted. "Thanks for calling, Majid." He skipped down the stairs, hung up the phone, and rushed into the living room where Agha Joon and Baba were sitting around the korsi. I couldn't hear what he said, but I heard Baba's angry words.

"How can you believe such a hoax?"

"This is what everyone is seeing now in the sky. Is everyone lying?" Reza shouted back. He rushed out of the living room and ran toward the foyer. A gush of cold air swept in as he opened the door. After a couple of minutes, he came back with the wooden ladder—the one Agha Joon used to climb up against the brick wall to trim the trees. "Who's coming up to the roof with me?" he said, dragging the ladder upstairs.

I didn't know what Baba meant by *hoax*. It was the first time I was hearing that word from him. My earlobe was burning from Mar Mar's toothpaste, and I was sizzling to know what was happening in the sky. I ran upstairs on the spiral staircase, and Mar Mar chased after me. Leila and Saba came out of their room on the second floor. "What's going on, Reza?" Leila asked.

"Do you want to see the moon?" Reza said.

"What's wrong with the moon tonight?" Saba said.

"Come see it for yourselves."

We all followed Reza in the corridor between his bedroom and my aunts' room. The end of the corridor was separated from the second-floor hall by a slim door. As a nosy girl, I had peeked into that dim space many times, but except for the shelves full of homemade pickles, vinegars, juices, and jams, I'd never noticed any way to the roof. Reza slanted the ladder to the wall above the pickle shelves and climbed up to the ceiling. There, for the first time, I noticed the trapdoor in the ceiling. A stream of moonlight illuminated the pantry as Reza pulled down the wooden door. Fine white dust sprinkled down from the ceiling like stardust, smelling of lime and plaster. Reza heaved himself from the upper rung on to the roof and disappeared in the night sky. Fearless and swift, I climbed the first two rungs after him. Leila grabbed me by my armpits and didn't let me move up the rungs.

"Koja? The roof is not for kids," Leila said.

I clutched the sides of the ladder. "But I want to see the moon."

"No, you have to go back to the living room. It's dangerous up there."

"How do you know? How many times have you gone up there?" I insisted.

"Moji!" she shouted. "You're going to come down, or I'm going to call your dad."

She separated my hands from the ladder, but I wailed and insisted on climbing. I threw myself in a tantrum on the icy mosaic tiles of the pantry. Mar Mar started crying when she saw me hitting the tiles. Reza peeked through the trapdoor and said, "What's going on, Leila? Why don't you put their jackets on them and bring them up here with you?"

Soon I was in my warm wool jacket, climbing the ladder in Saba's arms. She was the plummy, warm-hearted aunt who could never stand to see us cry. Between tears and the trapdoor dust, the moon shone like the wonder lamp. It was so bright that I stretched my hand to touch it. There was a dreaming girl in me who hoped the magic of the lamp would work, and I could fetch the gleaming moon. Mar Mar clung to Leila's leg beside the ladder, waiting for us to pass through the trapdoor. The roof was flat and covered with tar, like most homes in Tehran. The edges of the roof were not much elevated from the roof itself. I pulled against Saba's tight grip, wanting to go near the edge to see the city from above, but she didn't let go of my hands. Leila put Mar Mar down beside me and clenched her hand as well.

Mar Mar reached for my hand, as she often did when she was scared. We gazed at the sky and the neighborhood. Candle lights sparkled on the roofs like stars fallen from the sky. I couldn't see anyone from afar, but people were chanting slogans I didn't quite understand. Their cries turned into a fearsome rumble, like thunder coming close.

"Look at the moon! Can you see his face?" Reza said.

"Whose face?" Leila asked.

"Imam Khomeini's face. People have spotted his face on the moon everywhere in Iran tonight." He shouted the loudest slogan I'd ever heard in my life, "Marg Bar Shah!"

"Who's Imam Khomeini, Uncle Reza?" I asked.

"He is the leader of our revolution. He is a holy man," he said.

"Is he a moonfaced prince?"

"No, he is the man of God who is going to throw away all the princes and princesses of this country and bring a new republic. Enough of two thousand, five hundred years of monarchy in Iran," he said. He pointed to the moon. "Look, Moji! Can you see him? His glorious eyes, his beard, his turban?"

He kept chanting along with the invisible, ghostlike neighbors who were shouting the same words. Leila and Saba repeated the slogans after him. Every time they shouted, a thin fog rolled out from their mouths. They were excited and full of happy vibes, passing their energy through the air, breaking the silence of the night with their overjoyed cries. I heard Khomeini's name for the first time that night. The man whose face was claimed to be reflected on the moon, the man who would change the lives of all Iranians in an unforgettable way.

We stood on the roof shivering from the cold, gaping at the moon and desperately trying to find Khomeini's face. Maybe they saw a nose in the center, a beard on the lower half, an indentation of a dark turban on top and eyes hidden under unkempt eyebrows. Maybe they saw all this, maybe not. But I heard them chuckling and chatting about it in between their chants. Mar Mar held my hand the entire time, snuggling close to me. Even though she was one year younger than me, she had the patience of an old man. When all the chanting became silent, she brought her head close to mine and whispered, "Moji, I didn't see anything, did you?"

"No." I shrugged. "But maybe we'll see it when we get older."

I believe it was not only us who struggled to carve out a face in the full moon that night. We were, for sure, not the first nation to invent this phenomenon. Perhaps the Chinese had envisioned their princes and princesses on the moon, naming them full moon of the full moons before us. The name traveled perilous paths in deep hollows and high mountains from east to west, got translated to Arabic, and became Badr-al-Budur. Perhaps Arabs couldn't have invented the stories of *One Thousand and One Nights* suddenly out of the blue in one night. They must have heard the stories from Samarkand to Shiraz to Baghdad, and finally, an ingenious narrator gathered the stories and retold them in the lilting voice of a lady in dire straits to make them last for eternity in the hearts and minds of eastern people. Perhaps we were not the only nation who, in vain, dipped into the dark ditch of sorcery or soared into the sky to sketch the guise of a hero on the moon. It was mankind's imagination at work.

✳ ✳ ✳

A Shah on a Horse

*Then came forward the Persian sage and,
prostrating himself before the King, presented him
with a horse of the blackest ebony wood inlaid with gold
and jewels, and ready harnessed with saddle, bridle,
and stirrups such as befit kings.*

———

"The Ebony Horse"

Baba became ruffled by the "moon sighting" event that night. He didn't appreciate Reza taking us to the roof to observe—in his opinion—such nonsense. He didn't confront Reza that night but, as I found out later, he left early before dawn for the army base and asked Maman to leave Agha Joon's house as soon as she could.

It was snowing in Tehran when I woke up that morning. Snowflakes had gathered in the corners of the living room's French doors, covering the right angles of the windowpanes in soft white curves. Maman had spread the white tablecloth on the living room rug for the breakfast. She had placed lavash naans, leeghvan cheese, and different Azra-made jams on the sides of the tablecloth. Azra was sitting next to the samovar to pour tea for everyone. She didn't have a pleasant mood most mornings, and that morning was no exception. Maman picked a few whole figs from the jam bowl and placed them in the saucer in front of me.

"Spread them on your noon o panir and eat them after the tea."

I didn't like the small fig seeds scattering everywhere on the bread. The tiny seeds got trapped between my teeth, and I hated brushing my teeth again after breakfast. I took a bite from the bread and cheese, refusing to add the fig.

She cut two whole figs in halves and said, "You need to eat this, Moji. It's good for you." She was wearing her sapphire dashiki—a gift Agha Joon had brought for her from his pilgrimage to Mecca. She stared at me with her nut-brown eyes, waiting for me to swallow the fig.

I picked a half fig from its stem and said, "But I am full, Maman. My stomach aches already." Maman shook her head. I had no choice but to force the fuzzy half-sphere into my mouth.

"You've spoiled these girls as if they're the Shah's daughters in the Marble Palace!" Azra grumbled.

Maman glanced at Azra and shoved another half into my mouth. "They're just picky eaters. There is nothing wrong with the way they are raised."

"Don't nag, Moji. You need to finish your fig," Leila said. She was my outspoken, seventeen-year-old aunt in her final year of high school. Her luminous curly hair had caramel lowlights, and among her sisters, she had the fairest skin. She was almost always in slacks that covered her ankles and hid her slim body. She followed the unrest of the country carefully and had her own voice among the men of the house. Even though Agha Joon never attended formal school himself, he wanted his daughters to have higher education and supported their decision to go to the university. Leila was the most ambitious girl among his daughters and wanted to become a medical doctor. She was studying hard to prepare for the medical school exam the next summer. "People have reported from different cities, spotting Ayatollah Khomeini's face on the moon." Leila turned the morning newspaper to read the continued report from the front page.

"Leila jan, aren't there better stories to read?" Maman asked.

"Yes," Leila said, folding the newspaper, "but don't you want to know what is happening in the country?"

"Of course, I would love to," Maman said, "but this is not news. This is a lie, a shameful trick to exploit people's pure affection."

Saba glanced at Maman but said nothing. She was a year younger than Leila, had a reserved nature, and seldom joined the family's heated political conversations. She never failed to match her long maxi skirts with her earrings, even on lazy summer days.

I was too young to understand what Maman was saying to Leila, but from the gestures of my aunts and my mother, I could tell no one wanted to bring last night's topic to breakfast. I stood up and shook the bread crumps off my knitted wool dress. As I ran toward the door, Maman said, "Where're you going, Moji? You didn't finish your figs."

"I want to go to Agha Joon's room."

It was Agha Joon's habit in cold months, when there was not much to do in the garden, to get up early in the morning before sunrise, stroll down Sun Street, and buy a newspaper and a couple of fresh baked lavash naans for breakfast. Twice a week he went to his glaziery in Tehran's Grand Bazaar to oversee the workers. That morning he was home, working on his accounting books.

"You and Mar Mar need to get ready. We're heading home," Maman said.

"But Agha Joon wants to tell us the horse story tonight," I said.

"Maman, you said we're staying tonight," Mar Mar said.

"No, we're not staying. Baba is not coming back here tonight." She gathered our plates and swept the bread crumbs from the rug to the tablecloth.

"But I want to hear Agha Joon's story." I stamped my feet and jumped up and down on the rug.

"No!" Maman frowned.

I darted toward Agha Joon's room. I was resentful, feeling everyone was cruel at that moment. Maman, Leila, Saba, and even Azra, who didn't ask Maman to stay. I knocked on his door. "Agha Joon! Agha Joon!" He was hard of hearing so I kept yelling his name behind the door.

"Biya too," he replied in a loud voice. He had his pen in his left hand, his right hand lying over a giant book of numbers. He looked at me from above his half glasses and furrowed his broad forehead. "What's going on, Moji?"

"Maman wants to take us home now," I said. "She won't let us stay tonight."

"Baba asked your mother to take you home," he said.

"But Agha Joon, you promised you would read the horse story tonight." I was in tears. All week I had longed to come to Agha Joon's house to hear his stories. If we left, I had to wait another week. "Can you ask Maman to stay? She is your daughter. She should listen to you."

He sighed, took off his glasses, and rubbed his almost bald head. Even though I was young, I saw the signs of his surrender to my request. He acted tough and wanted to have the impenetrable façade of a cranky old man, but he was not even close. "Fine," he said. "Go get your mother."

Agha Joon read "The Ebony Horse" for me and Mar Mar that morning. Azra prepared some quick-made Barley aash for lunch, and we went back home in Maman's marina blue Volkswagen Beetle early in the afternoon. The sunshine had melted the morning snow, and the roads were covered with slush. Mar

Mar fell asleep in the car, resting her head on my shoulder. A few strands of hair tickled my ears as the Beetle jolted along the snow piles. Her dimples appeared even in her sleep. She must have been dreaming a pleasant dream. Cars drove slowly and kept distance from one another at traffic lights. I had started school in September, so I was able to pick up words on the signs, the store names, and the slogans written on the walls. I knew the streets Maman took to drive back home by heart. But in those days, the streets looked different every time we passed. Every night a new slogan was written on the walls. Paper placards were glued to the lampposts, and bus stop benches were painted with words. I remember there was something peculiar about a slogan written on most walls. It was a three-word death slogan. I knew the first two words, *death* and *to*. But I couldn't read the last word, since it was written in an awkward way and, most of the time, in red. Maman stopped behind a traffic light at the corner of a high school. A giant graffiti-like type of that slogan was drawn on the wall.

"Maman, what's written in red at the end of that sentence?"

She glanced at the slogan from her side window. "It's the word *shah* written upside down," she said. "It is the letter shin attached to alef and ha."

"Why do they write it like this?" I asked.

Maman shrugged her shoulders and didn't answer my question. She never answered when she was preoccupied with something. We were caught behind the traffic light for the third time. She pressed the lighter button in the dashboard, took a Winston cigarette from her brown leather purse, and lit it with the glowing lighter when it popped out. She glared at me with her all-knowing eyes in the rearview mirror and said, "You don't tell Baba what time we came home, chashm?"

"Chashm, Maman," I said.

She took a deep puff of her cigarette, changed gears, and crossed the intersection.

———————

Baba came home at night with a soldier who carried a giant rectangular cardboard box with him. We often had young soldiers who came to our house and helped Maman with everyday chores. They loved working in our house since she made delicious food for them and the house job was much easier in comparison to the army base work. Maman looked at Baba with surprise as the soldier passed the cardboard box through the front door. She warned us to move away from the door so he wouldn't accidentally hit us with that mysterious object. Baba helped him by holding and directing the opposite side of the cardboard. The young soldier placed it at the corner of the guest room, leaning on the wall. I had never seen such a gigantic object in my life. Mar Mar tried to peek through the narrow opening at the edge of the box.

"Go get a knife from the kitchen," Baba said to the soldier.

He fetched a sharp knife and came toward the box. Scared of the knife, we retreated behind the sofa and peeked at him as he cut the cardboard. After a few minutes, a majestic wooden frame of a painting emerged. Hooves and legs of a sable mare in grassland appeared next, and finally the imperial effigy of Mohammad Reza Pahlavi, the Shah of Iran, loomed large in the absolute silence of the room. Donned in his strapped, medallion-embellished uniform, a bejeweled crown on his head, he glared at us, auspicious and proud.

"What is this?" Maman asked.

"This is . . . a gift from His Highness for the years I served the army."

"They've accepted your early retirement?"

"Yes, they have."

Early in summer, Baba had applied for postgraduate programs at different universities in the United States, and late in November he heard back from the University of Alabama in Huntsville—where his cousin was a student. When he broke the news to Maman, she laughed out loud and said he must be joking. She said they couldn't be serious granting admission to a forty-some-year-old man from a country on the other side of the planet. Baba showed the official admission letter to her, bearing the raised stamp of the university at its bottom. A week later, Baba wrote his early retirement request to the army headquarters, but nobody—even himself—thought the request would be accepted.

Maman took a deep breath and became silent. The soldier saluted, and Baba dismissed him. After he left the room, Baba leaned on the doorframe and stared at Maman. She walked to the painting and gaped at Mohammad Reza Shah's crown screaming in the serenity of the scenery. She turned back and said, "I thought they'd never accept your early retirement in this time of need."

Baba nodded. "Well, the situation is perilous for the high-ranking officers. The major general is accepting retirement requests for the ones who want to leave the country."

"So, the situation is getting out of control, even for the army?"

Baba remained silent.

Maman raked her fingers through her hair and struggled to keep calm. "What were you thinking when you brought this home?"

"What do you mean?"

"Don't you think we would be in trouble with such gigantic portrait of the Shah in our apartment? At a time most Iranians loathe him?"

"We don't loathe him."

"Soon you're going to leave the country. What am I going to do with this, alone with the kids?"

"There was no room for objection, azizam. I had to accept it."

Maman didn't say anything else. She pursed her lips and went out of the guest room, a habit of hers when she got irritated by the conversation.

Baba peeked at us after she left the room. He noticed Mar Mar and me standing behind the sofa. He never wanted us to feel disheartened after their heated conversations. He winked at us as he tapped his legs and said, "Who wants to climb?"

We both ran toward him. One at a time, he held our hands and helped us climb his legs until we reached his neck. We played a game with the scar he had on his neck. The scar had a perfect circle shape, hairless and smooth. We tried to touch its center once we reached his neck. He'd told us the center of the scar was his most ticklish spot, and if we could touch it, he would giggle for a long time. He covered the scar with one hand while he held us with the other. We wrestled to remove his hand and touch the scar. We always won. He laughed and tickled our tummies in return.

After half an hour, we all started to pant. Mar Mar and I were both flushed and our bellies hurt from laughing. We collapsed on the floor to catch our breath. Baba sat on the sofa and leaned back to rest. Sweat had trickled down his hairline in front of his ears. He dried the corners of his face with his uniform's sleeves. I began to process the news. The man sitting on the sofa, my Baba, was going to America.

"Baba," I whispered, "are you going to leave us?"

Baba looked at me and smiled. "We're all going to go. I'm just going a little sooner to prepare a place for you to come."

"Why is Maman upset?" I asked.

"She'll be fine. She is a strong woman." He nodded. "We just have to live apart for a short time." He stood up from his place and paced toward the painting. He stared at the Shah and his black mare. "What story did Agha Joon tell you last night?"

"The horse story!" Mar Mar yelled with excitement. She sprang from the floor and darted toward Baba. I don't think she grasped the magnitude and consequence of Baba's news.

"Really? Like this one?" Baba said. Mar Mar stood beside Baba. She was shorter than his waist.

"Yes," she said, "Ebony. Agha Joon said her name was Ebony. The princess circled her hands around the prince and rode the horse with him. Did you know Ebony had a button behind her ear?"

"For what?" Baba asked.

"Mar Mar, her name was not Ebony. She was made of ebony," I said. I stood up and joined them beside the frame.

"The horse flew when the prince pushed the button," Mar Mar said.

"Really?" Baba furrowed his forehead with surprise.

Mar Mar nodded a few times. Her straight black hair swayed back and forth around her face. She felt triumphant to tell Baba something he didn't know. She sashayed in front of the portrait, joyful to have a new object to play with. Mar Mar stretched on her toes and touched the mare's ears. She pressed the ears, hoping something would happen.

I was enchanted by the beauty and charm of the painting like Mar Mar. The stealthy look in the mare's giant eyes invited us to caress her hair. It was a pitch-perfect portrait for the story Agha Joon had told us that morning. The sable mare was probably the same ilk of the ebony horse the Persian sage brought as a gift for the king. Even though I sensed the menace hovering around us, I had no idea how critical the country's political situation was getting.

Mohammad Reza Shah stared at us while we played with the mare. Caged in the frame, he had no power or authority to chase away two young girls fiddling with his horse. The case was the same outside in real life. People were chanting death slogans toward him from every rooftop in the country. His name was printed upside down in all streets and alleys, his glory washed away by waves of fury. He had no choice but to dismount the horse of power and leave the country.

The Shah's Statue

The King marveled and asked him, "What maketh thee weep, O young man?" and he answered, "How should I not weep, when this is my case!" Thereupon he put out his hand and raised the skirt of his garment, when lo! the lower half of him appeared stone down to his feet while from his navel to the hair of his head he was man.

———

"The Tale of the Ensorcelled Prince"

Leila and Saba shared a spacious bedroom on the second floor that had a view to the garden. The straw blinds hanging in front of the windows protected the room from direct sunshine and made the space dreamy—the way my aunts liked it. The V-shaped leaves of Corsican pines covered the window ledges all year long. I peeked through the straw blinds to watch the pigeons piling up pine needles for a nest at the far end of the ledge. The room was like a treasure island for me and Mar Mar. All we dreamed of having as young girls could be found in that room. Their makeup vanity set was made from black lacquered wood hemmed by a fine golden strip. I stood beside the mirror for a long time and watched Saba applying her makeup. She outlined a perfect arch for her eyebrows with the brow pen and plucked the hair outside the arch one by one. The eyeliners had the softest-ever leads, and her eyelids glittered the moment she finished coloring them. She sometimes let me roll her strawberry lip gloss over my lips. I still remember the stingy sweet sensation it left.

Old vinyl records were strewn everywhere on the rug. I never saw the records organized and placed on the shelves in that room. Colorful pictures of famous Iranian pop singers appeared on the record jackets on the floor and on the posters on the walls. Leila played the gramophone all day, sang along with the singers, and twirled from the bedroom to the hall, on the stairs, in the kitchen, and in every meter of the house. She knew the lyrics of those songs by heart. Her silvery voice echoed like the beautiful tones of a dulcimer through the rooms. "Can you turn off that music? Kar shodim be khoda!" Azra often yelled from the kitchen. But the music was loud, and Leila didn't hear anything—and even if she did, she never paid attention.

A few days after the moon sighting, Maman dropped us off at Agha Joon's house after school. She wanted to accompany Baba while he obtained his passport and other travel documents. Agha Joon had gone to the glaziery, and Azra was busy preparing dinner when we arrived. Mar Mar and I raced upstairs to my aunts' room as soon as we got there. Leila and Saba were getting ready to go out.

Leila was holding the hair iron in one hand and rolling up a thick lock of hair in her brush. "Why are you here today?" she said, surprised.

"Salam, Khaleh joon," I said, "Maman wanted to go with Baba to get his passport. Where are you going?"

She pressed the blades of the hair iron down on her caramel curls while holding the brush tight at the end. "To the street."

"Can we come with you?" Mar Mar asked.

Leila placed the hair iron on the vanity table and glanced at the straightened strands in the mirror. "No. You can't. We're going to attend an important demonstration. No place for kids."

Saba zipped her minijupe skirt and asked if I could button up her slate silk blouse from behind. She kneeled down so that I could reach her back. I parted her soft black tresses to reach the button and its loop. "Khaleh, what is a demonstration?" I asked.

Mar Mar put one of Saba's colorful headbands on her hair and looked at herself in the mirror. Maman usually placed headbands on her straight hair to keep it from falling into her eyes. She was fond of trying Saba's headbands on herself.

"Are you ready?" Reza knocked on the door.

"Almost. You can come in," Leila said.

Reza was surprised to see Mar Mar and me in the room. I told him the story and pleaded with him to take us out. It was fun to mingle and move around with them. They always went to cool places, lingered in front of cinemas, strolled in parks, and, most importantly, bought us chocolate-covered ice creams from Pasteur Confectionary. Reza said it would be fine for Mar Mar and me to accompany them.

"Are you serious?" Leila said.

"Why not?" Reza said.

"This is a real, true-to-the-cause action we're about to take. Why do you want to take the kids?"

"We're all in this together, young or old, it doesn't matter," Reza said. "They'll see the people's uproar and will cherish later that they were part of it."

Saba locked her golden hoop earring behind her ear and glanced at herself in the mirror. The earrings glittered between her tresses when she wiggled her head.

Reza glanced at Saba's tight minijupe skirt and furrowed his forehead. "Are you going to come like this?"

"What's wrong?" Saba asked.

"Well, one reason people are shouting in the streets is this."

He motioned his hand toward Saba from head to toe. "People don't want to see this French style, nude women everywhere."

"I'm going to wear my wool pants and a long coat on top," Saba said.

"But I thought these demonstrations are held to point out inequality and injustice, not how we dress!" Leila said.

"I understand, but at least change your skirt, Saba," Reza said.

Saba nodded and opened the closet. She slid the hangers on the wooden rod one by one and peeked at her different-length skirts, trying to decide which one to wear. She, unlike Leila, never confronted Reza.

"Why don't you two put your hats and coats on?" Reza said to us.

Mar Mar and I ran downstairs to fetch our coats. Azra came to the living room from the kitchen when Mar Mar was struggling to put her hand inside her coat's narrow sleeve. I had already buttoned up mine.

"Why are you wearing your coats?" she asked.

"Uncle Reza is going to take us out," Mar Mar said.

She helped Mar Mar slip her hand inside the sleeve. "Reza! Reza!" she hollered.

Reza walked into the living room. He was wearing a thick khaki coat over his sweater. "Bale khanoom joon?"

"Their mother will not be happy if she finds out you've taken the kids," she said.

"Well, then, she should not bring them here. If they're here, they're going wherever we go. Go get ready, Azra khanoom, you are coming too. It is time to celebrate."

"I can't walk too far with my knee pain," Azra said. "We are responsible for keeping Moji and Mar Mar safe."

"Don't worry, I'm with them. I want them to see these historic moments and remember."

Azra didn't insist anymore. Everyone trusted Reza. He seemed dependable and devoted to what he said.

A cold breeze swept our faces as soon as we stepped out of the house. Reza held Mar Mar in his arms, and I held Saba's hand as we walked from Sun Street to Vali-Ahd Street, Tehran's major north-south street. The closer we got, the sidewalks in front of the stores became more crowded. At that time, I didn't know what they meant by a *demonstration*. As soon as we turned from Pasteur Avenue to Vali-Ahd Street, I saw a sea of people in front of me. No car could pass. I clutched Saba's hand, terrified of getting lost in the crowd. Reza turned his face toward us and made sure we were behind him, holding on to each other. He raised his fist in the air and roared "Marg bar Shah" three times, like everyone else. It was the same death slogan I'd seen printed on the walls. We were pushed against each other and pulled back as if we were sailing ships in a tempest, unable to steer our way to a strand.

Mar Mar became scared. I heard her sobbing even though I couldn't see her face. I could distinguish her voice among the violent outcries. Between her sobs, she begged Reza to take her back home. I fidgeted as well, wanting to leave the demonstration. Leila picked me up and held me in her arms.

"Wasn't the best idea to bring them, Reza. I told you," Leila shouted out loud.

In Leila's arms, I could see Mar Mar's face. Tears had run on her cheeks and her lips were swollen red from the icy breeze. She tilted around to see where we were. I waved at her, elated to see her again. She beamed and dried her cheeks with her little fingers.

Every square meter of Vali-Ahd Street was filled with people. No space was left between the demonstrators' touching shoulders. I saw many pictures of Ayatollah Khomeini on placards floating among the crowd. He had such a ferocious frown and flaring eyes that no one, not even a six-year-old girl, could ever forget. Fists pumped up and down in the air. I imagined the people like the colorful fish in one of Agha Joon's stories. In revenge for the death of her beloved slave, the Vile Witch had turned the lower half of her husband, the King of the Black Islands, into stone. Then she had metamorphosed the citizens of the island into fish of different shapes and colors. In the crowd of demonstrators there were some women wearing scarves with not even a single lock of hair visible, some women fashionable like my aunts, some men with full beards, some men clean-shaven, and some with long hair like hippies. All bewitched, they yelled the same slogan over and over again.

We drifted to the heart of the crowd, 24 Esfand Square, where people had gathered around a bronze statue. The man in the statue wore military attire, a peaked cap on his head, and a sword strapped to his waist. With one hand on the sword and the other on his waist, he looked stern and sturdy. A row of soldiers had created a wall around the statue, safeguarding it from the people who had tried to climb the marble base and tear down the statue. Their commanders wore the same uniform Baba wore when he went to work.

"Khaleh Leila, is this the Shah?" I pointed to the statue.

"This is the statue of Reza Shah, the father of the Shah," she said.

"Why do people want the Shah dead?"

"Because he is a monarch and the age of the monarchy is over in Iran," Reza interjected.

"What is a monarchy?" I asked.

"Moji and Mar Mar," Reza said, "I brought you here to see the people's celebration. The son of the dictator you see up there is gone. Mohammad Reza Shah is ousted by the people. He has fled the country."

There among the people's jubilation, I heard the news of Mohammad Reza Shah's departure for the first time. We all faced the statue of Reza Shah, standing in the center of the square. The massive crowd chanted and screamed with joy. As dusk began to descend, Reza Shah's statue silently watched people wishing his son dead—incapable of executing any order or phrasing any objection to what people were saying against his dynasty. He resembled the half-stone king: cursed, condemned, and damned to a dark fate he had no way to flee. Was he in tears? From as far as I was, it was impossible to see.

A Woman Warrior

Then she considered awhile and said in her mind, "If I go
out and tell the varlets and let them learn that my husband
is lost, they will lust after me: there is no help for it but
I use stratagem." So she rose and donned some of her
husband's clothes and riding boots, and a turband like his,
drawing one corner of it across her face for a mouth-veil.

"The Tale of Kamar al-Zaman"

Baba left Iran exactly four days before the Islamic Revolution.
He got the United States visa the same day he went to the American Embassy on Roosevelt Avenue. Maman believed the dream
of Baba going to America was coming true faster than a sudden storm in early spring. After the Shah left Iran, Tehran's international airport, Mehrabad, was closed to prevent Ayatollah
Khomeini coming to the country from exile. But to everyone's
surprise, the temporary government started operating the airport after only a few days. Ayatollah Khomeini arrived in Tehran, and Baba flew to the United States.

We all gathered in Agha Joon's house before Baba's departure.
Azra made fesenjoon for lunch—a royal curry prepared with
ground walnuts and pomegranate sauce, the hallmark of a joyous ceremony in Persian tradition, served with saffron basmati
rice. Everyone except me loved the dish. We sat on the carpet
around the rectangular tablecloth Azra had spread out in the
living room. Agha Joon sat at the short end and leaned on the

cherry satin bolsters beside the wall. Baba sat at the other end. After the moon-sighting incident, this was the first time Baba and Reza were together in one place. Even though they kept their distance, they addressed each other with respect. There was an air of anxiety in the house, everyone fussing and fidgeting to make sure Baba's departure happened without delay.

Agha Joon ladled a scoop of fesenjoon on the rice in his plate and said, "Dast o panjat dard nakoneh, Azra khanoom."

"Thank you, Azra khanoom, for the fesenjoon. It is very delicious," Baba said. He passed the curry bowl to Maman, sitting next to him.

Mar Mar and I kept quiet while everyone praised Azra for preparing the delicious pomegranate sauce in the curry.

"So, when do you think the kids can join you in America?" Agha Joon asked.

"As soon as I find a decent place, I'll let you know."

Leila and Saba were sitting next to Maman, almost finished with their food. Leila had gathered her curls with a rubber band behind her head. She slid her plate from her side and said, "It would be so exciting to study in America. I've heard they have great schools."

"What's great about their schools?" Reza asked.

"One of my friends is planning to go to America. She says they have enormous libraries, ample resources for research, and excellent instructors," Leila said.

"There will be greater schools in Iran, Enshallah," Reza said. He nodded with certainty as he munched on his food.

"But who knows what's going to happen in this country," Leila said. She pointed to the TV stand in the living room corner. "Tomorrow they may close the universities, like the high schools and elementary schools that are closed right now. Everything is so unpredictable these days."

Throughout 1979, schools were closed on and off due to the

unrest in the country. Two days we went to school, three days we were off. I enjoyed going to school since I learned new parts of the alphabet every day. But I also enjoyed staying at home and playing with Mar Mar.

"It won't stay like this forever," Reza said. He placed his spoon on his plate and crossed his arms on his chest. "Imam Khomeini's movement will bring equality and justice to this country. Our resources will be spent for the Iranian people." He unfolded his arms and tapped the tablecloth with his fingers. "Our oil money will come to this sofreh, to help the people and to develop universities in Iran. He'll not let Americans steal our oil."

For a moment, everyone became silent. Baba put his spoon down and took a deep breath. He always ate with patience, and there was still plenty of rice on his plate. Maman bent over to fetch the doogh pitcher. The silence broke as she stirred the spatula in the pitcher, poured a glass of doogh for Baba, and handed it to him. Baba ignored what Reza said and turned his face to Agha Joon. "Zire saye shoma, the girls will be fine."

Agha Joon picked the small grains of rice that were scattered on the tablecloth and threw them on his empty plate. "Enshallah, don't worry about them."

"But we are going to miss having dinner together," Azra said. She shook her head and bit her thin lips, reminding us that this one was the last.

"And miss many other things," Reza said and turned to Baba, "like seeing the dawn of freedom in Iran!"

"Iran has always been free," Baba said with patience.

"Salavat befrestin," Agha Joon said. He scooted back and leaned on the bolsters. "Reza jan, he is traveling tonight. He has a long way to go. This is not the best time for a political talk."

Maman bent over the tablecloth and fetched the empty plates in front of everyone. The clatter of the plates put an end to Reza's argument. She rose from the floor, juggling the plates in hand, and headed toward the living room door. As she opened the door with her foot, she turned her head toward Agha Joon and Baba. "We'll be fine," she said, "don't you worry about us."

Agha Joon laughed. "Pir shi dokhtar. I'm sure you'll be fine."

Baba and Reza didn't say anything more. Leila and Saba gathered the utensils, folded the sides of the tablecloth, and carried it to the kitchen's back garden. Pigeons loved to eat the leftover rice that time of the year.

After dinner, we sat beside Agha Joon in the living room to hear the Kamar al-Zaman story. But I couldn't pay full attention to his tale. I heard Baba from the hall saying no to this, no to that, asking Maman not to overpack the already bursting suitcases. Azra had brought a few sealed packets of homemade dried figs and apricots as a farewell gift. She asked Maman if she could squeeze the fruits in between the clothes.

I imagined Baba getting lost exactly like Prince Kamar al-Zaman, who followed the bird that stole his ruby jewel into the bushes and got separated from his beloved bride. I ached to go to Baba. I wanted to circle my arms around his neck and feel his scar one last time before he left. I'd never been separated from him for more than a week or two.

"Agha Joon," I said. "Can I go to the hall?"

He paused reading and stared at me with surprise. "Don't you want to know what happens to Kamar al-Zaman?"

"Is Baba going to get lost?"

He laughed at me when he figured out my fear. "We have phones, we have maps, we won't get lost like the old days of these stories." He patted my hair and brushed away the strands that curtained my eyes. "But if you want to go to Baba, go. We'll finish the story later."

The hall rug was strewn with clothes, colorful food packets, and books Baba intended to take with him. Maman reorganized the suitcases to create more space. I hopped on the scattered things and crossed the room to reach Baba. He was sitting on the first step of the staircase.

"Wrap the books in the casual clothes. They won't bend or move around that way."

"Be patient, azizam. Have you ever found a torn book, or a broken glass in the suitcases I've packed?" Maman said.

"Never," Baba said. He noticed me going toward him. "Story finished?"

I shook my head. "Baba, are you going to come back?"

He opened his arms, and I sat on his lap. "As soon as you finish the Farsi alphabet, you'll fly and come to me."

He was wearing the wool sweater Azra had knitted for him during the fall. I remember her knitting two yarns, mixing the ivory threads with the turquoise blue. The color was so eye-catching I could hardly forget. I'd asked Azra to whom the sweater belonged. Never had I imagined Baba wearing it on the eve of his departure.

"Baba, but I am at letter shin. There are so many letters left, and the school is closed."

"You're a fast learner, aren't you?" Baba said. "How about you read yourself with Maman's help?" He winked at me.

Maman glanced at us as she heard her name. She placed Baba's brown corduroy coat on the row of wrapped books and folded the sleeves over the coat. Mar Mar darted from the living room and tripped on the dried fig pack.

"Easy, Mar Mar. Watch your step," Maman said.

She immediately rose and ran toward us. Baba pressed Mar Mar and me in his bosom and kissed our foreheads. The faint smell of his cologne brought back memories of the joyful moments we climbed his broad chest. The giggles he coaxed from our lips as we wrestled with him and defeated him on the floor. "Be good girls and listen to Maman," he whispered into our ears. "We'll be together before Agha Joon's figs are ripe."

I circled my hands around his neck and touched his scar. It felt smoother than ever at that moment. Baba didn't cover the scar like the other times. We were playing no game. I had to wait all spring to finish the rest of the alphabet, for school to end and to travel to America with Maman and Mar Mar. There were thirty-two letters in the Farsi alphabet, and it took one school year for children to learn the different shapes of them when they came in the beginning, middle, or end of a word. They disguised themselves and played tricks on us by changing shapes or becoming silent as they meshed with other letters to create words. It is hard to learn Farsi as a kid. Even though Baba assured me we would meet again, I fretted about his journey. *Safar* meant a perilous journey in Agha Joon's stories, and in my six-year-old mind, I was scared Baba would be ensnared in his safar or even worse, get killed by an ifrit. I believed faraway lands belonged to the ugly creatures who could take Baba from me. I didn't want him to leave.

———————

On February 10, 1979—one day before the Islamic Revolution— we returned home from Agha Joon's house. Winds had blown away the smoky fog that swathed Tehran most winter days. The sky was so clean that I could see Mount Damavand from afar, capped with pristine snow. We owned a condominium complex made up of three-story apartment buildings in the Narmak area of northeast Tehran. Baba had rented the upper two apartments, and we lived on the first floor, which opened to a shared front yard. That day, Maman drove us back earlier in the afternoon since the curfew was to start before evening. She didn't want to stay away from our apartment for too long since our tenants and neighbors could get suspicious. Everyone in our neighborhood knew Baba was a high-ranking officer in the Shah's army. Those days, people suspected high-ranking officers worked for the Shah's intelligence system, SAVAK. The notorious SAVAK identified and detained opponents of the monarchy in Tehran's horrendous prison, Evin. Stories of young students and revolutionaries being brutally lashed by cable wires or their nails being pulled out during interrogations circled in every gathering. Nobody wanted to have any relationship with SAVAK, not to say that Baba worked for that system.

The first thing Maman did after we got home was to get rid of the giant painting of the Shah in the guest room. She brought her sharp scissors out from her sewing kit to cut the canvas from the frame.

Mar Mar whimpered when she noticed Maman was cutting up the horse. "Why are you cutting Baba's gift?" she said. She was standing beside the frame, petting the horse.

Maman put the scissors down on the floor and pulled her close. She wailed in her arms. Maman patted her head and pulled back her bangs from her eyes. "We can't keep this painting in our house anymore, Mar Mar."

"Why?"

"It's not safe to keep it, azizam. Angry people can hurt us for having this painting in our house. Haven't you heard people saying death slogans to the Shah?"

"Why do people hate the Shah so much?" I asked.

She turned her face to me. "Because they think he has done bad things."

"Like what?" Mar Mar asked.

"Like killing people and stealing their money for himself and his family."

"But Agha Joon says kings have palaces and jewelry," Mar Mar said.

"How come Baba doesn't think like the other people?" I asked.

"People say many things. Only God knows if they're right," Maman said. "Mar Mar, do you want to help me collect the pieces? We can keep them like puzzle pieces and play with them later." She winked at me.

Mar Mar nodded and sprang out of her arms. Maman carved out the canvas, spread the painting on the floor, and carefully cut square pieces with her scissors. Mar Mar collected the squares on top of each other. The effigy of the Shah changed into a puzzle in less than an hour.

All evening, the new revolutionary radio spread the news of inner-city barracks and police stations falling one by one into people's hands. *Iran, Iran, Iran, land of blood, fire, and death* was played over and over again. The heroic song had become the emblem of resistance in the hearts and minds of Iranians. I got goose bumps every time I heard it on the radio. We slept in my parents' queen bed that night. Baba's empty place was too conspicuous, and we unknowingly tried to fill it. Maman placed Mar Mar in the middle so she wouldn't fall off. She had the tendency to move a lot in her sleep, and many times during trips she had fallen from the bed in the middle of the night. Maman locked all the windows and covered the voile sheers with thick Jacobean curtains so that outside noise and light wouldn't bother us. Still, I couldn't sleep. The violent noise of slogans and the sound of gunshots from the streets agitated me. I awoke from a shallow dream. There was a latticed night lamp on the wall across from the bed. Maman turned it on every night, and I often saw the blue light from the half-open door when I went to the bathroom. That night, the entire room glittered with cerulean blue dots diffused on the walls. I noticed

Maman sitting on the edge of the bed. She had a silk, strapped nightgown on and was rocking back and forth. Her shoulders shimmered in the soft light when she moved. I heard her sobbing silently, holding Baba's military peaked cap in her arms. Her chin touched the tip of the cap as she whispered words to herself. Was she talking to Baba? I couldn't catch her words. She clutched the opposite edges of the cap and neared its tip to her lips. Did she miss Baba as much as I did? She kissed the cap and placed it back in the chest of drawers where Baba kept his uniform accessories. It was then I realized I had never seen my parents kiss or embrace each other in front of us.

———————

The next morning, Maman awakened me and Mar Mar and told us we needed to get dressed to go to Agha Joon's house. Mar Mar was grumpy and didn't want to get up, but the notion of going back to Agha Joon thrilled me out of bed. Maman had parked her Beetle in the front yard. She took the travel bags she had packed the night before and went out to place them in the car.

We were still in Maman's bedroom when she hurried back to the house, hurled the bags to the floor, and shut the door swiftly behind her. We hurried to the living room to see what had happened. She rested her head on the door, trying to catch a breath. Her face looked as white as the door paint. Tiny pearls of sweat lined the upper rim of her eyebrows. With shaky hands, she locked the door.

"Maman, what's going on?"

She glanced at me and tried to hide her hands. "Nothing, azizam. Go have some breakfast. I've put some bread and butter bites on your plate." She led us to the kitchen. After she situated Mar Mar and me around the breakfast table, she poured some milk for us and rushed back to the living room. She totally forgot that Mar Mar only drank chocolate milk. Mar Mar complained, but Maman didn't pay her any attention. I'd never seen Maman edgy and anxious like that.

"Something's wrong, Mar Mar." I gulped down my milk. "We need to find out."

I got out of the chair and threw my bread and butter bites into the garbage. They had the nasty fig jam on them. I tiptoed out of the kitchen to see what Maman was doing.

"Maman will get mad at what you did!" Mar Mar yelled at me.

"Shhhh! Something important is going on," I said.

I snuck into the living room, but Maman wasn't there. She was in her bedroom, talking to Reza on the phone. I eavesdropped through the closed door.

"What do you mean, 'Are you sure'? The bullet has pierced the driver's seat! I found it in the hole it has made!" she said. "It must have been shot from one of the neighbors' rooftops, or, or our tenants . . ." After a few moments she said, "Reza, I don't know what to do. They wanted to kill him or threaten us." I heard her sobbing. "Now come on, don't blame him. Please, I don't feel safe." She listened for a while and all I could hear after that was *yes* after *yes* after *yes*.

Maman told us we would go to Agha Joon's house later that day, but she didn't say why she had changed the plan. I didn't dare to ask what had happened. Her anxiety terrified me and made me speechless. I peeked through the living room window: her Beetle was shining peacefully in the sun. I could see no bullet, no hole, no nothing. What was she talking about?

The events of that evening remain crystalline in my mind, as if I have recorded a movie clip and watched it hundreds of times. There was unspoken strangeness in the streets of Tehran that even a six-year-old girl roaming in the living room could feel. Gunshots pierced the sky nonstop. I could hear the "Allah o Akbar" slogan from every window and rooftop in our neighborhood. Our guest room window faced a street that ended in one of Tehran's important northeast squares called Haft Hose. Every time I pulled back the guest room's voile curtains and peeked through the window, I saw men running around in groups, carrying guns. I saw officers and cadets among them. They mostly belonged to the air force. I was already familiar with the military ranking insignias at that age. Baba had shown me pictures of different insignias when he'd found out I was interested in their shapes. My favorite was the eagle sitting under the golden crown, the emblem of the Shah's air force. It read, "High heaven is my house," beneath the great bird of prey. Maman kept the radio on at all times. The revolutionary songs filled the living room in between the nuggets of news about people's resistance in different cities. She didn't cook anything that day. Mar Mar and I ate the cold cheese and tomato sandwiches while Maman bustled around the kitchen, peeking through the window now and then. She called Agha Joon's house several times after lunch. Her fingers trembled when she dialed the phone. With a brittle voice, she asked for Reza every time. But he was not home, and no one knew where he was.

Early in the evening, I found Maman standing in front of the mirror in her bedroom, trying to gather her hair with a couple of pins on top of her hair.

"Maman, where are you going?"

"Go get your wool jacket and pants, Moji. We're going out."

She opened the closet door and searched through the clothes hangers until she reached her gray slacks, the ones she wore on busy school days. She yanked the pants off the hanger and quickly pulled them on under her skirt. She unzipped the skirt as she glanced at me in the mirror.

"Where's Mar Mar?" she asked. I shrugged. "Don't stand there! Go find Mar Mar and get ready."

Mar Mar had fallen asleep on the living room sofa, holding her doll tight to her chest. Maman leaped toward the sofa and combed Mar Mar's hair with her hand. "Mar Mar, wake up, azizam, we need to go out." She lifted Mar Mar from the sofa and motioned to me to follow her to our bedroom. She dressed me, then Mar Mar—who was half-asleep—in our merino wool jackets and pants, covered our heads with the pom-pom hats Azra had knitted for us, tied the hats' strings under our chins, and laced our duck boots tight around our ankles. Back in the living room, she shuffled a few of our clothes and belongings out of the travel bags she'd packed the night before and shoved them inside her sturdy handbag and a khaki backpack that belonged to Baba.

"We need to walk, and you need to be patient," she said to us.

"Are we not riding in the car?" I asked.

Maman shook her head and placed her index finger on her lips. We waited a few minutes behind the door as Maman listened for any sound coming from the staircase. We rushed out of the apartment as soon as she made sure no one was coming down the stairs. She clutched my hand with the same hand holding her handbag and carried Mar Mar in her other arm while the heavy backpack pulled on her shoulders. We hurried through the dark toward Haft Hose Square, hoping we could find a ride to Agha Joon's house.

Haft Hose Square had a large green area with seven connecting fountain pools in the center of the square. Maman used to take us to the park on sultry summer afternoons so that we could play in the cool wet breeze that blew from the fountains. We would splash the water near the edges of the pool and feed the colorful koi fish that had grown fat on cookie crumbs. I had chased Mar Mar many times beside the pools, counting them one by one, making sure they were seven every time.

That evening, the fountains were all turned off, and no kids were playing in the park. The stores encircling the square were open, but no one seemed to be buying or selling anything. The store owners and passersby had gathered in groups in front of the stores, talking to each other or following the news on handheld radios. It was supposed to be curfew, but no one paid attention to that. The storefront neon lights brightened the night sky, and their reflections shimmered on the smooth sidewalk. Sandbag trenches were built along the ditches all around the square. Men with bullet belts strapped to their shoulders and waists hopped in and out of the trenches. Maman dashed through the row of trenches, pulling Mar Mar and me with all her strength. I ran after her, sometimes tripping when I couldn't keep up. From the brick minaret of Narmak Mosque in Haft Hose, I could hear the "Iran, Iran" hymn again:

Iran, Iran, Iran, Burst of machine-gun fire
Iran, Iran, Iran, land of blood, fire, and death
Tomorrow will be spring, and there shall grow tulips in your
*   valleys*
From the blood of your martyrs and the tears of your orphans
Iran, Iran, Iran.

The revolutionary people played the song instead of azan—the call for prayer—which was broadcast every day at dusk. We were rushing to pass the mosque's gate when a young man hollered at Maman.

"Khanoom!" he shouted.

Maman froze in her spot. We all turned to the man. He was wearing a camouflage combat uniform with a bullet belt on his waist, and he had wrapped a keffiyeh scarf around his neck. He had a rifle in one hand and a box of baklava in the other. He approached us, brought the baklava box close to Maman and said, "Have some baklava, khanoom. Iran is free after all!"

In the glaring light of the mosque, I saw Maman's face had turned white. She stammered a thank you and took three baklavas with her trembling hand, one for each of us. She gave a sticky one to me and Mar Mar and said, "Eat! And thank agha." The guy stared at us while he rested his hand on the rifle. I swallowed the sweet wad and wished we could escape the armed men who surrounded us in the trenches.

We hurried along the seven pools of Haft Hose and passed a few intersections, all jammed with cars. Some drivers had flags of Iran in their hands and waved them from the windows of their cars. Some honked with the rhythm of the slogans men yelled out in the streets. Men carrying guns shot into the air, celebrating a new beginning for the country. I was terrified of the crowd. My hand hurt from Maman's constant pulling, and I had blisters from the pinch of the duck boots on my heels. She had pulled the laces so tight that my feet felt numb from the pain. I prayed from the bottom of my heart that we could magically fly above the city on Aladdin's carpet and get to Agha Joon's house.

It was pitch black when Maman finally found a taxi in a back alley, about three kilometers north of Haft Hose Square.

"Agha, can you please take us to Pasteur Square?" Maman asked the taxi driver.

"It's a long way, khanoom. The streets are all jammed," he said.

"My girls are tired, agha. We've walked a long way." She placed the handbag down on the ground and clutched the taxi's half-open window. "I'll pay you double the amount you normally charge."

He cocked his head and glanced at me and Mar Mar. We must have looked so miserable at that moment that he didn't ask for more and agreed to take us to Agha Joon's house. He was a young man who had an eagle eye and shifted the car's gears swiftly when he saw trouble along the streets. He drove through the alleyways, a different way than the route Maman usually took. As soon as he turned onto Sun Street, Maman leaned forward and said, "Khoda omret bede, agha. God bless you for bringing us here." He looked in his rearview mirror and said, "You're welcome, khanoom. It was not safe to be out in the streets, especially with your kids."

I don't remember how much Maman paid him, but I know he was overjoyed with the amount. He nodded his head with pleasure and wished us to be happy, healthy, and safe.

I could never forget the face of the man who offered the box of baklava to us on the eve of the Islamic Revolution. He often chased me in my dreams, forcing me to choke down things I never wanted to eat. His keffiyeh became the hallmark of fear, for it represented the revolutionary men who carried guns on the streets and forced us to follow the Islamic hijab in public, which was never before obligatory in Iran. Now that I look back, I can't fathom what Maman did on the eve of February 11, 1979. Any reasoning I bring tells me she should have kept the doors locked and remained in the house that night. She must have been brimming with agitation and anxiety to take two frightened little girls into the rabid ecstasy of people uprising in the streets. When I was older, I asked Maman why she was so frantic that night. "Moji, Agha Joon's house was my only refuge. I had to go back," she said. "It was not safe to stay in the house. The very people who had shot the bullet in the Beetle could've simply stormed in wanting to kill Baba. It was not safe to drive the Beetle and alert the neighbors that we were leaving, and it was not safe to go out. One has to pick her poison, and I decided to go to the streets."

The Dawn of Revolution

*Now the warmth of wine having mounted to their
heads, they called for musical instruments, and the
portress brought them a tambourine of Mosul, and a lute
of Irak, and a Persian harp. And each mendicant took one
and tuned it, this the tambourine and those the lute and
the harp, and struck up a merry tune while the ladies
sang so lustily that there was a great noise.*

———

"The Porter and the Three Ladies of Baghdad"

After the ghastly night of the Islamic Revolution, we didn't go back to our house for a few weeks. We stayed with my grandparents until Nowruz, the Persian New Year. Maman begged Reza every week to visit our house and make sure everything was fine inside the apartment. He often postponed going there until Agha Joon asked him to go. One night, he came to the guest bedroom after his visit to our apartment. We had unfolded the mattresses on the floor and were getting ready to sleep. Maman and I were sitting on opposite sides of the room, spreading the white linen over the mattress. Reza leaned against the doorframe and, without a word, watched us for a while. When we spread the blanket over the mattress he said, "I overheard the tenants talking about your husband in the stairway."

"What were they saying?" Maman asked, as she bent over to straighten the creases on the blanket.

"There are rumors about him fleeing Iran. I heard them say he worked for SAVAK."

Maman stopped for a moment and straightened her back. "Bastards!" she said. "How dare they speak of us like this when we've been so caring about them?"

"Well, who believes he left Iran to study in America four days before the Revolution?" Reza said. "America lovers are leaving Iran. They have every right to think he is a fugitive. He was a devout Shah supporter, wasn't he?"

"Yes, of course. He'd spent many years serving at the border while these rumormongers were lounging on their divans at home."

"Why don't you yourself explain this to them? You think they'll believe it?"

Maman finished tucking the last hem of the blanket under the mattress and rose from the floor. She stood right in front of Reza and said, "Be sure, I will."

Reza shrugged and left the room, shutting the door behind him. Maman stared at the door for a minute after he left. She combed her hair with her fingers and scratched her scalp in silence, as she always did when she pondered a serious matter.

"Maman, don't you want to sleep?" I asked.

She slipped out of her thoughts and glanced at me and Mar Mar. We were waiting for her to tuck us under the blanket as she did other nights.

"You go to sleep," she said. She covered our necks with the wool blanket and kissed us goodnight. Then she went to the corner of the room where she'd left her purse on the flower vase table, fetched her lighter and a Winston pack from the purse's side pocket, and slid out the door as she turned off the light.

As soon as she left, I tiptoed to the French doors and peeked through the voile curtains. The oldest fig tree in the front garden had become her sanctuary since we'd left our apartment.

She sat on the fig trunk where it divided into two big stems. The lighter's flame illuminated her face for a few seconds. She sucked the air through the cigarette filter in a long breath and swung the lighter to turn it off. The end of her cigarette gleamed in the dark.

"Is she smoking?" Mar Mar whispered.

"Yes."

Mar Mar jumped off the mattress and came beside me. We both observed her in the dark. Maman hesitated to smoke in Baba's presence, but since he'd left, she smoked often and in front of everyone. She hunched forward and hugged herself from the cold. I wished she'd just come back to sleep. Instead, she rocked back and forth while puffing three cigarettes in a row, lighting one with the glowing red tip of the other. She gave me goose bumps whenever she chain-smoked.

Spring was a busy time in Agha Joon's house. Everyone had to do something in anticipation of Nowruz. Two maids helped Azra with the spring cleaning. They washed the curtains and bedding, cleaned the windows, and dusted the furniture in the house. Azra made samanoo—a sweet pudding made with wheat sprouts. It was a difficult dessert to prepare, and I remember seeing her stirring the honey-thick, brown batter for hours in a large cauldron she placed on the portable gas stove. Every year, Reza brought the stove out from the basement and placed it at the center of the kitchen for all the cooking Azra did before Nowruz. We were forbidden to go into the kitchen. We could only stand at the door and watch her while she prepared the dish. The ambrosial aroma of samanoo spread the scent of spring in every nook and cranny of the house. My aunts arranged the traditional Haftseen table that we all gathered around at the equinox moment. They grew cress seeds on the surface of narrow-neck pottery jars a few weeks before Nowruz. I always wondered how the seeds sprouted on the jar. That year Saba showed me the trick. She placed a small ceramic jar inside one of her sheer nylon stockings and brushed the wet seeds on the surface of the stocking. She kept the jar full of water in a sunlit corner for days. The seeds sprouted, the roots twined through the filaments of the stocking, and the sprouts grew magically on the jar.

A day before Nowruz, Reza brought a batch of letters from our house. "You have a postcard from America," Reza yelled as soon as he entered the corridor.

Maman dashed down from the guest bedroom and snatched the letters from him. He had unlaced his boots and was about to hang his overcoat on the coatrack.

"Easy, easy." Reza laughed out loud. "Thank God you have a flunky at your service, khanoom joon."

Maman rushed back to the guest bedroom, Mar Mar and I following her to see what had come all the way from America. A blue envelope stamped with English alphabet was on top of the other letters. She tried to rip off the rubber band around the batch with her fingers, but the rubber was thick, impossible to tear by hand. Maman hurried to the kitchen and brought back a small knife. She cut the rubber band, slid the knife's blade under the envelope's folded edge, and opened it. A magnificent card bloomed in her hands. That card was the first objective evidence of Baba's survival in America. Under a thin semitransparent sheet, there was a glossy picture of a beautiful tulip field. I had no idea where the tulip field was, but I assumed it was the place Baba was staying. He had sent a picture of himself inside the card. With a blue-and-white-striped shirt, he had posed in front of a sloped, shingle-roofed house—the type I'd only seen in cartoons and movies from America. In silence, Maman read Baba's letter, tears glistening in her eyes.

"Maman, what has Baba written in the card?"

She kept Baba's photo and gave the card to me. "He's doing fine. He wishes us a happy Nowruz."

I glanced at Baba's script. He had written a few paragraphs for Maman, and I knew it because I could recognize many words in his handwriting. I saw Maman's name, my name, and Mar Mar's, all repeated in his paragraphs.

Maman embraced me and Mar Mar and said, "He wants me to kiss you for him."

Baba hadn't been ensnared by the ifrit after all. The postcard and the photo showed he had reached America safe and sound.

It was the best Nowruz I've ever had. Being at Agha Joon's house and spending time with lively aunts who sang while trying bright new dresses for Nowruz was joyful beyond a six-year-old girl's dream. Even for the picky eater that I was, the crispy, bite-size Nowruz cookies were enticing. That year the vernal equinox moment happened in the morning. Maman woke us early, dressed us in our new corduroy frocks, Mar Mar in russet red and me in navy blue, combed our hair, and sent us upstairs.

The guest room on the second floor remained mysterious to us since its lattice-framed door was locked throughout the year. It was the only room in the house that was decorated with French-style furniture. Azra kept her oldest chinaware in the glass-front cherrywood credenza. An antique Sarouk rug decorated the floor. The rich rosy flowers glowed in the black arabesque pattern of the rug. We gathered around the termeh that was spread on the oak table at the center of the room. Saba and Leila had placed the cress vases at the four corners of the termeh and arranged the seven symbolic items of Haftseen in gilded saucers. Azra wore her turquoise necklace on a white lacy shirt for the first day of Nowruz. She had colored her hair with henna and braided an arctic blue silk scarf in the tresses. She looked much younger with her hennaed hair. She heated a pan of samanoo and poured it in a china bowl to distribute shortly after the equinox moment. Agha Joon pinned his white kufi to his sparse gray hair and wore his pistachio-green robe—the one he donned only for Nowruz. He sat at the table and picked up the Holy Koran from the center of the Haftseen arrangement. The Koran's cover had a large golden diamond in the center embellished with tiny, entangled flowers. Under the diamond, in large font, I could read the word *Koran*, as the Arabic alphabet was pretty much the same as Farsi. Agha Joon recited a few verses in Arabic. I didn't understand a word, but there was a mystique in his pleasant posture and his calming tone that kept me quiet and still. The man with his pistachio robe reciting words in a poetic language that sounded magical to me.

Shortly after the equinox, we received our Nowruz gifts. From the first page of the Koran, Agha Joon brought out crisp new bills and gave one ten-tomans note to everyone. It was a lot of money at that time. We embraced each other and kissed—the way Iranians kiss—once on each cheek. We heard the hornpipes playing in the streets. My aunts danced to the blissful spring melodies. They had a special record they played on the gramophone for Nowruz. They even asked Maman to dance with them. I had rarely seen Maman dance, but she stood up and danced with the girls. They all wore their floral maxi skirts Agha Joon had brought from Mecca during his Hajj pilgrimage. The colors of their skirts mixed as they twirled, spreading spring flowers around the Haftseen arrangement. Mar Mar and I ran among the flowers, trying to wiggle our bodies to the rhythm of the song. Agha Joon and Azra clapped with joy. Reza held the Koran in his hands and kept his eyes on verses, trying not to pay attention to the music and the dance. Maman had placed Baba's picture against one of the cress vases. He smiled at us from America, missing Maman, Mar Mar, and me.

———————

On the twelfth day of Nowruz, Reza asked everyone to get ready to go outside after breakfast. Early before dawn, Agha Joon had left for a greenhouse in Rey—a small city south of Tehran—to buy saplings and flowers for his garden. Maman didn't feel like coming, but since everyone was going, she agreed to come. We all rode in Reza's olive 504 Peugeot. Azra sat next to Reza, and the rest of us squished in the rear seats—Mar Mar and I on Maman's and Leila's laps, Saba sitting in between.

Reza drove to Fakhriyeh Mosque in the neighborhood where he often attended prayers. He went to that mosque at noon and at dusk, a habit he had fallen into after the Revolution. I had seen Agha Joon praying on his prayer rug or Azra covering her head and body with a white floral chador, kneeling for prayer, but I'd never seen anyone in my family attending mosque. Like many secular families in Tehran, my grandparents did their prayers in solitude, and they didn't force their children to pray at home or at the mosque.

"Are we going to pray in the mosque?" I asked Reza as soon as I saw the minaret of the mosque.

He laughed out loud and looked at me in the rearview mirror. "Do your aunts look like they're going to the prayers?" he said.

"You're so funny, Reza," Leila said. "No, Moji jan. He's taking us to vote."

"Vote?"

"What's voting?" Mar Mar asked.

"You'll see it for yourself, soon," Leila said.

A long line had formed in front of the mosque's building, and people in different attires were waiting to get in. Some women had scarves or chadors, and some of them were like Maman and my aunts, their heads uncovered. The Islamic hijab wasn't yet obligatory, and women could still appear in public without a head cover. The street was packed with motorcycles and cars, no empty place left for parking. Reza dropped us off in front of the mosque's gate and parked the car in one of the back alleys. The sturdy chinar trees that flanked the street looked familiar to me. It was Vali-Ahd, the same street where we'd joined the demonstration a few months ago. Emerald shoots and budding leaves spread lacy shades on the people waiting in line. A gentle breeze swayed shadows on the shoulders of the people, and earrings and eyeglasses glittered in the dance of light and shade.

We joined the line. It wasn't cold anymore, so Maman had let me wear my navy-blue corduroy frock without a coat. I was wearing lace trim socks with my new Mary Jane shoes that day, trying hard to keep them clean. Mar Mar was wearing her Nowruz dress as well. We looked like twins. People seemed happy and kind, complimenting Maman on how darling we looked, and sometimes they pinched our cheeks, which I hated so much. Maman answered them cordially and explained we were one year apart; I was a finicky eater and Mar Mar was growing faster than me. It took us an hour to enter the mosque's double gates and get to the courtyard. The banners hung on the walls around the courtyard kept me busy while we advanced slowly. I recognized the letters I had learned and tried to read the words. Ayatollah Khomeini's picture loomed large over the mosque's main entrance.

"What are people doing here?" I asked Reza.

"Moji, we came here to vote for the Islamic Republic," Reza said. He raised me from the ground and held me in his arms. "You see people going inside? There are ballot boxes in the prayer hall. We'll go in and insert our voting cards in those boxes."

"What does vote mean?" I asked.

"It means we are going to choose our type of government. No more monarchy. No more Shah."

I recalled the days of the death slogans and the day Mohammad Reza Shah left Iran, but I didn't understand what Reza meant by choosing a government. The concept of democracy, especially an Islamic one, was a vague and ill-defined idea even for the adult Iranians. I knew nothing about democracy, though I was fascinated by the details of the voting process that day in the Fakhriyeh Mosque. The voting cards were peculiar rectangles divided equally by a dotted scissor line in two colors. The right side was red with a printed *NO*, the left side green with a written *YES*. All of my family members cast their votes that day. Even Maman, who had some reservations, tore the ballot card in half and pushed her *YES* ballot into the box. She, like the majority of Iranians, hoped the new republic would bring justice and equality for all, and even though the Islamic style of the republic was not well defined, many skeptical citizens still voted in favor of it. People were angry about the social disparity between the rich and poor and the luxurious life of the Pahlavi family. The extravagant "2,500 Year Celebration of the Persian Empire" that had been held by the Shah a few years before the Revolution made many Iranians furious at the lavish culture of the monarchs in Iran. One of the main promises of Ayatollah Khomeini was to distribute the wealth of our oil-rich country equally among the people.

When we came out of the prayer hall, Mar Mar and I chased each other in the courtyard around the ablution fountain. With the advent of spring, fresh blood was flowing in our veins, and the sunshine felt nice on our skin. We played a game, trying

to find YES cards among the thousands of red cards voters had
discarded on the ground. With our jet-black shoes, we tossed
the crimson sea of NOs that carpeted the courtyard tiles. The
two letters *noon* and *he* flooded the yard. But we couldn't find a
green card with *alef*, *re*, or *ye*.

On the Wings of the Roc

*I arose and, unwinding my turban from my head,
doubled it and twisted it into a rope, with which I girt
my middle and bound my waist fast to the legs of the roc,
saying in myself, "Peradventure this bird may carry me
to a land of cities and inhabitants, and that will be
better than abiding in this desert island."*

———

"The Second Voyage of Sindbad the Seaman"

Maman returned to our home after the Nowruz holiday to bring some of our toys, books, clothes, and school uniforms. She drove back to Agha Joon's house with the Beetle filled with our stuff and parked the car under the grape trellis in the front garden. In the afternoon, when everyone took a nap, I sneaked into the Beetle and searched for the bullet hole. I found a small round opening in the driver's side roof. Rays of sunshine passed through that tiny hole, illuminating the bullet's route. I was shocked to realize Baba could have been killed if he was in the car at that moment. The bullet would have pierced his brain.. I felt relieved that he left the country a few days before the Revolution.

After Nowruz, schools opened under the new Islamic government. I wore the same maroon pleated dress with a white knitted collar that I had always worn as my school uniform. There was still no obligation for girls to cover their hair. By the end of spring, I'd learned the Farsi alphabet, and I could read the newspaper headlines with some difficulty.

One day in May, Leila opened the French doors of the living room to the front garden and sat next to me, reviewing her biology book for her upcoming exam and supervising me as I did my homework. The flowers in Agha Joon's garden were in full bloom, the sweet scent of the honeysuckles sweeping into the living room with the breeze. Azra had boiled fava beans in their shells and served them in a large ivory and turquoise china bowl with salt and dried rose-petal seasoning. She'd started a sweater for me and was halfway through knitting hidden gem patterns with a purple yarn. Mar Mar was practicing the basic brioche stitches with large knitting needles. Maman had left early in the morning to apply for an entry visa to the United States.

"Khaleh Leila, can I go knit with Azra? I finished writing the last page."

"No. You need to read from the newspaper before you go." She closed her biology book and stretched her hand to fetch the front page of *Kayhan*. Agha Joon had scattered the newspaper pages around him, reading an article in the "Events of the Day" section. Leila slipped the newspaper toward me and asked me to read out loud. The lead story covered Ayatollah Khomeini's sermon about women on the birthday of Prophet Mohammad's daughter.

"You saw and we saw what women did in this nehzat. History has been witnessing to what women have been in this world and what a woman is." I raised my head from the newspaper and asked, "What does nehzat mean?"

"Means movement, a political or social movement," she said.

I shrugged and continued to read. I didn't understand the meaning of most of the sentences. "And the women that have risen in re . . . volt, revolt . . ." I paused and reread the sentence. "Khaleh, what does revolt mean?"

She grabbed the newspaper and read the rest of the sermon herself. "And the women that have risen in revolt were these same veiled women of the downtown areas of cities and of Qom and of the rest of the Islamic cities. Those who were brought up in the monarchial upbringing were not at all involved in these affairs." She shook her head and said, "Okay. It's enough for today."

I glided across the carpet and landed beside Azra and Mar Mar. As soon as I picked up my knitting needles from the yarn basket, Maman opened the garden gates. She parked her Beetle and paced toward the French doors. Her scarlet scarf had fallen around her neck, the knot under her chin had swayed to her shoulder. The black pins she carefully hid in her hair every morning were sticking out like porcupine spurs. She said a curt salam to everyone.

"Salam, baba jan," Agha Joon said. "Did you get the visa?"

Maman sat down and threw her bag in the corner. "They're not giving appointments for visas anymore."

Agha Joon folded the newspaper and asked, "What do you mean?"

"The embassy is almost closed. They're not providing consular services, except for the American citizens."

"What are you going to do now?" Leila asked.

Maman shrugged and rubbed her eyes with her hands. Dark circles had appeared under her eyes. She glanced at Azra and said, "Do we have tea, Azra jan?"

Azra put the half-knitted sweater on her lap and said, "I still can't grasp the idea of your husband studying in America at this age!"

"Come on!" she said, "I wish you would all stop criticizing him in this house."

"I'll bring you some tea," Leila said.

"She is tired, Azra. Why are you bothering her?" Agha Joon said after Leila left the room.

"What is she going to do with the kids?" Azra said. "They need their father."

"He's not dead," Agha Joon said, "he is alive. We'll find a way to help them get to America. Enshallah."

Mar Mar ran to Maman and showed her knitted shawl to her. "I've done all the stitches myself. See how long it is?"

Maman kissed Mar Mar's head and grabbed the shawl attached to the knitting needles. "It's very neat, azizam. All the stitches look the same."

I picked Mar Mar's yarn from the basket and rewound it as I followed her to Maman. "How are we going to get to Baba?" I asked.

She took the ball from me and said, "We'll see. Did you finish your homework?"

"Yes, Maman."

Leila came back with the silver tray and offered tea to everyone. Azra put her knitting needles back into the basket and handpicked a few fava shells for Maman. She grabbed the flower seasoning bowl, crushed the dried petals, and sprinkled the flakes on top of the beans. She slid the plate in front of Maman and said, "Eat some. You're starving."

That night, Maman didn't come to the guest bedroom to sleep. She sat on the fig tree stem and smoked for a long time. A slow breeze stirred the shadows of the fig leaves on her. The broad leaves shielded her face from the moonlight, and I couldn't tell if she was choking back tears or staring at the sky. The circular rim around the fountain pool glittered in the moonlight, and the frogs croaked now and then, breaking the ponderous silence of the night. I heard the shuffle of Agha Joon's leather mules on the terrazzo tiles. He was sleepless like us. He walked toward the fig tree and stood beside Maman, resting his hand on a thick bough. Maman crushed her cigarette under her foot and stood up from her seat. They spoke in whispers for a while, and Agha Joon embraced Maman and patted her hair. I wanted to run to the garden and squeeze myself between them. I wished I could hide my face in Maman's long skirt and unload the sadness I felt in my heart from the day's bad news. But I was scared to shatter their moment together, and I knew Maman would blame me for spying on her and not going to sleep early for school.

——————

The next morning during breakfast, Agha Joon announced he was going to take us out of the country. "Sefarat ke ghaht nist, we can go to Germany, England, or even Greece to find an American Embassy," he said, sipping his tea.

"Khoda omret bede," Azra said, praising Agha Joon for his decision.

"Where are you going?" Leila asked, surprised.

"Germany. We'll go to Germany first," Maman said.

"When did you decide to go?" Leila asked.

"We spoke last night. The political situation is getting more complicated every day," Agha Joon said.

"I read Khomeini's remarks in the newspaper yesterday," Leila said. "He was talking about Islamic training for women. I'm afraid they might not let us enter universities anymore." She placed her tea istikan on the saucer and put her hands on her lap. "I was thinking of coming to the embassy with you the other day," she said to Maman, "but now . . . I wonder if I can come with you on this trip?"

Maman gaped at her for a while, not quite realizing what Leila was saying. "You want to come to America?"

"Yes. I want to study in America," Leila said.

Everyone became silent. The only sound was Mar Mar stirring her tea with a spoon.

"My last exam is in two days. I'll receive my diploma in a couple of weeks," Leila said.

Agha Joon took a deep breath. He brushed his bushy eyebrows with his fingers and glanced at the fig trees quivering in the morning breeze. It was time for Agha Joon to pick the ripe figs. "How long have you been thinking about this?"

"I've been dreaming about it for some time . . . but now, with the situation getting worse day by day . . . I want to go to the university. I want to study medicine."

"Sakhteh tanhayi, dokhtaram."

"I know it's hard." She became silent.

Azra covered her face with her hands and shook her head. She wasn't happy about Baba going to America and leaving us back at home, separating the family. I wondered how she would take Leila's decision to leave. Saba stared at Leila with a somber look on her face. I could see her eyes welling up with tears. They'd grown up together and shared a bedroom all their lives.

"Why not?" Maman said. "She can come with us, and we can apply for a visa together. Agha Joon, shall I get five tickets to Frankfurt?"

————————

Maman packed our belongings in six enormous suitcases and moved most of our furniture to the basement. She rented our apartment to a couple with a newborn baby and asked Agha Joon to take charge of the old and new tenants. Every day we were getting closer to Baba, and the anticipation of seeing him thrilled my heart. Nothing could have delighted me more than traveling with Agha Joon in those days. My beloved Agha Joon, the silvery voice behind *One Thousand and One Nights*, the enigmatic voyager of journeys on the sea and sand, was going to take us to the wonderlands. He had read "Sindbad the Seaman" to us, and I wondered if he'd intentionally chosen that story. He depicted the vivid image of Roc, the gigantic bird with a long dazzling tail that lived on a mysterious summit and fed monstrous prey to her chicks. He told us how Sindbad bound himself to the Roc's ankle and flew over the Valley of a Thousand Serpents. I imagined us flying over dangerous valleys to reach Baba. Agha Joon was the savior who would unwrap his turban and bind his girls to the gigantic bird. Would he keep us safe from falling into the mouths of the starving serpents gaping at the sky? Sure, he would. Safar was not a perilous act anymore if Agha Joon accompanied us through the journey.

———————

On the airplane, I imagined sitting on the Roc's wings between Mar Mar and Agha Joon—Maman and Leila behind us—floating in the clouds. Flight attendants looked charming in their navy-blue suits and pillbox hats, wearing orange scarves around their necks and a small handkerchief in the front pocket of their coats. They spread urbane smiles in the aisles and brought us a Lufthansa Airbus A300 puzzle, a coloring book, and a box of six skimpy colored pencils I kept for many years. Agha Joon never cared about what I ate. Maman was busy talking to Leila in the seat behind us and couldn't control me during the meal. I ate the creamy pasta and tossed the chewy chicken in my crumpled white napkin. We peeked through the airplane's oval window and marveled at the splendid scenes of Earth we'd never seen before. The high chains of the Alborz Mountains faded into the seamounts of the Black Sea, and as the square patches of green land appeared, Agha Joon said, "We are above Europe. We're getting close."

———————

Munich was the first foreign city I clearly remember. We arrived there by a night train from Frankfurt, much of the travel foggy in my mind. I was exhausted, jet-lagged, and half-asleep. Agha Joon had come to Germany many times before, and he was familiar with Munich more than any other city in that country. He knew a little German, which gave him confidence and ease to travel on the metro system. We arrived in the morning and went to a hotel within walking distance from Marienplatz—the old town square in Munich. Maman called the American consulate as soon as we checked in, and they scheduled her appointment for the next day.

The next morning Maman and Leila left for the American consulate, and Agha Joon took us to Marienplatz after breakfast. It was a cloudy day in June and many people had gathered in the old town. The area was surrounded by tall buildings with a strange architecture I'd never seen in Tehran—except in scary movies. It was my first encounter with a Western city and its Gothic-style buildings. There were no cars on the cobbled streets, and people walked freely from one side to the other. The stores had rows of stalls packed with fresh bread, cheese, and fruit. The store names were written above their door shades from left to right, in contrast to the signs in Farsi in Tehran. Even though I didn't know the German alphabet, I noticed the striking individuality of letters that stood out in words. In Farsi, alphabet letters curled into one another to make the words and no letter preserved its individual shape.

Agha Joon bought some red apples, a big loaf of white bread, and a dull yellow Allgäuer Bergkäse cheese from the fresh market. We sat on the concrete pavement in front of the magnificent building known as the New Town Hall, ate our lunch, and enjoyed the carillon music when the giant clock on top of the tower chimed at eleven. On the pale green, patina-coated balcony below the clock, a few figurines started dancing around a royal couple, carrying colorful flags in their hands. The bells continued to chime for a few minutes throughout the dance, and people took pictures of the dancing figurines. Even though I enjoyed the show and the walk with Agha Joon and Mar Mar, I worried about Maman and wondered if she'd been able to get the visas.

That afternoon, when we walked back to the hotel, we received disappointing news again. Maman called Baba and sobbed as she told the story. Tears trickled down my cheeks when Maman cried. I realized getting to America was not as easy as I imagined in my dreams of riding the Roc and landing like a princess as the giant bird fanned her wing like a slide. Agha Joon peeked at Maman while she tangled and untangled the phone's wire coils. "There will be another day, another city you can try," he said after Maman hung up the phone. He believed in tomorrow and the possibilities that came with it, and I believed in my Agha Joon. He who held those enchanting stories in his chest, who knew the spell to take us to faraway lands.

We traveled in Germany for about three weeks, taking trains from one city to the next. We dragged our giant suitcases and many handbags, always in a rush, trying not to leave anything behind. When we traveled at night, Maman stayed awake, worrying we might miss our stop. One time she fell asleep in exhaustion, and I woke up with the train's whistle, alarmed we were close to a station. The train window was coated with vapor, making it difficult to read the signs outside. I had picked up the German alphabet here and there. Through the fogged window, I recognized a few letters in the *Cologne* sign as we passed. I knew we had to get off at that station. I sprung out of the bunk bed and shook Maman, who was asleep in the lower bed. "Maman, we are at Cologne!" She wiped off the window, and the signs for Cologne became clear as the train jostled to a full stop. We had little time to take out the luggage, so Maman pulled the window's emergency hammer and opened it. She yelled at Leila and Agha Joon to take us and any suitcase they could while she remained inside the cabin to throw the hand-bags and the smaller suitcases out of the window. I was petri-fied by the rush. Leila pulled my hand as if she were dragging a rag doll. I was afraid the train would leave with Maman. We ran on the platform until we reached the open window. Leila and Agha Joon collected the bags that Maman dropped out one by one.

The switchman noticed what they were doing among the bustling crowd. He blew a loud, long whistle that made ev-eryone in the station turn back and look at him. He waved his hand forcefully in the air, shouting in German and asking Maman to get off the train. I covered my eyes with my hands, scared to death about what would happen next. Mar Mar was screaming and crying Maman's name. At that moment, I wished we had missed the stop rather than being in that horrible, em-barrassing situation. I heard Agha Joon talking to the switch-man in broken German. I only opened my eyes when I heard Maman's voice soothing Mar Mar. She was smiling and shaking her head, saying "Es tut mir leid" to the man. Agha Joon and Maman were happy the guy didn't fine them for breaking the law by throwing the bags from the train.

From Frankfurt to Munich, to Cologne, to Düsseldorf, we heard the same response every time Maman and Leila returned from the American consulates. Agha Joon stayed with us while they lined up in the consulate hallways and tried to convince the consuls behind the glass windows to grant them an entry visa. I would anxiously wait for their arrival in the dim hotel rooms where we were staying. As soon as they would come back, I would search the contours of their lips for the beginning of a smile or a glint of hope in their eyes. But every time I was disappointed, wondering if we would ever join Baba. Maman traced the map with her fingers, followed the dotted train lines, and chose our next destination. She pondered what to say to the next American consul. The reason for denial was never quite explained—like all the other instances when people were denied entry visas to the United States because of political unrest in their home countries, probably the unspoken fear of waves of people fleeing a nation in turmoil to a country in peace.

When Maman and Leila lost hope in Germany, they decided to take their chances in Luxembourg. On the appointment date, we walked to a park near the American Embassy. It was a sunny day, unlike most days we journeyed in Germany. Mar Mar and I chased each other on the green lawn while Agha Joon watched us from a bench facing a fountain. After two hours playing in the park, we sat on a bench next to Agha Joon and declared our hunger. He didn't have anything with him. He looked at his watch and said, "The embassy will close soon. Your mother will be back shortly."

As soon as he finished his sentence, an old lady passed by. She had a dark brown beret on her head that covered her white hair, and her neat, knee-length raincoat was the same color. Mar Mar and I were wearing our lemon-yellow sleeveless sundresses, once again looking like twins. The lady stopped for a moment in front of us and looked at our sundresses with a wide smile. She asked something in a language we didn't understand. We smiled back at her, not knowing what to say. She opened her bag, brought out a giant red apple, and offered it to us. We looked at Agha Joon to see what he would say. Agha Joon nodded, and I fetched the apple from her. Agha Joon halved the tart apple with his hands and gave half to me and half to Mar Mar.

I believed the old lady was a pari from *One Thousand and One Nights* who came to save us from the troubles we had in Europe. She was a harbinger of good news, and sure enough, Maman and Leila got visas from the American Embassy that afternoon. Luxembourg had far fewer visitors than Germany, and somehow the news about the Islamic Revolution in Iran hadn't reached there yet.

Finally, after six months, it was time to see Baba.

Of Brass and Bronze

When they reached the top, they beheld beneath them a city, never saw eyes a greater or a goodlier, with dwelling-places and mansions of towering height, and palaces and pavilions and domes gleaming gloriously bright and scones and bulwarks of strength infinite; and its streams were a-flowing and flowers a-blowing and fruits a-glowing.

"The City of Brass"

"Don't forget the name of the flowers," Agha Joon said, when he kissed me at Frankfurt airport. "Write to me about them." He raised both hands and waved goodbye as we passed the security gate. Maman and Leila cried all the way to the airplane. I walked backward to catch the last glimpse of Agha Joon who was watching us as long as the departure corridor allowed him. He had accomplished his mission of passing us through the Valley of a Thousand Serpents and now, it was time for him to return home. I blew a kiss toward him before we headed to the plane, but I wondered why at that tender moment of farewell he mentioned flowers.

Baba appeared slim at the ground transportation area of the Atlanta airport. He was wearing a loose, white T-shirt I'd never seen him wear in Tehran. He hugged us for a long time and held Mar Mar in his arms while we walked to his car. He'd driven his metallic blue Chevrolet from Huntsville, debating all the way whether we would fit in his car with our luggage.

His kinky coils were more pronounced in Atlanta's hot and humid weather, and his scar had become darker, more like a fresh wound than an old lingering scar of the past. Every time he stopped at a traffic light, Mar Mar and I sneaked between the front seats, reached Baba's neck, and tickled his scar. We were too excited to sit still on the back seat. Baba turned his head, smiled, and winked at us every time. On the road, Maman told the story of our hopeless wandering in Germany while we enjoyed the view of Georgia's vast open spaces and farm fields. The striking green scenery differed from the images I remembered from our road trips in Iran. We passed many trees alongside the highways, some red among the green.

"The ones with white barks? Those are called white birch," Baba said when I asked.

Leila glanced at the fields from behind Baba and remained silent during the ride.

"Leila, I'm glad you came," Baba said, looking at her in the rearview mirror.

"I'm excited," she said.

Maman sighed. "We had a tough month. But I'm glad we're here at last."

It was almost dark when we arrived at Huntsville. I was eager to see Baba's house, and the tulip field from the photograph he'd sent for Nowruz. Thin bronze clouds streaked the slate sky, and green lawns stretched like dotted parallel lines along the streets. The houses were detached and surrounded by abundant green land in the old town district. Baba parked in front of a mint-colored house—the same one he'd taken a picture in front of. It looked very much like the neighboring homes with its low-pitched gable and shingled roof with wide eaves that shielded an enormous front porch. Posts rested on the railing, supporting the edges of the eaves. There was a rocking chair and a set of white wicker chairs on the porch. Mar Mar and I jumped on the rocking chair while Baba, Maman, and Leila carried the luggage inside. It was pitch black by the time they unpacked the car. The air was muggy and damp, the screeching sound of cicadas new to my ears. My skin felt sticky, and I was thirsty and tired. I nearly fell asleep in the rocking chair when Baba brought a cold pitcher of cherry red Kool-Aid for us. Maman and Leila came with drinking glasses. Baba poured the first drink for Mar Mar and the second for me. The tart-sweet taste of icy Kool-Aid was my first taste of America.

Agha Joon's first letter arrived in July, one month after we settled in Huntsville. He had written separately for Maman, Leila, and me. Maman cried as she read his lines many times out loud. Leila didn't read the letter in front of us. She locked herself in her room, only to appear an hour later with swollen eyes, sniffing her red nose every five minutes during lunch. Agha Joon's letter was the first ever letter someone had written for me. The fact that he was left-handed and had learned Farsi in maktab—an old-fashioned school for teaching the Koran and the Islamic sharia—made his letter illegible to me. He had learned Arabic first in order to read the Koran and taught himself Farsi by guessing the alphabet by their approximation. He was not used to writing three dots for letters that were unique to Farsi. This made it hard for me to guess what he meant—for example, *be* or *pe*, as they looked the same except that the letter *be* had only one dot underneath and *pe*, three. Maman had to read his letter for me.

The paper was cream-colored and rough on the fingers, a special one Maman called ahar—a paper treated with starch to make it sturdy and suitable for calligraphy. In black ink, his words slanted upward, and the rows got closer to each other as he reached the end. He'd signed it with his indigo blue seal at the bottom left. He had talked about flowers, of course, wanting to know how they looked in America. Trees, their names, fruits, if I liked them or I still refused to taste them. He'd asked about Mar Mar and whether I was behaving like an older, wise sister. At the end, he had mentioned the City of Brass, the last story he'd read for us on the torturous days of meandering in Germany:

> *On the couch lay a damsel, as she were the lucident sun, eyes never saw a fairer . . . And it seemed as if she gazed on them to the right and to the left.* Have you seen a beautiful princess like this? Or a city as elegant as the City of Brass?

The notion of that city left me perplexed. From the moment Agha Joon told the story, I was absorbed and frightened at the same time. The eeriness of the narrative glued me to the bed, yet the dark, gruesome picture of death scared me. All the people living in that city died from a lengthy drought and famine. Before dying—for reasons not told in the story—the living adorned the city with precious stones, purified the pathways and perfumed the alleys. The alluring princess of the city was dressed in a bejeweled gown, her eyes removed from the sockets after death and filled with quicksilver to glisten and look as if she were alive.

It took me a few weeks to gather the information Agha Joon had asked and write back to him. I penned the flowers, the pink azaleas, the false indigos, and the white camellias that filled the yards on our street. I wrote about the magnificent dogwood tree that grew tall and wide in front of the porch, its large four-petal flowers overlaying the leaves as if someone had sprinkled a fine white powder over the boughs when you looked from afar. I refused to write about the City of Brass. The loathsome picture of the adorned carcasses disturbed me. Why did Agha Joon even mention that city in his letter? Why did he want me to find a beautiful dead princess?

———————

Early in August, Baba enrolled us in McDonnell Elementary school for the upcoming school year. He asked the school principal to assign Mar Mar and me to two different first-grade classes. He wanted us to avoid speaking Farsi to each other in class. The principal accepted Baba's request and placed us in separate classes. I hated the fact that Mar Mar and I were both going to attend first grade. All I had achieved during the previous school year learning Farsi turned into rubbish! I looked as illiterate as Mar Mar in English and the ambience of the clever big sister had vanished. I'd bragged about my ability to read when we played together, accusing Mar Mar of not knowing the words. How could I start with her again?

"Baba, I don't want to be in first grade with Mar Mar!" I said in the car the first day he drove us to school. "I am one year, three months and three days older than her!"

Baba glanced at me and Mar Mar in the rearview mirror. She was leaning on her brown backpack, her soft black hair draping across the shoulder straps.

"Well, Mar Mar is growing faster than you," Baba said.

"But I've already passed first grade. The math is too simple for me."

"You know how to read in English?"

"Can't they teach me that in the second grade?"

"You want to eat more so you get taller and skip a grade?" Baba asked.

I didn't answer. I always got enraged when Baba or Maman talked about my eating habits and compared me to Mar Mar. Baba parked his Chevy in the parking area in front of the school. A vast green cotton field surrounded the school, and the cotton leaves shimmered in the sunlight as if the workers had greased the green leaves on every plant. Baba took our hands, and we walked on a concrete sidewalk toward the entrance. The school's name was written on a short brick wall in front of the building. Two white crape myrtles flanked the name, and their white conical flowers stretched out in every direction, as if the workers of the field had decorated the trees with spools of cotton thread. We passed a few wide, brightly lit corridors and turned a couple of corners. The classroom layout differed from what I'd pictured in my mind. In my school in Tehran, classes were separate from each other, every classroom door opening into a long corridor that faced the schoolyard. But at McDonnell Elementary, all the first-grade classes merged in a spacious square space, divided by low-lying cubby rows into four sections, leaving an empty central area. We stood in that space where other parents and children were waiting. They assigned me to classroom A and Mar Mar to classroom D. I held Baba's hand as tight as I could, but in my ears, I could still hear the throbbing of my heart. My mouth was dry. The white neon lights on the ceiling seemed so bright I had to squint my eyes in order to see. I glanced at Mar Mar, who was in tears. Baba kneeled down and hugged her. I tried so hard not to cry, not in front of Mar Mar, and not in front of Baba. At that moment, I wanted Baba to hug me more than anything in the world. How could we survive in those classrooms when we knew almost no English?

"Don't be afraid, Mar Mar. You'll be fine," Baba said.

"I want Maman. I want to go home," Mar Mar said.

"We'll come and pick you up soon, sooner than you think."

Baba caressed her hair and extended his other hand toward me. I was standing behind Mar Mar, watching them. He embraced me and whispered into my ears, "Take care of Mar Mar."

I nodded. Baba's comforting breath spread on the nape of my neck.

"Moji will be here with you." He pointed to my classroom. "You can see each other during class."

"But how can I say I need to go to the bathroom when Moji is not with me?"

"Raise your hand."

I parted my face from Baba's shoulder and looked at Mar Mar. A thin strand of black hair had stuck to her cheeks. Her dimples had disappeared. Warm teardrops drizzled onto my skin as I wrapped my arm around her neck.

"Baba," I said, "can you ask the principal to place us in one class?"

A loud bell rang, and a friendly voice spoke over speakers. Everyone became silent, a song was played, and parents chanted along. A lady gave a speech after the song. I understood nothing of what she said except her name, which I'd heard from Baba. It was the principal. Perhaps she was welcoming us on the first day of school.

Baba disappeared with the other parents and Mar Mar and I held tight to each other among the kids. The children around us were mostly fair skinned but a few kids had dark brown and coiled hair. Mar Mar and I were the only girls with black hair and peach skin. A blond girl came close to Mar Mar and asked something. Mar Mar stared at me as if I knew what she'd said. I shrugged my shoulders and said nothing. Mar Mar pointed to the name badge hanging in front of her chest, trying to introduce herself to the girl. The blond girl looked at the badge and laughed. The situation was hilarious: an illiterate little girl pointing to a name tag the other girl couldn't read. We all struggled to communicate with each other, whatever language we spoke.

I enjoyed the first day of school more than I expected. I had my own desk with a small wooden chair attached to it. In the desk's drawer, there was a yellow pencil box with tiny roses on it, two sharp pencils, a pair of children's scissors, a pack of twelve Crayola crayons, and a glue stick, which I loved to smell. There were twenty kids in my class. A sweet white lady, maybe a few years older than Maman, introduced herself as our teacher. Mrs. Berry was wearing a fine cherry red suit and had made a little bun on top of her head with her hazel-brown hair. As she moved about the class, small pieces of short hair jiggled playfully on her forehead. She started the class with a storybook, reading from the page and showing the pictures to us. Even though I didn't understand the words, I could deduce the story from the pictures, her gestures, and variations in her soft voice. She caught my attention by starting with a story. Perhaps she knew the magic that would turn me into an enthusiastic listener.

Mrs. Berry had a giant world globe on her table. As soon as she finished the story, she rose from her seat and fetched the globe. She placed her finger on the map and helped us see where we lived: In the United States of America, Alabama, Huntsville. After a few seconds, she pointed at me, twirled the globe, touched another place, and said "Iran." She wanted to introduce me to the class. She beckoned me to the front of the class and asked my name. I could only whisper. She asked me to speak louder so that everyone could hear—but I was still too quiet. So, she said my name out loud. "Moji? Am I right?" I nodded. The entire class repeated my name after her. I felt my cheeks burning like glowing pieces of charcoal. She tapped my back and guided me to my seat. On the first day of school, everyone found out I'd come from a different part of the world.

The bell rang, and suddenly Mar Mar was standing in front

of my desk. "My name is Mar Mar!" she shouted. Her dimples reappeared on her cheeks. She'd enjoyed the day—just like me.

––––––––––

One sunny day in September, Baba took us to a park outside Huntsville. Maman made cheese sandwiches with slices of tomato and cucumber and filled a thermos with hot tea. During the one-and-a-half-hour drive, Baba talked about the park. He said the park was named Noccalula, a name unlike any other I'd heard before. We fidgeted all the way and jumped up and down on the backseats, changing and twisting the sounds in the park's name. We made a game of Mar Mar chanting the funny names after me as we rode along.

It was midday when we reached the park. As soon as I got out of the car, I heard the distant humming of a waterfall behind the trees. We strolled on a narrow trail, tall green trees embracing each other alongside the gravel path. Mar Mar and I trotted on the green grass, thrilled by the natural sights and sounds that surrounded us. A smooth, square-shaped area appeared at the end of the trail. We raced to the paved area that was fenced against the rocky edge of the creek. Roaring water rushed down the sharply angled rocks and splashed deep into the plunge. The giant rocks were suddenly cut off as if an ifrit had gnawed the creek bed.

Encircled by red tulips, a bronze statue of a young girl stood close to the creek. We squeezed our faces into the black fence that separated us from the statue and stretched our hands in vain, trying to touch the girl. She had two strands of braided hair that reached her waist. A headband covered her forehead and a long feather poked up behind her head. The braided strands hung in the air as she leaned forward, facing the waterfall. She was standing on a smooth rock, staring at the creek.

"This is Princess Noccalula," Baba said from behind. He pointed to one of the three tablets installed around the statue. "Legend says she jumped from here into the water on her wedding day."

"Why?" I asked.

Baba skimmed through the written script on the plaque and said, "She was the beautiful daughter of the great Indian chief of Black Creek Falls. They were Cherokee Indians. Her dad wanted to marry her to a warrior from another Indian tribe."

"Why didn't she want to marry? Princesses are pretty in wedding dresses," Mar Mar said.

"Was he ugly?" I asked.

"She loved a man from her own tribe."

I placed my feet on the lower horizontal bar and tried to bring myself closer to the tablet. I could read *Noccalula* on top. Red tulips curled over the edges of the tablet, hiding the rest of the written words.

"Was she killed?" I asked.

Baba nodded. "They made this bronze statue in honor of the Indians who lived along this creek."

From where I stood, I couldn't see the plunge pool. I asked Baba to lift me up to have a better view. He handed the basket and the thermos he was carrying to Maman and hoisted me beside the fence. Up in Baba's arms, the waterfall appeared terrifying and magnificent at the same time. A small white cloud swathed the splashing water just before it hit the creek's surface. The undercutting of the waterfall was dark as if it had no end. The fallen rocks scattered on the riverbank looked smooth and polished to a lustrous sheen. I couldn't believe the princess had dared to jump off that height. "Why did she want to kill herself?" I asked for the second time. Mar Mar pulled at Baba's pants. She wanted to be next.

The red tulips around the statue wafted a faint, sweet aroma in the air. Princess Noccalula looked as if she were dancing, both hands bent at the wrists, fingers stretched out in the air. She gazed at the depth of water below her feet. I squinted to see her eyes: they were glistening with tears.

That night when we came back home, I wrote a letter to Agha Joon and told him I've found the dead princess in America. I told him about Noccalula and how she'd killed herself by jumping into the waterfall. There and then I realized why he insisted on the names of the flowers or finding the beautiful princess in America. He encouraged me to learn the culture of the new world. He wanted me to absorb the nuances of taste and temper like a thirsty plant sowed into a new soil. Noccalula was a queer name to me, but with her name came the story of the Indians who once lived along the curves of that creek. With names, the stories reached a seven-year-old girl from the other side of the world. With names came the aura and the aroma of the new land, the sunny days and the dark days, and the history of the country I had landed in.

The Eye of God

A number of naked men issued from it and without
saluting us or a word said, laid hold of us masterfully and
carried us to their king, who signed us to sit. So we sat
down and they set food before us such as we knew not
or whose like we had never seen in all our lives.

"The Fourth Voyage of Sindbad the Seaman"

One year of school in Tehran was not a total waste after all. It wasn't long before Mrs. Berry noticed my speedy progress in learning English and realized I knew more math than other kids in class. She divided us into different color groups based on our reading ability. Each group met with her separately while other groups did their assigned activity in class. The black group had only one student, and that student was me. It was the last group she worked with during the morning sessions. By December, she assigned second-grade study books to me and asked me to look up a word every night at home. We only had one American Heritage dictionary, which belonged to Baba. He helped me search each word in his dictionary. I wrote the meaning in my notebook and made a sentence with the word. Even though it was cumbersome to find a word and decipher the mysterious symbols in an adult dictionary, I loved to slide my fingers on the extra-thin papers and fumble with the adorned red edges of each page. The crisp sound of flipping papers made me feel older and wiser than a first grader struggling to do her nightly homework.

Before winter break, the first-grade teachers decided to decorate a huge Christmas tree that had been erected in the common area of our classrooms. Mrs. Berry announced there would be a competition between the first-grade classes, and the classroom that made the best ornaments would win a prize. She asked us to bring a few popsicle sticks and a small ball of yarn in red, blue, or white to school the next day. She said we were going to make an Eye of God in class.

Mar Mar and I ate a few popsicles and gave one to Maman, Baba, and Leila so that we could collect the sticks. From Kmart, Baba bought three balls of wool yarn in different colors.

"Eye of God? What kind of a craft is that?" Baba asked when he drove us to school.

"She will tell us today. I'm sure we'll win," I said.

"Who says so?" Mar Mar said.

"You'll see. We'll make the best craft. What are you going to make?"

"It's a secret. Mrs. Hamilton asked us not to tell anyone."

"How are you going to make it?"

"I'm not telling you, Moji! Nice trick!"

In class, I could not wait until we got to the art session. I was eager to see how the Eye of God looked when we hung it on the tree.

"First, y'all need to glue two sticks together in a cross." Mrs. Berry glued two sticks perpendicular to each other and then held them over her head. "This serves as the skeleton of your craft." She picked some red yarn, found the thread, and wrapped it around one stick. Then she wrapped it around the next stick and continued doing this until a small red diamond appeared on the branches of the cross. We all started weaving like her. We used the white yarn in the middle and the blue yarn for the outer layer. A blue diamond encircled a red-eyed white diamond when we finished.

"Mrs. Berry," I said, "why is it called the Eye of God?"

She nodded and said to the class, "Moji is asking a good question. There is a story behind it."

Everyone was busy, weaving the final blue over their crosses.

"We've learned this craft from the Indians of Mexico. They weave the Eye of God in silence, thinking of Him. They make these little crosses to bless their homes, their roads, their children." She raised the one she had woven and asked, "Does this remind you of something?"

Michael, a stout boy who always wore denim overalls, said, "Colors of our flag?" He was in the orange group, a group immediately below mine.

"Excellent, Michael. We made these to remember our men in Iran. May God bless them and bring them back home as soon as possible."

The color and configuration struck me the moment Mrs. Berry mentioned the flag. I had seen the American flag everywhere— when we strolled in our neighborhood, in our schoolyard, and on TV while Baba watched ABC news. I had seen it being burned and stamped on by angry people in Iran. I'd heard the news of Iranian students holding U.S. hostages in the American Embassy in Tehran, but I didn't pay much attention until that day.

"Now if y'all have finished, you can hang them on the tree," she said to the class.

I sprung out of my chair and ran toward the tree.

"Easy guys! Do it in silence."

I tiptoed the distance between my desk and the tree. Michael followed me. I wanted mine to be on the top branches, somewhere visible to everyone. I stood on my toes and stretched my hand as far as I could. I hung my Eye of God on a branch facing our class. My creation twirled on its little blue hanger. The white yarn I used had silver threads woven in with the white, and the silver threads glistened when the Eye of God swung, twinkling like a star.

"Why don't your people let our hostages come home?" Michael said. He was staring at me, one hand on his waist, the other in his jeans pocket. "You Iranians!"

I froze in front of him, not knowing what to do.

He took his hand out of his pocket, jumped high in the air, and snatched my Eye of God from the branch. He smashed it and shoved the broken sticks into his pocket. "Ya don't need to make these. You ain't American," he sneered. He turned his back and headed to our class as if nothing had happened.

My eyes filled with tears, but I didn't say anything. I had no idea why Iranian students had held hostages in the American Embassy. In my simple seven-year-old mind, I thought the terrible news of hostages would remain on TV and would never enter my classroom. It didn't occur to me—not even for a second—that I would be confronted by a classmate about a political crisis happening in Iran. I trudged back to my desk, thinking of my crushed Eye of God in his pocket.

On the way back home, Mar Mar was very excited. Their class had won the competition with their five-pointed stars made from thick art paper covered with colorful glitter glue. Their giant gold star sat on top of the tree, glowing like a splendid sun above the shining stars. She couldn't sit and squiggled in the space between the front seats. Glitter sparkled all over her hair and on her cheeks as she explained to Baba how they made the stars. I sank in my seat, leaned my head against the window, and listened to Mar Mar while we passed street after street. I fiddled with my fingers, trying to remove the sticky white glue on them that had turned dirty and gray.

Baba peeked at me in the rearview mirror a few times while

Mar Mar talked. "How about you, Moji?" he said. "How did you make the Eye of God?"

I shrugged. "Easy, I guess."

"Daddy," Mar Mar said.

"You mean Baba, Mar Mar?" Baba said.

"Yes, I mean Baba. Their art-crafts didn't shine like ours. That's why we won," she said.

"OK. But they tried their best." He winked in the mirror. "Moji, you may not be the winner all the time."

I nodded and said nothing. I spotted the American flag at every corner. I noticed a wreath decorated with white, blue, and red flowers hanging on our neighbor's front door. When Baba switched off the engine I said, "Baba, why are Iranians holding American hostages in Tehran?"

"You listening to the news?" Baba said.

"A boy asked me today at school."

"It's complicated. Why did he ask you such a question? Were you guys talking politics in school?" He laughed out loud.

I knew if I insisted, he would have asked about the details, and I was never good at telling lies. I didn't want to tell Baba what Michael did to my Eye of God. It hurt so much to think about, and I didn't want to make Baba angry about it. I feared he might come to school and talk to the principal. So, I decided to keep the fate of my Eye of God to myself.

On Christmas Eve, Baba's cousin, Hossein, invited us to his apartment for a potluck. He asked Maman if she could make an Iranian dish for the occasion. Maman eagerly agreed and decided to make ghormeh sabzi—a Persian herb stew. She bought the best cilantro, parsley, and chives from the market and spent all day chopping, seasoning, and frying the herbs. Mar Mar and I helped her by cutting the stems and washing the green leaves. The aroma of the scented greens brought back memories of Azra's kitchen. I missed the summer days Azra spread heaps of chopped herbs on white sheets in the roofed backyard to dry them for the cold months. Maman placed pieces of lamb and kidney beans in the slow cooker, crushed the dried Persian limes she'd brought from Iran, and sprinkled the lime particles on the lamb. Later she added the fried herbs and let the lamb braise in the lime sauce for hours and also made a platter of saffron basmati rice to serve with the stew.

A few guests had arrived before us at Hossein's apartment. He opened the door himself and welcomed us with a big smile on his broad face. He had visited us a few times since we'd arrived in the United States. He kneeled down to hug Mar Mar and me. He pulled out a pack of grape-flavored Bubble Yum bubble gum from his front pocket, gave each of us a pack, and kissed our cheeks. He greeted Leila with a gentle handshake and admired the cashmere cardigan she was wearing. She looked attractive with her caramel curls cascading down her lilac cashmere.

To my disappointment, there wasn't a single child in the apartment. None of Hossein's friends had children. Maman and Baba carried the foil-wrapped dishes to the open kitchen while Mar Mar and I said salam to the guests and sat on his roomy sofa. His friends asked our names and grades in school.

Hossein made room for Maman's dish on the dark granite countertop and said, "Welcome. We've been expecting your arrival since early afternoon."

"Expecting me or ghormeh sabzi?" Maman laughed out loud. She took the aluminum wrap off the stew and rice, and the aroma of the herbs wafted in the air. "It's tasty, one hundred percent homemade."

"I haven't had ghormeh sabzi for two years," Jalil said. He had a round face accentuated by an anchor-shaped black beard.

"Then please enjoy," Maman said to Jalil.

"Dinner is ready. Help yourselves," Hossein said. He stood beside the counter to distribute the plates and napkins.

Jalil ladled some ghormeh sabzi on his plate of rice and tasted a spoonful. "Fantastic!"

Hossein turned on the TV while everyone served themselves food. The news channel was showing a report on the status of the American hostages in Iran. The crisis had started on November 4, 1979, when a group of radical Iranian students stormed the U.S. Embassy and detained the employees inside the building. "So, what's the deal now that the Shah has left the New York hospital for Panama?" Hossein asked.

"One way or another, the Shah must be returned to Iran," Ali, another friend of Hossein, answered. He had the same bushy beard that the majority of Iranian students who captured the embassy had.

"I think it was wrong to seize the American Embassy, to blindfold, bind, and humiliate those poor employees," Leila said. She poured a glass of water for herself. "The embassy is considered a foreign nation's territory."

"Ah, ah, they are held on accounts of espionage. Do you really think Americans will sit aside and hail the glory of our revolution?" Jalil said.

"You might be too young, Leila khanoom, to remember the Shah's coup d'état with the help of Americans when all Iranians had their high hopes in Mosaddegh," Hossein said. He glanced at Leila's curls while she sipped from her glass. "Americans have a bad reputation for meddling in Iranian affairs."

"It is a demonstration of power," Baba said. "Khomeini wants to show to the world he has full command and that he is totally in charge." He was sitting on the sofa and eating from the plate on his lap.

Mar Mar and I were seated around the white cloth Maman had spread for us on the carpet. She sat beside Mar Mar and helped her eat the rice and stew while she supervised my eating. I separated the lamb from the rice and set it aside on my plate.

"Eat the lamb," Maman said to me.

"The stew has the nutrients. I'm eating the stew with the rice," I said.

Maman frowned at me but turned to Baba, wary of the hostage conversation becoming intense.

"They don't know what they want," Baba said. "These so-called Students of Imam's Line send confusing messages every day. One day their spokeswoman says the hostages will be put to trial. Another day she comes and says the hostages are going to have a memorable Christmas. Yet another day, she explains martyrdom to reporters and implies these poor Americans are being held hostage in exchange for the young Iranians tortured and killed in the Shah's prison. They don't know the tune. They are playing it by ear."

"I agree with you—their demands are not clear. What does she mean by memorable Christmas? Is she joking? Can anyone have a memorable holiday in captivity?" Hossein said.

"Imam Khomeini is presenting the glorious way of Islam to the world. He is demonstrating the hospitality of Muslims toward the Christian captives, that we are all brethren of one faith handed down from Abraham, the father for all Jews and Christians and Muslims," Jalil said. He waved his hands up and down as he talked. He turned toward Baba and said, "And about that bloodsucking Shah, sir, he ought to be returned to Iran, put to trial, and get what he deserves for the crimes against humanity he has committed. You cannot plow through sixty thousand lives and move on."

Baba shook his head and said, "Who says he killed sixty thousand people? Where is your evidence? Khomeini says so?"

"It's in the news, everywhere. The mothers of martyrs know it, deep in the wounds they carry in their hearts."

"Oh, such a grandiose image, sentimental, theatrical picture, blubbering out the immature emotions of the masses!" Baba said as his face flushed with rage. He placed his plate on the coffee table, leaned back on the sofa, and crossed his arms.

"Americans want to bring power back to the Peacock Throne. They've been caught red-handed in history for that," Ali said.

"Even if the Shah hadn't commanded killing at that scale, the majority of Iranians tend to believe it. They can't forget what happened in Jaleh Square on the seventeenth of Shahrivar or the many innocent people that have been tortured or killed in Evin Prison by SAVAK. Only in a fair trial will the pure gold be washed out of the dirty mud," Hossein said.

"We Iranians feed on rumors. Rumormongers we are. We've forgotten how the Shah modernized Iran and changed the world's perception of us. How do you think you are here, studying in America? Who empowered you as a civilized nation, eager to thrive? Who? Khomeini? With his anti-American doctrine?" Baba said.

"Now that's the show, sir, for you and me to believe the Shah was a devoted servant of his people. An ugly, dirty lie! Iranians know who he served. Imam Khomeini illuminated his traitorous face."

"Watch your mouth, young man!" Baba said. "Who are you calling a traitor?" He hammered his fist on the sofa's fluffy arm.

I had stopped eating and was staring at Baba, scared of what would happen next. Maman wasn't paying attention to me and Mar Mar anymore. She kept whirling the spoon in Mar Mar's plate, tossing the already mixed rice and stew. Mar Mar glanced back and forth at me and Baba.

"Salavat befrestin," Hossein said. "Jalil, go pour more ghormeh sabzi on your rice."

"Do you want a glass of water?" Maman stood up from the floor to fetch a glass for Baba.

Jalil turned his attention to the TV and sat on a stool beside the kitchen counter. Hossein leaped toward the TV to turn up the volume. The soothing sound of a Christmas carol chimed while an organ played in the background. Maman brought a glass of water for Baba and winked at him while she handed him the drink.

On our way home, Maman said that she felt the conversations at Hossein's apartment were unfriendly and not suitable for us. Even though I didn't understand some words and phrases Baba and others had used, I sensed the hostility in their voices. As I lay in the upper bed of our bunk bed that night, I eavesdropped through the thin wall between our bedroom and my parents' room. I had made a habit of listening to Maman and Baba's late-night conversations, since they often talked about something concerning me and Mar Mar.

I heard Maman saying, "But you shouldn't have argued with them."

"They don't know who the traitor is. They know nothing about history."

"Yes, they're young and ignorant."

"What will Americans, what will the world, think of us? That we are a bunch of barbarians, climbing walls, blindfolding, and tying up foreigners?"

"Well, azizam, you can't change what's happening in Iran by arguing with these students. They have the same mindset as the ones who captured the embassy."

"How will we be judged in history later on?"

I didn't hear a word after that. Their voices flickered and faded, as if Maman had placed a tiny, bell-shaped candle extinguisher on the flame. Maybe they kissed? I don't know. But the words Baba used lingered in my thoughts. Were we barbarians as he said? The word wasn't new to me. Agha Joon had told many stories about barbarians. He'd mentioned them in the Sindbad voyage stories. The ones who captured merchants and sailors, fed them with greasy food, and anointed them with coconut oil just to fatten them up to be roasted for the barbarian king. The king who only feasted on fat and greasy bodies. Were we acting like those barbarians? All I hoped that Christmas night was for the Americans to be freed and the hostage crisis to end, so that Michael or any other kid would not harass me because of them. I hated coconut oil, and the thought of spreading it on someone's body was repulsive. I didn't want to be called a barbarian. I wanted to be an Iranian with no other name.

The Iranian hostage crisis didn't end that Christmas or New Year as many had hoped. It dragged on throughout the spring. Every time Baba turned on the TV news, a counter on the left upper corner of the screen showed the number of days Americans had been kept in the embassy against their will. It had become routine to start the day hearing about the situation on public radio as Baba drove us to school. It seemed as if an evil ifrit had cast a dark spell on our life in America. Our neighbors suspected we were foreigners from our skin tone, our dark hair, and my parents' accents, but they didn't know what part of the world we belonged to. Maman and Baba didn't mingle with them.

One day in March, as we were preparing for Nowruz, Baba called us into the living room and gathered Mar Mar and me by his side. He said he had something important to tell us. Maman peeked at us from the kitchen while she mixed walnuts and egg yolks in a deep bowl. She had shelved the bowl on her swollen belly as she prepared our favorite Nowruz cookies. We were expecting a baby brother in May.

"From now on, if someone asks you where you're coming

from, you don't say you're Iranians," Baba said. "We've come from Jordan, understood?"

"Baba, where is Jordan?" Mar Mar asked.

"Why from Jordan?" I asked.

Maman stopped beating the batter in the bowl. The rhythmic sound of her fork broke off, and a deep silence ensued. We all looked at her standing in the doorframe, frozen, holding the fork in the air. "Jordan?" she asked, surprised.

"Because Americans are friends with Jordanians nowadays," Baba said. "Jordan is an Arab country close to Iran. If you bring a map, I'll show you."

Mar Mar ran to our bedroom and fetched the glossy world map Baba had bought for us a couple of months before. He unfolded the map and pointed to a country that resembled an upside-down V, somewhere close to the Mediterranean Sea.

"We could call it Iran's neighbor if we skipped Iraq."

"Baba, but we are Iranians. Why do we have to tell people we are from Jordan?" Mar Mar said.

"Baba, didn't you say we are from a great country?" I asked. "We are bigger than this tiny country. Why should we suddenly become Jordanian?" I touched the smooth brown mountains of Iran on the surface of the map.

"Never, ever doubt the glory of our civilization," Baba said. "We know who we are, but some of our neighbors might not know our country that well. They might mix us up with the bad guys who are holding hostages in Iran." He pointed to the TV stand in the living room corner. "Do you see the news every day?"

"Yes," we both said.

"I don't want anyone pestering you, knowing you are Iranian."

"Daddy . . . mmm . . . Baba, what does civilization mean?" I asked.

"It means we had, well, still have, a well-organized society in Iran. We have great art, music, and literature that we are proud of. Our people admire beauty from ancient times."

"Baba, will those barbarians let the Americans come home?" I asked.

"Do they know Marcie is waiting for her brother to come home?" Mar Mar asked. "Didn't they see her crying on TV?"

"Where did you pick up that word, Moji?" Baba asked.

"From Sindbad's stories," I said.

"I see," Baba said, nodding his head. "Well, let's not call them barbarians, but they have committed an outrageous, uncivilized action against the Americans."

"What do you mean by uncivilized action?" I asked.

"La elah ella Allah!" Maman said from the kitchen. "Don't you girls have homework?" She had spooned the batter onto the cookie sheet and placed the tray in the oven. She came to the living room and said, "Will you let these *Jordanian* girls do their homework and muse on their nationality change for a few days before you lecture them about civilization?"

Baba laughed out loud. "Sure, my Jordanian lady."

Maman sat on the coffee sofa beside me and pulled me close to kiss my head. She combed her fingers through my hair as she glanced at the map shining under the light. I folded the map carefully on its creases, trying to restore its original shape.

"Baba," I said, "can you buy us a world globe, like the one we have in our class?"

"Is this map not enough for you?"

"The mountains are raised on the globe, and the oceans have rims. Can you please? I've seen a couple in Kmart."

"You like geography?" Maman asked.

I nodded and said, "Maman, there're too many islands, too many eccentric names written on our globe."

"Eccentric!" She patted my hair and winked at Baba.

"Next time we go to Kmart, we'll go to the school aisle." He leaped from the sofa to turn on the TV.

––––––––––

Carla, our neighbor's daughter, was a year younger than Mar Mar. She was taller than both of us, and she wore dresses all the time. Her mother must have been fond of dolls, buying so many clothes for Carla and dressing her like a doll. Pleated or plain, she wore colorful dresses when we played. Her freckles darkened in sunshine like chocolate spots on her cheeks, and she always tucked her soft, light brown hair behind her big broad ears. She was an only child who loved playing with us and eating Maman's saffron rice. Every day at quarter past five, she knocked at our front door and said sholom since she couldn't pronounce salam the way we said. We had tea parties with our dolls and colored our Wonder Woman coloring books when she was at our house. Late in spring, we rode our bikes back and forth in the street. I was the fastest even though I was the smallest, and I often had to wait for Mar Mar and Carla at the end of the street.

One Saturday morning in April, when the dogwood tree in our yard was in full bloom, we cycled the neighborhood many times. Toasted by the sunshine, we grew thirsty by noon. We pulled up to Carla's house, panting over the handlebars of our bikes, trying to catch our breath for the next race. Carla's mother came out to the porch to fill the food bowl for their black cat. She was wearing a snow-white bouffant dress that covered her skinny legs and made her look like a dandelion on a thin green stem. She called to us as she poured the cat food in the bowl. "Y'all wanna come in for some Kool-Aid?"

Carla nodded. "Let's go inside."

Mar Mar and I had never gone to their house. We stayed where we were.

Carla noticed the hesitation and said, "We'll be back soon." She followed her mother and disappeared into the foyer. "Come on in!" she yelled from inside.

I glanced at Mar Mar. "Shall we go in?"

Maman didn't like us going to the neighbors' houses, but we were both thirsty and tired. We decided to go in for five minutes to drink the Kool-Aid and then return to our bikes. A cool, dark hallway led to their living room. Unlike our bare rooms, their entire house was decorated with fine wooden furniture. A tall grandfather clock emerged at the end of the murky hallway. It struck twelve as we meandered past the decorated walls. The bay window in the living room had off-white voile sheers covered by aster-patterned curtains. Mar Mar and I sat on the white cotton sofa facing the windows, and Carla slid onto the love seat in front of us while we waited for her mother to bring the Kool-Aid. An old gramophone, similar to the one Leila and Saba had, played "You Needed Me"—a hit love song I'd heard many times those days. Withered and parched, we faded in our seats, listening to the song.

Memories flooded back as I glanced at those curtains hanging in front of the windows. Maman used to take us to Zartosht Street in central Tehran to buy textiles for sewing dresses. The stores in Zartosht Street were famous for their upholstery fabrics, curtains, and clothing. I would touch the curtains while Maman haggled over prices with the sellers. Aster flowers, with their lavender petals embracing the marigold anthers, were my favorite pattern. The flowers, kittenish and coy, lived on a rough, starched cotton background, and the petals turned a slightly different shade as I caressed them. I could smell the dampness of the sea, as if they bore the sea mist in their threads.

Once I asked Maman if she would sew a gypsy skirt out of those aster-patterned curtains for me. I dreamed of dancing around the house, floating the skirt in the air, and spreading the scent of the sea.

Amid the melancholy of the moment, I suddenly noticed the oceanic blue of a world globe in the far corner of the room. The giant globe shone like a star on its cherry wood stand, attracting me like a magnet. The next moment, I found myself beside it, fondling the raised amber mountains.

"You like the globe?" Carla's mom asked, jolting me out of my dream. She'd entered the room with three ice-filled glasses of cherry Kool-Aid.

"I love world globes and maps." I ran back and sat on the sofa.

"Come, drink the Kool-Aid and let's see what ya know." She placed the drinks on the marble table in front of the sofa.

Carla jumped out of the love seat and gulped down the Kool-Aid in three seconds.

"Moji? Am I right?" she asked Mar Mar.

"No, Mom, she's Mar Mar. She looks bigger, but she's not," Carla said.

"Carla always talks about y'all."

"Thank you, ma'am," Mar Mar said as she picked up her glass from the tray.

"Ya gals need to come here more often. Carla enjoys playing with you." She sat in the love seat, placing one leg on the other, twirling her pointed kitten heels in the air. "Now tell me, where are you from?"

I placed my Kool-Aid back on the tray and darted to the globe to spin it to the Middle East. The blue sphere twirled a few times before I could locate Iran on the map.

"Mar Mar and I were born here!" I touched the raised Alborz Mountains. "On the foothills of this silent volcano, named Damavand."

"Oh," Carla's mom said. She rose from the love seat and came toward me. She bent down to look closer at the globe. "But this mountain chain is in Iran."

"Yes ma'am. We were born in Tehran, the capital of Iran. Our country was called Persia before, and we are Persians. Persia was a great empire. Have you heard anything about our history?"

"Ha! But I thought ya gals are from Jordan."

Mar Mar shook her head in silence. I suddenly remembered all about Jordan and noticed what a huge mess I'd made.

"Yes, I mean, I mean the Persian Empire stretched to the Mediterranean Sea in the old times. It included Jordan as well," I said. "Iraq and Jordan were part of Persia before." I slid my trembling fingers from the mountains to the blue sea.

"I see," she said. "You know a lot about history, don't ya?" She moved back to the love seat. "You want some more Kool-Aid?"

"Thank you, ma'am. Can we go back to our bikes?" Mar Mar said.

"Yeah!" Carla screamed. "I'll win this time."

Mar Mar and Carla rushed out of the room. I stumbled after them, ashamed of the conversation I'd started, mortified by the identity I'd revealed, and terrified of Baba's reaction once he discovered I'd broken his rule. A gush of remorse washed over me as I realized that I had endangered myself, Mar Mar, and the whole family.

———

For a few days, at a quarter past five, we expected Carla to appear at our door. But she didn't come to play with us. We wondered if she was sick, so I decided to check on her one afternoon when we were biking outside. Mar Mar sat on her bike beside the porch while I knocked on their door. After a few seconds, Carla's mother opened the door.

"Hello, ma'am," I said. "Can Carla come and play with us?"

"Carla is not home. She's gone with her father to see her grandma," she said. She was wearing a lemon-colored lacy dress with a teal blue belt that day. She placed her hand on her waist and said, "She won't be back for a few days." She shut the door without a goodbye.

I shrugged as I turned back to Mar Mar. As soon as I got on my bike, Mar Mar said, "Moji, look!" I followed her eyes and glanced at their bay window. Carla was peeking at us from the corner of the aster curtains. She waved at us and smiled. Suddenly, she turned her head back and dropped the curtain.

Two weeks after the incident at Carla's house, all our neighbors knew we were Iranians. There was a giant maple tree close to the cemetery where kids gathered under its shade after school. They had roped the inner tube of a truck tire and hung it from a thick branch of the maple tree to make a tire swing. Mar Mar and I sometimes went there and took turns riding the swing with the other kids. One day after a thunderstorm, we biked all the way up the hill and parked our bikes against the short wall of the graveyard. The dogwood petals that had been blown off in the storm covered the sidewalk like a white floral carpet. As always, we said hello to the other kids and joined the circle around the swing. I noticed that the tall boy I stood beside stepped away from me. No one said hi to us.

"Who's the last in line?" I asked.

"You ain't going to swing today. You and your sis," the tall boy yelled back at me.

"Why?" Mar Mar asked.

" 'Cause you keep our hostages!" the girl on the swing shouted back.

She jumped off the tire and stamped on the green grass in front of Mar Mar. She pushed her hands against Mar Mar's chest and said, "Ain't you Iranian? Carla's mom told us you are!"

Mar Mar fell back on her hands on the wet grass.

The tall boy snatched the swing's rope and pulled it toward himself. "You have no turns. Go back home!" he yelled.

Mar Mar and I walked back to our bikes, leaning lonely against the wall under the dogwood tree. I saw Mar Mar's tears trickling down her cheeks. She wiped her face with her dirty hands. A streak of mud lined the lower rims of her eyes.

"Don't cry, Mar Mar." I tried to cheer her up. "We'll go home and play together." But my heart broke when I saw her crying. She was the most patient girl I've ever seen in my life. She never cried when we quarreled or when Maman reprimanded her for something. It hurt to be accused of holding hostages when we had nothing to do with the crisis. I had buried the story of the Eye of God in my heart. I wanted to calm Mar Mar, but how could I console her when I was deeply hurt myself?

We never biked in the neighborhood again.

Back to the Sea

*Were it not that thy heart loved me and that
thou promotedest me over all thy concubines, I had
not remained with thee a single hour, but had cast
myself from this window into the sea and gone
to my mother and family.*

———

"Julnar the Sea-Born and Her Son
King Badr Basim of Persia"

One night in May, I woke up to Leila's whispered voice talking
to someone on the phone. I rubbed my eyes in the dark to
see the round clock on the opposite wall. The short hand was
pointing to three. Who was Leila talking to so late at night? Mar
Mar was still asleep in the bed below. As soon as I stepped on
the first rung to get out of bed, the bedroom door opened and
the living room light seeped into our room. Leila was standing
at the door.

"Are you awake, Moji?" she whispered.

"Yes, khaleh," I said. "Who was on the phone?"

"Baba called," she said, "your mom just gave birth to a baby.
They're both healthy, and he is a big boy."

I jumped down from the second rung and ran toward her. I
was so excited I didn't know what to say. Mar Mar startled in
her bed as I jumped to the floor. She squinted her eyes to see
us in the light. "What's going on?"

"Mar Mar," I said, "Maman has given birth to a little boy."

Mar Mar rose from the bed and came to us. She joined me in Leila's arms. "Mobarak bashe," Leila said to both of us. "You're going to have lots of fun with the new baby."

All day in school, I was longing for the moment I could see Maman and my little brother in the hospital. It was Mother's Day, and we had made cards for our moms at school. I wondered how Maman felt after giving birth. She looked tired during the last few months of her pregnancy, and she had trouble moving around. I hoped she could become the agile and energetic mother I'd known before.

The drive from school to the hospital took forever. I couldn't understand why Baba was driving so slowly, stopping for more than five seconds at every stop sign. It seemed like traffic lights stayed red longer than usual and every single car drove faster than us. I was standing in the space between the two front seats, not able to sit still in the back.

"Baba, how far is the hospital?"

Mar Mar leaped from her seat and squeezed herself between me and Baba's seat. "Baba, how does he look? Our teacher said all babies have cute button noses."

"Mar Mar, put your backpack in the seat, at least. You are squishing me like a tomato!" I yelled.

"You've been standing here the entire ride. I want to ask Baba a question."

"I've asked before you. You just meddled in."

"Easy girls, you need to sit back." Baba laughed out loud. He turned into the visitor parking outside the hospital. "We're almost there."

"Baba, what are we going to name the baby?" Mar Mar asked.

"We shall see," Baba said.

He turned off the engine and unlocked the doors. I jumped

out of the Chevy, trying to get to Maman sooner than Mar Mar. On our way to the lobby, I wondered how Maman and Baba had picked our names. Baba carried our backpacks in the elevator and said, "Don't forget to wash your hands before you touch the baby."

As soon as the elevator door opened, we saw a picture of a blond mother holding a naked newborn in her arms in a wooden frame on the wall. Baba pushed a button beside a green double door, and we waited for someone to answer. An old lady's voice asked Baba's name and after confirming it, she opened the double doors. The mother-baby floor smelled like roses in bloom. Flower vases embellished the nursing station and a floral ornament hung on every patient door—Mother's Day flowers. Baba stood beside a door in the hallway and motioned us to go in. The day had been so long I couldn't believe I was finally seeing Maman and the baby. And there she was, my mom, sitting on the bed, holding the baby to her bosom. Wrapped in a fluffy blanket, a miniature human was suckling on her breast.

"Ghorboonetoon beram," Maman said as soon as she saw us. Her eyes brimmed with tears, and her lips slanted upward with a faint smile. "Come here." Her hair was unkempt, but her cheeks were satiny and bright from the pregnancy weight she had gained.

Mar Mar and I bent over the bed to see the baby. Maman pulled her nipple out of the baby's mouth and brought him close to us. Eyes closed, he slept peacefully.

"Look at his nose," Mar Mar said with joy. "Maman, can I hold him?"

"I'm first. I'm the older sister," I said.

"Remember what I said?" Baba said to us.

We darted toward the bathroom, trying to grab the soap in a race.

"Moji, older sisters should have patience!" Mar Mar yelled as I snatched the soap from her hand.

"You should wait your turn, Mar Mar! I am one year, three months and three days older than you."

Leila laughed. "Dava nakonin hala." She'd come in the morning to help Maman during the day. "You girls want some kaachi?" she asked.

"What is kaachi? Is it delicious?" Mar Mar said.

"It's a dessert made especially for women who've given birth," Leila said. "It's basically a liquid halva, sweet and rich. I got the recipe from Azra a few days ago."

I noticed the pot on the window ledge. As far as I remembered, it was the first time Leila had made a dish. Maman let each of us hold the baby for a short time. He had the cutest little nose dotted with tiny white spots, and his eyebrows barely had any hair. Leila ladled some kaachi into two bowls for me and Mar Mar. Baba took the baby from Mar Mar and kissed his little feet.

"We have named him Mohammad, the one who is praised," Baba said.

"We'll call him Mo," Maman said after Baba. "May Allah bless him all his life."

I ate a few spoons of kaachi as I listened to Maman and Baba. Like that bowl of doughy dessert, my heart was a mélange of sweet and rich emotions. I was overjoyed with the baby's arrival, yet I felt detached from the little creature that had suddenly become the center of my family's universe. I couldn't feel the kinship bond yet—like the one I had with Mar Mar. Was that little boy going to be like Mar Mar to me? I twirled the spoon in the bowl, fascinated by the curves that lingered on the surface of the kaachi. I couldn't understand Maman's emotions at that moment. Why did she cry when she saw me and

Mar Mar? Was she becoming estranged from us because of the new baby?

Mohammad, I thought, was a beautiful name.

Early in July, Baba took us to Guntersville State Park, near the banks of the Tennessee River, about an hour drive from Huntsville. Mar Mar and I were excited about the trip since Baba had told us we could swim in the park's lake and play on the beach. I had pleasant memories of the Caspian Sea in northern Iran from the time we spent our vacation in a well-equipped private resort built for the Shah's high-ranking officers and their families. Mar Mar and I loved to collect seashells at the beach, a game we had almost forgotten. Thousands of little sea creatures lived near the shore, where the foamy water sank into the sand. We were scared of those creatures crawling on our feet. We stayed far from the shore and played in the dry sand until Maman and Baba carried us in their arms, past that frightening place where the water met the sand. I wondered how other kids weren't afraid of those crawling little monsters and went barefoot into the water. With puffy water wings, we floated on the water like fluorescent bobbers on the end of a fishing line. Maman and Baba swept our legs out from under us and pulled us under the water as we played. "Look what a glittery whitefish I've caught!" Maman said as she caught me and kissed my cheeks.

But Maman was indifferent about the Guntersville trip. She said she would rather stay at home and take care of Mo, who was too small to enjoy the beach. Baba frowned at her and said that the baby would be fine in his bassinet. She didn't argue with Baba and gathered our beach towels as we jumped up and down on the sofa, excited about the trip.

At the park, children swam in the shimmering lake. The crystalline sand glittered in the sunshine as if a one-eyed thief had dragged a sack full of jewels behind him, not noticing they were falling out of the bag. Baba found an empty picnic table with an umbrella stretched above it and asked us to unpack there. That day we wore strapped sundresses with handkerchief hemlines, dresses Maman had sewn for each of us from the same fabric. Maman's hemline reached below her knees and ours kissed our ankles. Mar Mar and I were wearing swimsuits under our dresses, ready to jump into the water as soon as we got to the lake.

"Maman, are you coming with us?" Mar Mar asked.

Maman gathered her hair with a rubber band and repositioned her straw hat on her head. "I'll watch you from here," she said. She cleaned the bench with a kitchen towel and straightened her dress to sit.

"But Maman, we want to play with you like before!" I said.

"Someone has to watch Mo," she said. She bent to peek at Mo, who was asleep in his bassinet. "Baba can come with you."

"I can watch Mo if you want to go with the girls," Baba said.

"No. I'd rather sit here beside him."

Baba didn't insist. He unzipped the bag to fetch his swim pants. I felt the uncomfortable silence between them as we got ready to go into the lake.

Mar Mar and I floated in the tepid water and played with each other as Baba watched us from nearby. Despite the calmness of the moment, I felt ill at ease. Was it because Maman didn't join us like before? Or was it because I was in a new place not as familiar as the Caspian Sea?

The cinnabar sun tinged the tops of hickories and red maples when we came out of the water and wrapped our towels around us. We were almost ready to go when Mar Mar suddenly noticed a cut on her ankle. It was a straight cut, covered in sand

and sea moss. She started crying as soon as she saw the blood. Maman inspected the wound and fetched a bandage from her purse. She always had calming creams and cleansing wipes in the zipped pocket of her bag. She sat on the bench, held Mar Mar on her lap, and said, "It'll be just fine, Mar Mar. Don't cry." She rubbed the sand from the wound with a clean towelette and applied the bandage. But Mar Mar continued to cry. "You know what Azra did when I had a wound on the beach?"

"What?"

"When I was a little girl, I had a cut on my foot, deeper and bigger than yours," she said. "Azra split a cucumber in half and rubbed its end on my wound."

"A cucumber?" I said.

"Did it help?"

"Yes, it did. It sucked up the salt from the wound. It stopped burning," she said. "There is a lake in Iran called Urmia. It is a salt lake, did you know? You can never drown in that lake because you'll always float on the salty water. But few people dare to go in."

"Why?" Mar Mar asked. She'd forgotten to cry.

"If a tiny drop of that salty water splashes into your eyes, it'll burn badly. People usually don't go into the water because of that. But we had a secret remedy."

"What is a remedy?" I asked.

Maman looked at the crimson lake and smiled. It was the first time I saw a faint smile on her lips after she'd given birth.

"A cucumber?" I said.

She nodded. "Yes, Moji. We used cucumber for burning eyes. We rubbed it on our eyes as soon as the water drops sprinkled on our face. Azra had the secret remedy for all pains."

The straw hat shaded her eyes. In the dying light of dusk, I couldn't tell if they brimmed with tears. She dried the corners of her face with her arms. At that moment, I wished I had a cucumber I could split in half and rub on her eyes. Never in my life could I stand to see her lamenting eyes.

Maman started smoking again. I found a Winston packet deep in a kitchen drawer one day when I was searching for a straw. I smelled the familiar odor in her hair, but I never thought she would chain-smoke again until the night I saw her on the porch. I woke up from a nightmare and went searching for her, but she wasn't in her room. Terrified and trembling, I saw the smoldering tip of her cigarette sparkling like a cat's eye on the porch. She was bent forward in the rocking chair, inhaling the fumes into her lungs. Earlier that day, Baba had taken Leila to Birmingham and wasn't back yet. She had been accepted to an undergraduate program at the University of Alabama in Birmingham, and she had to move before her classes started.

I ran to the porch and said, "Maman, I had a nightmare!"

She startled and crushed out the cigarette in a saucer she had in her lap. "You scared me, Moji!"

She placed the saucer on the floor and opened her arms for me. We rocked back and forth for a few minutes in silence. I was surprised she didn't ask about my nightmare. Usually, she asked about the details and then advised me not to pay attention to it. I wanted to ask why she'd left Mo in the bedroom and was smoking alone in the dark. But I didn't dare. Deep in my heart, I knew I wasn't going to hear a pleasant answer, if I received any answer at all. I counted five cigarette butts in the saucer. I said nothing and let my ears relish the lilting music of her heart.

Baba came home later that night, exhausted and sleep-deprived. It was not usual for Baba to wake up late. But that Sunday morning, we had finished our breakfast long before he came to the kitchen. He complained of a severe headache and asked Maman if she could give him some Anacin. Maman was rinsing rice for lunch in the kitchen sink. Mar Mar and I were coloring our Wonder Woman coloring books on the kitchen floor. Colored pencils were strewn everywhere, under the table and chairs. Dazed and with eyes half closed, Baba stepped on a few pencils as he walked to the table, and the sharp point on one of them pierced his big toe. A drop of blood dripped onto the floor. He moaned and leaped toward a chair to inspect his toe.

"Can't you two play outside? Why do you spread your pencils on the floor?" he huffed.

Maman snatched a paper towel and gave it to Baba. He cleaned the blood and looked closely to see if the pencil tip was still in his toe.

"They can't go outside and play. Nobody plays with them. They're trapped inside."

Baba raised his head and looked into Maman's eyes.

She looked straight at him, her hair unkempt, her right shoulder showing from the scoop neckline of her slack gown. "We are all trapped," she said.

"What do you mean?"

"I mean what I said. We're trapped like those poor hostages. Trapped in this house, in this suffocating prejudice that surrounds us. If it wasn't because of you, because of the trust I had in you and your plans, I wouldn't have left Iran for a single day!"

Baba froze in his seat, the paper towel pressed to his toe. The water ran into the strainer, washing broken kernels of rice into the sink. I could hear their gravelly sound as they swirled down the drain. Mar Mar crawled close to me and pressed my arm. We watched Baba and Maman in silence, stupefied and startled, as if we were waiting for an explosion.

"Don't blame the kids for staying inside and coloring their

books on the floor!" Maman yelled. "Don't blame anybody. It was the worst time to come to America. It was wrong, just wrong!"

She bent over the table and snatched up an envelope that lay near the breadbasket. She pulled the letter from its torn envelope, unfolded the papers, and smashed them in front of Baba. Without glancing at us, she picked up Mo from his bassinet and walked out of the kitchen. She slammed the bedroom door after her.

Baba grabbed the letter with his bloody fingers and skimmed through the lines. As he turned to the second page, Mar Mar and I gathered the pencils from the floor and sought refuge in our bedroom, not knowing what was going to happen next. I wondered what important message hid in that letter Maman showed to Baba.

Baba made rice and dill in the rice cooker and served it with plain yogurt for lunch. It was the first time he ever cooked for us. He asked me to go to their bedroom and ask Maman to join us for lunch. Maman didn't answer when I knocked on the door. I begged her to come have lunch with us. I heard Mo crying in the room. He became silent after a few seconds. Maman must have picked him up to nurse, but I didn't hear her say anything. We had lunch in complete silence, unlike every other weekend when Mo cried or Maman talked with Leila and Baba. I came to realize I had never had any lunch, dinner, or breakfast without Maman. She was the ever-present pillar supporting my life.

———————

After lunch, Baba went to Leila's empty room to rest. With his headache ratcheting up, he asked us not to make noise while we played. As soon as he left, I sneaked into the kitchen to read the letter Maman had shown to Baba. Baba's bloody fingerprints had dried on its corners. It started with "My dearest daughter," but it wasn't Agha Joon's handwriting. The letter informed Maman about what was happening with our tenants and that they were refusing to pay rent. They were trying to gather a statement from the neighbors saying that we'd fled the country in order to present it to a newly founded organization called Bonyad Mostazafin to confiscate our apartments. Agha Joon had also mentioned that his vision was becoming blurry and he needed to have surgery for the "pearl water" in his eyes. In the end, he said Reza had transcribed the letter for him and that he wished he could see us one more time.

I couldn't understand what he meant by "pearl water." At first, I thought he was referring to another story from *One Thousand and One Nights*, something to do with an ifrit's magical power, sprinkling poison from a seashell into his eyes. But then I wrote off that idea, knowing Agha Joon would never speak of sorcery—not in real life. I guessed that "pearl water" was some kind of a disease Agha Joon had contracted in his eyes.

Mar Mar and I watched *Love Boat*—our favorite TV show—all afternoon. As the *Pacific Princess* cruised in the ocean, stories of love and betrayal played out in that magnificent ship's ballrooms. *Love Boat* was an escape for us from the lonely days in America to the lovely nights we gathered in the house on Sun Street. The show embedded stories within stories of people with different backgrounds, strangers to each other, sailing the ocean together, their paths crisscrossing in one ship. I wished from the bottom of my heart that we could board the *Pacific Princess* and sail back to Iran. I wished I could sleep on the terrace and listen to Agha Joon's enchanting stories while I gazed at the stars. I felt disheartened that something bad was happening to his eyes, and I hoped with all my heart to see him once again.

It was almost dark outside, but there was still no sign of Maman in the living room. Baba woke up from his siesta and asked whether Maman had come out of her room. He turned on the TV and changed the channel to ABC news. In the dim, luster-less silence of the room, a glaring blue caption appeared at the bottom of the screen: Day 267, July 27, 1980.

"A few of his old friends are mourning his death as many of his countrymen seem to be rejoicing it. But here in the United States, the death of the former Shah of Iran in an Egyptian hos-pital today is being discussed mainly in terms of how it may affect the Iranian hostage crisis." On the screen, the image of Mohammad Reza Shah appeared. "The end came for the ex-monarch at midmorning in Cairo while the former empress, his four children, other family members, French and Egyptian doc-tors, and one of his American spokesmen were at his bedside. He was reported by his American spokesman, Mark Morse, to be lucid and alert almost to the end of his life."

Baba was standing about a meter from the TV when we heard the news. His pose at that moment is etched in my memory. If I had doubts about his loyalty to the Shah, that Sunday evening erased them all. Eyes glued to the screen, he didn't blink. He was so still it hardly looked as if he were breathing. He looked like a figure engraved on a plaque, staring at a disaster.

I believe there are a few particular days in our lives that im-pact our fate more than any other day. Sunday, July 27, 1980, was one of those days for my family and the nation to which I belonged. The day the death slogan Iranians screamed from the rooftops and wrote on the street walls became true. "Margh Bar Shah" was finally fulfilled, and the Shah was dead and gone. The Revolution entered a new phase with the inability to put the Shah on trial. No Shah could be returned for justice in ex-change for the American hostages. The Islamic Republic had to look for new mottos to move forward, and new enemies to fight.

Two months later, when the war between Iran and Iraq began, we returned to Iran. Baba abandoned his classes at the university and dropped out of school. With the Shah's death, he lost hope that the situation in Iran would return to the prerevolution state. I could see why he hoped the Shah would return to Iran and seize power once again. After all, the Shah was brought back to power one time before with the help of Americans in Operation Ajax in 1953, against Mosaddegh's democratic government. So, on day 267 of Iranians holding American hostages, on the Sunday evening of the Shah's death, Baba made the decision to go back to Iran. Maman had the postpartum blues, and she wanted to be with her family more than anything. She felt desolate in America. We were losing our apartments, our income, and more importantly the bond among ourselves. Baba put himself in danger for the sake of his loved ones. He went back to fight for what belonged to us and to keep the unity of our small family.

And Where, Oh My Mother, Is My Father?

> *Then the boys all laughed and clapped their hands at him
> saying, "He does not know who is his papa: get out from
> among us, for none shall play with us except he know his
> father's name." Thereupon they dispersed from around him
> and laughed him to scorn; as his breast was straitened
> and he well nigh choked with tears and hurt feelings.*

"The Tale of Nur al-Din Ali and His Son
Badr al-Din Hasan"

I could hear the throbbing pulse in my ears as we landed at Mehrabad Airport. It was hard to wait in the aisles to get off the plane. After almost two years, I was about to see Agha Joon and Azra again. But as soon as I walked down the stairs, I noticed a stark difference in the appearance of the land and people around me. My eyes were so accustomed to Huntsville's vivid shades of green that I'd totally forgotten the gray and clay of my homeland. Camouflage-uniformed men with guns wandered in the hallways between the gates. Women, the ones who worked in the airport and almost everyone who had come to greet the passengers, wore hijab on their heads. Maman had also covered her hair with a small silk scarf, her long black tresses dangling on her shoulders.

To my utter disappointment, neither Agha Joon nor Azra had come to the airport. Saba and Reza were waiting for us instead. The biggest surprise came when we saw Saba among the welcoming crowd. None of us recognized her at first. She was wearing a black chador, covering every inch of her body, as if she had transformed into a shapeless, black rolling sack without hands or feet. Maman placed her hands on her face in astonishment as soon as she saw Saba, wondering if this was the sister she'd left in Tehran. I felt I was being engulfed by a bulky dough when she hugged me with that sack. She embraced Maman and Mar Mar, kissed Mo in Maman's arms, but refused to shake hands with Baba. Baba stared at her with surprise and drew back his empty hand. Reza appeared different as well. His beard had grown many inches longer, and it had become an essential part of his face. His collarless white shirt hung over his pants, and he had folded down the heel of his monk shoes to make them like the sandals of the mullahs. He greeted us with a smile but didn't ask a single question about our life in the United States. Agha Joon never mentioned anything about Saba or Reza in his letters other than them being fine. I felt the icy wall that separated them from us. They had metamorphosed into the alien creatures of *One Thousand and One Nights* during the past two years.

This was not the encounter I'd dreamed of on the way back home. I flew between the fluffy clouds, longing for the radiant rays of kindred love that had illuminated the house on Sun Street. I was waiting for the moment I could hug Agha Joon and tell him about our life in America. I wanted to circle my hands around Azra's neck and fill my lungs with the rose perfume she wore in the triangle of her long neck, her shoulders, and the rim of her floral chador. The sweet scent of home inhabited that triangle, different from the saccharine-filled marshmallow fragrance I'd gotten used to in the United States. A poignant pressure squeezed my heart as I entered the gloomy, polluted dusk of Tehran.

———————

Maman grieved for the abandoned garden as soon as Reza opened the gate. "He can't see anymore," she whispered in a weepy voice.

It was late October and the vines in Agha Joon's garden had lost their leaves. They looked crooked and grouchy, lying lifeless as we passed under the trellis. There was no scene more disheartening than a garden deprived of the caring hands of its gardener, no one fretting over the fate of the fragile boughs in the snowy cold.

My eyes filled with tears when I noticed Agha Joon couldn't differentiate between me and Mar Mar as he welcomed us into the living room.

"Where have you been, my darlings?" he said. He held us close to his chest. "Mashallah, you've grown so fast."

"Agha Joon, Moji is on your right side," I said.

"Mar Mar is getting taller than you, ha?" He pinched Mar Mar's cheek between his fingers.

"Agha Joon, I've learned a lot about flowers from my teacher," I said. "Can you read us a story tonight?" I realized immediately what a stupid question I'd asked.

Mo was babbling in Maman's arms. As soon as Azra reached for him, his lower lip quivered, and he pulled himself back to Maman. Azra laughed and said, "Stranger, am I?" She ended up kissing his little feet.

Maman gave Mo to Baba and embraced Agha Joon. "Ghorboone cheshmat beram!" I could hear her sniffling as she muttered the affectionate words for his cloudy eyes.

"Alhamdolellah you all came back healthy. He was impatiently waiting for you," Azra said as she hugged us and kissed our cheeks several times.

"Hopefully you will regain your vision soon," Baba said. He shook hands with Agha Joon and embraced.

We sat down on the floor in the living room, leaning against the bolsters while Azra poured tea from her golden samovar and treated us with her cardamom tea and halva.

"When is your eye surgery?" Baba asked as he sipped his istikan of tea.

"It's hard to find an eye doctor these days," Agha Joon said. "Many are leaving the country, and the ones who are staying don't have a set schedule. But Enshallah, in a few weeks."

"I'll be with you Agha Joon," Maman said. "Whenever it is."

We took the guest bedroom on the first floor that overlooked the garden. The room seemed smaller than before, maybe because I was older and taller, or maybe because Mo's crib occupied one corner. Saba had graduated from high school but couldn't attend any university at the time due to the Cultural Revolution that happened the year after the establishment of the Islamic Republic—all colleges and universities were closed. Mar Mar and I hoped to see Saba more often, but she was hardly ever at home. She left early in the morning, came back late in the evening, and most of the time didn't attend dinner with the family. Agha Joon asked about her every night, and Azra gave the same answer: "Who knows where she is." To my surprise, we usually ate dinner in silence, and no one pursued Saba's absence further. I guessed that a dramatic clash must have happened between Saba, Agha Joon, and Azra before we returned to Iran. She wasn't the warmhearted aunt I knew from before. There was no sign of the shiny skirts or colorful shawls with matching earrings that dangled as she walked. She only wore the black chador every time she left the house.

One morning Saba forgot to lock her bedroom when she left, and Mar Mar and I sneaked into her room as we had in the days before the Revolution. To our astonishment, everything had changed. There was not a single photo of the pop singers anywhere. Instead, she had hung a gigantic poster of air force officers hailing Ayatollah Khomeini, an iconic photograph of the Shah's army surrendering to him in February 1979 at the height of the Iranian Revolution. The old gramophone was not in her room either, and we couldn't find a single record anywhere, not even in her closet where she used to keep her favorites.

Azra passed by Saba's room and saw us fumbling with papers and a few revolutionary pamphlets on her desk. "What are you doing in Saba's room?" she said. "She'll be mad if she finds out."

"Where's the gramophone?" I asked.

"We wanted to play a Googoosh song. Where are the records?" Mar Mar said.

Azra stepped in and said, "Zahmat nakeshin! She burned the albums in the front garden."

"Why?" we both said in shock. We couldn't believe she had burned those beautiful jackets with the records.

"Something is going on in her head," Azra said. "She's brainwashed."

"Brainwashed?" I asked.

"Someone has poured water into her brain?" Mar Mar asked.

Azra laughed. "Do you remember any of Agha Joon's stories? How ifrits transformed beautiful girls into ugly old ladies in an instant? This is what the Iranian Revolution has done to the youth in the country." She snapped her thumb against her middle finger in the air. "Like that!" She motioned us to get out and locked the door. "They've forgotten the past. They've become absolutely new creatures, alien to their families."

I looked at Mar Mar to see if she understood something. She shrugged and curved down her lips. I didn't understand either.

Baba was called to the army court a week after we arrived in Tehran. He received a letter informing him of the date he had to show up in court for further investigation. Because of the special circumstance of his early retirement and his stay in the United States, the new army authorities suspected him of being a royalist. He was summoned to provide an explanation.

Early at dawn, Mar Mar and I woke up to the noise coming from the foyer. Mo was asleep, but Maman and Baba's mattress was empty. I peeked into the foyer through the half-open door. Azra had thrown a fistful of espand—the incense she used in welcome and farewell ceremonies—into a small cylindrical censer. The aromatic seeds popped one after another on the glowing charcoal, fuming white smoke in the air. Freezing wind howled below the door, swaying the cloud of espand in the foyer. Maman stood beside the door, leaning her foot against the wall like a one-legged crane. She was wearing her sapphire dashiki and was holding the Holy Koran in one hand. Agha Joon stood next to Maman, all waiting for the moment Baba opened the door. Maman held the Koran up in the air so that Baba could pass under it before he left the house.

"Hold it higher!" Azra said. "He can't pass without bending his head."

Maman raised the Koran higher without a single word. She was dead silent, as if someone had sewn her lips together. I'd never seen her as somber as that early November morning. Baba passed under the Koran and stretched his hands to take the Book from her. For a few seconds, they both held the corners of the Koran, staring at each other.

"Take care of the kids," Baba said.

Maman let go of the Koran and covered her face. Her muffled moan seeped through her fingers and echoed between the walls of the foyer. Baba gave the Koran to Agha Joon and pulled Maman toward him. He pressed her to his chest and rocked her back and forth in his arms. She trembled as she cried. He kissed and caressed her hair.

"What have I done?" Maman wailed. "What have I done?"

Azra shook her head and sniffed. She twirled the censer around Baba's head and whispered the farewell ode on her lips.

"He'll come back, Enshallah. Why are you acting like this?" Agha Joon said.

Baba opened the door, said goodbye, and disappeared in the dim light of the dawn. Maman leaned against the wall and crumpled to the floor. "What if he never returns?" she said. "What if they arrest him and don't let him come back?"

White smoke had fogged the foyer. I could see Maman's slim body shaking with her sobs. Nothing could stop her tears, not even Agha Joon's soothing words. The occasional popping of espand seeds broke the brooding silence. Mar Mar and I cried as she cried, and Mo started squirming in his crib. He woke up to the dawn of Baba disappearing to the ill fate that many Iranians feared: the horror of being arrested by the arcane Islamic army.

I don't recall a trace of fear in Baba's face when he left. He was a learned man, an experienced antiguerrilla leader who'd spent many years of his service near the border between Iran and Iraq. He had encountered more terrifying situations in life than being called by an army court. But in those days, no one knew what was going to happen to the officers who were called for an investigation. Maman had every reason to blame herself, and I blamed her too on that gloomy morning. What if he never came back as Maman feared? Wouldn't it have been better for us to stay in the United States? To bear the solitude that surrounded us in America rather than return to that horribly changed homeland, to that unhomely, alien-feeling country that was taking Baba from us?

Baba didn't come home that afternoon, the day after, or the weeks following that cursed dawn. We didn't receive any call or letter to tell us what had happened to him. We didn't even know where he'd gone. Those days, speedy trials were held—unbeknownst to the public—in small dungeons in buildings occupied by the Islamic Revolutionary Guard. No one knew exactly who the interrogators were, who the judge was, or how the crime was defined. No light of information escaped the black hole of the army courts.

Maman was afflicted in body and mind. She refused to eat and had lost a significant amount of weight. She locked herself in the guest bedroom, chain-smoked, and ignored us as if we didn't exist. She had become a stranger to me. I couldn't believe the elegant lady who straightened her black hair in front of the mirror and gathered it with pearled pins á la mode had transformed into this unkempt woman who resembled the evil witches of *One Thousand and One Nights*. She sprung out of her dark den, disheveled and perturbed, only when Reza came home in the evenings. She snatched the *Kayhan* daily newspaper from his hands and incessantly searched for the list of executed former members of the Shah's army. At first, Mar Mar and I watched her in astonishment when she mourned over the gory images of generals and officers executed by the firing squads. In later days, as soon as I heard Reza ring the doorbell, I would pull Mar Mar by the hand into the backyard outside the kitchen. I would cover my ears with my hands. I didn't want to hear Maman wailing over those newspaper images. I didn't want to be part of the merciless world that had nothing to offer but lifeless faces oozing blood from bullet holes. An eight-year-old mind is capable of understanding death. I understood Maman's futile effort to relieve the pain that was crushing her chest. I fled the moment everyone was waiting for: the moment of hearing the news of my father's execution.

Deep in my heart, I couldn't believe he was dead. I held out hope he would come back. If we had stayed in America, Christmas would be coming soon. We would have put up a pine tree in our class and decorated it with stars and glittering globes. Maybe we would be making the Eye of God again since the American hostages were still being held captive in the U.S. Embassy.

In Azra's yarn basket, I found the turquoise and ivory balls of yarn that had remained from Baba's sweater. I touched them. They had the same softness the sweater had every time I hugged Baba. I grabbed them and pressed them hard to my chest. How I wished I could hug him one more time. I found two straight twigs in the front garden and made a cross. Taking turns, I wrapped the turquoise and ivory threads around the twigs. I made an Eye of God for Baba. I hung it to the highest hinge of the French door in the living room where Mar Mar and I slept. I stared at it every night before I went to sleep. *Dear God*, I whispered to myself, *if Indians believed the Eye of God brought their dear ones back, I beg you, I plead to you, please bring my Baba back.*

———————

Azra's kitchen had become a sanctuary for me and Mar Mar. We helped her prepare ingredients for the meals she made. I enjoyed making noodles for aash reshteh, a soup made of fresh vegetables and homemade noodles during cold months. She gave us two zinced trays and dusted our hands with wheat flour. She sprinkled the flour on the trays and then dumped two fluffy balls of dough she'd prepared the night before onto the trays. We pressed the dough until it was a thin layer on each tray. I loved playing with the dough. It engulfed and consumed my anxiety as I pressed my fingers against that malleable mass. Azra praised me for making a nice, even dough spread, and she showed me how to roll the layer of dough from the opposite sides toward each other until the two resulting tubes came side by side. She brought her sharp, long knife and cut the twin tubes into slim segments. The fluffy dough transformed into a bundle of long noodles. We helped her hang the soft noodles on a cotton rope she'd put up in the backyard.

"It'll take a few days until they dry," she said. "Then we'll break the dry noodles into small pieces and pour them in the aash."

"Why do you have to break them into pieces?" I asked.

"Because long noodles cling together in the broth. They won't cook completely."

I held my tray as she picked the noodles off of it and hung them on the rope.

"Noodles keep our strings tied together, they say."

"What does that mean?" I asked.

She took the last string from my tray and said, "It's an old saying. We wish for the noodles to keep us connected when we eat them."

"Will they connect us to Baba?" I asked.

She turned her face from the noodles and smiled. She patted my hair with her floury hand and whispered, "Enshallah." Then she took the empty tray from my outstretched hands and asked Mar Mar to raise hers. "When all the leaves have fallen from the trees, I'll make the aash."

The first snow of January covered the bare boughs when Azra cooked her first aash. There was still no sign of Baba. No phone call, no letter under the garden's gate, and not even in the newspaper where Maman searched every day. The tenants continued to live in our apartments without paying rent. Maman neither had the stamina nor the interest to get out of Agha Joon's house and dispute the property ownership claims the tenants had provided to Bonyad Mostazafin.

White icy film had covered the ground in the front garden the morning of Agha Joon's eye surgery. Reza went outside to warm up his Peugeot to take Agha Joon to the hospital. Before taking his woolen shawl from the coat peg, Agha Joon walked back in the foyer and knocked on the guest bedroom door. He had pinned his kufi to his hair and was wearing a long brown coat over his suit. Mar Mar and I stood beside him, hoping to see Maman if she opened the door.

"Dokhtaram, I'm going to the hospital," he said, "are you coming with me?"

After a few seconds, Maman twisted the doorknob and opened the door. She looked well-groomed, but huge, dark shadows circled her eyes. She had covered her hair with her blue silk scarf and had her leather raincoat on over her slacks.

"I'll come with you, Agha Joon," she said.

She stared at me and Mar Mar as if she hadn't seen us for ages. She caressed my hair with a brief stroke and said, "Your hair is growing long, Moji. You need a haircut."

Mar Mar clung to the side of her raincoat and pulled Maman to herself. Maman bent down and hugged her, and her long black tresses spilled onto Mar Mar's shoulders from beneath the blue scarf. My eyes filled with tears when she hugged me. The thick cigarette odor was in her hair. She embraced Agha Joon and tapped on his back. "I'll never let you go alone, Agha Joon." She sobbed in his arms. "I won't let you slip out of my hands like him."

"He'll be back, dokhtaram. He has done nothing but risking his life in the high mountains. They'll free him, Enshallah."

Maman took Agha Joon's hand and led him to the foyer. Snowflakes blew inside as she opened the door, but they melted into tiny droplets of water as soon as they touched the tiles.

A day later, Reza took us to visit Agha Joon at Farabi eye hospital. The doctor had successfully removed his right lens, and he admitted him to the post-op ward for observation after surgery. In a two-patient room, Agha Joon lay in the bed closer to the window that faced the Corsican pines in the hospital's park. His right eye was covered with a white cotton patch, and Maman was sitting beside him in an uncomfortable metal chair. A plain gray curtain divided the two patient beds from each other, and an old man, about the same age as Agha Joon, was in the second bed. He had an eye patch too, but on his left eye.

"Nave haye khoshgelam," Agha Joon said, with a hoarse voice as soon as we entered the room. We ran to him and hugged him, each of us on one side of the bed. His wide chest had room for both of us.

Azra placed the bouquet of roses we'd bought from the neighborhood florist on the rolling table in front of Agha Joon. "Khoobi, Agha?" she said

Agha Joon bent his body forward to smell the flowers. "Bah bah," he said, "I am fine, Azra khanoom. Dastet dard nakoneh."

Maman stood up from the chair and took Mo from Reza's arms. She offered her seat to Azra and kissed Mo's head. "Any news?" Maman asked Reza. She had placed the newspaper over the window ledge before we arrived.

Reza shook his head.

"Agha Joon, what did they do to your eye?" Mar Mar asked.

"They took a little round lens out of it," Agha Joon said.

"Why do they call your disease pearl water?" I asked.

Agha Joon smiled. "They call it pearl water because the clear lens in the eye turns white and blurry like a pearl. That's why I couldn't see."

"Agha Joon, will you be able to read again?" Mar Mar asked.

"Agha Joon, can you tell us a story?" I said. "It's been a long time since you told one."

"Moji, you always pick the worst time! He is sick, don't you see?" Maman said.

"It's fine, aziz jan. I can tell a story."

Everyone became silent to hear Agha Joon's story. Even the old man sleeping in the next bed listened. He started the tale of Ajib, a little scholar boy who had lost his father mysteriously. The father's disappearance haunted Ajib throughout his young life. The children at school teased him for not knowing his father and naming the grandfather as his dad. The grandfather takes Ajib to Basra to search for his father. "Basra was a large city in the Islamic world. It was the go-to city at that time."

"Did Ajib find his dad?" Mar Mar asked.

"Yes, in a very sweet way . . . by a pomegranate jam."

"Pomegranate jam?" Mar Mar asked.

"Did they find him in Basra?" I asked.

"Agha Joon, why don't you tell the rest of the story later?" Maman said.

"Maman, but this is the most interesting part of the story!" I said.

She looked at her watch and motioned to Reza to take us home. Agha Joon became silent. He was obviously tired and needed someone to intervene. Azra stood up from the chair and trudged to the bed. She stretched out her hands and combed his sparse gray hair with her ivory comb. It was a gift Agha Joon had bought from Mecca, she had told me once when I'd asked. An image of a turbaned man brushing a girl's long tresses was engraved on it. Agha Joon didn't move as she combed his hair. After a few strokes, he took her wrists, brought her wrinkled hands close to his lips, and kissed her fingertips.

On our way back home, I mused about Ajib's tale. I became certain Agha Joon didn't pick that story randomly. Was he trying to kindle the hope of Baba's return in my heart? Is that what he meant by a sweet ending—like a pomegranate jam? How could he be so sure?

The reason Mar Mar and I couldn't go to school after we returned from America was the mere fact that we didn't have an "understandable" report card for the school administration. A few days after we arrived, Maman took us to the elementary school near Agha Joon's house to see if we could attend classes. Elementary schools had been in session for more than a month. The school principal asked for proof of residence and told Maman we needed to take the placement exam by the end of the first trimester. Maman bought our grade books, fourth grade for me and third grade for Mar Mar, and intended to help us study the books in preparation for the placement exams. But after Baba disappeared and she locked herself in the guest bedroom, study time was canceled. Azra urged us to study, but she couldn't help us since she had limited written language skills.

I read the passages in the Farsi language book. Even though there were many unfamiliar words, I studied them by reading the definitions provided in the gray vocabulary box at the end of each lesson. I especially liked the *Religious and Islamic Teachings* book for its prophet stories. Unlike kids who grew up in religious families, I'd never heard the stories of the prophets before reading that book. Maman and Baba never attended mosque prayers, and I never heard a single sermon in my entire childhood. The stories in that book introduced a new world that fascinated me. They were in sharp contrast to the *One Thousand and One Nights* stories that were full of love affairs, magic, and mystery.

After Agha Joon came home from the hospital, Maman took us to the nearby elementary school to take the placement exam. She gave each of us a plain scarf she had brought from America and showed us how to fold one end over the other and drape it on our heads. She tied a tight knot under my chin and shoved the hair above my forehead under the scarf. "Make sure no matter what you do, you keep this on your head."

At the age of eight, it was the first time I wore a scarf to go outside the house. We had no option but to observe the hijab if we wanted to attend school. Women were threatened in public if they didn't comply with the Islamic hijab, even if they were only little girls like us. The revolutionaries squirted acid on the faces of women who didn't have scarves or cut the showing skin on their legs with razor blades while they rode their motorcycles on the streets. Many women were arrested and tortured in confinement by their legs being placed in bags full of crawling beetles—or at least this was the story being told. The Islamic Republic enforced hijab by spreading fear among women and punishing those who didn't abide by the new law. The hardest part for me was keeping the scarf in place. Like a salamander, it slithered on my hair as I moved. All the way to school, I had to keep pulling the scarf forward. The two ends became unequal from the constant tightening of the tie under my chin. I had a maroon uniform over loose pants that Maman had sewn for me and a thick woolen coat over the uniform.

We passed the same streets we used to stroll with Leila and Saba when they took us to the Pasteur Confectionary. Everything appeared different, yet the same. I tried to remember how it used to be to understand the difference. The stores along the streets were the same, the walls were worn out with the same surly mottos, chinar trees were leafless and bare, and the cars had the same models and makes as before. But the people? Their clothing had changed. Men were wrapped in stone-gray coats, women enveloped in jade black chadors or brick-brown manteaus. There was also something changed in their faces. When you passed them on the street, there were no smiles, laughter, or happy eyes.

We passed the army uniform shops on Sepah Street. Those stores had the best army uniforms in Tehran. I remembered the day I came to the Parcham store with Baba when he wanted to order a new uniform for work. The mustached, round-bellied tailor measured Baba's shoulders, chest, waist, and hips with his green measuring tape and jotted down the numbers in a little notebook he kept in his pocket. He chewed his stumpy pencil between his teeth and said, "I'll make your uniform with the best breathable denim we have in the market, sir." I liked the insignias and medals hanging on the walls with their colorful bands, figures, and shapes, like the lion holding a sword in its right paw, wearing a golden crown, with the sun rising behind the lion's back—the emblem of the nobility and superiority of the Shah.

"Maman, this is the store I came to with Baba once," I said.

She stumbled as we passed Parcham's display window. I let go of her hand and stepped in the shop's doorway. I wanted to see if the round-bellied tailor was still there. Maman ran between the glass door and me, cutting my way.

"What are you doing?" she said. "It's getting late."

But she didn't pull my hand back to the sidewalk. She stood beside me in the doorway, staring at the insignias and uniforms behind the glass display cabinets. All the swords and lions and crowns were gone. There was no longer any trace of the Shah's army symbols. Mar Mar rested her head on Maman's leather coat. Maman caressed her head over her white scarf and put her other hand on her mouth. Our agony was etched and framed in that bitter moment. Oh Maman, where is my Baba? Who has taken him from us? Where is he lost in this land?

———————

Hajar Elementary School had the most perfect square yard imaginable. At the far end of the yard, opposite to the school's gate, faucets sprang out of the cement wall, and water flowed from them into one long, narrow groove. A circle of chinar trees stood in the middle of the yard, allowing children to sit and play under the shade when they had leaves. On that day, a sprinkle of powdered snow had covered the faucet handles and the edge of the gutter around the trees. We entered a long corridor that had windows to the outside street at one side and doors to the classrooms on the other. The first room was the administrative room, which was separated into two sections by a gray wall. The inner section had a "Principal's Office" sign on it. A staff member greeted us and offered us chairs to sit on. After a few minutes, the assistant principal, Ms. Hamid, came out of the principal's office. She wore a long navy manteau that almost reached her galoshes. A black khimar covered her head and torso down to her waist. She gawked at Maman from above her round glasses, as if she were the one who was going to take the exam. With her tight leather coat and her floral silk scarf loosely tied under her chin, Maman resembled a fairy among the fire angels in that room.

"So, Moji is sitting for fourth grade and Mar Mar for third?"

"Yes ma'am," Maman said.

Ms. Hamid had two folders with some papers in her hand. She opened one that had my name on it. "You live on Sun Street?"

"Yes."

"Do you have proof of residence with you?"

Maman brought a folded paper out of her purse and gave it to her. "Here is the signed paper from Fakhrieh Mosque's imam."

Ms. Hamid glanced at the paper and said, "How long have you been living at this address?"

"I have been living there, God, for almost my entire life before I got married. But my girls are living with me and my parents at this address since we came back from America."

"Oh, I see. When did you come back?"

"About three months ago."

"What were you doing there? I see they went to school there?"

"My husband studied in the United States."

"You are living with your parents? Is your husband still in America?"

"No. But he travels a lot."

"Well, here is the imam's signature certifying you live at this address. That's all we need."

Tiny drops of sweat had covered Maman's wide forehead like drops of condensation on a chilled ice glass. She took her embroidered handkerchief from her coat pocket and dried her face.

"Are you ready?" Ms. Hamid looked at me and Mar Mar. "Let's go to the library."

She closed the folders in her hand and motioned us to follow her. Maman blew us kisses in the air as we approached the door. Before we left the room, Ms. Hamid faced Maman and said, "You can come pick them up in two hours. And . . . they should have navy or black scarves. The color they're wearing is not suitable for school."

She took us to a dinky, windowless room on the second floor. Two bookcases with a scant number of books on the shelves

caught my attention. The books appeared thin, some resembling flyers rather than books. Having seen the bright library
filled with thousands of books in McDonald Elementary School,
I felt a pinch in my heart as I entered that room. I wondered
what stories they had in the thin books of that small library.

"Mar Mar, sit here, and you, Moji, sit there." She pointed to
two steel folding chairs with tablet arms near the door and at
the far end of the room. "You sit and I'll bring the exam papers."

We situated ourselves as she left. Mar Mar's tiny body had
sunk into her loose manteau and pants. Her head, covered with
the white scarf, looked like a giant pinboard attached to her
body. In her new shape, she looked nothing like my little sister.

Mar Mar turned her face back to me and whispered, "Moji,
I'm scared."

"Don't be, Mar Mar," I whispered back. "You'll do your best,
I'm sure."

"But what if I get things wrong? I'm not good at reading
Farsi."

"You'll be fine. You read well at home the other day."

She nodded and smiled. My assured tone calmed her down,
but I wasn't sure myself. At that moment, I was glad Mar Mar
couldn't hear my fast heartbeat or feel my own nervousness.
She rested back in the chair and stared at the library door.

The exam was not as terrible as we expected. The questions
were mostly from the books we'd read, and the math and spell-
ing sections were easy. After about an hour and a half, the assistant principal asked us to turn in our papers. She mentioned
there would be an oral exam for me. I had no clue what she was
talking about. What was she going to ask? Mar Mar looked at
me and shrugged in surprise. She placed the exam papers in
our individual folders and brought out the *Religious and Islamic
Teachings* book from underneath the folders.

"You are going to be nine soon?"

"Yes ma'am," I said.

"What's the significance of nine for girls?"

"That I am mature enough to say my prayers?"

"Indeed," she said. "Now, can you read this story for me?"

She opened the book to a certain page and placed it on the tablet attached to my folding chair. I recognized the story the minute I saw the picture of the wheat field on the page. After I read the passage she asked, "Do you know what it means when we say this world is like a harvest field?"

I knew what she was trying to ask. She wanted to test my knowledge of life after death. I talked about the resurrection day and the final judgment according to the Islamic teachings. She listened carefully until I stopped. "Who taught all this to you?" she said at last.

"I read them myself," I said.

She smiled and patted my head. "You know the Islamic teachings better than the girls who have remained in Iran." She pinched my cheek and said, "Mashallah. We need to talk at recess time when you start school."

I felt relieved when we came out of that library. After so many weeks since Baba had disappeared, her words brought a small solace to my grieving days. I took Mar Mar by the hand, and we went back to the office.

On the last day of school before spring break, Mar Mar and I came home early after our exams. Azra's maids—who cleaned the house every two weeks—had washed and spread the linens on parallel ropes in the front garden, and they were cleaning the glass panes of the French doors. Maman and Azra were in the living room, each with a tray full of lentil and half-split peas in front of them, picking the pebbles out of the grains. Guests would pour into Agha Joon's house during Nowruz.

Mar Mar and I decided to play hide-and-seek between the linens before lunch. The tiny embroidered flowers on the fabrics wiggled as we ran after each other between the ropes. The shining glow of white linens reflected on the terrazzo tiles and created a milky halo around the sheets. The upper part of the linens had dried, but water still dribbled from the lower hems. The fresh fragrance of lazhuward—the dark blue powder maids used to cleanse and disinfect the linens—was in the air.

"Don't touch the white sheets!" Maman hollered from the living room.

"Yes, Maman, we won't," I yelled back.

It was my turn to close my eyes, count to ten, and find Mar Mar somewhere in the garden. I looked for her shadow slinking between the sheets, knowing she was slow to choose where to hide. There was no movement anywhere but the fluttering of the sheets. I went between columns, every crevice of the garden, among the short boughs of the fig tree, underneath the grape tree trellis, but I couldn't find her. I shouted her name so that she could hear.

"You can't hide in the house. The rule is to hide in the garden," I said, facing the living room.

The young maid who was almost finished cleaning the glass glanced at me and smiled. I thought Mar Mar had slipped into the living room from the door that was left ajar. I cupped my hands on the newly cleaned glass and peeked into the room. I didn't see her anywhere.

I ran back among the sheets. Suddenly I saw a tall shadow reflected on the last column. I looked down at the tiles: a pair of ragged brown loafers kissed each other at the heels. They looked unfamiliar to me. The scrawny shadow on the linen doubled in size from above the waist. The phantom was holding something in his arms. Who was he? How on earth did he get into the garden? I ripped aside the linen to see for myself. And there in front of my eyes stood Baba holding Mar Mar in his arms. If it weren't for Mar Mar resting her head on his shoulder, I wouldn't have recognized him. His temples had arched into his face, and there was hardly any cheek left. He had grown a grizzled beard. I'd never seen him with a beard. I rushed to him and pressed my fingers into his thighs. I wanted to make sure he was real. He put Mar Mar down on the tiles and lifted me up in the air. I pressed him so hard to my chest that I couldn't breathe. He smelled of the same earthy scent he had when he came back from missions near the border. I slid my fingers along his scar, the scar that bore all my childhood memories in its circular rim. I couldn't believe Baba was back.

He kissed my cheeks and whispered into my ears, "You've grown so beautifully, Moji,"

I was blessed to see him and to be in his arms once again. I wanted to shout, "Baba is back!" but my throat was gripped with joy. It was much the same for Mar Mar, who was silently clinging to his feet. The halo of white sheets surrounded us like heaven and secluded us from the cruel world that once had taken him from us.

Baba took our hands, and we walked toward the house. Just before he turned the doorknob, he placed his index finger on his lips. We tiptoed into the foyer, trying not to make any noise. Maman had finished cleaning the lentils and was heading toward the kitchen, holding the tray with both hands. She sensed our presence and turned her head before she entered the kitchen. She jolted when she saw Baba. The tray dropped to the floor and banged on the tiles, and the lentils scattered all over the hall and the kitchen floor. Baba leaped toward the kitchen doorway and embraced Maman, picked her up from the floor, and twirled her in the hall. The lentils crushed under his loafers as he spun Maman. In her chokes of joy, Maman kept saying, "Ghorboonet beram! Khoda ra shokr bargashti."

We watched them in shock; we watched them with joy. Azra came into the hall when she heard the noise. She froze in the living room doorway when she saw Baba. She leaned on the frame and pressed her hands on her chest. "Agha! Agha!" she yelled.

Agha Joon opened the door to his bedroom and stepped out. He must not have heard the tray's loud crash or Maman's joyous shrills. But he was sensitive to Azra's voice when she yelled his name. Baba parted from Maman and walked to Agha Joon. The two men embraced for a long time; their shoulders shivered as they both cried. Agha Joon dried the tears that dropped on his round, thick glasses. I'd never before seen him cry.

"Alhamdolellah!" he said. "Alhamdolellah."

Baba didn't say anything about his detention or his whereabouts in front of us. "Later," he said, when Maman asked. He was too exhausted to go through the pain of telling the torment at that moment. I studied him carefully as he held Mo in his arms and nuzzled his face against Mo's soft cheeks. I couldn't believe he was back. It felt like the tales of *One Thousand and One Nights*—too fantastical to be true. Mar Mar and I clung to him wherever he went. We didn't want to lose him ever again. Later, Baba told us they detained him with no charges against him, waiting and hoping for some evidence to show up while they searched his records. He was among the few lucky ones who were released after a few months.

Nowruz came with all its beauty and bounty. Azra's wheat sprouts grew nice and tall for our Haftseen table. Agha Joon fully recovered from his eye surgeries and could see the world clearly again. Like every Nowruz, he bought the saplings and flowers he wanted to plant in his garden. Saba and Reza came home earlier and spent time with the family, helping with the festive arrangements. New life ran under the skin of the house on Sun Street. Even in those days of political insecurity and uncertainty, wordless joy wormed its way into our lives.

Part Two

✳ ✳ ✳

The Fables of the Ancients

Our sire died and left us much wealth, and we divided
amongst us his treasures and talismans, till we came to the
books, when we fell out over a volume called "The Fables
of the Ancients," whose like is not in the world, nor can its
price be paid of any, nor is its value to be evened with gold
and jewels; for in it are particulars of all the hidden hoards
of the earth and the solution of every secret.

———

"Judar and His Brethern"

Three years had passed since we returned from America, and
we still lived with my grandparents in the house on Sun Street.
Despite Baba's official complaint to the court, our tenants continued to occupy our apartments and didn't pay a single toman
for the rent. Baba began working in a private telecommuni-
cation company that belonged to one of his cousins. Maman
started teaching—after two years of unpaid maternity leave—in
the same middle school where she worked before the Islamic
Revolution. Uncle Reza married a girl from a religious family
and moved out to an apartment closer to Agha Joon's glaziery
in Tehran's Grand Bazaar. They had a little girl and were expecting another child in a few months. Agha Joon seldom went to
the glaziery and spent most of his time in his beloved garden,
attending to his flowers.

In June 1983, we received a call from my elementary school
that I'd passed the written exam for entering Farzan School,

the only high school for the gifted and talented girls in Tehran. Maman and I had to appear for an interview as the final step for acceptance.

On the interview day, Maman said that she would never wear a chador, even if it increased my chance of getting in Farzan School. "We are who we are. They can like me with scarf and admit you, or you go to a regular school," she said to me in the cab on our way to the school. We were stuck in a traffic jam. Maman glanced at her watch and shook her head. It was close to nine, and she didn't want us to be late for the interview. She paid the driver, and we got off in the middle of Kakh Square, close to the school.

We whisked through an alley that was flanked by chinar trees and had a few multistory buildings. Farzan School was a one-story brick structure squeezed between the tall buildings at the end of that alley. A row of white mulberry trees shaded the classroom windows all the way to the end of the schoolyard. Ripe mulberries had scattered under the trees, and spots of crushed berries had given the concrete pavement a polka dot pattern. A chubby calico cat lay on the last window ledge, dozing off in the trees' cool shade.

A crowd of students and parents had gathered around a notice board on a tripod in the schoolyard. Parents searched for the classroom number their girls had been assigned to for the interview. Every girl whose name appeared on the board was nominated by her elementary school principal based on her fifth-grade scores and had passed a two-step written exam. Maman spotted my name and found my interview classroom. The school entrance opened at the center of the yard, and two long corridors appeared on each side of the entrance hall. According to the wall signs, we had to proceed to the east corridor. Parents and students hovered around the benches in front of the classrooms, waiting for their turn for the interview. A girl was sitting alone on the bench in front of our classroom. As we got close, she stood up and offered us her seat. Maman praised her for the kind gesture and asked her to sit. She was taller than me and unusually fair skinned for a Persian girl. Her hazel irises drew immediate attention in her round face.

"My name is Nusha. What's yours, friend?" she asked.

"I'm Moji," I said.

"Do you have an interview with Ms. Taba as well?"

"I think so. I'm supposed to go to classroom three."

"Which school are you coming from?" Nusha asked.

"Hajar. And you?"

"I am coming from Taghva School. It's in the Shemiran area. Where are you coming from?"

"I'm coming from central Tehran. Pasteur Avenue."

"I see. You have a friend from your school?" she asked.

"No, I'm the only girl from my school."

"I have one. Her name is Nadia. Can you see her there?" She pointed to a girl with a milky scarf at the far end of the opposite corridor.

A lady with a chocolate brown manteau and a light scarf walked out of the classroom. Nusha rushed toward her and yelled, "Mom, how did it go?"

The lady hushed her and said, "I think it went well." She greeted Maman and introduced herself. I wondered what type of questions the interviewer had asked Nusha and her mom. I was already nervous when I heard my name from inside the classroom.

A small fan was spinning at full speed on the teacher's metal desk. Even though the air conditioner blew cold air from the ceiling, it was swelteringly hot in the room. Ms. Taba pointed at an olive chair in front of the desk with her hand fan and asked me to sit. A silver ring encircled the sides of her ginger scarf right under her chin. She had pulled the sides so tight inside the ring that I thought she might suffocate any minute. She flapped the fan rapidly in front of her face, opened a yellow folder, and scanned through the papers inside. I recognized my handwriting. I hoped she didn't notice the rapid rise and fall of my chest under my manteau.

She stared at me from the upper rim of her narrow glasses and said, "Moji? Is this what they call you at home?"

"Yes ma'am," I said.

"You've given creative answers on your written exam," she said. She turned to a page where I'd drawn imaginative shapes out of circles. She slipped the paper toward me and pointed at a specific shape. "This is interesting. What is it?"

"Oh, that, that is a celestial planisphere," I said.

"Celestial planisphere?" she said, surprised. "What is that?"

"It is a mystical globe. The owner can face the globe toward any country on Earth and see the cities and their people in that sphere."

"Oh!" she said. "Where is this that you've drawn?"

"This is Lake Karun in Egypt. Somewhere near the Sinai Desert that has fish as red as coral reefs."

She glared at me with her widened pupils, as if she'd never heard such a weird story. "Where did you get this idea from? This . . . planisphere?"

"From a book called *One Thousand and One Nights*. My grandfather used to read it for me when I was a child. Now I try to read it myself. The language is difficult."

"I see . . . I noticed you mentioned that book as your favorite book in the written exam. That's a voluminous book full of stories. Tell me a story from that book."

I told the story of the red fish in Lake Karun. I wanted to impress her with my reading skills and my affection for books. I elaborated on the allegory of the Moors of Morocco and their chivalrous quest to find *The Fables of the Ancients,* or the book of all knowledge, that was hidden in a treasure trove, guarded by a cipher only known to those red fish.

She listened while she opened and closed her fan, and stared at my nails as I moved my hands in the air. I thanked God I had bathed and cut my nails the night before the interview. When I finished the story she said, "Do your parents let you read such books?"

I remained silent.

"That book starts with the story of an unlawful relationship between a queen and her slaves."

"My grandfather never asked my parents when he started to read that book to me," I said. "But that book has many stories about the epic battles of the Islamic army conquering the infidels in different parts of the world. My grandfather focused on those stories."

"I see!" She closed her fan with a snap and hammered it on the desk. "Ok, you're done. Why don't you ask your mother to come in?"

"Yes ma'am." I moped out of that suffocating room.

Maman looked at me with worried eyes. "Why are you so flushed?"

I shrugged. "Maman, she wants to talk to you."

Maman sighed and went in. Nusha ran toward me from the other corridor and grabbed my hand. "How did it go?" she asked. "Did she ask you about the shapes we drew?"

I nodded. I didn't feel like talking to anyone at that moment. I was sure I had ruined the interview. I'd heard all sorts of things about the students who had been rejected from entering the university for failing those interrogation-style interviews. Never in my mind had I imagined them questioning me for reading a storybook. But I realized my grave mistake. How could an eleven-year-old read a forbidden book like *One Thousand and One Nights* and still be admitted to a gifted school reopened after the Revolution with a new Islamic agenda?

"What did you say you've read?" Nusha asked.

"What did you say?" I asked.

"I said I've read *Suvashun, A Persian Requiem.*"

"What's that book about?"

"It's a novel about a family in Shiraz during World War Two."

"Is it interesting?"

"You want to read it?" she said. "If we get into this school, I promise I'll bring it for you. How about you? What did you read?"

"Where is your friend? Is she done too?"

Maman exited the classroom with a smile. I was glad she had come to my rescue, but I was puzzled by her smile.

"How did it go?" I asked.

"It went well," she said and winked at me. "Did she keep looking at your nails?"

"Yes!" Nusha and I both yelled at the same time.

"I thought I had ink on my nails, the way she stared at them," Nusha said.

"Shameful!" Maman said. "They even want to know if we're painting our nails."

We said goodbye to Nusha and left the building. On the way back home, the traffic jam had disappeared. It was early afternoon in June and the streets were not busy anymore. Everyone had sought shelter from the heat inside the cool stores. Maman hugged me in the cab and said, "Don't worry, Moji. I'm sure you'll do fine. Here or in any other school."

Despite Baba's hesitations and concerns, I started high school in Farzan all-girls school in September 1983. He feared the school would train me in the new Islamic way of the revolutionaries—brainwashed and alien to our Persian culture—but since Farzan was the most advanced and equipped school in Tehran at that time, he enrolled me after I got accepted. We were the first sixth graders selected after the Islamic Revolution.

As soon as I entered the school's auditorium, Nusha waved her hand in the air, signaling that she had saved an empty chair next to hers. Nadia was sitting beside her at the end of the third row. The auditorium quickly filled with students. I walked down the middle aisle, stepping over the feet and backpacks of the girls already sitting in the row. I greeted Nadia and Nusha, excited to be close to the stage. They both wore black scarves and gray manteaus like every other girl. The pistachio-green curtains in front of the stage were the same color as the velvety chairs. A subtle current moved the curtains back and forth, and a bright circle of light beamed from the projector onto the curtains.

Somebody said "Takbir," and we shouted, "Allah o Akbar" in response. A deep silence engulfed the auditorium as the school principal entered from the back and walked down the aisle. She stepped onto the stage and moved toward the bright light at the center. Her photochromic glasses changed to dark green as soon as she entered the circle of light. Her cheeks appeared so rosy in her square face that I thought she'd put a blush on them. Later I found out she had a kind of acne that gave her those ever-blushed, bumpy cheeks. In contrast to all the elementary school principals who wore black, Ms. Zadie wore a coconut-colored manteau and a shiny black silk khimar that covered her hair, neck, and shoulders.

After a long hesitation during which she stared at us from the stage, she took the microphone from its black pole and said, "Welcome to Farzan, dear students! We congratulate you for being accepted to this honorable school. Soon you will realize the fine education you will receive here compared to your home schools. Proud you shall be and grand you shall feel for your achievement, for being chosen one out of every two thousand schoolchildren, and for having the honor to sit in these chairs. Before you, dear pupils, many intelligent students have studied here, in the same classrooms and the same chairs you will occupy. But forget not . . ." She paused and pulled her khimar forward on her head. "But forget not, that every illustrious intellect demands higher accountability. We have suffered from reckless intelligentsia who had forgotten their commitment to their society. You are here because of your intellects, your gifts. But do not forget that by entering this school, you have taken the pledge of devotion to our Islamic Republic. You are standing on the cusp of an epoch in the history of Iran. You, dear students, have the greatest responsibility on your shoulders, to study hard and to be accountable toward your country. May you all flourish and succeed."

I looked back at Nusha and Nadia in bewilderment, not quite understanding what she meant. I saw the same confusion in their eyes. We all felt relieved as she finished and stepped down from the stage. Her shiny black shoes clicked on the stage's wooden floor as she left us baffled by her speech.

Nusha and I were assigned to one class, Nadia to the class next door. As soon as we entered our class, we noticed the stark difference in the number of students from our elementary school days. Coming from crowded elementary schools, we were used to being jammed together with three kids sitting on one bench. But in Farzan School, we had the luxury of individual chairs and sharing a wide green table with only one other girl. Nusha and I sat together behind a table in the first row. Our classroom was at the far end of the west corridor, where we could see the school's back wall from the last window frame.

The balmy breeze swayed the pistachio-green curtains hanging at the classroom windows. Queen, the calico cat, jumped inside the class from the wall. We laughed out loud as she meandered through the tables and mewed for food. As the older girls told us later, it was her ritual to slide through the open window every morning and make a chaos in our classroom. The older girls were finishing their last year of high school, the remaining students of the prerevolution era. No new student was admitted to Farzan School after the Revolution until the new administration designed a new selection process. The school had remained in a reduced staff mode for a few years until my class started. There were one hundred girls, all around eleven or twelve years old, who entered Farzan that year.

"What did she mean by saying we are standing on the cusp of an epoch?" Nusha asked during our first recess. Nusha, Nadia, and I were sitting on the limestone steps in the schoolyard, eating our lunch. I mixed the rice and ghormeh sabzi in my lunch bowl.

"By epoch she meant the Islamic Revolution, I guess," I said.

"Yes, I understand that. But why did she talk so awkwardly?" Nusha said, munching her food. "She is fearsome. No one budged while she talked."

"Same in our class," Nadia said. She took the slices of tomato out of her sandwich. "I hate squished tomatoes, and my mom never listens to me."

I was delighted to see another finicky eater like me. But unlike me, she was chubby. I couldn't figure out how she'd become so sweetly curved if she was as picky as me.

I nodded. "By the way, Nusha, have you brought *Suvashun* like you promised?" I winked.

"You think I forget?" she said. "I didn't know you were accepted, but I brought it hoping I would see you again. I love that book. I keep it close to me when I sleep."

"How are you going to lend it to me if you love it so much you sleep with it?"

"You'll see for yourself," Nadia said.

The Fortress of Mystery

Indeed it was said that she had collected a thousand books of histories relating to antique races and departed rulers. She had perused the works of the poets and knew them by heart; she had studied philosophy and the sciences, arts and accomplishments; and she was pleasant and polite, wise and witty, well read and well bred.

———

"The Story of King Shahryar and His Brother"

The library at Farzan School was a fortress of mystery. The senior girls told us the old librarian had straight white hair braided down to her waist. They claimed the braids gave her the magical power to know the place of every book on the shelves. She would know specific words in paragraphs of the books, and if a girl uttered a phrase, even a word from a certain book, she would find the location of the book in one breath. One day, the white-haired lady vanished from the school and never came back to her beloved library. Rumor had it she never retired—as the school administration claimed—but was detained on account of being a member of Hezbeh Toodeh, the major communist party in Iran. She faded into the same dark fate other individuals who fought with the Islamic regime had, and the library became lackluster after her disappearance.

The first day I visited the library, when I was browsing a book on the "New Books" shelf, I heard a soft voice behind me. "Do you need help finding a book?"

I turned and there, for the first time, I saw Shirin. She was the new librarian appointed by the school administration. She was about Leila's age, maybe a couple years younger, with the same height and build. Her hazel, highlighted hair was soft and straight, peeking out from beneath her cream-colored scarf. Her honey-colored eyes were streaked with gold. With her up-turned eyes, she reminded me of Badr-al-Budur, the princess in the Aladdin story. She had a birthmark on her forehead, slightly lighter than her skin tone, that looked like a country map to me. I couldn't say which country, but I imagined it to be a country from the East. Nusha later told me it was a firebrand, or a daagh, as it is said in Farsi. She said that people who gen-uflected and placed their foreheads on the prayer clay for long hours had it. I rejected the idea since she was young and I couldn't imagine her praying like an old man.

"Yes," I said, "I am looking for a poem." I recited the verse at the beginning of *One Thousand and One Nights*.

"I think I know this poem," she said. "It's at the opening pages of *Alf Layla Wa Layla*. Let's see if we still have it in our library."

I was surprised she knew the poem, but I remained silent, letting her lead me to the book. We passed three columns of bookcases until we got to the section that was labeled PERSIAN LITERATURE. The faint, musty scent of vanilla and grass filled my lungs as we passed through that aisle. Tomes of poetry with rag-ged covers surrounded us in silence. The gleam of milky light from dome-shaped pendant lamps scared away the shadows from the shelves. The titles were readable and clear, and I could see hundreds of divans—poetry collections—on the shelves.

"This, I believe, is what you're looking for. It is the most popular Farsi translation of *Alf Layla Wa Layla* by Abdul-Latif Tasooji." She stretched out her hand and fetched a thick old book from the top shelf. It had a leather-bound hard cover, and higher quality paper than the copy Agha Joon owned. She carried the book under her arm as we walked back to her desk.

"Do you like reading stories?"

"Yes, I do. I was curious to see if there were copies of this book in this library."

Shirin nodded with a smile and said, "Well, this is apparently the last copy. Do you know the origins of *Alf Layla Wa Layla*?"

"I know the stories. My grandfather used to read them to me."

"How interesting . . . you most probably know that the author is unknown, but the stories are from the folklore of ancient Persia. Some scholars believe the author might be Queen Homay, the daughter of King Bahman, who reigned around 500 BC. The oldest text of the book was written in Pahlavi, the language of Persians before Islam. The book was called *Hezar Afsan* at that time. Unfortunately, the original Pahlavi text was lost, and the only available translation after that was *Alf Layla Wa Layla* in Arabic, which was later translated back to modern Persian by Tasooji in the nineteenth century."

"Do you read a lot?" I asked.

She glanced at me as she placed the book on the desk. "What's your name, young lady?"

"Moji."

"Moji, to answer your question, I do. I read a couple of hours every day." She closed the book and slid it toward me. Her long narrow fingers slipped into the gilded groove of the book's title as she pulled back her hands. Her nails were short and she wore no rings or bracelets. "Well, I hope you enjoy reading the book. It's a fresh start for the first week of school. This library has thousands of books if you enjoy reading."

After a few weeks, during which we became close friends, Nusha shared her observation about the books in the library with me.

"You see, if you pay attention to the number on each book's spine in any given row, you'll realize many books are missing," she said.

It was a cloudy Thursday afternoon in November, and we were both reading in the library during our free time. I didn't want to show interest in what she was trying to present as a great discovery, but I stood up from my chair after half an hour and wandered between the shelves. I couldn't take my eyes off the numbers. To my surprise, she was right. There were too many gaps between the serial numbers on adjacent books to be explained by students borrowing them.

"Can you believe twenty books in this row are gone?" Nusha whispered into my ear. She had followed me into the aisle. "Look at this one! You see?" She kneeled on the camel hair carpet. "Who's interested in this book?"

I glanced at the title, *Samak Ayyar, Volume III*.

She pursed her lips and said, "Who, tell me, who even knows this book to borrow it? This is a five-volume book my dad has in his library. Where are the other four? Someone must have forgotten to take this out of the library."

I didn't know such a book existed, let alone know what it was about. Many times during those first few weeks of school, Nusha had mentioned titles of books I'd never heard. From the bits of information she blurted out during recess, I figured they had a huge library in their house. She thought that many books had been taken out of Farzan's library because the new administration found them unsuitable for students.

"Well, this is just a guess. We can certainly ask," I said.

"Do you honestly think they are going to give us a real answer?"

"Why not? We can ask Shirin. She's a bookworm. She knows a lot about the library."

"Ah, you trust her? She is one of them."

"What do you mean, she is one of them?"

"She's the principal's sweetheart. Haven't you noticed?"

"No, I haven't observed any such thing. And why do you think she's not going to tell us the truth?"

"Look, Moji, you're far too simpleminded in this matter, you naive girl. How many books have you read in your lifetime to know these revolutionary people? Aside from that *One Thousand and One Nights* that you keep boasting about!" She smirked as she put her hands on her waist. "Which, by the way, I've spotted in our library."

"I've read many books. I've read in English as well, when I was in America," I cried.

"Ah, I see. How many books do you have in your house? Do you even have a bookshelf for books at home?"

I sprang up from the carpet. No one else besides the two of us was in the fiction and fables section at that moment. I ran back down the aisle without a word, feeling the burning in my cheeks. I glanced at the librarian's desk on the way out to see if Shirin was sitting behind it. To my disappointment, I didn't see her through the film of tears covering my eyes. She was not in the library.

On the way home, the other girls were making a racket on the bus. I couldn't sit in the first row behind the driver where I usually sat because I was late and my usual seat was taken by a girl named Zara, who peeled oranges all the way from school to home. I hated the fact that she peeled the orange skin with her black, inky hands, making the pith look dirty and dark, and above all, offering the sticky, juicy segments to the girls on the bus. I decided to sit in the third row, far from her and at a reasonable distance from the noisy girls who congregated in the back seats and chattered all the way home. I missed Mar Mar. If she were there on the bus, she would have known in an instant that something was wrong with me. Nusha had hit my heart's bull's-eye by asking that question. All those years I had lived in the house on Sun Street, it never occurred to me why we didn't have a library in that big house. I pictured every nook and cranny of my grandparents' house—now almost our house as well—in my mind and couldn't remember a single bookshelf aside from the one in Saba's room that was filled with Islamic books.

It was dark when I got off the bus. I could hear the evening azan from Fakhrieh Mosque. Mar Mar opened the door as soon as I rang the bell. She saw the uneasy look on my face but said nothing. Maman was in the kitchen with Azra, chatting about Reza's wife's pregnancy. Mar Mar followed me to the living room, eager to hear the stories from my fascinating school. Agha Joon was leaning against the cherry red bolsters, reading the *Kayhan* newspaper. I untied my black scarf, took off my manteau, and threw them at the corner of the room. Agha Joon asked about my day in school as he glanced over the pages.

"Agha Joon," I said, "how come we don't have a library in this house?"

Agha Joon lowered the newspaper and stared at me through his thick glasses. His eyes seemed two times larger since he'd started wearing those magnifying lenses.

"Library? Who builds a library in a house?"

"My friend Nusha said they have a big library in their house."

"What do they do with the books if they are in need? Do they eat them when there is famine?" He laughed out loud.

"They read them, Agha Joon. Books are food for the mind," I boasted, as if I knew more than anyone in the house.

Mar Mar squeezed her eyes, with a *now-what* look on her face.

"This house is adorned with flowers. Have you not seen them when you run around?" He stroked the Kashan rug near his feet.

I glanced at the fine silk rug that covered the living room tiles. The rug's woven flowers twisted around each other, creating a curved paisley pattern in every corner of the room.

"Every rug in this house is a piece of jewelry. We can sell them if we are in need."

"But Agha Joon, at school they say knowledge is the greatest treasure, more precious than anything!"

"You carry the knowledge within you, not in the books of your library," he said. "You know what they call the people who possess books but don't read them?" He folded the newspaper and set it aside. "They call them hamal-al-ketab, the ones who carry books like a donkey, but whose minds are empty."

"But, Agha Joon! When you read books, you live in their world, you gain knowledge. What do these rugs add to our lives?"

Agha Joon sighed. Mar Mar shook her head, signaling I had crossed the line and become too loud again. "I am a glazier, Moji. I am no scholar. Did I ever tell you the story of the little boy who fixed broken glass?"

"No," Mar Mar said.

He told us the story of little Ismael, who was orphaned at the age of eight and had to work to earn money for himself and his mother. He was hired as an apprentice to his uncle, who was a glass mender in Tehran's old bazaar. He roamed between the bazaar's narrow alleys with his master, hoping to find a broken glass in the chambers' windows. They had a donkey that carried plain glass in one side of its saddlebag and stained glass in the other side. Rays of sunshine beamed through the circular openings in the bazaar's domed ceilings like pillars of light as they strolled through the passages. The little boy was in love with the reflection of light on the stained glass. He chased the reflections on the walls and jumped up and down trying to catch the colorful rays as the donkey moved forward in the narrow alleys. One benevolent day, his master was hired to replace all the broken stained glass of the lattice window frames in the Atigh Mosque, the ancient mosque of Tehran's bazaar.

They spent the whole winter working on the sash windows, removing the wooden frames and replacing the broken glass with new stained glass. The little boy played with the putty as he mashed and spread it between the glass and its frame. He watched the young mullahs walking in and out of the mosque's library as he repaired the lattice doors. Ismael wondered what they read in the Atigh Mosque library, so every time his master took a tea break, he sneaked between the bookshelves and browsed the books.

"Did he know how to read?" Mar Mar asked.

"Yes, his father had sent him to maktab to learn the Koran when he was five," Agha Joon replied.

I had heard from Maman that Agha Joon went to maktab when he was a child. I knew he had taught himself Farsi from the Arabic alphabet and the words of the Koran, but that was as much as I knew about his past. He never talked about his parents or his childhood. I glanced at the deep cuts he had on his hands. The scars he carried from the years he had fixed the sharp broken glass in windowpanes. "Is that where he found the book of *One Thousand and One Nights*?" I asked.

Agha Joon smiled. "The little boy found a fascinating book among the books in that library. He was mesmerized by its first story. He continued to read slowly and silently, hidden from his master's eyes, whenever he had a chance. He read the book page by page all through the winter as they repaired the lattice frames, glass by glass.

"How did he own the book if it belonged to the mosque's library?" I asked.

"One day, the library's mullah found little Ismael squatting on the floor, running his little fingers between the lines of that strange book. The mullah took the book from the boy but soon found out the book didn't belong to the mosque's collection of

Korans and holy scriptures. He gave the book to the boy, who has kept it ever since."

"But how would you have known its stories if you didn't possess the book?"

He wasn't listening to me anymore. His eyes were fixed on the rug, on a red flower tangled between the leaves.

"He kept the stories forever in his chest."

A thin, fluffy layer of snowflakes sprinkled the outside window ledges, and the glass panes, covered with a thin layer of frost film, kept any fragile rays of sunshine from peeking into the classroom. There was no sign of Queen since the temperature had dropped, and I wondered where she'd taken refuge since the windows now remained closed and locked. We started the day with mathematics class. Our math problems were getting harder and more complex compared to the ones we had the first few weeks of school.

Nusha said salam as soon as she saw me. I turned my head away and sat in my chair as if I hadn't heard her. I had decided to ignore her when I went back to school. She needed to be taught a lesson not to boast about her home library. I knew it would be absolute torture for her to tolerate my silence. But as I was taking my solutions book out of my backpack, to my astonishment, she said, "I am sorry for my behavior on Thursday, Moji. What I said was wrong and rude."

She had such a sincere, sorrowful sound to her voice that I couldn't keep the vow I'd made to myself. I shrugged and said, "That's fine, Nusha. People live in different homes. Not all homes have libraries or fine Persian carpets. And you don't need to own one thousand and one books to read them."

"I know. I am sorry, Moji. Can I invite you to our house as

an apology? My dad said we can spend the whole time in his library."

"I have to ask my mom."

Our math teacher walked in, and everyone rose from their seats. I felt ill at ease to go to Nusha's house, but visiting their library was a tempting offer. As soon as math class was over, we were friends again, as if nothing had happened. Nusha was preoccupied with her theory about the books being taken out of the library on purpose and insisted the books should be somewhere in the school since the administration didn't have the time or the money to pay someone to get rid of them. I repeated the idea of asking Shirin. She hesitated but didn't reject it at once.

"Well," she said. "Why don't you ask her next time?"

———

Every time I popped into the library during recess, Shirin was busy with a student, finding a book or checking one out. It was Saturday, the first day of the week, and everybody was rushing into the library, remembering a forgotten task or returning an overdue book. I decided to stay close to her desk and help her out with stamping library cards. There were a few brief moments I felt I could ask her, but I held my breath and remained silent until the last recess.

"You sure you don't want to go wash your hands before your last class?" Shirin glanced at my fingertips. "You have ink all over your fingers."

"I think I still have time, Ms. Shirin. Is there anything else I can help you with?"

"You've been a great help so far." She nodded. "But if you insist, do you want to carry the book trolley to the last row with me?"

We rattled through the bookshelves, row by row. She was wearing her faint perfume that attracted me like a parrot to a pistachio jar. It smelled sweet like the angabin Azra mixed with tahini paste for breakfast. We stopped near the last row at the far end of the library. Shirin pulled the trolley down the aisle as I pushed it to help her. Her scarf had slid down her head, and I could see the hazel strands of her hair glistening under the direct light. She picked up a large volume from the trolley's top tray, and while she searched for the book's correct location, she asked, "Is there something you wanted to ask, Moji?"

"Hmm, no, I mean, yes," I blurted out.

"Is there a particular book you are looking for?"

"Yes. I mean, I have searched for *Samak Ayyar*. It's a book in five volumes."

"It's a book of stories within stories. They're quite fascinating. You'll be immersed in them."

"But I couldn't see any other volumes except for volume three. We think, I mean, I think, it's strange that the other volumes are missing. Is it possible that, that, some books have been removed from this library?"

Shirin was facing the bookshelf at that moment. I could see the side of her lip slanting upward as she heard my speculation. I thought she was going to be surprised by our novel discovery, but she bent down to take another book from the trolley's lower tray as if nothing had happened.

"Those volumes might have been removed before the reopening of the library, and volume three left out by accident." She pulled her scarf forward to cover her hair.

It became apparent to me that Shirin knew about the missing books. I imagined Nusha tittering as I told her the story. *Didn't I tell you she is one of them?* Her voice echoed in my head.

"But I can get you that book if you want to read it," she said.

I nodded, but I felt my heart racing. Why did she want to bring those books for me if they were deemed unsuitable by the school administration?

"Thank you. Are they, I mean those books, somewhere inside the school?"

She winked and wiggled her fingers up in the air. "Maybe."

The search for the hidden books started the day after I spoke with Shirin. Nusha and I thought about places that could serve as storage for the books. We suspected Shirin wanted to give us a clue by moving her hands in the air. Maybe she meant somewhere close to the roof?

The west corridor in Farzan School had classes on one side and the library on the other side. The east corridor had the same design, except that the prayer hall faced the classes. Lunch breaks were the best opportunity to investigate every corner of the school. Nusha and I wanted to go alone, but Nadia insisted she wanted to accompany us. Against her will, Nusha revealed our speculations about the hidden books. Nadia was amazed by the idea of searching the school. The condition for Nadia to be included in the book hunt, Nusha said, was to take an oath that she would never disclose the findings of our quest to anyone. She scribbled her pledge on a piece of paper, signed it, and gave it to Nusha. We all agreed to be at the entrance hall five minutes after the lunch break began the following day.

The first two lunch breaks were hopeless. We searched every classroom and corridor, but there was no hidden path leading to the treasured books. The prayer hall was nothing but an empty spacious salon surrounded by plain walls that didn't even have shelves carved in them. The only place we suspected and still hoped to find the books was the school auditorium. It was separated from the main building by the schoolyard. The auditorium's entrance opened in front of the school's east wing. From the newer russet bricks that decorated the exterior walls, it was apparent the auditorium was built as an addition to the school a few years later than the main building. A broad, low-stepped staircase with terrazzo mosaics led to the balcony and continued to the roof.

On the third day of the hunt, we gathered at the auditorium entrance and decided to climb the stairway and search around the balcony. As we passed the balcony level, rusted heaters and fans, crusted paint buckets, brushes fixed into hardened paint, brooms, and broken chairs were stacked in the stairway's landing. A fine white dust had spread over the mosaic tiles there, proving no one had been in that corner for a while. A giant cobweb covered the landing's high window, and a few flies and ladybugs were entangled in its shiny silken net. The pungent odors of turpentine and toluene filled the air, coming from the half-open, drying paint buckets. Ten steps above the landing we noticed a slate-colored, wooden trapdoor about half a meter above the stairs.

"That is the door to the hidden books, I bet," Nusha said.

"It's dirty and dusty here," Nadia said. "Can we hurry?"

"You shouldn't have insisted on coming if you're obsessed with cleanliness," Nusha said. "We haven't even opened the door yet!"

"What if the door is locked?" I asked.

"There is no lock, can't you see?" Nusha said. She leaped the last two steps and landed close to the trapdoor. "All you have to do is push with your whole body."

The trapdoor was swollen and stuck, and she couldn't get it to budge even a centimeter. "Now you girls need to help!" she shouted as she hammered the door with her hips. Nadia and I joined the rhythm and slammed the door with our hips as hard as we could. The door squeaked as we hit it, and after twenty-some attacks, it surrendered and we were flung into what appeared to be the attic. It was dark and musty inside, and we couldn't see anything. I fell on the floor, palms first. Thick dust soiled my manteau and my hands. I stood up and tried to shake and clean my clothes. Dim light beamed into the attic from the narrow rim of the high windows. As our eyes got used to the dark, we saw hundreds of books piled on top of each other, dust spreading over their covers and hiding the titles on the floor. We walked through the attic strewn with burlap sacks full of books. Empty sacks were left in the corners. It was obvious the books had been carried in an unconcerned and careless way. We could hardly read the titles in the dark, but finally, we had found the treasure.

"We should bring a flashlight tomorrow," Nusha said.

"We shall come here every lunch break to investigate the books," I said.

I was thrilled by our triumph. All those books beckoned to be picked up and cared for in my arms. I wanted to clean the book covers with a cotton duster and slide my fingers on the forgotten words. I craved the excitement that lurked in the pages of those books. We danced around the books, prying into the secret world we had found. One thing that still baffled me was the fact that Shirin had given us the clue. Why did she lead us to the attic if she followed the same line of thought as the principal and the other staff?

Over the following weeks we entertained ourselves with hundreds of books in the auditorium's attic. Nadia faded away after the first two weeks since she wasn't as enthusiastic a reader as we were. Every single lunch break, Nusha and I fetched the flashlights we hid under a broken chair in the staircase, saturated our lungs with the addictive vanilla and toluene scent that filled the attic, and nibbled on pages in different books. We found Russian novels like *War and Peace*, *Anna Karenina*, *Crime and Punishment*, and *Notes from the Underground* piled like marble pillars that reached the bottoms of the high windows. Books that I had never heard of, authors I'd never known in my life. Nusha enjoyed lecturing about Tolstoy, Dostoyevsky, and Gogol. It gave her an ultimate sense of pleasure to introduce the masters of Russian literature to me. I was humbled by the amount of knowledge she had. One day in that freezing attic I asked, "Have you read all these books, Nusha?" I was browsing through the first volume of *War and Peace*.

"Not all of them, of course. Not that one in particular. But I've heard about them since I was very young. My father used to teach Russian literature in Tehran University before the Revolution."

"If you have these books in your library, why are you still searching for them?"

"Girl, have you seen me touching that Russian pillar of yours?"

"No."

"Exactly. I am interested in special forbidden books, ones you have no idea about!"

She pointed to the stacks of books whose titles I couldn't understand, or even read the authors' names correctly—books like *The Communist Manifesto* by Karl Marx and Frederick Engels, really only a slim booklet, and a book about Historic Materialism, or something like that. I always assumed stories were the most admirable form of writing and never imagined how a twelve-year-old girl could be interested in books that sounded like gibberish to me.

"What are these books about?" I asked.

"My brother has asked me to find and read them."

"How does your brother know about these books?" I turned and pointed to the Russian books and said, "And why would you listen to him and read those instead of these?"

"Moji, did you ask your mom for permission to come to our house?"

"Yes. She said it would be fine."

"Then I'll tell you that day. It's a long story." She glanced at her watch and said, "We need to pick up some books and leave. Break is over."

———

I snuck *War and Peace*, *Anna Karenina*, and some other novels out from the attic, one at a time under my puffer jacket. I stole some of Maman's parchment papers from the sewing closet and wrapped the books in them before I left the attic. I tucked the books between my manteau and the jacket's inner layer and zipped the jacket all the way up to my chin. We peeked down the stairs and made sure no one was in the entrance hall before we left the auditorium building. When we reached our class-room, we pretended we had borrowed those books from the li-brary. Covered in parchment paper, no one suspected they were smuggled out of the attic.

When I reached home, I sighed and felt relieved. I could touch the pages with pleasure without my fingers turning blue in the bitter cold of the attic. I had all the time in the world to delve into the stories without fear of being caught red-handed in the land of forbidden books. Anna Arkadyevna mesmerized me. I fell in love with her story.

———

During a general assembly in December, Ms. Zadie complained about the scant number of students attending noon prayers. "We have noticed you do everything but attend the namaz. The reason we have extended your lunch break is not for you to chase after the ball or jump incessantly on the elastic cord. We are told by our prophet—peace be upon him—that the best thing a Muslim can do during the day is to pray to Allah. I have observed you fleeing from the prayer hall! From now on we are enforcing namaz by calling the azan overhead and reminding you to attend."

It was not wise to go to the attic that day at lunch break. For the first time in my life, I decided to attend the noon congregation and pray with an imam. I told Nusha she should come too. She asked me to go ahead and said that she would join me after a few minutes.

The white walls in the prayer hall invited everyone to silence. The arched windows facing the school's backyard let the faint light seep through the sheer curtains. Scotch-tape lines marked the carpet for students to stand in rows behind the imam. Girls teetered around the lines, struggling to stand shoulder to shoulder. Most of them had brought their floral chadors for the prayer. Few girls made sure their chadors completely covered their hair. Some had a piece of sepia clay in front of them, and they placed their foreheads on the clay as they genuflected during the prayer. There was a box full of those clays in different shapes beside the door. The girls who didn't have their own piece fetched one from that box. I took a heart-shaped one as I entered the hall and stood on my toes to see if I could find Nusha in the crowd. I couldn't spot her anywhere. I suspected she was stubborn enough to go to the attic all by herself, even on such a dangerous day. I noticed Shirin standing beside the clay box.

"How are you, Moji? Haven't seen you in the library lately," she said in a cheerful tone.

"I am fine, Ms. Shirin. I'm busy with assignments during the breaks."

She nodded her head. "Do you want to stand beside me during namaz?"

"Sure. I would be happy to."

I followed her as she walked to the front row. As soon as the girls recognized her, they emptied a space for her there. In the front of the prayer rows, there was a special place called mihrab. It was the spot designated for the imam to stand and kneel during namaz and give sermons. The mihrab was embellished by a fine hand-woven Persian rug. Shirin stood behind it and asked me to stand beside her. I stepped forward and squeezed myself between her and a tall girl who was adjusting her chador.

"I don't have a chador," I said.

"No worries," Shirin said. "Neither do I. But you can cover your hair and elbows up to your wrists and that is suitable for namaz as well." She slid her scarf forward and a long, braided hazel tress freed itself from beneath her scarf.

"Can you help put my hair inside my manteau?" She struggled to do it herself, with no luck.

Her hair felt like a frisky trout trying to escape my hand as I slid it back into her manteau. On the fair skin of her neck, just below the hairline I saw a delicate henna tattoo. It was hard to tell the tattoo's exact shape, but it resembled the tail of a bird, with its torso—I imagined—extending on her right shoulder and her chest. I was shocked to see that tattoo on Shirin's neck. Until that day, all I knew about henna tattoos were the ones on Azra's hands and nails. I never liked henna and didn't let her put one on my hands. But Shirin had such a tattoo on her neck, a patterned one, a delicate bird someone must have spent hours drawing on her chest.

We all stood shoulder to shoulder, waiting for the imam to appear. Ms. Zadie emerged from the last row and sauntered toward the mihrab. Shirin gave way and paid respect as soon as she saw her. There were other teachers standing in the front row as well. Ms. Zadie greeted everyone with salam and stepped on the prayer rug while a girl sang the azan. Ms. Zadie brought out her white chador from her brown leather bag and wore it over her khimar. It had a chin cover and was sown in the front.

She placed her hands on her ears and a loud Allah o Akbar silenced the buzzing murmur of the hall. No one budged or uttered a single word. The only voice I could hear was Ms. Zadie's modulated hymn. I'd heard those verses of the Koran many times, but I didn't know their Farsi translation. I wasn't sure about the order in which we had to kneel, genuflect, or rise, but I did the same as everyone else. Only I made one mistake. I interlocked my fingers while I stood in the row, not sure what to do with my hands. It didn't take more than a few seconds for Shirin to intervene. Without a word, she opened the lock of my hands and laced her fingers in mine. She held my hand all throughout the namaz. I was baffled by this and didn't know what to do. I didn't dare to pull my hand away.

As soon as the azan girl announced the end of the prayer by singing salam, Shirin said my name. Everyone was still sitting on the carpet, calves under thighs. She turned her face toward me and whispered in my ears, "We are not slaves to Allah. We stand like lovers in front of the Beloved. Don't lock your hands the way Sunnis do."

I didn't understand what she meant. Perhaps she wanted to teach me something about the way Shia Muslims prayed. I nodded and said nothing. She slid her hand under her scarf to bring her braided hair out of her manteau. Ms. Zadie turned back to shake hands with the teachers in the first row after the prayer. She shook hands with me and said, "Nice to see you in the first row, Ms. Moji. May Allah accept our namaz va ebadat."

I thanked her and glanced at Shirin. She nodded and smiled back.

The girls' loud chatter filled the prayer hall. They stood up from their spots and folded their chadors to put them back in their bags. I darted toward the door to get out and find Nusha.

"Wait a second, Moji, before you go back to your class," Shirin said from behind.

I stopped and wondered what she wanted to ask.

She lowered her voice and asked, "How are you liking *Anna Karenina*?"

"Oh, I, I, I am not sure!"

"*He walked down, for a long while avoiding looking at her as at the sun, but seeing her, as one does the sun, without looking.* Amazing, huh?" she said.

I froze in the middle of the hall as if an ifrit had cast a spell upon me. Still and silent, I stared at her eyes. The golden streaks in her irises appeared sharper than ever.

"You need to come back to the library so we can talk about the meaning of the namaz you just did. It's shameful to stand in front of the Beloved and utter words you don't know. You must learn what you say." Then she winked and said, "Come Moji, maybe we can chat about Anna too."

She turned her back and walked to the door. I could see the last knot of her braided hair reaching her waist from under her scarf, just like what I'd heard about the old librarian lady of Farzan School. Had the old lady settled into Shirin's soul?

The Celebration of Light

*Sharrkan awoke not until his horse stumbled over
wooded ground. Then he started from sleep and found
himself among the trees; and the moon arose and shone
brightly over the two horizons, Eastern and Western. He
was startled when he found himself alone in this place and
said the say which ne'er yet shamed its sayer, "There is no
Majesty and there is no Might save in Allah, the Glorious,
the Great!" But as he rode on, in fear of wild beasts,
behold, the moon spread her glad light over a meadow
as if 'twere of the meads of Paradise; and he heard
pleasant voices and a loud noise of talk and
laughter captivating the senses of men.*

———

"The Tale of King Omar bin al-Nu'uman and His Sons"

We celebrated Yalda, the Iranian celebration of light, on December 21, 1983, the longest night of the year. Agha Joon bought a giant watermelon from the fresh market, believing no one could have a sweet Yalda unless they tasted a slice of watermelon. Azra cut the leathery skin of three pomegranates and separated the seeds from their paper-thin membranes, gathered the diamond-shaped seeds in a big plastic container, and transferred them to a crystal bowl for the ceremony. Baba came home with a basket full of nuts he'd purchased from Pasteur Confectionary. Reza came to our house with his wife, Nastaran, and his girls early in the evening. Nastaran was a stout girl from the northwestern part of Iran and observed the hijab completely, even in front of family members. Baba knocked at the living room door and said *Ya Allah* before he entered the room in her presence. She gave permission as she quickly brought the hems of her chador close together under her chin, a gesture I thought brought formality to our family's usually affable atmosphere.

The blood-red pomegranate seeds, the fresh cubes of watermelon, and the sweet aroma of honey-glazed walnuts solidified the sense of celebration in the living room. Maman lit the gilded candles while she arranged the nuts and fruits on the termeh. The flickering candlelight illuminated faces in a peculiar way, making eyelashes longer, eyebrows broader, and lips almost unnoticeable. Saba joined the celebration that night but kept herself at the corner of the termeh, far from the feast.

"Let us thank Allah for being together and for having His blessing for this sofreh," Agha Joon said at the beginning of the ceremony. "It's hard for some families to prepare even a single item on this colorful tablecloth during the time of war." He placed a few cubes of watermelon on his plate.

"Especially when our soldiers are offering their blood for our country," Reza said. He put a few spoons of pomegranate seeds in a small cup, poured some salt on it, and offered it to Nastaran.

"Any news from the border?" Baba asked Reza. Uncle Reza had a close friend by the name of Ahmad who was a key member of the Islamic Revolutionary Guard. He often had more accurate information about the battle with the Iraqis than the media did.

"They're preparing for a major offensive," Reza said.

"Which part of the border are they planning to attack?" Baba asked.

I could feel Baba's enthusiasm in his vibrant voice. Every time people talked about the war, he became interested in the conversation and inquired about the tactics and maneuvers the army was using. He criticized the inexperienced Revolutionary Guard officers and brooded over the soldiers of the Shah's army who were lost forever. Flickers of the glorious past sparkled in his eyes, from the time when he was in charge of his battalion near the northern border between Iran and Iraq, the life he'd spent in active duty in the high mountains of Kurdistan.

"They are eyeing the southern border, the freeway from Basra to Baghdad," Reza said.

"La elah ella Allah," Azra said. "Haven't they killed enough of our young men?"

This was the Arabic phrase I'd heard many times when my family expressed their deep misery.

"Only Allah knows how many innocent boys are going to get killed this time," Agha Joon said.

"Well, when these novice officers barely know war tactics on the ground and use the 'human wave' instead of armor, massive casualties are inevitable," Baba said.

"What is the option when the imperial powers are backing the Iraqis in this war?" Reza said. "To let go of our land?"

"No. But nations are often not defeated by their enemies. They're defeated by their own failure to contrive ways of handling critical situations, by lack of a stratagem for success. When almost all of the experienced officers of the Shah's army are executed or exiled, when all the cunning men who could handle real war are eliminated, victory is not far-fetched for the enemy."

"But they were betrayers, loyal to the Shah, backing their imperial masters," Reza said.

"It is clear they are not winning this war, Reza jan," Agha Joon said. "Even to inexperienced eyes, it is evident that our army is losing far more lives than the Iraqis."

"Hundreds of fallen soldiers are named every day in the media, in each alleyway of this city, in every city in Iran. These teenagers, who are barely trained, are just used as a human shield. The 'Army of Twenty Million' as Khomeini says!" Baba shook his head in deep rage.

"Our principal's brother was martyred a few days ago near Hawizeh," Maman said. "She said they're going to bring his remains along with a few hundred more martyrs to be respected and buried this Friday after the prayers." She picked out the black seeds from the remaining pieces of watermelon on the tray.

"These caravans of caskets covered with flags. Some of the coffins are empty, only carrying the soldier's plaque," Azra said. She struck her right hand with her left with a sullen look in her eyes. "What are the mothers feeling when they can't even say goodbye to the body of their beloved son? Tane jigar gooshe kojast?"

"Human wave or no human wave, at this point what else can we do? Sit back and offer our homes to the Iraqis?" Reza said. He turned to face Baba, clearly wanting to hear an answer from him.

"They could've finished this bloody war peacefully and respectfully when the port city of Khorramshahr was liberated from the Iraqis a year and a half ago," Baba said. "This is nothing but Khomeini's propaganda to spread his version of Islam. His pretension, his ambition to be the sole Islamic leader of the world!"

"No! I disagree with you. The future will prove you wrong. Imam Khomeini is the God-sent leader who is here to save our souls, and our war is a holy one, as Imam says, hagh alayhe batel, light against darkness." Reza glanced at Azra and continued, "And speaking of our country, I wanted to tell you earlier, but I didn't want to break the news on the phone." He placed his pomegranate cup on the termeh and brushed his beard with his palm, coiling his fingers under his chin.

"What news?" Azra asked. She had a small crystal cup of pomegranate in her hand, taking one spoonful at a time. The spoon froze in the air, midway between her lips and the cup.

"I have enlisted to fight at the front line."

Azra dropped the spoon and cup, and the pomegranate seeds scattered all over her ivory dashiki, some getting caught in the laces of her V-shaped neckline like ruby jewels. She placed her hands over her gaping mouth, trying to muffle the moan that sprung out uncontrollably.

"You didn't, Reza. Tell me you didn't!" Azra cried.

"La elah ella Allah." This time it was Agha Joon. He leaned back against the cherry bolster and distanced himself from the sofreh.

"Your daughter was just born a few weeks ago. This is the worst time to enlist for war, Reza. How could you even imagine doing this to your family?" Maman said. She turned to Nastaran, who was calmly looking at Reza. "Nastaran, did you not object to this?"

"Who lured you into this? Who whispered into your ear to go enlist? Tell me, who? Ahmad?" Azra asked. She hammered her bosom a few times with her interlocked hands.

Reza remained silent, trying not to fuel the fiery situation. Even the candles, I felt, ceased to flicker at that moment. Faces were frozen in astonishment. Maman leaned toward Azra, who was sitting next to her, and plucked the pomegranate seeds from her dashiki. Still shivering, Azra held her hands clenched at her chest. Maman caressed Azra's straight hennaed hair and embraced her, trying to calm her down.

Azra's cry woke Sami, Uncle Reza's newborn baby. She'd been sleeping in her travel bassinet all throughout the evening's con-

versation. Nastaran rose from her spot and stepped toward Sami's bassinet in the corner of the living room. Tears glistened
on her cheeks as she, for a moment, let go of the hems of her
chador to pick up the baby. She tucked Sami under the chador
and lulled her with a somber song. I was curious to see her reaction to Reza's announcement, but she didn't say a word. To my
astonishment, she didn't object to Reza's departure like Maman
or Azra. She acted like the hundreds of revolutionary women I'd
seen on TV—proud of their husbands going to war.

 No one stretched a hand to pick a treat from the sofreh after
the news. Candles burned down, the molten wax suffocating
the wicks. I fiddled with the corner of the termeh, not knowing
how to react to the bitter situation. The embroidered flowers
felt coarse and grainy, like thorns pricking my fingertips. Was
that delicately woven termeh always so rough to the touch? I
looked at Mar Mar. She was sitting in front of me, watching the
whole scene in silence. I saw the same affliction in her tearful,
glistening eyes that I felt. We shared the same woe, the same
sorrow-stricken emotion that no word could relay. Like a single
bitter almond among the basket of nuts, Reza's news poisoned
the ceremony's sweet taste.

"When are you going to leave?" Baba finally asked and broke
the silence.

"Next week, Enshallah."

"Where are they going to station you?"

"After a few weeks of training in Tehran, they're taking us to
Abadan, and only God knows where from there." Reza turned
to Azra and said, "Ahmad never said anything. I enlisted with
Amir. He is coming with me."

"Amir? Uncle Zabih's son?" Maman asked.

Reza nodded.

"How did you decide to go with him?" Maman asked.

"He comes to the glaziery these days. We've been talking

about the boys who are volunteering to go to the front line. He was eager to go. He enlisted, and I decided to go with him."

Azra covered her face with her hands and shook her head in despair. Amir was her brother's son. He was a tall young boy in his late teens, as I recalled from the few times I'd seen him at family gatherings. They lived in the southern part of Tehran, where the Revolutionary Guard recruited the majority of its soldiers. Boys were encouraged to register to gain heavenly rewards. I remembered the interviews with young boys broadcast on TV. They said they were ready to drink the sweet, scarlet sherbet of martyrdom and fly to heaven to join their brethren killed in war.

Saba, who had been silent all through the night, drew close to Reza and rested her hand on his shoulder. "I am so proud of you, Reza."

Agha Joon shook his head and said, "Why didn't you tell me you'd enlisted the past few days when we were at the glaziery?"

"I wasn't sure it would be received well," Reza said.

"I wouldn't have objected," Agha Joon said. "I've always respected your choices in life. But to shock your mother on Yalda was not a wise decision."

"She would've disapproved on any occasion." Reza glanced at Azra, his forehead puckered with compassion. "But regardless, can Nastaran and the girls stay with you while I'm gone? I don't want them to be alone."

"Why do you even ask, Reza?" Agha Joon said at once. "She is welcome to stay in this house as long as she wishes."

———

That night, I tossed and turned in my bed, unable to sleep. I pictured the dusty rocket-propelled grenades as they thrusted back forcefully into the soldiers' shoulders after firing. Gory images haunted me in the dark: a fallen khaki helmet, blood spilling out of a blown-open skull, a soldier—Uncle Reza—falling in a trench. I couldn't grasp the reason behind Reza's enlistment. How on earth could he leave his sweet daughters behind and volunteer to die in a damp, dirty trench? How could Baba be in accord with Reza in the most disagreeable situation of fighting under the Islamic Republic flag? Something beyond their usual disagreement surfaced in the conversation, which didn't make sense to me. Baba didn't approve of the Islamic regime's tyranny. But in his heart, he carried the love for his country even after his imprisonment. Baba and Reza both loved Iran, each in his way, and no matter how differently they regarded the Islamic Republic, they were both ready to defend their country with their lives.

The Stolen Kiss

They drank and each played with each, till their
cheeks flushed red arid their eyes took a darker hue and
Ghanim's soul longed to kiss the girl and to lie with her
and he said, "O my lord, grant me one kiss of that dear
mouth: perchance 't will quench the fire of my heart."
"O Ghanim," replied she, "wait till I am drunk and dead
to the world; then steal a kiss of me, secretly and on such
wise that I may not know thou hast kissed me."

———

"The Tale of Ghanim Bin Ayyub"

With a written permission from Maman, I rode the school bus
with Nusha to her house. She lived in the mountainous part of
Tehran, where the houses had modern architecture and a Western look, unlike those in our neighborhood. After twenty minutes of driving uphill in a never-ending, slushy alley, the bus
stopped in front of a navy iron gate. As soon as we got off, Nusha buzzed the electric doorbell. Their servant opened the gate,
and we entered a sloped garden that led to a marble villa at the
top of the hill. The sun had already set, but the villa's windows
glittered and lightened the garden. The steps leading toward the
villa were wide and shallow, covered with icy snow. When we
were halfway up the steps, the servant opened the door.

"Salam, Nusha khanoom, welcome," she said, and stretched
her hand to invite us inside.

Nusha guided me to the library that opened into the foyer.

"Would you like to have some hot chocolate milk, Moji khanoom?" the servant asked.

"Thank you, ma'am," I said after a pause. I didn't recognize my name at first. No one had called me khanoom before.

"Bring some butter and jam with the chocolate milk," Nusha said without looking at her. "You don't need to call her ma'am, Moji. She is our servant." She pulled a wooden chair from a small round table and asked me to sit. She then ran out the door, leaving me in the absolute silence of the books that reached up to the ceiling.

Two white abat-jours with turquoise shades illuminated the library. Beside one of the lamps at the far corner of the room, was a grand piano. I dropped my backpack on the parquet floor near the entrance and marveled at the rug in the library. All the fine rugs we had in our house had cherry-red backgrounds with tiny vibrant flowers. The rug embellishing that library had an eye-catching, sky-blue background with giant ivory lilies, like a reflection pond.

I walked toward the grand piano to see it up close. The ebony lacquer caressed my fingertips as I touched its smooth surface. *Petrof* was written in gold at the center above the keyboard and beneath the music stand. A few sheets of music by Rimsky-Korsakov stood on the stand, ready to be played. I wondered who played the piano in that house. On an elegant, chestnut desk there were pictures of Nusha's family in different frames. I recognized Nusha and her brother standing beside each other in one frame, smiling at the camera, brother circling his hand around sister's neck. In another photo, Nusha's parents appeared glorious in their wedding clothes. A bust of a long-bearded man sat beside the frames, looking straight into my eyes. I didn't know who he was. Bookshelves covered the walls, even the lower part of the wall with windows facing the garden. The parquet's pine scent and the blue hue of the objects in the library transfixed me in a state of awe.

"You like our library?" Nusha asked.

I turned my head toward the door. "It is magnificent. Good for you."

"He's your favorite writer. Did you recognize him?" She pointed at the bust. "Tolstoy."

"Oh!" I said. "He looks heroic and magnificent."

The servant came back with two cups of hot chocolate and a snack tray of bread and butter nuggets. She placed the tray on the round table and asked us to help ourselves.

"My parents are not home. They just came back from St. Petersburg and are visiting a friend tonight. But Manuch will be home soon from the university."

"What's he studying in the university?"

"Chemical engineering at Sharif University. Lucky he started school after the Cultural Revolution when the universities opened again."

"Did he have an interview?"

"Of course, he did! But they couldn't find anything against him, so they accepted him."

We went back to the round table. She placed the hot chocolate in front of me and said, "Dad worried they would reject Manuch because of him."

"What does your dad do, now that he doesn't teach at the university?"

"Travel!" She snorted. "But mostly he spends time at home in the library."

She grabbed a nugget and dashed to one of the bookshelves. She sat on the floor and pulled out a giant hardcover book from the bottom shelf. "Come here. I want to show you something."

I kneeled beside her and looked at the book. On the book's glossy dust jacket, a young lady in a cream bouffant gown was pulling a silk shawl from a stool. Nusha flipped the book so I could see the continuation of the painting on the back. A young lad was kissing the lady's rosy cheek in a rush. Nusha opened the book to show me the masterpiece printed on the cover. The excerpt written beneath the painting was not in English.

"*Le Baiser à la dérobée*," she said, "*The Stolen Kiss.*"

"Do you know French?" I asked.

"An oil painting by Jean-Honoré Fragonard. Not much . . . but I have a private tutor. Dad bought this book from the Hermitage in St. Petersburg. It's about the famous paintings in that museum." She touched the smooth shiny image and said, "Look at the pleats of her silk skirt. You can even see the contours of her left leg beneath the silk. Isn't it magnificent? The fine painting of light and shade?"

I had nothing to say. I had no clue where the Hermitage was, nor did I know anything about the paintings in that museum. Far more astonishing than the shining pleats of the woman's skirt was the hasty look on the lad's face as he took the kiss.

"There are many nude pictures in this book." Nusha winked. She turned to another page, and the naked body of a reclining lady appeared. "*Danaë*, by Rembrandt. Here, take it. I've looked at these a hundred times." She handed the book to me.

"Marvelous," I said. "How did your father bring this book into the country?"

"I knew you would ask," she said. "Mom tore the inner layer of the suitcase from the edges, wrapped the books in a couple folds of soft cloth and spread the cloth between the inner layer and the outside of the suitcase. Then she sewed up the edges so that you couldn't tell anything was in there."

"They're lucky the custom officers didn't catch them," I said.

"For sure. Or they would have been in trouble having these beauties in the nude."

The doorbell rang, and the servant opened the door. It was Manuch coming back from the university.

"You enjoy. I'll be back soon," she said.

From the softness of the ivory pages to the subtly raised scripts, I couldn't take my hands off the pages. I stared at the striking images in that book. Danaé looked astounding in her elegant feather bed. She was waving at someone not depicted in the scene. Who was she waiting for in the bed? What was the golden angel sprinkling on her head? What was the old man doing there, lurking behind the curtain? Her upright, firm breasts and the dark mysterious triangle of her genitals fascinated me and gave me a sense of shame. I lingered between the glossy pages, examining the naked bodies in detail. Each body looked mysterious in its own way, beckoning me to unfold the passion hidden in its curves and contours. The faint, fair skin of those flawless heroines appeared completely different from the fallen soldiers I saw every day on TV. The bloody and blistered corpses of young soldiers were advertised as pure and unblemished bodies by the regime. I pondered the sharp contrast between the culture that defined beauty in those fine, naked bodies and the culture that considered a bleeding martyr as a sublime symbol. I tried to read the descriptions written in French. Alas, I didn't know French and couldn't understand a single word. I envied Nusha and everything she possessed in that heavenly blue library.

After a few minutes, Nusha came back with Manuch. Contrary to what I'd pictured in my mind, he was a short young man with a thin amber goatee and fine copper-brown hair already growing sparse on the top. I put *The Paintings of the Hermitage* down and rose from the floor to greet him.

"Welcome to our house," Manuch said. "Nusha is glad to have you as a friend." He pulled a chair back and signaled for me to sit. Nusha sat next to me, and he went to the opposite side to sit across from me. I straightened my back and placed both hands on my legs, trying to stop them from wiggling. I remembered I hadn't combed my hair after I'd taken off my scarf.

"How is school these days? I heard you found a treasure in a cove." He smiled and winked at me. He leaned forward and placed his elbows on the table, grabbing them with his hands. "I understand you are an avid reader, like Nusha. Very good, very good."

"Thank you, sir," I said in a low tone.

"Oh, just call me Manuch. I like to be called by my name."

"Nusha, have you shown her the library? The books you are reading now?"

"Yeah, but she is more interested in fiction. She loves *Anna Karenina*."

"That's nice," he said, nodding. "But maybe you want to give her the books you're reading now. It's important for you girls to understand the theories and concepts prevalent in our country."

He rose from his seat and walked toward the window. He reached for a stool beside the window and pushed it over to a bookshelf. From the highest shelf, he fetched a few books and brought them back to the table.

"I'm glad you girls have found some good Farsi translations of communism books in your secret place. It's really hard to find the Farsi translations these days."

He slid a couple of books toward me. "Why don't you browse these books? I know they are in Russian, but the pictures, even the shape of the book says many things. You get the feel."

I glanced at Nusha, trying to comprehend her reaction. She was listening to Manuch like an obedient trainee listening to her guru.

"These books are about Lenin and the Bolshevik Revolution. Take a look. Nusha, why don't you bring *The Communist Man-*

ifesto you just finished a few days ago? She might be interested to know more about the foundations of the revolt by the proletarians against the bourgeois and the basis of communist ideation."

"It's a hard-to-follow book," Nusha said.

"Yes, I know. Books about theories and concepts are not as appealing as stories, but how can you live in such an epoch and be naive about the underlying motives of our revolution?"

"Epoch . . . I remember Ms. Zadie used that word in her opening speech this year as well. I always thought our revolution was an Islamic one," I said.

Manuch shook his head. "This is exactly why you have to recognize the power of the proletariat. The Islamists have hijacked the efforts of thousands of our sincere comrades and misnamed the revolt of the common people as an Islamic one."

"What do you mean by proletariat?" I asked.

"Ha, that's a good question. You may start with *The Communist Manifesto,* and we can meet again here after you've read a couple of good books."

"I'll give you those books, but you need to be careful not to show them to anyone," Nusha said.

"Nusha, why don't you invite Moji back in a few weeks? I need to leave for a friends' meeting."

After Manuch left, Nusha picked up *The Paintings of the Hermitage* from the floor and handed it to me.

"Take this one as well," she said. "It's way more interesting than the dry stuff Manuch suggests we read."

"Does he always talk like that?" I asked.

"Like what?"

"I mean he sounds like a scholar when he talks."

She laughed. "Yeah, he is well-read and always confident. He knows Russian, French, and English quite well. He takes after my dad. They are both very assertive."

"Do you really read that stuff?"

She nodded. "Yes. It's important to read and to not be igno-rant like many others."

I said nothing. I had many new concepts flitting and floating through my mind that I needed to explore. I felt my hands tin-gling and going numb and noticed that my fingernails were turn-ing blue at the base. I felt cold, estranged, and overwhelmed.

It had snowed again when Baba came to pick me up. He brought with him the sweet aroma of the sesame sangak bread he'd bought from the neighborhood bakery. I tucked myself in the back seat and raised the collar of my wool coat up to my nose. Snowflakes covered the windshield between the swift strokes of the wiper blades. Mist covered the windows, creating halos around the streetlights glistening outside.

"Did you have a good time with your friend?" Baba asked.

I remembered a time I would have answered him without pause, explaining everything that had happened in detail. But on that gloomy night, something stopped me from revealing my bewilderment to him. I didn't want to answer his question with a simple yes or no, as if I was a little girl coming back from a birthday party. I'd never heard sympathetic remarks in my fam-ily about Mujahedin or Hezbeh Toodeh, the major communist parties in Iran. I had an inkling I should not reveal any piece of the conversation I had with Manuch to Baba.

"They have a huge house and an elegant library full of books," I said. "Nusha gave me a nice book about the paintings in the Hermitage. Have you heard of that museum, Baba?"

"Yes, I have. Tsars used to live in the Winter Palace that now is the museum," he said. He glanced at me in the rearview mir-ror and asked, "Why did she give you such a book?"

"Oh, her parents had brought the book from St. Petersburg. I loved the paintings. She said I can borrow the book for a while and examine the pictures. I can study the bodies. It is useful for our drawing class."

"It sounds like an interesting book," he said.

We were on Vali-Asr Street, getting close to home. Baba drove slowly as the slush had already frozen on the asphalt and the fresh new flakes covered the dirty, frozen snow. He focused on driving, trying not to skid on the slippery black ice. "Well, I'm glad you had a good time."

I was glad too, that it was snowing and he couldn't pry more information out of me. I longed to be left alone more than any other night. I had ideas of materialism on my mind, the image of a kiss on my cheek, and a backpack of books I could tell no one about.

The Reed Warblers of Basra

*He espied King Badr Basim in his form of a
white-robed bird, with red bill and legs, captivating
the sight and bewildering the thought; and, looking
thereat, said in himself, "Verily, yonder is a beautiful
bird: never saw I its like in fairness and form."*

―――――――

"Julnar the Sea-Born and Her Son
King Badr Basim of Persia"

As soon as Uncle Reza left for the front line, Agha Joon replaced
his old broadcast receiver with a brand-new Philips radio–
cassette player he'd bought from Tehran's black market. Every
evening, he twisted the black tuner on top of the radio to find
the BBC Persian shortwave frequency. He didn't budge from
his spot until the news broadcast was over. Sometimes the frequency was lost, and Arabic or Turkish music filled the living
room instead. Short bursts of singing rang out in our house as
Agha Joon turned the tuner back and forth by minuscule de-
grees to find the British broadcasting again. I imagined a naked
belly dancer as I heard the singer saying *ya habibi* in a thick,
Arabic accent. The Turkish singers were almost the same as Iranian singers before the Islamic Revolution: beautiful women
with bright red lipsticks, golden necklaces, and décolletage
gowns. They stood in front of microphone poles, singing the
nostalgic songs of lost love. Baba often joined Agha Joon, both
men sitting close to the radio, staring at the silver cover of the

cassette player as if it was soon to announce the end of the
world. No one could talk, whisper, or even sigh as they listened
to the news. Azra wasn't allowed in the living room during the
BBC show. She couldn't help but clasp her hands and cry whenever she heard the death toll. She was too fainthearted to endure
the ritual. Mar Mar and I had to study in complete silence, like
jinni trapped in a lamp. The reporter's irksome voice pierced
my eardrums as Agha Joon turned up the volume. He was hard
of hearing and didn't want to miss a word about the war. They
didn't trust the Islamic Republic's broadcasting since it only
echoed the bravery of Iranian soldiers and didn't report much
about retreats or casualties. Every night the BBC ritual was followed by dinner being served in front of the TV as the eight
o'clock national nightly news aired. Images of soldiers running
in khaki combat helmets, men in trenches carrying heavy RPGs
on their shoulders, young boys smiling in front of the camera
and showing the V-sign for victory filled our nights.

In February 1984, we heard the dreaded military operation
march from the national radio once again. I was on my way
home from school. *Dear listeners, pay attention please! Dear
martyr-fostering nation, pay attention please! In a few moments,
we will announce important news from the front line.* The military march overpowered the chatter of girls on the bus. Every
time our troops led a major attack against the Iraqis, the national radio would broadcast the operation march. *Our coura-
geous heroes have once again achieved an epic victory over the
Iraqi infidels. Our dauntless soldiers passed the Hawizeh marshes
in a surprise amphibious attack. Many Iraqi infidels were sent to
hell. Iran's Islamic flag is once again erected in the Hoor Al Azim.*

I wondered about Uncle Reza. We hadn't heard from him in
six weeks, and we were all anxious to know where he was. Was
he on the front line, where the offensive operation was taking

place where so many soldiers were killed with each wave of attacks? The school bus stopped in front of our cul-de-sac. I hopped down the steps, eager to get home after the long ride. A hejleh, a kind of decorative glass chamber, came into my view as soon as the bus passed the street. It hadn't been there in the morning. In Iran, when an unmarried, young man dies, a hejleh is lit to honor his death. Those days, hejlehs illuminated many streets in Tehran for the young soldiers who had died in the war. I went close to see whose picture was attached to the glass. Candle-shaped lamps lit up the small pieces of glass adorning the hejleh's surface. There was a photo of a young boy behind the glass. I'd never seen him, nor did I know his name. The neighbors must have heard the news of his martyrdom that morning. A Koran-reciter's voice filled the cul-de-sac from two loudspeakers placed inside the chamber.

I saw our mailman riding his motorcycle at the end of the street. He was still delivering mail to the houses on Sun Street late in the afternoon. Many people were expecting letters from their loved ones on the battlefield. I called him when I noticed he was heading toward our house. He saw me waving my hands in the air and stopped his motorcycle beside the hejleh and searched inside his enormous, oilskin mailbag.

"Do you have any letters for us, Mr. Mailman?"

"I think I do." He looked at the photo of the dead boy. "May God bless his soul," he said in a sorrowful voice. "He used to open the door and collect the mail in house number three. I hadn't seen him for a few weeks."

He handed the letter to me. It was from Uncle Reza, posted a week before from Abadan.

I darted into the garden as soon as Mar Mar opened the door. "Where is Nastaran?" I asked without saying salam.

"Salam! What's going on?" Mar Mar asked.

"I have a letter from Uncle Reza," I said as I held the letter in the air.

"She's upstairs trying to put Sami to sleep."

I skipped the stairs two at a time and hollered across the staircase, "I have a letter!"

Nastaran opened the door to Reza's old bedroom, where they'd been staying for the past few weeks. She was rocking Sami to sleep.

"Is it from Reza?" she asked.

I nodded and handed the letter to her. She snatched it, dashed into the bedroom, and sat on the edge of the bed. She gave Sami to me while she tore the envelope with her trembling hands. Maman and Mar Mar rushed into the room. Azra trudged behind them, panting as she walked toward the bed.

"What's he written?" Azra asked. She sat beside Nastaran on the bed.

Sami started crying in my arms. All the noise we made had woken her from her nap. I tried to rock her back and forth while Nastaran read the letter. A picture fell out of the folded letter. Reza had started his letter with "Besme rabbe shohada va sediqqin." I had heard that phrase in school, referring to God Almighty, the Master of the martyrs. The one and only Allah, in whose name the soldiers were sacrificing their lives. Many warriors started their testaments with that phrase. The words brought a sense of finality to what came next in the letter.

Dear Nastaran,

It feels like spring here, beside Hoor Al Azim. At night, a cool breeze carries the scent and moisture of the marsh to our station. Last night I couldn't sleep. I went out and walked around the camp before the dawn prayer. Pink and orange auroras appeared on the horizon above the marshland. Green reeds are growing ev-

erywhere in batches in the marsh. They quiver and bend
in the breeze and make soft waves in the reed bed. In the
morning silence, I heard a mysterious bird singing, as if
a young man was playing music on an old reed. Later,
when I asked a native soldier in our group, he told me
about the Basra reed warblers that live in the marsh. He
said it is rare to hear them sing. The natives of Hawizeh
believe if anyone hears their song over the squawks of
the white herons flying over the Hoor, he will have
good luck.

Our journey has been a memorable one so far. Brothers help each other here in countless ways. Amir and
I don't feel desolate or homesick. In the near future,
maybe even an hour after the ink dries on this letter,
we're going to ride on the speedboats and pass the Hoor.
We'll catch the Iraqi infidels by surprise, and we'll defeat
them. They ought to be taught a lesson, one they will
never forget. No one should ever dare to attack our land.
May Allah be with us in these hard times. Kiss Azra and
the girls for me, and give my regards to Agha Joon and
everyone else.

With love, Reza

The picture showed Uncle Reza and Amir side by side, Reza
resting his hand on Amir's shoulder. They both had khaki helmets on their heads and dark olive overcoats zipped all the way
up to their throats. A sapphire pond filled the background, and
green reeds stuck out of the water in the distance. Amir was
smiling and waving at the photographer. Reza had the same
stern look I'd always seen in his eyes.

The letter fell to Nastaran's lap. She wiped the tears that trickled down her face with her sleeve and circled her arm around
Azra's neck. She kissed her on the cheek. The two women sat

on the edge of the bed in silence and in shock. I was the only person in that room who moved as I tried to soothe the baby.

The house on Sun Street changed into a battlefield. The national radio broadcast the news of the Kheibar Operation from dawn to dusk and the serenity nesting in the corners of the house was shattered by the shrills of the military march. Once we discovered where Reza was stationed, the war felt closer, as if it was happening in Agha Joon's garden. Never before had I paid attention to the war. The war was a tragic mishap that befell a world far from me. But when I heard Reza's words, a vision of him steering a speedboat to escape a barrage of gunshots stuck in my mind. I'd heard that Iraqi helicopters flew close to the ground and shot Iranian soldiers like reeds being scythed in the marsh. I'd seen soldiers fall in trenches, bleeding to death in their comrades' arms as they whispered their last goodbyes. The national TV never failed to show the gruesome war images to goad young men into enlisting for the front line. The eight o'clock news ended with the same sad folkloric melody I'd heard many times before, an elegy sung by a soloist with a southern Iranian accent. I'd only paid attention to the beginning of the song before, since it started with a strange, intimate nickname used for little boys. *Mamadi, you were not here to see* was all that I knew from that song. But as the war felt close, the rest of the words revealed their meanings to me:

> *Mamadi, you were not here to see*
> *The city is freed*
> *The blood of your comrades*
> *Becomes fruitful finally.*
> *Oh, where is Major General Jahan Ara?*
> *Oh, where is the gleaming light of our eyes?*

After you left, the flowers have withered
The palms of our city have died.
Mamadi, you were not here to see
Your armor remains in our palms
Your name in our memory.

The Battle of Marshes

He bared his sabre and bore down on them, he and his,
but the Franks met them with hearts firmer than rocks,
and wight clashed against wight, and knight dashed upon
knight, and hot waxed the fight, and sore was the affright,
and nor parley nor cries of quarter helped their plight; and
they stinted not to charge and to smite, right hand meeting
right, nor to hack and hew with blades bright-white, till
day turned to night and gloom oppressed the sight.

———

"The Tale of King Omar bin al-Nu'uman and His Sons"

We received no information from Reza until a few days before
Nowruz. The second trimester exam season was upon us, and
Mar Mar and I had stayed home to study. One morning, I was
reading my geography book when the rotary phone rang in the
hall. Mar Mar picked up the phone, and a man who didn't introduce himself wanted to talk to Agha Joon. Azra hurried out
of the kitchen and took the phone from Mar Mar. After a few
seconds of yes and no, Azra tapped her chest with her fist and
hunched forward to reach the banister of the staircase. "Is he
dead?" she wailed. "Sarkar to ro khoda rast bego, are you trying to prepare me?"

Mar Mar and I looked at each other, worried and surprised.

"Which hospital?" Azra said. "How is he?" As soon as she
hung up the phone, she hollered into the hall room. "Nastaran!
Reza is injured. Bacham o avordan bimarestan! Mostafa Kho-

meini Hospital, I need to go there now," she said in tears. She pushed her shaky hands against the banister to straighten her back and murmured, "Reza janam," as she trudged toward the foyer.

I darted to her bedroom to get her scarf that was always hidden somewhere in the closet. I heard Maman talking to Nastaran on how to get to the hospital. Maman had to go too since she was the only one of the women who knew how to drive. They said Mar Mar and I needed to stay and take care of the kids, but I didn't want to stay home. I wanted to find out what had happened to Reza and how he'd been injured. They had taken him to the hospital close to my high school. Mostafa Khomeini was the army trauma hospital in Tehran, well equipped to take care of wounded soldiers. I tried to find an excuse to go with them. I told Maman I'd left my geography notes and class assignments in my locker—which was true—and I needed to pick them up from school for the exam. I said I was lucky they were going that way, or I would have had to ask Baba to take me in the afternoon.

Maman squinted as she heard my story. "They may not let you in the hospital," she said. "I don't know their policies on child visitors."

"I am not a child anymore, Maman," I said. "I'll be twelve in two weeks."

"Yes, but you are tiny," she said. "They don't check birth certificates. Besides, I am not sure visiting a hospital full of wounded soldiers is suitable for you."

"But Maman, how come you let us see all the dead and wounded on TV?"

"I don't have control over the news and the TV shows. I can't erect a screen in front of your eyes every time they show a battle scene. And, of course, those men are not your uncle lying injured in a hospital bed," she said.

Azra was already in the front garden, yelling at us to hurry.

"I promise, Maman, I promise. I won't be scared or throw up or faint. I can stay in the school or in the car if they don't let me in."

Maman shook her head. She didn't want to argue with me any longer. "Fine," she finally said. "Go put on your scarf and manteau while I warm up the car."

On the way to the hospital, Azra, Maman, and Nastaran talked about Reza and fretted over his injuries. Nastaran kept asking Azra if she could remember more of the conversation she'd had on the phone. Of course, she was so stressed she couldn't even remember the room number, let alone any detail about how he'd been injured. I pictured Reza lying on the bed, one leg completely covered in white plaster and one arm hanging in a sling. I imagined he would be asleep when we entered the room, opening his eyes with excitement, and instantly asking for Sami.

The hospital's reception hall was full of flowers. White and pink gladioli were arranged like open Japanese fans in straw baskets and lined beside the smoky glass wall. Red roses in tall vases stood at the bottom of a spiral staircase there in the hall. People carried baskets of carnations and chrysanthemums as they entered the hospital. I had never seen so many flowers gathered in one place in my life.

The receptionist, a young soldier sitting behind a round glass table, asked Maman who we wanted to visit. Maman said Reza's name as she stooped forward to peek at the bulky registry book in front of the soldier. He turned the pages to find Reza in the alphabetically sorted book. His khaki sleeve brushed a glass vase with more roses as he rolled his fingers down the rows of names. I leaned on the glass table to breathe in the roses' aroma.

"He is in room 204 on the second floor," he said. He glanced at me bending over his table. "Be careful, young lady, you could knock over the vase. And you won't be able to go in."

Maman frowned at me for leaning on the table. "She's twelve years old, sir. She studies at the high school next to the hospital. She is just small," Maman said.

He looked at me from head to toe, trying hard to believe I was twelve. "Do you have any sort of ID?" he asked. Luckily, I had my school library card in my purse. I gave the card to him. He examined my face and the picture ID. Azra intervened and said, "Pir shi pesar, we've come a long way. I can't stand here any longer. Let us go upstairs."

The soldier handed the library card back to me. He raised his hands and said, "You can either go up the staircase or use the elevator. Room 204 is close." I ran toward the stairs, but Maman grabbed my hand. She thanked the soldier and said we would rather use the elevator for Azra's sake. Then she said to me, "Can't you just calm down and not make a show of yourself?"

———

Reza was asleep when we entered the room. To my surprise, no white plaster covered his limbs. An oxygen mask cupped his nose and mouth. Azra walked toward the head of the bed and grabbed Reza's face in her hands. Tears glistened in her eyes as she kissed his cheek above the mask. Reza opened his eyes at the touch of her lips. After a few seconds, he recognized Azra and pushed his hands against the bed as he struggled to sit. He started to cough as soon as he moved.

"Noore cheshmam koja boodi?" Azra said, weeping and shaking her head.

Nastaran and Maman drew closer to the bed, Maman at his feet and Nastaran gripping his hand.

"Khoda ra shokr bargashti, Reza," Nastaran said.

"What has happened, Reza jan? Why are you coughing so much?" Maman said.

Azra moved back and withdrew her hands while Reza continued to cough. He tried to talk, but the coughing cut short his sentences. A nurse with a white scarf and navy blue cloak came into the room. She had a small cup of pills and a glass of water in her hands. She greeted us and asked Reza to remove his mask. Then she gave the pills to Reza one by one, asking him to swallow carefully between his coughs.

"Try not to talk. Your lungs need to heal," she said.

"What is wrong with his lungs?" Nastaran asked, frightened. "Is his chest injured?"

"No, he has pneumonia. Perhaps the doctor can explain better for you. He needs to stay in the hospital for a few weeks," she said.

"What has happened to him?" Maman asked.

"Let me get the doctor," she said. "He's still around."

Reza was gasping for air. I came close to his bed and stood beside Maman. Sunlight shone through the tall windows and brightened the room. I was happy to see my uncle again. He had been present in every crucial event of my life, and I had witnessed the other version of the Islamic Revolution's story through him. Through his eyes, I had seen the people's uproar and a nation's utter belief in a hero. It was wonderful to see him alive, even with his disabling cough. I stretched my hand to caress his shins. I longed to hug him, if only Azra would ever step aside.

"How are Somi and Sami?" Reza asked.

Nastaran circled her arms around Reza's neck. Her white chador covered Reza's face. "They're fine, Reza jan, they're fine," she said. "Thank God you're back."

A tall man with a grizzled beard entered the room and introduced himself as Dr. Sharifi. He was wearing a blue tie and a clean white coat buttoned all the way up to his collar. Nastaran stood up, pulled the chador over her head and grabbed the hems under her chin. Maman welcomed the doctor and stretched her hand to shake hands. She immediately noticed her mistake and drew her hand back. She'd forgotten we were in the army hospital. Dr. Sharifi smiled and winked, signaling he understood why she withdrew her hand. With the stylish tie and the pleasant smile, he belonged to the same school of thought to which Maman and Baba belonged. He turned to Reza and asked, "How are you feeling, Reza?"

"Better," he said.

"Well, young man, you should be. Your family is here. You're all united again."

"Aghaye doctor, bacham khoob mishe?" Azra asked.

"Hopefully he will, madar jan. He is recovering from the pneumonia," he said.

"Khoda omret bedeh. Thank you for taking care of my son."

"Your son is lucky, khanoom." He smiled. "Many boys weren't as lucky as him. They either drowned or burned in the marshes. Their bodies are yet to be found. But Reza was brought to one of Tehran's best trauma hospitals," he said.

Reza rested his head against the pillow. He stared at the shoots emerging from the branches outside. Chinar trees danced in the breeze and tapped the windows with their burgeoning boughs. Reza's mind was not in the room with us. He was somewhere else, probably somewhere between the tall and slender reeds in the marsh. He took a deep breath, but then his staccato coughs captured him once again.

I woke up to the harsh rasp of a metallic object rubbing against something. The scraping sound was coming from the front garden. Maman and Baba were not in the room, but Mar Mar and

Mo were still asleep on their mattresses. It was early in the morning, a few days after Nowruz, and schools were closed for the spring break. I pulled the voile curtains away from the French doors to peek at the garden. The windowpane was freezing cold. I saw a young man moving his hand back and forth, honing a giant knife with a whetstone. He had on a heavy overcoat and had pulled his woolen hat down over the ears. He had tied a young sheep to the grape trellis.

"Mar Mar, wake up! Agha Joon has bought a lamb."

Uncle Reza was supposed to be released from the hospital that morning. I rushed to the kitchen to find Maman. Everyone was awake and at work. Azra was going to make aash reshteh to celebrate. She was sitting on a clean white cloth she'd spread on the tiles with fresh batches of parsley, mint, dill, and spring onions surrounding her. She opened the mint batch, trimmed the thick end stems, and threw the thin leaves into a deep drainer. The mixed scent of green onion and mint wafted around the kitchen. She loved cooking aash for the ambrosial scent that came from the cut leaves. Nastaran had a tray full of white beans in front of her, pulling one row of beans toward her at a time. She separated the tiny pebbles from the beans, making sure Azra didn't pour them into the aash. Maman had folded her sleeves above her elbows and was rubbing small balls of dry whey in a shallow ceramic bowl of water.

"Good morning, everyone," I said. "Can I help?"

"Salam azizam, of course you can," Maman said. "Go wash your hands and come help."

Maman let me take over her job after I folded back my sleeves. I rubbed the kashk balls in the ceramic bowl. The tiny balls shrank and gradually dissolved in the water, making a thick creamy sauce. Maman used this kashk sauce to garnish the aash.

Agha Joon had brought the giant zinced trays from the basement for the sacrifice ceremony. He had pledged to slaughter a sheep and donate the meat to the poor. I'd seen the gutting and skinning of sheep before. Every year on Eid Ghorban—the sacrifice feast—Agha Joon bought a sheep and gave away the meat like hajis in Mecca. He was a haji himself, having attended the pilgrimage three times in his life. In the past, I'd been astonished to see how skillfully the butcher blew into the sheep's leg after he'd cut the throat and severed the head, tearing the skin from the fascia beneath. He would hang the carcass from a giant hook under the trellis and skin from the neck, the red meat emerging from the white fluffy fat as he peeled the skin. Then he handed the raw meat to Agha Joon to slice and divide in equal portions on the zinced trays. Except for the pungent odor of the raw lamb that clung to the knives and trays, I loved the ceremony. The entire family worked together to prepare the fresh meat for the poor. The grown-ups were happy and in an elated mood, letting us swing under the grape trellis or play hide-and-seek in the garden. The day Reza came was as beautiful and green as those Eids in the past.

Baba drove Agha Joon's gold Chevrolet to bring Reza home. We heard the car purring as Baba turned into our quiet cul-de-sac. Mar Mar and I raced toward the gate, hollering Reza's name and trying to beat each other. Agha Joon came after us and asked the butcher to drag the sheep outside the house. We opened the gate wide for the butcher and the lamb.

Baba stooped beside the passenger seat to help Reza get out of the car. Reza grabbed Baba's shoulder and pushed against the doorframe to rise from the seat. He squeezed his eyes from pain as he stood up. "Are you okay?" Baba asked. Uncle Reza took a deep breath and coughed. He circled his arm around Baba's neck to walk home. I'd never seen Baba and Reza this close to each other, as if the mist of disagreement between the two had vanished in the spring sunshine. Azra appeared with the incense burner, smoldering espand seeds on blazing charcoal. The fresh aroma of espand wafted in the air as she neared Reza. Agha Joon held Reza's head in his hands and kissed his forehead. Azra twirled the burner around Reza and whispered prayers.

"Noore cheshmam, khosh amadi," she said. She pulled Reza to her bosom, one hand caressing his neck, the other holding the hot burner away from Reza's hair.

Nastaran held Sami in one arm while she gripped the chador under her chin. Somi clung to her mother's chador. Reza came close to Nastaran and wrapped his arms around her, one cheek nudging Sami's soft cheek, the other rubbing against Nastaran's cheek over the white chador. Nastaran sobbed like no other day. Somi jumped up and down, wanting to be held. I was thrilled to see Uncle Reza again. Eyes blurry with tears, I wasn't sure when my turn would come to hug him.

The butcher led the sheep by its rope and brought its neck to the ground near where Reza was standing. His knife was sharp from all the honing he'd done early in the morning. He placed his foot on the sheep's shoulder and stretched out its neck as far as he could. He cut the throat in a flash, blood splashing out like a fountain from the animal's neck. A sudden gush of blood flooded the ground. The sheep jolted rhythmically, and blood spewed out the veins with every thrust. The butcher let go of the sheep's head and straightened his back once the sheep became still. Everyone was silent, watching the animal die. Reza stepped over the blood puddle that was already clotting around the edges.

Agha Joon raised his hands toward the sky. "Ya Allah," he said, "may you accept this sacrifice. May you take the spilled blood as our earnest bestowal. May you bring health and happiness to all who abide in this house, Ameen, ya rab al alamin." He brushed his face with the palms of his hands.

After lunch, we gathered in the living room to rejoice over Reza's return. Tea leaves and cardamom seeds brewed in the china teapot on Azra's golden samovar. She sat beside the samovar and poured tea for everyone.

"Behdooneh is good for your cough," Azra told Reza. She poured boiling water into a tall glass half-filled with the quince seeds. The seeds gave away a gelatinous juice that thickened the water as Azra stirred the mix. She placed the glass on a small tray and asked me to give it to Reza. He stretched his feet on the mattress Maman had spread for him, leaned against the bolsters, and took the glass from the tray.

"Reza jan, tell us what happened," Baba said. The steam rising from the tea blurred Baba's face as he drank from the hot glass.

I was eager to hear Reza's story, just like Baba. I wanted to know how he'd survived the battlefield.

Reza pulled away the black seeds with a spoon and sipped the quince syrup. Then he said, "We were sailing around in the speedboat for about an hour when we heard a helicopter chopping the air above us. We aimed the machine gun toward the chopper as soon as it came close, but they opened fire on us, denting our boat and killing the boy behind the machine gun. I jumped into the marsh just before the boat exploded." He handed his syrup back to me and sighed. "I swam with every bit of strength I had in my muscles. I kept myself close to the reeds, hiding my head underwater every time I heard a helicopter flying above."

"How long did you swim in the water?" Baba asked.

"Vallah, I don't remember. Maybe for a day. Dead bodies were floating on the marsh. Hundreds of them, riddled with bullets, half-burned, sometimes I couldn't even distinguish the faces,"

Reza said, his voice trembling. He cleared his throat and covered his eyes with the tip of his fingers, trying to hide his tears. "I don't wish anyone to be in that hell of a battle."

I glanced at Maman and Azra while they listened to Reza. Azra's head bobbed with Reza's broken voice, and she tapped her hand unconsciously on her leg, mourning for every soldier killed in that marsh. Maman cupped her hand around her mouth, her eyes brimming with tears.

"The choppers kept coming back, taking pictures of the floating bodies. They opened another barrage of gunshots to kill anyone they assumed was alive." He straightened his back and tried to fold his legs under his body. The cough returned as he continued to speak. "I was soaked, shivering from cold, and swimming aimlessly in the marsh. I spent the night in the water, floating between the reeds. Early morning, I felt a heaviness in my chest. I couldn't breathe, as if someone had trickled acid down my throat."

Agha Joon scratched his bald head above his kufi. The creases in his forehead looked deeper as he listened to Reza's horrifying story. "La elah ella Allah," he said, shaking his head.

Nastaran wept silently under her chador. I could see her torso shaking. The only person who seemed untouched was Baba. He listened carefully to Reza and peeked at the front garden every now and then. Perhaps he was evaluating the combat situation in his mind.

Reza closed his eyes and took a deep breath. "I don't remember how long I struggled to breathe. I became unconscious after that. All I can say is that I saw the blur of some men with black goggles and heavy masks pulling me out. With my eyes half closed, I heard them shouting, 'Take off his shirts, take off his shirts!' They tore off my uniform, took off my boots and socks and wrapped me naked in a blanket." He paused and shook his head. "For a few seconds, I thought I was dead, and those men were angels preparing me for the next life." A bitter smile shaped on his lips.

"Where was Amir during all this?" Baba asked.

Reza became silent as Baba named Amir. The water simmering in the samovar was the only noise breaking the silence.

Finally, he said, "He was in another boat about ten meters ahead of us. I lost track of them when I jumped into the water. I don't know what happened to him."

"I've been calling Zabih every day since you came," Azra said. "No news."

Reza looked out the window and said, "I think I was the only survivor on our boat."

Uncle Zabih called on the eleventh day of Nowruz, three days before we went back to school. Mar Mar and I were working on our homework that was due after spring break. We didn't hear Agha Joon's conversation with Uncle Zabih, but from the wailing that spiraled through the house, we assumed something terrible had happened. Mar Mar and I stormed into the living room. Azra and Maman were striking their hands and punching their chests, mourning for Amir. Deep in our hearts, we knew this was coming. Not having news for weeks meant either Amir was dead or captured by the Iraqis.

Uncle Zabih told Agha Joon that Amir's funeral service was going to take place in Behesht e Zahra—Tehran's largest cemetery—the morning of the thirteenth day of Nowruz. It was the first time in my life that I would attend a funeral ceremony. I was surprised Maman didn't ask us to stay home. Every single member of my family attended the funeral that day, even Reza, who had barely recovered from his pneumonia. The fact that I'd never encountered death in the family ignited my curiosity. Never had I set foot in Behesht e Zahra, nor did I have any imagination about burying a body. Rumor had it that the Martyrs' Foundation—a newly founded organization after the Islamic Revolution—organized the ceremony for every martyr and took care of some costs to help the families.

On the day of the funeral, the emptiness of the barren land gave me goose bumps as we approached the cemetery. A mist formed in front of my face from the cold as soon as I got out of Maman's Beetle. There was no sign of spring in the southern part of Tehran. "Keep your jackets buttoned up at all times," Maman said to us. She had parked close to the mortuary where they washed and shrouded the corpses. The graves spread in every direction I looked, endless and innumerable. There was no upright headstone anywhere. The flat gravestones covered the bare desert like a huge black and gray quilt. Here and there, men and women were sitting or standing close to the graves, moaning, touching and tapping the stones with their fingertips. Children were running around and playing between the graves, oblivious to the dead. On TV, I had seen aluminum stands, tulips, roses, and flags flying above the martyrs' graves. They must have been buried somewhere else, somewhere different from the barren desert here in front of me.

We walked toward the mortuary, Maman holding Azra's hand, Mar Mar, Saba, and I following them. Maman was wearing a black chador for the first time I'd seen in my life. She looked completely different—spiritless and dim.

"Maman, why are we going to the mortuary?" I asked. "Didn't you say they don't wash the martyrs?"

"Yes. But his body is still there, kept in the coffin," she said.

In the coffin, she said, and I wondered how he looked in the coffin. Was he torn apart? Were they going to show him to us, like the images I'd seen on TV? Did I dare to look inside the coffin?

The mortuary had separate sections for deceased men and

women. They didn't allow any opposite sex in the two sections. We had to wait outside while Baba, Reza, and Agha Joon went inside with Uncle Zabih and his other sons. Amir's sisters were whining and dusting their heads with soil outside the mortuary. They all looked the same, fine white powder covering their black chadors. Azra started sobbing when she saw them. They embraced each other, put their heads on each other's shoulders, and cried. They were loud and relentless, as if their grief would never end. The fact that Amir's mother had died a few years before made things even worse. His sisters kept calling their mother's name, saying she was blessed not to see this day—the day her son's body was pierced and slabbed. I was disheartened by their words and their wretchedness. I was curious to see the procession, but at the same time, their desolation made me miserable. The world seemed dark to me at that moment. Why did we have to go through this?

I heard men shuffling out of the mortuary in a group, saying *La elah ella Allah* repeatedly. They were wearing black shirts, and some men had keffiyeh around their necks. Amir's three brothers appeared first, with three other cousins carrying the coffin. They each bore the coffin's weight on one shoulder. Agha Joon and Uncle Zabih followed them in the first row with the other older men. Uncle Zabih looked crumpled, trudging with heavy steps. Reza came after them, brooding and walking with difficulty. Baba stood out in the crowd with his striking white shirt. He was among the few who never wore black in the mourning ceremonies. Amir's sisters started ululating in sorrow as they saw the coffin. I had seen women ululating in wedding ceremonies, sticking their tongues to their palates and making a continuous cry in celebration. Their ululation reminded me of how we grieved for the young in my country—we mourned for his never-happening wedding ceremony.

Iran's flag covered the whole coffin. Stripes of vivid green and fiery red flanked a wide band of white silk in the middle. Allah's name was embroidered with golden threads at the center of the white band. Allah occupied the place where the Lion and the Sun had been on the old emblem of Persian Shahs. The flag's golden fringe brushed the coffin's edges. Two stout men I'd never seen before led the procession. They wore green headbands on their forehead that read *Ya Hossein*—the name of the third imam in Shia belief. They roared a slogan as the crowd headed toward the grave: *In gole par par mast. Hedyeh be rahbar mast. This is our flower, bereft of its petals. This is the gift to our leader.*

We walked a long way, following the men in the crowd. My toes squeezed and felt numb in my new Dove wedge shoes. Two times the men placed the coffin on the ground to take a breath and change shoulders. We passed several blocks of graves, each numbered with a wooden sign. After half an hour, we reached the block I'd seen many times on TV: the block of martyrs. In contrast to what they showed us on TV, I saw mothers crouched on gravestones, crying for their beloved sons. Some men had knelt on the ground, whispering elegies for their lost children, some splashing buckets of water on the graves to wash them and dust off the dirt. I saw a forlorn place, different from the glorified cemetery they advertised. There was no patriotic soundtrack in the background. All I heard was the melancholic reciting of the Koran.

I felt a pinch in my stomach as the men's *La elah ella Allah* became louder. We were getting closer to Amir's grave. For the third and last time, they placed the coffin on the ground, beside a narrow, deep hole. The soil mounted beside the grave was still soggy, giving off the unforgettable smell of freshly dug earth. The two stout men pulled the flag back to open the coffin, for Amir's sisters to see him for the last time. Their ululation pierced the sky. They gathered all their strength for this last goodbye.

"Don't look when they expose the body," Maman had said to me and Mar Mar as we marched toward the grave. But I peeked from above the sitting women who'd clutched the edges of the coffin. Amir was not washed in rose water or shrouded in white cotton. He still wore his green helmet and his boots, the same khaki uniform I'd seen in the photo. His face was not disfigured, but there was a small bullet hole above his right eyebrow, and a narrow streak of blood had stuck to his forehead. When they lifted him out of the coffin, I saw the back of his head when the helmet slid forward on his face as they grabbed the body to bury it. His skull was all smashed, and clots of blood covered the white particles of his brain.

None of Amir's brothers could bring themselves to enter the grave. It is a ritual in Islam for a close male family member of the deceased to descend into the grave and recite the last prayer while shaking the corpse. One of the men wearing a headband jumped in, sang the prayer, and placed a heavy, flat stone on Amir's head. He was quick, knowing well what to say and what to do. Later I heard from Baba that they were members of the Martyrs' Foundation, trained to lead the funeral ceremony. He shouted that Amir was a gift to Imam Khomeini so many times that Amir's older sister couldn't take it anymore. "To ro be Khoda bas kon. Stop it!" she yelled at him in between her cries.

Amir's body disappeared little by little as they shoveled the soil into the grave. Uncle Zabih sat beside Azra, resting his head on her shoulder. Azra's gray hair was showing from beneath her black chador. She hadn't hennaed her hair for many weeks, and she didn't realize her chador was almost falling from her head. Uncle Zabih trembled as he called Amir's name over and over again. Tears glistened on his cheeks in the sunshine. Maybe he hoped his son could hear and respond. But Amir was dead silent among the moaning women and stunned men staring at the fast-filling grave.

I always wonder if I should have avoided looking inside the coffin, as Maman had suggested. Why did she bring me to that horrendous place if she really didn't want me to see? Now I only come to one conclusion: she wanted me to realize the true nature of the lies the Islamic regime was spoon-feeding to us in the media. She wanted me to see how gloomy and dull that deified cemetery appeared in reality, despite the revolutionaries' effort to glorify the culture of martyrdom in the country.

I felt sick to my stomach after I saw Amir's blown-apart skull. I stepped back from the grave and distanced myself from the crowd for some fresh air. The martyrs' aluminum stands surrounded me in that block. A framed picture of a young man gazed at me from every stand. They all looked to be in their teens or twenties. Some of them didn't even have a first-time beard on their faces. Their dates of birth were so close to mine. Amir had been seventeen, only five years older than me. The painful reality tormented me in that moment. If I were a boy, I could have been in Amir's place, dead and gone at seventeen, losing my only chance of living and experiencing the world. How could those martyrs accept such a deal? How could they be sure that after dying the archangels nurtured them in Allah's presence? How could they believe in those ideals and surrender their lives? There, in the martyrs' block, I realized what it meant to sacrifice oneself for a deified cause.

At the center of the martyrs' block, I saw Behesht e Zahra's blood fountain. Red water spewed from the wide fountain, gurgling over the pool's circular steps. I wondered if they had erected that structure to symbolize all the blood that was spilled as a sacrifice to the Islamic Republic. I saw pictures of Ayatollah Khomeini everywhere, attached to the light poles or stuck beside the martyrs' pictures in those aluminum stands. Who was this Khomeini that all that blood was spilled and presented to him as a gift?

The Enigma of Shirin

*Hending in hand an iron knife whereon was inscribed
the name of Allah in Hebrew characters, she described a
wide circle in the midst of the palace-hall, therein wrote
in Cufic letters mysterious names and talismans; and she
uttered words and muttered charms, some of which we
understood and others we understood not.*

———

"The Second Kalandar's Tale"

"Today, we come to Euclid's fifth postulate, also known as the
parallel postulate," Ms. Borhani said and drew a straight line on
the green board at the front of our classroom. We had geometry
on Thursday afternoons. The mulberries in the schoolyard had
ripened, and their sticky nectar had scattered along the window
ledges. Queen, lying in the shade, licked a ripened black mulberry that was squished in front of her whiskers and listened
to the teacher's monotonous voice as she explained Euclid's ele-
ments. Like Queen, we all dozed off on the parallel lines while
they stretched and continued forever.

Ms. Borhani pushed up her thick glasses with her chalky fingers, leaving a white mark on the tip of her nose. "Now I want
you to prove that you can draw one and only one parallel line
from a point out of a straight line," she said. "Nusha, can you
repeat what I said?"

Nusha startled when she heard her name. She straightened

her back in the chair and repeated Ms. Borhani's statement in one breath.

"Good! I give you ten minutes to prove this."

Ms. Borhani wiped the chalk marks from her navy manteau and walked back to her desk. Five minutes later, someone knocked on the classroom door.

"Come in," Ms. Borhani said with a loud voice.

A girl from another class walked in and gave a white envelope to Ms. Borhani. She whispered something close to Ms. Borhani's head and then left the room.

She opened the envelope while we gaped at her. "Keep your eyes on your paper," she said. "You have only one minute left."

As soon as she read the letter that was in the envelope, she glanced at me. She crinkled her forehead and said, "Moji and Nusha, you need to go to Ms. Zadie's office!"

Suddenly I felt a heavy stone dropped deep in my chest. I looked at Nusha, wondering if she felt the same. I worried that the school staff had seen us slinking into the attic. I wasn't going there as regularly as before, but Nusha kept asking me to go with her during the noon prayer. I tried my best to show my face in the prayer hall every now and then. We both stood up and trotted toward the door, other girls gawking at us as we went. We hurried down the corridor and exited the school's main building. The school administrative building was located on the other side of the schoolyard, attached to the auditorium. The first room in that building was Ms. Zadie's office.

"I bet they've discovered our visits to the attic," I said. My hands were trembling in fear.

"Keep calm, Moji," Nusha whispered. "We don't know yet."

Ms. Mirza, our tall and heavy assistant principal, was pinning a notice to the news board as we entered the building. As soon as she saw us, she shook her head and shouted, "You two stay right here! I shall inform Ms. Zadie that you're here. Moji, you need to go in first!" She knocked and entered Ms. Zadie's office.

I wished there was a bench in the hall where I could sit. I felt dizzy and nauseated. Something was immensely wrong or they wouldn't have pulled us out of mathematics class. I tried to move closer to the wall so I could lean on it before I fell, but my feet weren't coming along.

"Nusha, I knew this would happen. We should've stopped going to the attic after the noon prayer warning," I whispered. Before Nusha could answer me, Ms. Zadie's door opened and Ms. Mirza signaled me to go in. She left me in Ms. Zadie's office and shut the door behind her.

"Salam, Ms. Zadie," I said in a mousy tone.

Ms. Zadie was sitting at her desk scribbling a letter with a fountain pen. She didn't respond to my salam, nor did she pause her writing. The folds of her shiny black khimar fluttered as she slid her hand on the paper. A large framed portrait of Khomeini hung above her seat. He stared at me with his fierce black eyes and thick frowning eyebrows, as if I were soaked in sin. I pulled my scarf forward almost to my eyes, trying to hide all the curly, disorderly hair on my forehead. I stood beside the door, still and silent, my heart jolting my chest with every racing beat.

"Ms. Moji," Ms. Zadie said. She raised her head from the paper, placed her pen on her giant oak desk, and looked at me for the first time. "You have wronged all the calculations I had made about you. I never expected such shameless disobedience from one of the most respected students in our school." She pressed her elbows on the desk, leaned forward, and roared, "How dare you sneak into the forbidden places of the school at the holy time of prayer?"

She stared at me through her dark square glasses, her cheeks flaming red more than ever. I lowered my eyes and stared at the marbled mosaic tile floor. I didn't dare look into her eyes. I wished I could shrink and sink in the cracks between the tiles under my feet. Tears trickled down my cheeks but I didn't dare wipe them from my face.

"How long have you been going up there?" she said.

I didn't say anything.

"Answer me!" she screamed.

"I . . . I . . . I . . . Just a few weeks before Nowruz, ma'am."

"What sort of books were you reading up there?"

"Some novels. Anna, I mean Russian, some Russian novels," I said.

"Anna? What Anna?"

"*Anna Karenina* by Tolstoy."

"Don't you realize if we deemed those books suitable for you, we would've kept them in the library? *Anna Karenina*? Instead of reading about the Islamic scholars? Reading novels at the high time of prayer?"

"I'm so sorry, Ms. Zadie. I . . . I'll never go up there again."

She took a deep breath and sank into her leather chair. She remained silent for a while. The more she kept silent, the more I felt she was going to take a serious action against me.

"Well," she finally said, "being sorry is not enough. I have called your father, and he is on his way to school. We need to investigate more into this matter, and you need to be disciplined for your misconduct."

Someone knocked on the door. "Come in," she said.

Shirin's head appeared in the doorframe.

"Ms. Shirin, come in."

Shirin glanced at me as she walked inside. She had a peculiar smile, signaling that she knew what was happening in the room.

"Ms. Mirza said you asked to see me."

"Yes, indeed. Please have a seat." She pointed to the tea table and four low chairs placed at the center of her office. "I wanted to ask you, since you've praised Moji on many occasions, if you were aware of her missing the noon prayers and reading the illegal books up in the auditorium's attic."

Shirin situated herself comfortably in the low chair and straightened the creases of her chocolate manteau with her hands. "Moji never told me she was visiting the attic," she said. She turned her head toward me and studied me from head to toe. "But I was aware of her growing interest in novels and works of fiction."

"Oh, how interesting, and how did you know of her interest?" said Ms. Zadie.

"We talked about Russian novels, *Anna Karenina* in particular, as she was interested in Tolstoy," she said, smiling at me. She faced Ms. Zadie. "I know she has made a terrible mistake, but to her benefit, I should say that she often attends the noon prayer. Do you remember the day she was standing in the first row beside me?"

Ms. Zadie nodded.

"I blame it on her zealous curiosity and her fervent desire to read. I can definitely guide her enthusiasm and help her not to make such grave mistakes again."

"I am sure you can. That's why I wanted to hear from you. Curiosity is a powerful force, and a dangerous one if it's not streamed in a righteous way."

"I believe she understands the magnitude of her mistake. Yes, Moji?" Shirin asked. She winked at me with a faint smile, the expression on her face not visible to Ms. Zadie.

"Yes. Ms. Shirin, I do," I said, and I wept.

"Well now, Ms. Moji, you are not to come to school next week," Ms. Zadie said. She turned to Shirin and continued, "I am giving her a second chance since you trust her. If it weren't because of you, Ms. Shirin, I would have given her file to her father today to take her to another school." She looked back at me and said, "Dismissed."

I came out of Ms. Zadie's office soaked in sweat and tears. My underwear was stuck to my wet skin, and the sides of my scarf were saturated with the mixture of snot and tears. I sighed in relief. The interrogation was over, and thank God, they didn't decide to expel me from school. The punishment was not as terrible as I'd imagined.

Nusha was still in the hall, standing beside the news board. She glanced at me with wide, worried eyes. "They figured out?" she mumbled in a low tone.

I nodded and stood close to the news board beside her, not knowing what to do next. I wondered who had seen us going to the attic and reported us to the school staff. Shirin came out of Ms. Zadie's office shortly after me.

"Your turn," Shirin told Nusha.

Nusha glanced at me one last time before she went in. The bold look I'd seen in her eyes had suddenly vanished, and she slumped forward in defeat. I wondered what fate she would suffer in Ms. Zadie's office. Certainly not better than mine.

As soon as Nusha disappeared, Shirin looked at me and said, "We need to talk after you're back at school, Moji. Meet me in the library next Saturday when you're back."

"Yes, Ms. Shirin," I whispered.

The last knot of her braided hair swayed under her scarf as she left the administrative building. What puzzled and tormented me most at that moment was the way Shirin acted in the entire scene. Was she the one who reported us to Ms. Zadie? Was this a plot laid by her to trap Nusha and me? No doubt she knew we were visiting the attic, but why didn't she say that? Why did she wink at me when Ms. Zadie couldn't see? I never told her a single word about my interest in Tolstoy. How did she know I loved Anna Arkadyevna Karenina?

On the way back home, I had a crushing headache. Even the soft laughter of the girls at the back of the bus annoyed me and worsened the throbbing in my head. Zara was the first girl who noticed how pale my face was.

"You've seen a ghost in Ms. Zadie's office?" She cackled a harsh laugh. She had seen me coming out of the administrative building that afternoon. She had physical education for the last session of the day, and they were playing basketball in the schoolyard. "Why did you go to the office instead of attending class? You got punished for something?" she said.

"I wasn't feeling well. I have a terrible headache, and I don't feel like talking right now."

The corners of her wide mouth quirked up in disbelief, showing the bits of orange between her teeth. "Grumpy Moji! Grumpy Moji!" she sang and slipped back to the last row of seats on the bus.

It felt like the longest ride of my twelve-year-old life. I didn't know how to approach Maman and Baba. What were they going to do with me when they found out? Were they going to punish me as well? Baba was for sure being informed by Ms. Zadie and was not supposed to be home when I got there. How could I rectify the situation at home? What excuse could I give that they would believe?

I was expecting Mar Mar to open the door for me, but to my surprise, Maman appeared at the gate. She had a worried look in her eyes, showing that she was alarmed by what had happened at school. Without a reply to my salam, she said, "Baba called and asked me to take you directly to our room. You need to stay there till he gets home." She narrowed her eyes. "What mess have you made at school?"

I wished Mar Mar was in our room, squatting on the floor and doing her homework like other days. I could seek refuge in her arms and tell her the story before the second interrogation of the day started. Alas, Mar Mar and Mo were in the living room with Agha Joon and Azra. Maman closed the door behind me and left me in the silence of our bedroom. Every signal I received showed a tempest on its way. Where could I cast my hope to be saved? I took off my scarf and manteau, sat beside the French doors, and peeked at the front garden. Figs hadn't ripened on the old fig tree yet, but sparrows chirped here and there, pecking at the green figs high on the branches. My headache was not going away. I cracked open the door, hoping a fresh breeze could sweep in and brush away my pain.

After an hour, which seemed like a day, the doorbell rang and Baba appeared at the gate. I tried to figure out his mood from his gesture and his gate, but I couldn't see the contours of his lips or the crinkles around his eyes. In the dusk, it was hard to distinguish anger in his poise. After a few minutes, Maman and Baba entered the room. Baba had a stern look on his face, his shoulders pulled back as if prepared for one-on-one combat. Maman looked vexed, the furrows in her forehead more prominent than before.

I immediately rose from my seat. "Salam, Baba," I said.

He shook his head but didn't reply. "Close the door. I don't want anyone to hear what we say."

I closed the French door and stood beside it. Maman and Baba situated themselves on the mattress spread beside the wall.

"Come and sit here," Baba ordered.

I dropped to my knees in front of them, and I could hear the throbbing of the swollen veins in my ears. "I am so sorry, Baba, for what has happened. I promise I won't break any school rule again," I said.

"It is not about breaking the school rule that I am concerned right now," Baba said. "I need to know what you've been reading the past few months."

"Have you brought the books home?" Maman asked.

"If you've brought them home, go get them. We need to see them all."

I had stacked the books beside Azra's jams and pickles in the second-floor pantry that led to the roof. I thought no one would bother going there and poking through the shelves, between the old magazines and booklets, among the cherry jams and pomegranate sauces. I moped upstairs, hoping I could hide the books I'd borrowed from Nusha. But Maman came after me, dogging my every single move. She shook her head when she saw the mountain of books in the pantry.

"All this time, you didn't say a word to us about these books?"

I was almost in tears. Maman helped me bring the books downstairs to our room. Baba browsed through the books page by page, lengthening the torture by reading the notes I'd scribbled in the margins and the sentences I had underlined. I was getting flattened by the mounting pressure, like the white sheets Maman pressed with her hot iron. The words of love between Anna and Count Vronsky that resonated in my heart screeched into my ears as Baba read them out loud. I can't remember a more disgraceful time in my life than that night. They were unearthing my hidden treasures one by one, tormenting me with the shame of my exposed emotions. I wished a dark abyss would open under my feet and devour my whole being, rescuing me from the ignominy suffocating me in front of my parents. How could Baba and Maman do this to me? How could they allow themselves to dredge up my innermost sentiments by reading my notes?

Maman stared at me in silence while Baba placed the books aside. The red cover of *The Communist Manifesto* appeared among the stack.

"What is this?" Baba raised his voice. "Did you find this in your school's attic as well?"

Maman cupped her mouth with her hands, trying not to shout or say anything.

"Answer me!" Baba roared.

I covered my face and whined. I couldn't sit straight anymore. I squatted and placed my face on my knees. "I am so sorry, Baba," I yelled.

"Moji, where did you get this?"

"It was ... it was ... the school attic. I ... I ... I didn't take it," I mumbled.

"I can't hear you."

Maman came close, raised my head, and straightened my back.

"How did this book end up here?" Baba said.

"Nusha took it first and then gave it to me with some other books from their library."

"Do you know what could have happened if you were found reading this book? You could have been arrested!" Baba shouted. "Do you not live in this country? Are you naive, or acting as if you know nothing of the situation we live in?" Baba tapped his forehead with his hand. "Moji, oh, Moji, what have you been doing all this time?"

I gasped for air in between bouts of sobbing, feeling dizzy and light-headed. Maman rubbed my back and tried to calm me. It was hard to see Baba with the teary film that blurred my eyes. Even though I sensed carrying those books could be dangerous, I never imagined the magnitude of the danger I might be bringing on myself and my family.

"We struggle to keep you from the Islamists' poisonous ideas. Not to offer you, with our own hands, to the Communists. Are you reading *The Communist Manifesto* without saying a word to us?"

"Baba jan, I never knew they could arrest me for carrying these books."

"Even worse! Teenagers are being executed just for carrying

a page of this book. Don't you know? Do you not hear when we talk?"

"Did you give any of these books to Mar Mar?" Maman asked.

"I only gave her some Chekhov plays." I showed the book among the stack.

"Does your school know you've carried the books home?" Maman asked.

"No, I don't think so. They punished me for going to the attic and not attending the noon prayers," I said.

"I don't give a damn if you missed the noon prayers. I told Ms. Zadie they can't force you to pray. But I do care about what you read and who you mingle with. From now on, you will not step into Nusha's house again. I will arrange for her family to come pick up the books. And you are required to show me or your mother what you read."

I froze in place. My feet began to tingle under the weight of my body. "Baba, but Nusha is my best friend." I hoped he would at least lessen the punishment.

"What kind of friend knowingly puts you in danger?" He shook his head. "Is that clear?"

"Yes, sir," I said.

"Dismissed. Go wash your face and clean the snot covering your face."

———

When I looked in the mirror hanging in front of the washbasin, I saw Mar Mar standing behind me. I had left the bathroom door ajar, and she had stepped in when she noticed me washing my face.

"What happened, Moji?" she whispered. She circled her arms around my neck and held me to her chest. "Why are you crying?"

I turned off the faucet and hugged her in return. At that moment, Mar Mar's hug meant the world to me. I felt relieved in her arms. Tears welled up in my eyes again. "They found out I've been going to the attic. I can't go to school for a week."

She brushed the hair away from my eyes and pressed my hands in hers. She shook her head and bit her lips when she noticed my puffy eyelids. "What did Baba and Maman say to you all that time?"

"They want to know every single book we read from now on."

"Why? Do they think we should not read those books?"

"Mar Mar," I said, "there were books in the stack that Baba thinks could have gotten me in trouble."

"Like which one?"

"Baba said people can get killed by reading them," I whispered.

"Really?" Mar Mar shrugged and raised her voice. "Books can get you killed?"

"Shhhh," I said. "I didn't show those books to you. The ones I borrowed from Nusha."

Mar Mar nodded. "What were they about?"

I saw Maman peeking at us in the mirror. I let go of Mar Mar's hand. "Dinner is ready," Maman hollered from the hall. "Come out of the bathroom, Moji and Mar Mar."

"I'll tell you later, Mar Mar," I said with a broken voice. "Go eat. I'm not hungry."

———

Maman didn't insist I eat dinner with the rest of the family. The clatter of the dishes and the smell of the lentil soup came into our room, but I didn't feel hungry at all. I spread my mattress and went to bed early, trying to distance myself from the day's events. But it was impossible to forget what had happened. Every word that Ms. Zadie or Baba had said echoed in me, as if I was trapped inside the Cave of Wonders, words hitting the walls and bouncing back to me. What if Baba wasn't exaggerating? Could I be arrested for reading *The Communist Manifesto*? Our house was close to the prime minister's headquarters on Pasteur Avenue. There were Revolutionary Guard members at every inspection post. What if one of them stopped me and searched my backpack? How could I prove I was just reading and not believing in communist ideas? They were violent and never gave anyone a chance to defend themselves. Would they execute me in front of a firing squad—like the people I'd seen in the newspaper? How careless and naive I had been, thinking I wouldn't get caught reading those books at my pleasure. What would have happened to my family? Would they have arrested Baba again? What about Mar Mar? Would they have interrogated her as well? I pressed my fingers against my eye sockets in the dark, and flashes of light twinkled in front of my eyelids. How could I be so inconsiderate of my family?

———————

During the week of punishment, Nusha and Manuch came to pick up the books. I was baffled by the conflicting emotions I felt toward her. I was delighted to see her again, knowing she was the only soul in the world who shared my agony, but I was also disturbed by the fact that she put me in danger by giving me those dangerous books. She was wearing a gray scarf and a dark manteau, and her skin looked jaundiced under the fluorescent lights over the trellis. The luminous girl I remembered from the first day of school had completely vanished. Manuch looked tired as well, nothing like the enthusiastic young man I saw in that blue library.

"Please come in and have some tea. I just brewed it before you got here," Maman said.

"Thank you for your generous offer, ma'am. I have a lot of work to do for finals," Manuch answered.

"How have you been?" I asked.

"I'm fine," Nusha answered.

In the background I could hear Maman talking to Manuch about his studies at Sharif University.

"Did you have to stay home for a week as well?" I whispered. Nusha shook her head. "I can't come back to school, Moji."

Deep in my heart, I knew she was going to give that answer, but I had tried to trick myself and ignore the facts, hoping she would get the same punishment I did. Her case was worse than mine. She hadn't attended any noon prayers and didn't have a powerful supporter like Shirin.

"They expelled me from school." She shrugged and leaned against the trellis pole. It was hard for both of us to hear that word. We knew the stigma it bore. "Dad thinks he shouldn't have sent me to that school in the first place," she said. "It's not a suitable learning environment for me."

I wanted to mention the danger she'd brought to my life by carrying those books around, but I hesitated to say anything after I heard what she said. Nusha and her family were well aware of the situation themselves. What was the point of confronting her at that moment?

"I am sorry to hear this, Nusha," I said. "What are you going to do?"

"It's almost the end of the school year, Moji. There's no hope any other school would accept me. My parents don't want to send me to any other school."

"What do you mean?"

"They're thinking of sending me abroad for the next school year. Somewhere in Europe, maybe Paris," she said.

"Oh, do you have anybody there? Are you going alone?" I furrowed my forehead in surprise.

She shook her head. "Boarding school, maybe."

For a moment, I imagined myself in her position. It scared

me to death to leave Iran and go to another country all by myself. I couldn't last a day without my parents and Mar Mar. "Are
you not scared to go alone?"

She lowered her head and rolled her sneakers back and forth
in the groove between the mosaic tiles. "It's scarier to stay in
this country, Dad says." She looked back at me with tearful eyes.
"What else can I do?"

Pain pierced my heart. Not seeing her in school was a sharp
cut on top of my already weeping wound.

"Do you want to bring my books?" Nusha said finally.

I ran back to our room to fetch the books. As I grabbed them
one by one, I remembered all the moments we had together in
school, sitting at the same table, talking about books and all the
tiny, trivial things that weaved us together. I already missed her
lively poise and her stubborn attitude, the wonders we shared
while exploring new horizons in hidden books.

Manuch and Maman had finished their conversation when I
got back. They were waiting for me under the trellis.

"Keep in touch with Nusha. She enjoys your companion-
ship," Manuch said to me.

"I'll send you letters when I am settled," Nusha said. A faint
smile appeared on her lips. She kneeled to unzip the backpack
she'd placed on the tiles. She put the smaller books in first and
opened the zipper wider for *The Paintings of the Hermitage*. The
book had a small tear on the top right corner of its glossy cover.

"I'm sorry it doesn't look as good as when you gave it to me,"
I said. "I accidentally tore the front cover with my fingernail."

She examined the cover under the fluorescent light. She
browsed through the pages and ran her fingers along the paintings. "Why don't you keep this one for yourself?" she held the
book out toward me. "As a gift from me!"

I couldn't believe she gave that book to me. I looked at Maman to see if she was fine with me accepting that expensive book. To my utter surprise, she nodded and said, "You are so kind, Nusha jan. Moji would love to have this book."

I thanked her and grabbed the book from her hands. I kneeled down beside her and hugged her, *The Paintings of the Hermitage* squeezed between our chests. I didn't want to let go of her; she was my first best friend. Nusha and Manuch said goodbye to us and disappeared in the silvery light of the lamppost that illuminated Sun Street.

I often wondered what happened to Nusha and whether or not she ever got out of the country. She never sent a letter to me.

After that night, I never saw her again.

———

The first thing I noticed in the class on Saturday morning was the empty olive chair beside me. Now I had the entire table to myself. No one pushed my notebooks to my side of the table for more room. No one said salam with a cheerful voice, asking, "What did you read during the weekend?" Nusha's empty place was more conspicuous to me than to anyone else, and her absence pinched my heart.

"Moji, where were you last week?" a tall girl shouted from the back of the class.

I wasn't sure how fast the rumors about Nusha and me had spread.

"I wasn't feeling well," I shouted back.

"What kind of sickness did you have? Diarrhea?" another girl jeered in the noisy classroom.

"Where is your soulmate? Was she sick as well?"

I shrugged, pretending I didn't know anything.

We started the class with mathematics. Ms. Borhani reviewed Euclid's fifth postulate and proved it for the second time. Like a repeating nightmare, I was back in the world of parallel lines. A week of torture squeezed between the never-ending lines. Every minute of that class, I longed for the bell to ring and recess to start. More than anything in the world, I wanted to see Shirin.

––––––––––

They had changed the lighting above Shirin's desk during the week I was out. Her birthmark looked more glamorous under the new bright light. She was wearing a pearl-white manteau and a teal blue scarf with an oceanic pattern. Waves on her scarf brushed the hazel highlights in her hair as she tilted her head to scribble dates on library cards. She noticed me as soon as I entered the library. I didn't know what to expect from her, but I was thrilled to see her beaming face. She glanced at me as she wrote on cards and answered questions, waiting for the right moment to approach me.

Shirin turned to a student she was helping. "Why don't you search under ecosystem, under I, for Iran, while I talk to another student?"

"Yes ma'am," the girl said.

Shirin rose from her seat and signaled for me to follow her out of the library. I felt a cannonball sink deep in my stomach. Where was she taking me? It scared me to follow her, but I couldn't bring myself to stop. It was as if she had an invisible leash around my neck. She strolled along the corridor without saying a word. Girls rushed around, bumping my shoulders right and left as I trailed after her. She stopped in front of the prayer hall, searched her pockets, and brought out a key chain to open the locked door.

"What did you do at home last week?" she said as she turned the key and opened the padlock with a click.

"I . . . I . . . helped my Agha Joon pick sour cherries. My grandma makes jams in May."

"Did you help her make jams?"

"Yes. I pitted the sour cherries for her."

She paced toward the mihrab and then straightened the creases of her manteau as she kneeled and sat on the prayer rug.

"You like jams?" She smiled, loosened the tie of her scarf under her chin, and took it off her head. I saw her full braided hair for the first time as she pulled the long braid forward and let it fall on her breast. She combed her fingers through the hazel highlights on top of her head.

"I like the sour cherry jam," I said. "Fig jam is the worst with its tiny seeds."

She tapped her finger on the prayer rug. "Sit."

I kneeled and sat down in front of her. The tall windows of the prayer hall were behind her, and the milky light seeping through the sheer curtains created a crisp silhouette of her against the window. She looked misty, curved, and thin. The prayer hall seemed to loom larger than it had on other days. No one was singing prayers or giggling at jokes before the noon service started. The strange silence amplified my anxious thoughts.

"What did your parents say?" she whispered in her soft voice.

I hesitated to answer. I didn't want to describe the shameful moment with Baba and Maman.

"Did they punish you?"

I nodded.

"Were they astonished when they saw the books?"

"Yes. They were both shocked. My mom kept asking how I smuggled the books out of school."

"Did they find out about Anna too?"

"Yes. Baba read all my notes out loud . . . Ms. Shirin . . ." I tried to find the courage to ask the question that had been bothering me for a long time. "Can I ask you something?"

"Go ahead," she said.

"How did you know I love *Anna Karenina*?"

She chuckled. "You think it is hard to figure *that* out about you?"

"But I never spoke with you about that book, or about the other Russian novels I read."

She sighed. "Was your father angry when he saw your notes?"

"He was furious." I lowered my head and stared at the woven flowers on the prayer rug. I became certain she knew everything. She must have visited the attic after us and noticed the missing books. I wondered if she had intentionally stacked those novels in front of the trapdoor to be picked up first. Did she flap her fingers in the air to lead me to the attic and lure me into reading those books?

"Moji, it's hard to bear the moment your parents discover your secret world. I know the embarrassment and the anxiety. But I am so glad Ms. Zadie didn't realize some books were missing, or you wouldn't have been able to come back to school."

"I didn't want my dad to read the lines I'd marked. I wanted no one to read my notes."

"I know, Moji," she said. "I know." I couldn't make out the expression on her face, but her voice was as calm and serene as ever.

"I was ashamed." I burst into tears. I tried to wipe off the tears with the ends of my scarf.

She took my hands off my face and caressed the corners of my eyes with her fingertips. "My dear Moji," she whispered as she dabbed the teardrops on my skin. Her icy fingers calmed my burning cheeks. She hugged me and caressed my hair that was slipping out of my scarf. I closed my eyes and listened to the music of her life, the soft whistle of air moving in and out her lungs. Her breathing lulled me into tranquility. I smelled the addictive scent of her myrrh perfume on the nape of her neck where I could see the feathers of her tattoo. She smelled sweet like the honeysuckles that grew in Agha Joon's garden in spring.

She held me to her bosom for a long time, longer than any namaz I'd whispered in that prayer hall. Her hug captured me and pulled me out of misery. It soothed my aching heart like the thick, dark honey Azra applied to our open wounds, which had a tingling burn at first but then healed the ailing skin. Part of me wanted to shelter in her chest and hold her forever. But the other part feared this cunning, tattooed girl who might have planned to trap me in a situation only she could cure. She was leading me into a murky path where I wasn't familiar with the twists and turns. I couldn't see where she was heading, but I was charmed by her soothing words and her attractive mystery.

The Quest to Mount Qaf

*Thou must know that the lord Solomon committed this
castle to my charge and taught me the language of birds
and made me ruler over all the fowls which be in the
world; wherefore each and every come hither once in the
twelvemonth, and I pass them in review: then they depart.*

———————

"The Story of Janshah"

One afternoon in September 1984, a week after we had gone
back to school, our Persian literature teacher took us outside to
hold the class under the mulberry trees. Because she was short,
Ms. Talebi always wore orthopedic platform shoes to school.
She was the only teacher who would wear those prescription
shoes, since at that time in Iran—five years after the Islamic
Revolution—women could only dream of wearing any type of
raised heels in public places.

She asked us to write a passage about an event we remembered. "Be specific and use details," she said, and her plummy
cheeks became more prominent as she smiled. I scribbled down
the words floating in my mind. My story was about Amir's funeral and the blood fountain I'd seen at the center of the martyrs' block in Behesht e Zahra.

It started raining before I finished my piece, making the girls
chuckle about being outside and getting wet under the mulberry trees. Even though I was the last girl to put down my pen,
I raised my hand to share my writing with the class. Ms. Talebi

silenced the chatter and asked me to read before we moved our stuff back inside. The girls became quiet as I read my piece, and the bustle of returning to the class came to a halt. Ms. Talebi walked toward me and took the paper from my hands. Drops of rain that had fallen from the mulberry leaves made small spatters on my paper, dissolving letters here and there. She glanced at my writing and said, "I need to see you after class."

After the tragic event of the hidden books, I dreaded going to the administrative building. From the moment Ms. Talebi finished her sentence, I worried I'd written something wrong in that piece. I blamed myself for volunteering to read when everyone wanted to rush back to class. My heart began racing as I neared the administrative building on the opposite side of the schoolyard. I stood near the teacher's lounge and hoped Ms. Talebi would see me once she finished talking to another teacher.

"Come in, Moji," she said as soon as she noticed I was standing at the door. "We were talking about you!"

I slogged my way through the lounge and kept my eyes sewn to the tiles. Teachers were holding glasses of tea and talking around a big circular table in the center of the room. Some teachers were sitting in armchairs placed against the walls. I wished Ms. Talebi was closer to the door and hadn't hollered my name across the lounge. She asked me to sit next to her in an empty chair.

"Ms. Shirin came to me the other day and asked for my recommendation for the Dawn Ceremony project."

I stood in front of her in silence, hesitating to sit in a teacher's chair.

"You're writing well, Moji," she said. "All of us in Persian literature group have noticed this. Ms. Shirin wants to direct a play, and she's asked us to recommend someone who can write the script. I had you in mind, and today, after hearing what you wrote in the limited time you had, I think I can recommend you with confidence." She rose from her seat to take a glass of tea from the large tray the school caretaker had just brought in. Her high heels clacked as she paced toward the center of the lounge. She came back with a steaming glass of tea in hand and said, "You like the idea?"

"Oh, I, I'd be happy to help, but I've never written a play in my life."

"You think we expect you to be a writer from the time you were in a crib?" she burst out, the tea in her glass tilting, almost spilling on her manteau. "Don't worry, we can help." She took a sip of her tea and said, "Do you remember the book of poetry called *Mantiq-ut-tayre* by Attar? Don't you dare say no, since I've talked about it in the history of Persian literature class many times." She jolted with laughter.

"Yes, Ms. Talebi, I do remember."

"She wants to create a play based on that story. So, you need to read the book if she decides you're going to write the play."

"I haven't read anything from Attar," I said.

"I know. I don't think you can read that book on your own." She slurped the remainder of the tea and said, "Start reading the book and skip the prologue and epilogue for now."

The drizzle that had started during the literature class turned into a storm. Frenzied wind whirled the gold and amber mulberry leaves around the trees and piled them up against the rusty brick wall. I was enthralled by Ms. Talebi's exciting news. My literature teacher's confidence in me was encouraging. Like the fallen leaves, I wanted to twirl in the rain, spin until I was drenched, and drop completely soaked under the mulberry trees. I was chosen to write the play with Shirin! She had left her library position to become the developmental counselor who oversaw our extracurricular activities for the new school year. To work with her on a script was like a dream.

———————

A week after my conversation with Ms. Talebi, Shirin introduced the idea of the play to our class. She summarized the story as the journey of a thousand birds to Mount Qaf and their quest to find Simorgh, the majestic king of the birds. "Out of one thousand birds that started the journey, only thirty birds reached Mount Qaf, and only in unity were they able to find Simorgh." We were all intrigued by the idea of acting out the play.

Nadia raised her hand in utter delight and asked, "Have you thought of what we should wear?" She was the fashionable girl among us and always wore trendy dresses to private parties. We knew that from the photos she sneaked into the school.

"Of course!" Shirin said. "For such a huge play, we need to have attractive makeup and shimmering dresses for the actors. As charming as the birds look in nature."

"Can we bring makeup to school?" Nadia gaped in astonishment. Cosmetics had become a great taboo after the Islamic Revolution. Using makeup was considered seductive, so it was forbidden for girls to use it in public. The school administration repeatedly told us it was shameful and disgusting for a Muslim woman to paint her face when she appeared in public. They said a devout young woman was expected to use makeup only at home, for her husband. No student was allowed to bring makeup to school, let alone wear it in class.

Shirin laughed. "I know you're all interested in makeup," she said. "You can bring your moms' Revlon eye shadows and Lancôme lipsticks, with my permission, exclusively in preparation for the play."

Girls cried out in excitement, some snorting with surprise.

"But this doesn't mean you carry them in your bag starting tomorrow." She laughed again. "Or the next thing you say to Ms. Mirza or Ms. Zadie that I permitted use of cosmetics in school."

"What about the costumes?" Zara said. "Can we bring a décolletage nightgown to school?" She turned to the class and winked.

Girls burst into laughter.

"Where do you wear that kind of dress, Zara?" Shirin asked.

"Nowhere, Ms. Shirin. I've seen them in the movies."

"And where do you see such movies, Zara?"

"I mean, I heard from my mom, as she'd seen in theaters before the Revolution."

Shirin remained silent for a few moments. The girls became silent as well, not knowing how she would react. The school administration had changed the student dress code for more strict Islamic hijab observation after the summer break. Now we were obliged to wear khimars that covered our shoulders and upper chest, in place of the scarves we had loosely tied under our chins before.

"Listen, you girls!' she said. "This play is not about cosmetics and costumes, even though I know you all love that part. The story of the birds is an allegory, and I want you to delve into the meaning as you prepare for the play."

"How did you come up with the idea of this story?" Mandy asked from the last row in the back. She was a tall, bony girl who was popular in school and had gotten high scores in every subject the year before.

"Aha! I knew you smart girls would ask this question. You'll soon realize how the story is applicable to the current situation we live in. For now, I would recommend you to buy *Mantiq-ut-tayre*—Attar's book of poetry—or borrow it from school or the public library near your house and start reading it. Many of you might even have it at home."

"A book of poetry?" Zara asked in surprise.

Shirin squinted as if she was puzzled by the question. "I believe Ms. Talebi has already introduced Attar and his work to you. Hasn't she?"

"Yes, Ms. Shirin," Mandy said, "Zara doesn't remember. She doesn't like poetry. She likes films."

Zara, who was sitting in the middle row, turned back and gave Mandy a nasty look. Mandy ignored her and continued to look at Shirin.

"It's difficult to read, Ms. Shirin," Zara said.

"I surely understand. That's why I want you to start reading the book and do your best. You'll read and memorize the script for the play, which we've decided to ask Moji to write."

"How did you choose her?" Mandy asked.

"The Persian literature teachers recommended her. She writes well. Don't you agree?"

"Yes, Ms. Shirin," the girls said.

I blushed at that moment. I shied away from being conspicuous among the other students. It made me uncomfortable to be praised in class. I lowered my head and stared at my shoes, trying to avoid their heavy looks. I felt the burden on my shoulders, not knowing how I would write the play. Bewilderment engulfed me as I wondered whether I should have accepted the offer. It was the first time in my life I was going to be seriously challenged, and I was not sure I would succeed. There was also strangeness to Mandy's question that unsettled me. I tried to escape the reputation of being the teacher's pet to our developmental counselor. Most girls didn't like to be close to the school administrators, and even though I was fond of Shirin, I didn't want to be identified with her in front of my classmates.

———

The weather was still pleasant so I could spread a straw mat on the terrace, bring a pitcher of ice water filled with cucumber slices out with me, and read under the Corsican pines. I began *Mantiq-ut-tayre* at the first appearance of Simorgh, the majestic bird, in a moonless night. It was in China, Attar said, that a feather from Simorgh floated in the air and the rumors of his fame became known to man. Since then, every man kept an image of that feather in his heart, hoping to see Simorgh in his lifetime. Thus began the search for Simorgh, and men sought him in every country on Earth. How could a single floating feather create such chaos in the world? How could all the beauty be derived from that single fallen feather of Simorgh? I would read *Mantiq-ut-tayre* that afternoon and many afternoons to come. I would read so long that all the ice cubes in the pitcher would melt and fine drops of water would cover the surface of the glass and magnify the cucumber slices floating in the water. It was not easy to decipher the hidden meaning of the verses in the language of birds.

Even though Ms. Talebi helped me with the questions I had, the content of the book was far beyond my novice understanding of Islamic mysticism. I wondered why Shirin had picked this story for a junior high school play. The more I probed into the arguments the birds made to excuse themselves from the journey to Mount Qaf, the more I was surprised by their wayward explanations. The hoopoe, leader of the birds, told stories from human life to convince the birds to make the journey. People in those stories responded to their circumstances in stupid ways. The hoopoe could never convince me—how could he satisfy and move the birds? After reading the book for the third time, I began to feel the terror that fretted the birds. I gradually absorbed the dreadful ambience of Mount Qaf—the Simorgh's abode.

Wednesdays when we had free time at the end of the school day, I went to Shirin's office to read and edit the scenes I'd written during the week. I struggled with the hoopoe character. Every time I went to her office, she would pull a chair beside her desk and offer me the seat. I would read the hoopoe's lines, and she would shake her head and ask me to rewrite those sentences.

One time, I became so frustrated that I threw my pencil on the paper and crossed my arms. "Ms. Shirin, I'm not sure why you don't like the hoopoe's lines I've written. What's wrong with his answers?"

She leaned back in her chair and looked at me for a while. "I am afraid you didn't grasp the concept of Hoopoe's leadership."

"I've read the book three times. I am not putting anything in his beak that is not already in the book."

"I know. But something is missing in your dialogue. You need something that shows the essence of his role in the journey."

I sighed and stared at the lines on the paper. "I wish I'd never accepted writing this script."

"Moji!" Shirin said in a raised, irritated voice. "You're disappointing me. I thought you had the perseverance to perfect any work given to you. Am I wrong?"

"No. But honestly, I don't know what you're looking for in Hoopoe."

Shirin shook her head again. "That's a different discussion! We can talk about the hoopoe as long as you feel it's necessary, but to make an excuse in the middle of the task is what I don't expect from you."

The desk lamp had created a golden circle of light on the table. My pencil's shadow darkened half of the birds' names in the lines of dialogue. The hoopoe answered the birds on every other line. I grabbed the pencil, and the shadow disappeared.

"Let's read the verses where Attar talks about the hoopoe again." She leaned forward and reached for *Mantiq-ut-tayre* at her side. Her scarf was pulled back on her head so I could once again see the hazel highlights in her hair. Those hazel strands glittered under the desk light as she flipped pages in the book. She'd attached dozens of small notes to different pages to mark them, and she'd made notes in tiny script in the margins. She found the page where a bird asked Hoopoe why he was the chosen one. The bird's main objection was that the leadership position had been bestowed upon the hoopoe in spite of him having the same creation as other birds. *How come we are the lees and you get to be the purest of wine?*

"But I thought . . .," I said, interrupting her reading, "I thought the hoopoe was elected by the birds because of his capabilities. He was not chosen by the divine. There is a clear section about the election process in the book."

"True. And that is exactly what I want to tell you." She rose from her seat and scanned the bookshelf beside the window. The books were neatly organized on the shelves, starting from the thick, glossy hardcovers to the thin paperbacks. Some of them had English titles. I always wondered how well she knew English. Most of the books had small papers jutting out of their top edges, like flat birds sitting on a slanted power line. She kneeled to get a closer look at the bottom shelf. She pulled out a couple of books and then pushed them back in their spots. "It used to be here," she said, shaking her head. "I can't find it now."

"What are you looking for, Ms. Shirin?"

"I wanted to show you an image of the hoopoe I had in one of my books." She suddenly knocked her head with both hands. "Oh, I remember now, I took that book home." She came back to her seat and said, "In that calligram, which is basically calligraphy in the shape of a bird, Allah's name—the word *Bismillah*—is depicted in the hoopoe's beak. It is referring to the Koranic verse about the hoopoe. In King Solomon's story in the Koran, the hoopoe is the king's messenger. I'm sure you've come across the relation between the hoopoe and King Solomon as you've read the poems."

"Yes, that's his given name in Attar's book, the 'Solomon's bird.' But what does that calligram have to do with—"

"On some occasions, Moji, an image can tell you a thousand words. Divinity, my dear, is something that is bestowed upon certain individuals and not achieved by human effort."

"What do you mean, Ms. Shirin?"

"I mean it is true that the birds choose their leader in the story, but they could have not chosen anyone but Hoopoe. The divinity had fallen upon the hoopoe from the day he was born. The birds only acted to reveal his true identity."

I must have had the most puzzled look on my face, hearing that explanation from her. "I know it's surprising for you," she said, "but what you are missing in your lines of dialogue is this. The process of election in Islamic theocracy is totally different from the election process in Western societies. We only cast our votes to reveal the one who is already chosen by Allah."

"So, who is choosing the leader? Allah or us? I am confused."

"We are and we are not. Allah reveals His choice through us. The hoopoe in the story of Attar is the chosen one, the flawless and perfect bird capable of leading the flock to Simorgh. The birds only happen to unveil his destined role."

She opened a whole new world in front of me at that moment. I wondered if all I'd learned about the role of human effort in pursuing perfection was wrong. "Is that why you said this story has never been as relevant to our society as today?"

She smiled. "You got it, Moji. You got it just right. We are the birds, Imam Khomeini our hoopoe in the quest for Allah."

I remained silent for some time, gazing at the golden streaks in her eyes. The question of Khomeini haunted me once again in her office. I never identified with people who loved Khomeini so much. I believed there was a sort of derangement in their emotional perception and their chain of thought, loving this man to the point they sacrificed their whole lives for him. But at that moment, I could see why millions of Iranians revered this clergyman, this ayatollah. He was the ultimate leader who was destined to guide them in their quest to Allah. And didn't *ayatollah* mean *sign of God*?

I was so behind with the play's revision that Shirin invited me to her house to finish the script with her on Friday. Aside from visiting my fifth-grade teacher for her daughter's birthday—who happened to be my classmate—I'd never stepped foot into my teachers' homes. Maman was aware of the writing process, so she gave me permission to go to Shirin's house. To my surprise, Maman offered to drive me to Shirin's apartment, even though it was in the western part of Tehran. She lived in Ekbatan—one of Tehran's newly built apartment complexes at that time.

We arrived early in the morning. Maman parked the Beetle in the parking lot in front of the building and pushed the doorbell button beside Shirin's apartment number. Shirin answered the buzz and opened the lobby door for us. As we rode the elevator up to Shirin's floor, I could hear my heart throbbing in my ears. I tried to stay composed, not wanting Maman to notice my anxiety. But how could I keep calm when I was about to see Shirin in her house?

Maman clapped the door knocker, and after a few seconds, Shirin appeared at the door. She was wearing a snow-white floral dress without any headscarf. Maman had never seen Shirin in person. All she knew about her were my scattered anecdotes of my encounters with Shirin at school. She was warm and welcoming and invited Maman in for a glass of tea, which she eagerly accepted. I was certain she wanted to inspect the house and the people living in it to make sure I would be safe there.

We stayed in the living room while Shirin went to the kitchen to prepare the tea. Framed photos of two army soldiers hung on the wall. One of them appeared younger than the other, but there was a striking resemblance between the two. They both had dark eyes and bushy beards, one grizzled and the other as black as hot tar. I noticed the LA insignia on the chest pocket of both men's uniforms.

Maman pointed at the pictures and asked in a hushed voice, "Her family members are in the Revolutionary Guard?"

I didn't know.

Shirin returned with two china teacups and a bowl of sugar cubes on a serving tray. I glanced at her as she stooped and held the tray in front of me. The brilliant blue roses on her dress matched her oval zircon earrings. The dress had a tight waist, and the hemline of its full skirt kissed the naked shin above her ankles.

"Thanks for bringing Moji here. I'm sure it will help her immensely to finish the script." She placed the empty tea tray on the wooden coffee table and sat in front of Maman.

"You're welcome, Ms. Shirin. I hope everything goes well with the play."

"Hopefully it will. The girls are enthusiastic about it. They can't wait until we start rehearsing."

Maman finished her tea and placed the empty cup in the saucer on the side table. She started playing with the edges of the silk scarf she'd placed on her lap. "Hopefully we haven't disturbed your family this early in the morning."

"Oh, not at all," Shirin said. "Nobody is home except me. Mother goes to Behesht e Zahra every Friday morning. She wants to talk to her martyred husband and son."

"I am very sorry, Ms. Shirin," Maman said in a low tone.

"Thank you." She glanced at her father's photo and said, "He died two years ago in Kurdistan. My brother was beheaded one month after him, also in Kurdistan." She bit her lips, her hands squeezing the blue roses of her dress.

"How horrible!" Maman said. Her gaped mouth and fixed

gaze on the photos showed her utter surprise. "I'm so very sorry to hear this. It must've been terribly hard for you and your mother."

The corner of Shirin's lips lifted in a bitter smile. She turned her eyes toward the window and looked at the bare chinar trees outside. "Mother misses them a lot. She spends every Friday with them. That's her way of coping with their absence."

"So hard, so sad." Maman shook her head.

I had never heard Shirin talking about her family. I was shocked to find out she'd lost her father and brother. She had never made a reference to their martyrdom. In the past two years, in every single ceremony we had about the war between Iran and Iraq, she had remained silent, with not even one teardrop filling her eyes. I wondered how she could be so resilient about such a horrifying disaster.

"Would you like some more tea?" Shirin asked to change the subject.

"Oh, sure. Thank you," Maman answered. I could tell she was dying to find a private moment to talk to me. As soon as Shirin left, Maman rose from the sofa and came to me. "What a horrible story!" she whispered. "Did you know any of that?"

I shook my head.

"Most probably they were killed by the Kurd secessionists in guerrilla combat. They must have been devout Islamic Revolutionary Guard members. Not everyone goes to those areas of the border." She cupped her face in her hands and sighed loudly. "I don't want you to come here again," she said in a hushed tone.

I nodded and said nothing. My jaws were locked. We heard Shirin's wooden sandals clacking on the parquet floor as she came back to the living room. Maman rushed back to her seat and grabbed her scarf. Shirin had fresh cups of tea on the tray.

"Ms. Shirin, I have to pick up Moji's sister from her volleyball practice. I'm afraid I can't stay for another cup of tea." She tied her scarf around her neck and picked up her purse from the sofa.

Shirin placed the tray on the coffee table. "Bashe, that's fine. Thanks for bringing Moji here today."

Maman hurried to shake hands with Shirin and kissed my forehead before she left. "Call me as soon as you're done!"

I hadn't spoken a word since I'd come to Shirin's house. Even after drinking the tea, my mouth felt completely dry. I pressed my hands against my thighs to keep them from trembling. I rose from the sofa as soon as Shirin returned to the living room after walking Maman to the door. She motioned with her hand for me to sit. The silence in the room was suffocating. I could hear the cars that parked outside and turned off their engines. I didn't know what to tell her. What word of condolence could spring out of my mouth? Did she even want me to refer to those frames hanging on the wall? What about Maman's warning? Why didn't she want me to come to Shirin's house again?

"Are you done with the final scene?" Shirin said, tearing me from my chain of thoughts and bringing me back to the room.

I nodded.

"Then let's go to my room and start."

I followed her down a dark corridor that led to her bedroom. Nothing decorated the corridor, and it was so dark that I couldn't guess the color painted on the walls. We passed a bathroom and a bedroom. From the half-open bedroom door, I saw a picture of a young couple in wedding clothes hanging beside an oval mirror. The dark violet bed cover had been neatly made. Her mother must have woken up early to make the bed and tidy up the room before she left. Once we reached the far end of the hallway and Shirin twisted the doorknob to open the bedroom door, bright light flooded the corridor.

I could have never imagined what I saw in that room. Intricate Persian calligraphy adorned every inch of the walls. Birds in different shapes perched on tiny tangerine twigs, each bird made of curved Persian alphabet letters that spooned one another with compassion and care. The birds were drawn in delicate pen and ink, in every possible shade of blue. No doubt Shirin had spent hundreds of hours depicting those letter-made birds on their boughs. Images of birds and flowers were woven into the carpet, and books were strewn on top of it like bowls of ambrosia for the heavenly birds. *Mantiq-ut-tayre* nested at a higher level, on the royal blue and ivory quilt of her bed.

Shirin pulled out the chair behind her desk and pushed aside the ink pen collection to create more space. A stack of calligraphy stencils occupied the corner of the desk and ink jars lined up in a row along one edge, almost touching the wall. From lapis to lazhuward to irtyu, her room brimmed with different shades of blue. Why had I never noticed so much blue in her before? Pungent aromas of henna and brown sugar wafted from a ceramic bowl covered with a plastic wrap. The henna paste looked fresh, like it had been made early that morning.

"Sit here, Moji. I hope the scent of henna doesn't bother you." She took the ceramic bowl from the desk and placed it on the nightstand.

"Not at all," I said, "I'm used to it. My grandma colors her hair with a mix of henna and coffee powder. I love the smell of coffee in her mix."

She sat on the quilt, propped the pillow against the wall, and rested her head on the pillow. "My ears are yours."

I read the last act I'd written out loud. Every word I uttered brushed more anxiety off my chest, and I felt peaceful once again. We worked all morning and a couple of hours after lunch. She believed I had nicely represented the unification of thirty birds to become Simorgh at the end of the quest in the final scene.

"I love how you pictured the hoopoe as the front part of Simorgh. Oh, I remember . . ." She jumped down from the bed and fetched a book from the floor. "I wanted to show you this the other day."

The book was about the Islamic art of calligraphy. She placed the book on the desk and flipped the pages to find the image. There on a sheet of straw-colored paper was an outline of a bird drawn in black and gold ink. A small crown of feathers characterized the bird as the hoopoe. With his head craned backward, he was looking at his black, bold wing. Inside the wing, three cedars had grown in different directions—a symbol of the hoopoe's abode. Tiny golden curls embellished the torso and the long, curved neck, and the word *Rahman*—the merciful—stretched from his back all the way to his eye. The tail feathers flared ostentatiously in every direction, and the word *Bismillah*—as Shirin had told me at school—was written on his beak in fine black ink.

"Amazing," I said.

She nodded and came closer to the desk. She leaned over me to reach the stack of stencils at the corner. The blue roses on her dress kissed my cheek. From the stack, she pulled the stencil copy of the hoopoe image she'd just shown to me. She had carved out the curved alphabet on the bird's torso. I remembered the tattoo of the mysterious bird on her neck.

"I learned this art from my paternal aunts during the years we visited them in Abadan." She sighed and slid her long fingers on the stencil's inner curves. "They used to draw floral patterns on my hands. But I animate my calligraphy and draw birds. It's soothing to bring verses to life by shaping them like birds. They become nice body tattoos."

"What bird did you tattoo on your neck?"

"Oh, the one I had last year you mean?"

I nodded.

"It was the Simorgh. Mother helped me print it on my chest. She knows how much I love my bird tattoos." Then she stared at my neck and chest for a few moments, measuring the sizes with her eyes. "This hoopoe pattern is new. Would you like to have one on your chest?"

I was astonished by Shirin's offer. To have a tattoo painted on me by my counselor was something I could've never foreseen happening at her house. At twelve, I haven't even pierced my ears. How could I have a tattoo on my body? I'd never even tried my grandmother's henna on the tips of my nails—how could I let Shirin draw a bird tattoo on my chest?

"I'm fine," I said. "Thank you!"

"It's only temporary. It'll fade in a few weeks."

She reached for my fingers and gently turned my hand to glance at the palm. A sharp, tingling sensation traversed my nerves as she mapped the lines on my palms with her fingertips. She uncovered my forearm with her other hand and patted my bare skin. "You have a nice skin tone, Moji," she said. "The henna will turn to an attractive auburn color on your skin. The cold, clammy feeling when it dries is relaxing."

I didn't know how to respond to her offer. What if Maman found the tattoo on my chest? What if a feather revealed itself under the first undone button of my blouse?

Shirin sensed my doubt. She retracted her hands and distanced herself by reorganizing the stencils on her desk. She closed the calligraphy book and embraced it to her chest. "You need to step in, Moji," she said. "The road to Mount Qaf is arduous and challenging. Remember the first of the seven valleys to Simorgh?"

My eyes were fixed on the row of blue inks. I remembered: the Valley of the Quest. It all started with a wanton desire. She was standing on my shoulder like a God-sent angel, holding a book to her chest, waiting for me to start the quest. I tilted my head upward and looked at her eyes. What mystery lay in those golden streaks that I could never say no to her? I nodded and surrendered in utter silence.

She grabbed the henna bowl from the nightstand and left the book of calligraphy in its place. From her closet, she brought a wooden box containing the tools for henna tattoo. She unfolded a cotton apron with amber stains all over it and wrapped the strings around her neck and waist. With strong, measured strokes, she mixed the henna into a smooth paste and poured the paste into a thick plastic bag with one corner cut off.

"You want to lower your top while I wet the towel?"

The hardest part for me was to expose part of my chest in front of her. I unbuttoned the top buttons on my blouse, pulled my arms out of the sleeves, and lowered it to right above my breasts, holding the fabric in place by squeezing my arms against my sides. Except for the times Maman scrubbed my skin in the bath, I'd never shown so much skin in front of anyone—and certainly not since returning to Iran after the Revolution. I always wondered how I overcame my sense of shame in Shirin's bedroom and let her stare at my naked skin. She collected my curls and created a bun on top of my head so that no strand of hair would fall on my chest. "Ready?" she whispered into my ear.

I nodded. I felt her icy fingers through the stencil paper when she glued her hand to my chest to keep the paper in place. I don't know if she felt the throbbing of my heart. Every minute I expected her to ask, "What's wrong, little bird? Calm down." But she didn't say anything and spread the henna paste in absolute silence. I struggled with shame, and my nipples became erect when her hands and wrists would brush my breasts as she applied the henna. But to my utter surprise, I didn't want her to stop. I enjoyed those soft, accidental touches. Unlike what she had claimed, I felt no cold sensation as the henna dried. Anywhere she spread the paste burned as if she'd placed a hot iron on that patch of skin.

After half an hour, she gave me a hand mirror to see the bird. The body parts of the hoopoe appeared one by one as she rubbed off the dried clumps of henna with the damp towel. He perched audacious and lively on my chest. The word *Bismillah* was imprinted on the beak, on the spot above my heart. I was ready to tread into the Valley of the Quest. I was marked to become a soldier for Allah.

Our Feather Vests

*And, when Janshah knew of his sire's command, he
caused the artificers to fetch a block of white marble and
carve it and hollow it in the semblance of a chest; which
being done, he took the feather-vest of Princess Shamsah
wherewith she had flown with him through the air: then,
sealing the cover with melted lead, he ordered them to
bury the box in the foundations and build over it
the arches whereon the palace was to rest.*

"The Story of Janshah"

On the way back home, I tried not to attract Maman's attention
while she drove. Occasionally, I bent my neck and peeked under my blouse. I wanted to make sure the bird was still sitting
on my chest. From my viewpoint, I could only see its rump and
tail. To see the beak, I had to get home and go to the bathroom.
The house on Sun Street had many mirrors in different geomet-
rical shapes decorating the walls, but the full-length mirror was
in the cloakroom next to the bath.

When we parked in the front garden, I told Maman I needed
a bath. Never before that Friday had I thought of the logistics
of bathing. I remember I often took a shower twice a week,
once on Friday, once during the week, sometimes with Mar
Mar, sometimes alone, and, rarely, with Maman. Bathing was an
austere, painful ritual in a Persian woman's life that we had to

master before she let us bathe alone. She didn't think we were clean until the dark gray tubes of dead skin grew larger as she scrubbed the coarse knit washcloth smeared with the white balls of sefidab exfoliating clay on our skin. Then she soaked us in a tub full of water treated with starch to soothe our raw skin. She had watched me bathing myself multiple times before she deemed my scrubbing sufficient enough to allow me do it without supervision.

I locked the cloakroom door and turned on the faucet in the bath. I didn't want anyone to suspect I was standing in front of the mirror, staring at my body. Maman always made the bath so hot and humid that a thick layer of water vapor blurred the mirror. Or perhaps I never before paid much attention to the reflection of my body while I undressed for a bath.

It was freezing cold in the cloakroom, making me reluctant to take off my blouse. The hot water pelted the porcelain floor tiles and splashed down the drain while the steam wafted the acrid scent of Azra's olive soap into the air. My fingers fumbled as I tried to take off the blouse. It took much too long for the hurry I was in. The hoopoe shone in its glory as I pulled off my underwear. Shirin had painted the bird perfectly. Each feather was distinct from the others in fine, auburn lines. He stared at me with the pride of a genuine beautiful bird in his eyes. There I stood, all naked in front of the clear mirror, staring at the image of my body previously unbeknownst to me. I had luminant, toned skin but hardly any curves. The backs of my hands were cracked from the bitter, dry cold. My waist was so narrow it looked disproportionate to my hips, and my calves lacked the seductive fullness of most young women's legs.

I slid my fingers on the bird's beak, the part Shirin had spent the most time painting. It was the patch of skin that still contained the feverish memory of her touch. I dreamed of her hands rolling on my skin, pressing my breasts. The feather lines snaked down toward the space between my breasts. I pet the hoopoe and slid the tips of my fingers down the longest feather and then continued down between my breasts and on to my naval. It seemed as if a thousand receptors lay in the triangle of skin below my naval and between my legs. I stroked that triangle of skin. The steam clouded the cloakroom and fogged the view of my naked body. I didn't want the pleasure that added up with every throb of touch to end. I could hardly breathe. Eyes closed, I didn't want to see anything. If only that moment could last forever. I sat down on the cold built-in bench in the cloakroom, lightheaded and floppy, not knowing exactly what had happened to me. How much time had passed? Was anyone suspicious of the shower that seemed to take forever? I flung myself into the bath and let the hot and pleasurable water run on my hair and my skin. It caressed my body and the majestic hoopoe that was now a part of my skin.

The play rehearsals took place on the school auditorium stage. Twice a week, for the last session of the day, we gathered there, and girls read and tried to memorize their lines. Shirin had assigned the roles based on students' physical appearance, their ability to recite the poems, and their acting talent. Closer to the show date, we stayed after school to get in even more practice. Mandy was the hoopoe, Nadia the peacock, and Zara the hawk. I was an introvert and fearful of acting and being the center of attention. Shirin knew that and never asked me to act. Instead, I helped the girls by repeating the script and the poems as they struggled to memorize.

One afternoon in January, a few days before the play, Shirin asked girls to wear the costumes they had brought to school for a dress rehearsal. In the dressing room backstage, two full-length mirrors stood in their metallic frames side by side. They gave rusty screeches as the girls looked at themselves while tilting the mirrors on their hinges. Stereo speakers in different sizes, black snaky cords, cans of spray paint, and boxes of decorating papers covered the dressing room's corners. Students' backpacks and costume boxes were strewn all across the large mosaic tiles as if an excavator had plowed the room for hidden gems. Everyone screamed with joy, jittery with excitement at taking off their veils and showing their hair. It was so unusual for us to see one another's hair, let alone to see our bodies without manteaus covering their shapes. I was surprised to see my classmates had grown taller and stronger than me. As they undressed, I noticed that many bra cups held bulkier breasts than what was visible underneath the loose manteaus. I was glad I didn't have to undress in front of my friends. Mainly because I didn't want to reveal the hoopoe perched on my chest. Compared to the luxuriant, leafy stems of my classmates' bodies, I resembled a bare bough. Nadia, who was fond of hair, shrieked in a frenzy as soon as Zara took off her khimar and pressed open her dented hair clip, letting her raven black hair shower her shoulders.

"You look absolutely gorgeous!" Nadia said.

"Oh, thank you, Nadia. My sister straightened my hair last night. I was hoping it would stay smooth until this afternoon. Your hair is pretty too."

Nadia combed her fingers through her dark brown hair, trying to untwine her tangled locks. "I use almond oil after the bath, or I can never comb my hair."

Mandy undid the last button of her manteau and said, "Imagine the beaks on our faces. I can't wait to see how funny we'll look with them." She looked at herself in the mirror, cupping her hands around her nose and mouth.

"Your eyes will sparkle like stars, no doubt," Nadia said.

"Moji, have you seen Ms. Shirin's calligraphy on my beak?"

Mandy stepped back from the mirror and stooped to open the costume box she'd placed beside her backpack.

"No, but I'm sure she has written the most delicate Bismillah on the beak," I said.

"How do you know?" Zara asked me.

"She is glued to Shirin. She might have seen it in her office," Nadia said. "They're like conjoined twins."

"Yeah, I figured that was why Shirin wanted her to write the script," Zara said.

"But that was Ms. Talebi's recommendation," I said. "Don't you remember?"

Zara shrugged and continued to brush her hair, as if she didn't hear me.

Mandy straightened her back and unfolded the tissue paper wrapped around the beak. The black calligraphic words emerged on the rusty-brown rolled paper beak. She pulled the rubber string attached to it behind her head and situated the beak on her face. The beak pressed against her face and made her cheeks look fuller. The Bismillah on the beak was prominent and easily readable. She recited a few of Attar's poems, loud and clear.

"Excellent, Mandy," I said. "You're so confident and prepared."

"Yeah, Shirin knew who to pick as the leader," Zara said. "But I'll give the hoopoe a hard time."

"You will get your answer for every question you ask," Mandy said.

Nadia had already taken off her spaghetti-strapped tank top. The fair skin of her nude torso glowed under the dressing room's bright lights. She slithered the emerald green maxi dress up around her waist and asked Zara to zip up the back of it. The dress clung to her body, especially around her breasts. The embellished lace on her chest and upper back sparkled as she twirled in front of the mirror.

"Oh, lá lá," Zara said with a thick French accent. "Boys will die for those breasts."

"Can you please stop?" Nadia yelled.

"Girl! I'm just complimenting you!"

"I don't like to be complimented like this. It is rude. I don't like it," Nadia said. "It shows a lack of female delicacy."

"Ok, dokhtar jan. I'm sorry!"

"Do you think I am like you, mingling with boys all the time? Changing boyfriends twice a year?" Nadia said, continuing to harass Zara.

"You're tough under that deceivingly soft skin. I pity your boyfriend!"

"I don't have one. And by the way, what happened to the tall skinny boy you had ice cream with last week?"

"Who dares to have a boyfriend these days?" Mandy pitched in.

"You mean Mehran?"

"Whatever his name is."

"We got caught by the Islamic Committee in Tajrish square." Zara laughed out loud.

"What?" Mandy shouted.

"My mom and his father came to the Committee headquarters in Tajrish and swore we were cousins. They let us go after they took a written oath from them."

"Aren't you scared you'll get hurt by those Committee guards?" Mandy asked.

"I'm not a mouse like some people," she said, and winked at Mandy. "And I am always careful. That one time was an accident."

"I am not a coward, if you're talking about me," Nadia said. "I act like a lady, not making myself available to every foolish boy. And I don't want to get expelled from school."

"Zara, she's right. Do you know the truth behind Mina's change of school story?" Mandy said.

"Yes," Nadia and Zara said together.

"No," I said.

"She was on our school bus and is our neighbor," Mandy said. "Apparently, Ms. Zadie spotted her with a boy in Vali-Asr Street after school."

"She was stupid, hanging around with a boy near school," Zara said.

"I saw her writing the boy's phone number on her forearm on the school bus. I told her it's dangerous to carry his number with her. She paid for her carelessness," Mandy said.

"Then you better be careful when you're having ice cream with your friends," Nadia said to Zara. "Lucky you live far from school."

"How about you, Moji? Do you have any fun besides writing scripts and reading *Mantiq-ut-tayre*?" Zara asked.

"Oh, for God's sake Zara, can you leave her alone?" Nadia said.

"I don't," I said. "I don't know any boys."

"She's small," Nadia said. She came close to me and pinched my cheek between her fingers. "But I'm sure she'll grow into an elegant lady. Don't you get her into your boy business."

"Good afternoon, girls," Shirin said as she entered the dressing room.

We turned our heads toward the door, surprised by her sudden appearance. We looked at each other, wondering if she'd heard our conversation.

"Are you ready?" she asked.

"Yes, Ms. Shirin. We are trying to put our costumes on," Zara said.

"You look stunning, Nadia." Shirin peered at her in her costume. "We need to have glitter on your face on the day of the play. A peacock should be perfect in her beauty."

"Thank you, Ms. Shirin."

"Where are your beaks? You need to put them on so I can listen to you recite the poems while wearing them."

She pointed at Mandy's beak and said, "It's legible and elegant on your face." She turned to me and said, "You have the scripts?"

I fetched the copies from the box I'd placed close to the door and distributed them among the girls. As they started reciting the verses, a hundred strings of questions laced my mind, one after another. I knew the poems by heart, line by line, but what annoyed me was the astonishing chasm I felt between me and my friends. We had all been selected to thrive in Farzan School, but what detached me from the world they were referring to in their chats? Was it because I was late to puberty and the female hormones hadn't had enough time to affect my brain the way it had theirs? Where was the zeal, the urge, the fascination to connect with, or the temptation to reach for the opposite sex?

I gaped at the bird-girls twirling around me, strutting from one side of the stage to the other, swishing their tails and chattering with joy, calling Simorgh over and over again. I wondered if they had delved into the mystical meanings of those poems. Did they know this was all a classy counterfeit to catch them? To make them tread into the Valley of the Quest? I wondered if they have stepped onto the path? Had they already nudged their beaks in the sea of self-indulgence and desire like me?

I watched Shirin as she trotted around the stage between the girls, repeating the verses, bringing the journey to life. She had taken off her khimar, and her long, braided hair was swinging as she paraded back and forth, adjusting the positions of the birds in each act. Of course, I had seen her many times when she was talking to me or directing a speech to us, but to see her graceful moves on the stage, her agility and her artful dexterity, filled my heart with happiness. Was it because of this fine, mysterious creature who had burrowed a hundred inconspicuous holes in my heart that I had paid no attention to boys? Was it because of Shirin that I had closed the shutters on letting the gleaming glee of girlhood into my life?

I wasn't sure what exactly happened to me in the cloakroom, but I couldn't talk to anyone about it—not even Mar Mar. I was ashamed, and it felt too personal and totally private. At the age of twelve, I hadn't got my periods yet, but Maman had briefly told us about the monthly bleeding since Mar Mar had got hers a few months earlier. Even though she was a year younger than me, she'd grown more and had become taller than me. I assumed this pleasure-seeking behavior had something to do with the changes happening in me, but I didn't know if it was related to the start of monthly periods or whether I was doing something harmful to my body. I decided to search the school library, but finding such information seemed unlikely to me. Other than the scientific books, I felt sure they had pulled other relevant books from the library.

One afternoon when the library was almost empty, I searched for sexual changes in the human body on the reference shelf. I fished out a few physiology books and browsed the pages that talked about the human reproductive system. Other than information about hormonal changes and female monthly cycles, I couldn't find much about sexuality or sexual desire. Disappointed by the science section, I looked at Books of Clarifications— or Risalas—at the far end of the library. Those books were written by high-ranking clerics about Islamic rituals for everyday life. During lunchtime talks with my classmates, I'd heard there were bizarre and ironic questions and answers written in them. Some older girls made jokes about the problems and laughed out loud when they described the situations. I shied away from those discussions, but I always wondered how open and straightforward the daily rituals mentioned in those books were. Sexuality was part of life, so I thought I might find information about sexual desire in them.

Among the mostly voluminous tomes stacked together in our library, the thin Risalas begged to be picked. With shiny and clean covers, pages that were never dog-eared or folded, they screamed their loneliness on the shelves. Hardly anyone borrowed them. The authors were clergymen with sophisticated Arabic epithets I couldn't even pronounce correctly. Khomeini's name sounded familiar among them. His Risala was available in many copies, so I picked one and dashed into a dark corner to find the critical sections I wanted to read.

For every single human action, there appeared a command in Khomeini's book. From the way a person needed to clean herself before prayers to how to bury the dead, there was a ritual described. There were sections about finance, traveling, breastfeeding, sex with women, men, and even sex with animals in that book. Page after page, I was astonished to find out even the most absurd human behaviors had a "what to do" explained next to them. I skimmed the sexual commands section, trying to find something about touching oneself. *Masturbation* was the term he had used. The commands were mostly written for men—only a few referred to women. There was a detailed explanation on how to rinse the body and wash away the languid state. But what jolted me in that lonely corner was the phrase he had written about masturbation. *Sin* was the word Khomeini had used. *Who shall play with oneself and seek indulgence in his body has committed a great sin.* I felt stupefied when I read how he said Allah hated the people who committed such sin and how distant those individuals had placed themselves from Him.

Wasn't sexual desire a natural reaction in our bodies? Weren't we supposed to grow into adult human beings capable of reproducing offspring? Why a sin? *A sin so great that provoked Allah's hatred?* At some point, I couldn't digest his words anymore. They were too harsh and too furious, like the picture I'd always seen of him, ready to punish or kill anyone he deemed sinful in front of Allah. I closed the book and placed it back among the other Risalas on the shelf. Baba and Maman never trusted this man in Iran's political events. Why should I trust his words in what seemed only natural to me? What about Shirin? How could I approach her with such a personal matter? Did she have the same opinion as the Ayatollah?

During the month of January, we heard the air raid siren wailing in the skies of Tehran. The fact that the closest Iraqi border was about eight hundred kilometers from Tehran made it hard for the Iraqi MiGs to fly in the Iranian airspace without being detected by radars. There had been a few air attacks, but besides hearing the news from the national radio and television and seeing the caravans of martyrs brought from the border to Tehran, we had been fairly secluded from the war. Hearing the sirens let us know that Saddam Hossein had expanded the war zone and included Iranian cities into the battle plan. The Iraqi Airforce launched a series of air raids over Tehran and several other major cities to retaliate for the Iranian offensive in Basra.

One day when I came home from school, I noticed thick blankets hanging behind the French doors from inside. I called Maman and Mar Mar when I entered the house, but no one answered. I heard someone hammering on the second floor. Maman, Mar Mar, and Saba were all in our bedroom, covering the windows with blankets. Saba was standing on the three-step stool, two big nails jutting out of her mouth. She had a hammer in one hand and the side of a wool blanket in the other. She had already punched a few nails into the blanket and was making a few more holes in the wall to hang the blanket in front of the window.

"Did you hear the sirens at school?" Mar Mar asked before anyone else, excited about the news.

"Yes. We went under our tables each time."

"We did too. Our school assistant said if the air raids continue, they might close the schools. She said we should listen to the radio every morning before we come to school."

"Same as us. What are you doing?"

"We have covered all the windows downstairs and most rooms upstairs."

"Mar Mar, can you give me a couple more nails?" Saba said. She had almost reached the other side of the window.

"They've asked us to cover the windows so that the inside light doesn't give away our location to the Iraqi jets," Maman said.

"Two Revolutionary guards came to our door this afternoon," Mar Mar said. "They had guns strapped to their shoulders. They wanted to talk to the men of the house!"

Saba stepped down from the stool and glanced at the window. Azra's striped red and blue wool blanket was punched in several places and suspended in the air. I wondered how Azra had let her delicate blankets be ripped apart like that.

"Do we have enough blankets to sleep tonight?"

Saba laughed out loud. "Azra has a cave filled with blankets and sleeping mattresses."

"You've covered almost all the windows in short time," I said.

"Well, when gunmen come to the door, you need to be quick," Maman said.

To have the Revolutionary guards come to the door and order us to block the windows was something that only happened to the houses on Sun Street. After our neighbor, Prince Shapour Gholam Reza left the country, the prime minister's administration occupied his palace. The security measures had tightened around our house, and people could not pass Sun Street and other streets in the neighborhood as easily as before. We all had to have ID cards showing our address for the Revolutionary guards handling the prime minister's security to let us in. Many times, our guests called us and asked Baba or Agha Joon to come to the security checkpoint to identify them and accompany them on Sun Street.

Later that night, we heard the air raid siren for the second time. We had finished dinner in the living room when the program following the eight o'clock news was suddenly interrupted, and a red notice banner appeared on the screen. A man's voice forcefully warned us that the air raid would happen in a few minutes and that we had to abandon our workplace and seek refuge in a shelter. Saba and Maman turned off all of the lights in the house in the blink of an eye. We all stayed away from the windows and gathered under the central staircase in absolute darkness.

Baba held Mo in his arms. Mo was afraid of the dark and started crying. Baba patted his back and tried to calm him down. "You're a young man, Mo. Soon you have to protect your sisters," he said.

Maman held Azra's hand and brought her to the staircase. It was hard for Azra to rush. "Ya Allah, Ya Allah," Azra whispered under her lips. She kept moving back and forth in her place, trying to keep calm. Agha Joon carried the handheld radio with him. He tuned into the national radio station on low volume so that we could hear the white siren signaling that the air raid was finished.

We stood silently, listening to the muffled sounds coming from the sky. We could hear the MiGs flying closer to us. After a couple of minutes, the bombs started hitting the ground, one after another. One explosion was so.loud and so close that it jolted us under the staircase. The house shuddered and a few windows shattered from the shock. "Ya Allah, help us! Ya Allah, save us!" Agha Joon shouted in the dark. Without a word, we all came close and clung to each other. Agha Joon grabbed my hand, Mar Mar clutched Saba's blouse, and Maman gripped Azra with one hand and Mo's feet with the other. At that moment, all the memories I had from that square area of the hall came to my mind. The night Reza peeked at the staircase window to see the moon, the day Baba twirled Maman in the air after his release, the call Azra received about Reza's battlefield injury—all the bittersweet moments I had witnessed in that corner of our house. My eyes brimmed with tears. We had come close to each other by the calamities descending from the sky. I couldn't believe that was going to be the end for me and my family, dying in an air raid in the house on Sun Street. I loved my family deep to my bones, and I didn't want a single scratch on anyone's skin. But we were among the fortunate that night, and when the white siren finally came, it was the music of relief.

I woke up early in the deep darkness brought to our room by the hanging blankets. I missed the view of the garden in early mornings when I would sit beside the window and listen to the hum of the pigeons walking on the ledge and the faraway croak of the crows. I would pull the curtains away to see the sprinkles of snow powdering the evergreen needles of the pines. The exhausting war between us and the Iraqis had moved further into our lives, penetrating our bedrooms and straining joy from us.

Later in the day, we heard about the number of homes turned into rubble and the number of civilians who died in the attack. We had no real shelter in our homes, and nobody knew when the fighter jets would fly over Tehran again, or where the bombs would hit next. Our house could simply be next. But surprisingly, Mar Mar and I weren't afraid of the raids. Maybe we were too young to grasp the magnitude of the attacks, or maybe we were raised in a constant state of turmoil, accustomed to threats happening every day. We had learned to ignore the menace surrounding us as a survival skill.

———

The Dawn celebration of the Islamic Republic's establishment continued in Tehran's schools despite the Iraqi air raids. *The Conference of the Birds* show was considered the hallmark of the students' efforts and was scheduled for the last day of the ten-day ceremony. Mothers were invited to see the show in the auditorium. Maman didn't want to come to the ceremony since she believed we should mourn—rather than celebrate—such a disaster in our country, but having observed my tireless efforts to write the script, she didn't reject the idea at once. "Why haven't they invited your dad?" she had asked after she'd read the invitation letter from school.

"Because girls are performing in costumes and are not wearing hijab for the show." She had nodded in surprise and said, "Maybe . . . then I shall see."

As the mothers entered the auditorium one by one, I stood on tiptoe to see if I could spot Maman in the crowd. I had reserved a seat next to mine for her since I wasn't performing and my work was finished backstage. She entered wearing her ivory manteau and with her sapphire silk shawl hanging loosely on her hair. I was delighted to see her in the auditorium.

Luckily, the red air raid siren didn't sound during our performance, so we didn't have to leave the auditorium throughout the show. A few times during the acts, I noticed Maman turning her face and staring at me. I repeated all the sentences the birds said in a hushed voice. She looked at me in admiration and surprise, as if she were seeing her daughter in a new light.

I wondered if she could believe her curious little girl had transformed into this studious young girl who had put in her hardest effort to comprehend the mystic words of Attar on the journey of the birds to Mount Qaf. I wondered if she could imagine what valleys her daughter had passed as a wayfarer on the path.

The show ended with a bang. Birds clung together as one, shaping the majestic Simorgh on the stage. They chanted the final verses of *Mantiq-ut-tayre*, celebrating their unification to become the king of the birds. Mothers unconsciously started to applaud, which soon transformed, guided by the school staff, into chants of Allah o Akbar. They must have been very excited, almost forgetting that now, in the Islamic Republic, Allah o Akbar was the way to applaud. No clapping, no cheering, nothing but the words of Allah.

Maman pulled me close and kissed my cheeks once the curtains came down. She embraced me in her arms and said, "Azizam, afarin. I am so proud of you, my dear Moji."

Even though I was plagued by anxiety, her admiration and affection peeled thick skin of worry from my heart. Her embrace always relieved me of my inner conflicts and strains. I dared to ask her if she wanted to meet with Shirin. "Sure, azizam," she said. "She has helped you a lot."

We passed a few rows of seats to get close to the stage where Shirin was still talking to a couple of girls. Maman stood beside the first row in the aisle, waiting for me to fetch Shirin. Girls were shrieking with joy, making it impossible for Shirin to hear me calling her. I stepped up onto the stage and walked toward her.

"Ms. Shirin," I yelled, "my mother wants to meet with you if you have time."

Shirin turned around and noticed me. I pointed to Maman leaning against a seat in the first row. "My pleasure. I'll come and meet with her," she said.

She hugged a few girls on the stage and then walked down the steps toward Maman. She shook hands with Maman, and after a few words of gratitude, she said, "You have a talented and hardworking daughter."

"Thank you, Ms. Shirin. I saw her efforts in reading and understanding the text. It was not easy for her."

"Absolutely. We love her manners in school. You have raised a fine daughter indeed."

Between their praise, I was hoping Shirin would mention something about the afternoon activity that day. The school staff was going to duct-tape all the windows to keep the shards of glass contained in the case of an air raid. I wanted to stay and help as it was my only hope to be alone again with Shirin, but she mentioned nothing about staying after school.

I barged in. "Are you going to tape the windows this afternoon, Ms. Shirin?"

"Yes." Shirin looked at me in surprise.

"Can I stay?" I looked at Maman. "I can help a couple of hours in the afternoon and come home with the metro bus before dark."

Maman was not in the mood to say no, and I suspected that after such a nice appraisal, neither of them would deny my request.

"Sure. But do they need students to help?"

"We always appreciate students helping," Shirin said. "But don't you want to go home with your mother and enjoy the rest of the day with your family?"

"I love helping our school," I said.

Maman smiled. "Well, if you like to help, of course you can stay. But make sure you come home before dusk."

———

For every new roll of duct tape, I detached the almost-impossible-to-find end of the tape with my thumbnail and handed the roll to Shirin or Ms. Mirza, who had climbed onto the stools placed beside the windows. There were a few other students like me who had stayed. One of them handed the scissors to the teachers as I handed the tape. From the top right corner down to the opposite left, Shirin unrolled the tape and stuck a wide strip of it diagonally across each windowpane. The constant tearing sound of the tape filled the room, along with occasional thwacks of the empty rolls hitting the floor. Nobody said much of anything other than the repeated success story of the show. I was losing hope. I couldn't find a moment to be alone with Shirin, and even if I did, she was extremely focused on taping the windows. I had never seen her so uninterested in me. She didn't make any eye contact with me, and that unsettled me the most.

When we finished taping the windows in the last classroom, it was getting cloudy and dark, and I still hadn't had a chance to talk to Shirin. I killed time until all the other students left. I was lucky none of them lived close to my house, or they would have offered to go home together on the bus. As I finished putting the scissors in the school office stationery box, Shirin asked, "Don't you want to go home?"

Last year, if I lingered around, she would have approached me and asked if I wanted to tell her something. Why wasn't she asking me anymore? Had I done something wrong at her house that she didn't want to get close to me again? After that Friday in November at her house, I was longing to see her alone. Many times, I had gone to her office hoping to see her, but she was always either busy with other students or not in the office.

"I need to talk to you, Ms. Shirin."

"But your mom is expecting you home before dark."

"I know. But it's important for me to talk to you. I mean, I have been trying to see you for quite some time. You've been busy."

"Okay then. Let's call your mom and I'll tell her I'll bring you back home this evening."

She suggested we go to a teahouse close to the school. She said there was something in that teahouse she would like me to see, and I agreed right away. It was the first time I had met someone outside school in a teahouse, and her offer was beyond what I'd wished for. To have tea with my beloved Shirin sounded like a dream.

The Kakh teahouse was in the middle of Palestine Street, a few blocks from our school. The revolutionaries had changed the name of Kakh Street to Palestine—in solidarity with the Palestinian people in their conflict with Israel—but the teahouse owner had insistently kept the old name. I had seen the new beverage ads written on its smoky glass display window when I took the metro bus home, but I'd never been inside. The first thing that caught my attention was a colorful mural facing the entrance. Shirin led me to a small table close to that painting, and when we sat down, I could see it in better detail. A handsome young man with a sliver of a mustache was lurking behind some shrubs, spying on three beautiful girls bathing in a teal blue sea. On the shore, there were three piles of feathers heaped on sand. At first glance, I thought someone had gutted the birds and left the feathers near the beach.

"I wanted to show you this painting," Shirin said. "Do you remember the story of Janshah and Shamsah from *One Thousand and One Nights*? This is a scene from that story." She glanced at the counter holding different types of baklavas and said, "The owner of the teahouse is fond of the book's stories and once in a while changes the painting on the wall."

Scattered images from that story came to my mind. Suddenly

I remembered those heaps on the sand were feathered vests of three fairies who had descended from the sky to swim in that teal blue sea. Janshah—the young man behind the shrubs—falls for Shamsah, the youngest of the fairies, with her perfect round face and long black hair.

The server, a tall young man with a Turkish accent, brought us the drink menu and greeted Shirin. "How do you do, Ms. Shirin? How is your sire?" Shirin responded respectfully and asked for a mint tea from the menu.

"Do you want to try the mint tea?" she asked

"Sure. I'll try whatever you choose, Ms. Shirin."

"Two mint teas with rock candies on the side, please." She handed the menu to the server, leaned forward, and placed her elbows on the table, her hands relaxing over the opposite forearms. She looked into my eyes for the first time that day and said, "Do you remember you mentioned *One Thousand and One Nights* in your entrance exam?"

"Yes, I do. I was mesmerized by its stories."

"On the admission committee, Ms. Taba advised against you and argued that your parents had not supervised you well, letting you read a banned book that had inappropriate, adult content. I argued—against everyone's opinion—that they should accept you because of your curiosity and your honesty in telling us you'd read that book."

I clearly remembered the admission interview and the hesitation I sensed in the interviewer's words and tone. Shirin was alluding to something I had struggled to understand.

"Now, I am all ears, Moji. What's your question, my dear?" she said in a soft voice.

I gathered all my strength and looked straight into her eyes. The golden streaks in her irises bothered me more than ever. I wanted to ask about the Valley of the Quest and the sins a wayfarer may commit. I wanted to ask about the sin the Ayatollah had said would provoke Allah's hatred. But I didn't know how to tell her about my experience in the cloakroom, and I shied away from revealing it. So, I changed my mind and pursued the subject she'd brought up in the conversation.

"Why, Ms. Shirin? Why did you fight to get me into the school without knowing me well?"

The server brought the mint tea in two large glasses. He placed the bowl of saffron-tinted rock candies at the center of the table between us. Shirin picked two uneven crystals and threw them in her glass. The larger crystal cracked into smaller pieces as it reached the bottom of the tea glass.

"Why did you help to keep me at school when I was about to get expelled?"

Shirin nodded and twirled the teaspoon in her glass, staring at the rock candies dissolving in the mint tea. "Do you remember Janshah's story? How he treaded one thousand miles in demons' lands in search for Shamsah? Do you know how many years he struggled to find her?"

I didn't remember the number of years.

"Seven years. Seven bleak years." She took a sip of her tea. "Do you know why?"

I kept silent. I didn't touch my tea.

"Janshah saw a gift in Shamsah. He saw the golden sun in her heart. Do you see the glowing halo the painter has depicted around Shamsah?"

I focused on the young girl's face. Shirin was right. Unlike the other two, she had an innocent baby face with a button nose and a curved chin, and fine golden arrows radiated from her face.

Shirin drank the last sip of her tea and pushed the glass aside. There were still a few tiny crystals of rock candy remaining in the bottom of her glass. "Do you remember how Janshah captured Shamsah in the story?"

I glanced at the painting, hoping to find the answer. "He stole Shamsah's feather vest so she couldn't fly back to her family?"

"You got it, Moji! For many years, he buried the vest inside the marble pillar of the palace he'd built for her. Their carnal love lasted until she smelled the scent of her feather vest and discovered its hiding place. As soon as she carved out the vest, she flew back to her kingdom, and Janshah, in agony over his departed love, searched for her for seven years." She leaned back in the chair and continued, "You see, my dear Moji, we are all like Shamsah. We are ensnared by our sins. Until we find our hidden feather vest, we are captivated by the charms and pleasures of our bodies. We have to try and find it and fly back to our true home." She leaned forward, stretched her hand across the table, and patted my head, "And to answer your question, yes, I fought for you because you have that glowing sun in you, my dear Moji."

Suddenly, we heard the red siren outside the teahouse, signaling another air raid. The server turned on the radio on the counter.

"You should have taped the windows today!" the manager yelled at the server. "If this glass breaks because of a bomb falling near us, we'll be torn into pieces!"

We bolted from our chairs and sought shelter under the teahouse counter. The manager and server kneeled close to us in that small space. Shirin crossed her arms around me and held me tight to her chest, shielding me from the window with her body. Her long hazel braid pressed into my chest, working its magic and bringing us together at the most unexpected moment. Once again, I inhaled her faint fragrance of myrrh. A hundred memories were pinned to that scent, the moments I had lived beside this mysterious, tattooed girl who had captured my heart. In the darkness under the counter, all I felt was the warm body of my beloved Shirin. I wished for the air raid to go on forever.

Why would I ever want to search for my feather vest?

Lovesick

She shone out in the garden in garments all of green,
With open vest and collars and flowing hair beseen:
"What is thy name?" I asked her, and she replied, "I'm she
Who roasts the hearts of lovers on coals of love and teen."

———

"The Story of Janshah"

I spent most of the Yom Allah of 22nd of Bahman—the Birth-day of the Islamic Republic—ruminating over the talk I'd had with Shirin at the teahouse. The show was done, and I had no schoolwork to do over the holiday. With my Persian poetry study book open in front of me, I sailed between her words and docked along the hidden islands of meaning in our con-versation. There was certainly more to explore in what she'd said. I closed my eyes in rapture, reimagining and reinventing the minutes we spent together under the teahouse counter. The sweetness of the situation saturated me. I didn't want to leave the mattress, even when Maman called me for lunch. I didn't feel hungry. Azra had made aash reshteh—the family's favorite soup—and Reza and his family had come to visit. Between Mar Mar's yelling and Maman's constant orders, I had no choice but to appear for lunch.

The national TV station showed waves of demonstrators chanting "Death to America" and hailing the Islamic Repub-lic in turn. The narrator kept commenting on the bravery of the people who had attended the demonstration, even under

Saddam Hossein's brutal attack of our cities. *The whole nation is united against this coward puppet of the USA, the infidel Saddam Hussain.*

Saba had left home early in the morning to attend the demonstration. I was surprised to see Reza at home and not going to the Yom Allah ceremony himself. After he returned home from the front line, he seldom argued for the Islamic Republic with Baba. He was a fervent Khomeini supporter, and his being present for family lunch on such a historic day was surprising to us all.

Azra served the aash among talk about Saddam's air raids on Tehran. Reza spoke of the damage he'd seen in the area close to the bazaar—homes in ruins and civilians being pulled out with bare hands from mounds of white dust and broken bricks. I listened to him with a sense of indifference when he described the screeching ambulance sirens and the rescue teams running around the destroyed buildings. I was desensitized to news of human suffering after so many years of living in crisis. Like all the youth in my country who had experienced the terror of a bloody revolution and the scourge of a prolonged war, I witnessed catastrophe every day under the Islamic Republic. I was emotionally dissociated from the family conversations as if I were in a trance, hearing the horrible news but incapable of perceiving the pain behind it. I played with the noodles in my bowl, spinning them around the spoon instead of eating them. I couldn't eat a single spoonful.

Maman was the first person who noticed I wasn't eating. She narrowed her eyes and pointed to my soup with her chin. "You didn't touch your aash, Moji."

"Don't you like the aash?" Azra asked. She placed her bowl on the sofreh and bent forward to reach for the salt. "Do you need salt?"

"It is very delicious, Azra jan, but I'm not hungry."

Maman puckered her forehead in surprise. "You haven't taken even a spoonful," she said. "How do you know it's delicious?"

"I don't feel well, Maman. Maybe I am getting a cold," I said, hoping they would leave me alone.

"You see how small and withered she looks?" Azra shook her head. She pinched my arm to show everyone I had no fat on it. "You need to take her to the doctor."

"Doctors won't make kids eat, Azra jan." Maman leaned forward and reached with her hand to touch my face. She placed her fingers on my forehead. "You don't have a fever."

"She is not growing well. There is something wrong with her," Azra said.

Baba stared at me and raised his black eyebrows. Small wrinkles appeared around his lips. "Moji, are you not feeling well?"

I lowered my eyes and clutched the edge of the sofreh. I wished they would stop talking about me. I felt embarrassed being the center of the family's attention. "I am fine, Baba jan," I said. I took the spoon and force-fed myself. The noodles slithered down my throat like white worms. I gulped down the broth from the bowl, hoping it would wash away the filth I felt in my throat. But my stomach couldn't tolerate the aash. A few minutes after I placed the bowl down, I rushed to the bathroom and threw up all I'd eaten. It became clear to everyone that I was sick.

I spent most of the rest of the afternoon on my mattress—the most desirable place on Earth to me. Maman and Baba came to the bedroom after lunch. Baba sat beside me, took my hand, and pressed his index finger on my wrist to feel my pulse. He looked at my eyes and lips while he measured my heart rate. He asked if I'd eaten something suspicious the day before. Maman felt I had too much stress from the show, and I needed to rest.

But Baba didn't buy her idea and worried there might be more to the sickness than excessive stress.

"Maybe your mother is right," he said.

———————

Mar Mar checked on me frequently as I lay staring up at the ceiling all evening. She brought a glass of mint tea on a small silver tray. She placed the tray beside the mattress and spun the spoon to dissolve the rock candies in the tea.

"Azra says it's good for your stomach," she said. "She has crushed rock candy in it. Do you have pain under your stomach or your back?"

"None," I said.

Mar Mar slid close to the mattress and caressed my hair. "Why are you sick, Moji?" she said in her soft voice. I knew she didn't believe I had stomach flu. She sensed something deeper was troubling me.

My chin quivered. I could never conceal my feelings from her.

"What's wrong, Moji. Tell me." She bent forward and kissed my cheek.

Tears welled up in my eyes. I sniffed and tried to swallow the tears. "I don't know, Mar Mar. I don't feel well."

She nodded and dabbed the tears that had pooled in the corner of my eyes. "Maman wants to take you to the doctor tomorrow."

"I can't go with her. I have algebra and trigonometry class. I have to go to school."

She shook her head in despair.

I sat on the mattress and took a sip of the mint tea. The taste of mint tea and rock candy was forever linked to Shirin. I placed the glass back on the silver tray. How could I tell Mar Mar about the months I wrestled with my love for Shirin? How could I reveal the secret tattoo, the cloakroom, the longing for her touch and her hug, and the story behind the feather vest? I couldn't take more than one sip.

———————

The second trimester exams started in March, a few weeks after the show. I missed the chance to see Shirin every day since during the exam season we only went to school on exam days. Before exams, it had become a feverish habit of mine to wander around her office and peep through the door as she talked to other girls. After every exam, as soon as I handed my paper to the teacher, I dashed down to the administrative building to find Shirin. But every time I found her office closed. I would knock on the door a few times, but I never heard a response. I worried she'd become sick, but I didn't dare to ask Ms. Mirza or any other teacher because I was afraid my passionate love for her would reveal itself by seeping through my words. Distraught at her absence, I went home and prayed I would see her on the day of my next exam, but every day I despaired when I found the door still locked. Different horrifying scenarios haunted me through the days, but I soothed myself by thinking if something bad had happened to Shirin, the school staff would have announced it during the morning assembly.

I continued to have no appetite. I gave the food Maman packed me for lunch to the other girls at school, who seemed always hungry. Days passed, and I only drank a packet of apple juice most days, just to keep me from fainting during the exams. The appearance, the smell, even the thought of food made me sick. At dinnertime when I had to force-feed myself in front of the family, I slinked into the upstairs bathroom shortly after dinner and threw up everything. My cheekbones became more prominent, millimeter by millimeter, as I refused to eat. Yellow, thin, brittle hair replaced the dark hair on my skin.

After the last exam, I went to Shirin's office with a faint hope I would see her before spring break and give her the Nowruz greeting card I'd written to her. I found her door ajar and the ceiling light switched on. My heart started pounding in my chest, and I couldn't swallow as I peered through the door. No one was in her room. I sneaked in and took a deep breath, trying to ingest the scent of her myrrh perfume that remained in the air. I slid behind the desk, opened the *Atlas of the World* sitting on its surface, and ran my fingers across the teal blue seas and rusty mountains drawn on the maps. She must have rolled her fingers on the hills and hollows of that book. Everything she had touched excited my neurons and brought back my memories of her. Her name meant *sweet* in Farsi. She was the sweetest incident of my life—my redeemer, my love. She showed me the path a wayfarer must take to reach Mount Qaf. She taught me how to redeem a lost soul. I missed her so much.

"What are you doing here, Moji?" Ms. Mirza asked. She was standing at the door, her hands on her hips.

I jumped out of the chair. "Salam, Ms. Mirza, I . . . I . . . I came to see Ms. Shirin."

"Obviously! Why are you sitting at her desk? She's not here today."

"I came to see if I could borrow her *Book of Calligraphy* for the spring break."

"Well. She is not coming back until after Nowruz. She has gone to Germany with her hus- . . ." She cleared her throat. "Why do you need that book?"

"I wanted to practice drawing some calligrams from that book," I said with a broken voice.

"Okay. Why don't you take the book and go before your

school bus leaves? I'm sure she wouldn't mind me lending that book to you. I'll tell her when she's back."

"Yes, ma'am," I said. I leaped toward the bookcase, fetched the book from the lowest shelf, and fled the office as fast as I could.

I killed time until every bus disappeared from the school's alley. I roamed the streets around the school all afternoon. I couldn't digest what I'd just heard. How blind I was that I couldn't see this coming. I walked around the Kakh teahouse and paced Palestine Street many times. I wandered beside the teahouse, staring at the smoky glass, desperately trying to see the painting on the inside wall. The conversation between Shirin and the teahouse server when we were there that day slapped me in the face. He had asked about her sire. It didn't occur to me he was referring to her fiancé. It didn't register in my mind that her father and her brother were both dead and there could be no sire in her life aside from a future husband. How stupid I was to miss the clues, her distance from me the day we were taping the windows, her conversation about our desires and our sins, the hidden feather vest, all the details of the story of Janshah and Shamsah, the story of a departed love, the agony of Janshah in pursuit of his beloved for seven years. How could I not see this day coming?

It was late when I got home. I noticed the living room furniture being taken out to the hall. We had started spring cleaning a few days before, and now velvet bolsters, the TV and its stand, and all the coffee tables and vases decorating the corners of the living room were lined along the wall. Mar Mar was vacuuming the living room carpets with the electric vacuum cleaner, but she turned off the vacuum cleaner as soon as she saw me. Maman was standing on a stool, sliding curtain hooks aside in the ceiling track, and she had the damp, clean voile curtain hanging from one elbow. She turned her head toward the door and asked, "Where have you been?" She froze in her position on top of the stool. "Weren't you supposed to come home early today?"

"I didn't do well on my trigonometry exam," I said.

"Okay. But where were you all this time? I called the school office, but no one answered. School was closed early today."

"I walked around the school thinking about what I need to do for the final trimester," I said.

She placed the last hook on the track and released the snow-white curtain in front of the blanket covering the window. She knew I was lying. Her mother's instinct warned her there was something gravely wrong with me. "We need to talk once your father is back. You can't just come home two hours late and tell me you were wandering around the school, pondering your exam."

The damp voile curtain spread the fresh scent of bleach in the room. Mar Mar looked at me in sympathy and started the vacuum cleaner again. She didn't believe me either, but I knew she felt pity for me. I avoided making eye contact with Maman. It was useless to explain further. I was drained of any strength to argue with her. I wasn't even scared of her threat. What could Baba and Maman do to make my situation any worse than it already was?

Like the day I came back home from Shirin's house, I went into the cloakroom, took my clothes off, and stared at the reflection of my naked body in the mirror. Except for a few fine feathers on my lower chest, the hoopoe tattoo had disappeared. But the memory of her touch was still there on the fading lines of henna, tormenting me. I felt the pain of her absence in every remaining tail feather curl. Tears welled up in my eyes, drowning the last bit of Solomon's bird, the keeper of my secret love for Shirin. I turned on the hot water faucet and let the steam cloud the bath. From the bathroom shelf, I fetched the rough washcloth Maman used to slough off our dead skin and soaked it in the hot water bowl. I scrubbed between my breasts and flayed the skin that had nested the hoopoe for so long. I sloughed off the patch that housed the memory of her touch. Tiny drops of blood emerged as I rubbed the bristled washcloth on my skin, and it burned as if I had placed a glowing hot iron there. But as soon as I saw the blood on my chest, I felt relieved. Warm tears streaked down my face and vanished among the vapor drops covering my cheeks.

It was midnight when I woke up in my bed. I could hear Mar Mar's regular breathing beside me in deep sleep. I didn't know when she had come upstairs to sleep. She must have thought I was dead tired after the bath and didn't wake me up for dinner. I was thirsty, and my throat was dry. I couldn't even remember the last time I ate or drank anything. I wanted to go to the bathroom, so I placed my hand on the wall and tried to stand up. But as soon as I rose and took two steps, I felt dizzy and nauseous. I screamed Mar Mar's name just before I fell.

I have only patchy memories of what happened after that. I heard Maman moaning and calling my name, but I couldn't open my eyes or say anything. I couldn't move at all. I could only hear a distant melody, a sad tune someone was singing into my ears. I sensed Baba lifting me from the mattress and taking me downstairs. Even though I couldn't respond, I felt the position of my body in space. I have no idea how long passed, but later I felt a light flashing in my face, and I opened my eyes. I saw that the flashing light was coming from the streetlamps we were passing, and I realized I had never before seen the streets of Tehran from that viewpoint. Maman had placed my head on her lap in the back seat of the Beetle and was caressing my hair. I felt her lips kissing my cheeks.

"The emergency entrance is in the alley, not in the main street!" I heard her yelling at Baba.

"I know, azizam. Calm down!" Baba replied.

In the emergency room, I opened my eyes every time they pricked me with a needle. They had hard time finding my veins because of severe dehydration. The bright lights and white coats disturbed me, I couldn't muster the will or strength to answer the doctor's questions. I knew who I was. I knew I lived in the house on Sun Street. I knew I had lost my beloved Shirin. And all the pain of pricking and poking needles into my forearms was incomparable to the pain I felt of her loss in my heart. Their hopeless efforts could not quench the glowing flame that burned throughout my entire being. The heat of her love had parched me to my bones, and even if they infused oceans of water into my veins, they couldn't satisfy me.

A Yarn for Life

Tell Whoso hath sorrow
Grief never shall last:
E'en as joy hath no morrow
So woe shall go past.

———

"The Story of King Shahryar and His Brother"

I stayed in Sasan Hospital during the Nowruz holiday. The doctors in the hospital believed I was malnourished and needed a workup. My small stature, the amenorrhea—as they called my not having periods—and the fact that I showed the characteristics of a high achiever made them think I had some type of eating disorder. I never took them seriously about the eating disorder. I knew exactly why I was sick, but I couldn't tell anyone. I believed doctors didn't have the capability to understand that a young girl could have such repugnance for food. I received many bags of intravenous fluids during my hospital stay, and Maman and Baba came to see me every day. Mar Mar came with them once and brought a world of joy with her. Maman always brought homemade food for me because no Iranian believes hospital food will do any good for the sick, especially when the primary reason to stay in the hospital is an aversion to food. I remember staring at my plate filled with saffron rice, beef stew, and kidney beans for hours. I still didn't have any desire to eat.

"This is ghormeh sabzi, your favorite dish. Why are you not eating, Moji?" Maman kept asking me.

My parents withered day by day. I could read the anxiety on their faces. Maman begged to take me home every morning when she saw the doctor. She believed she could take better care of me at home. I wanted to go home, too. Who wanted to stay in the hospital when everyone back at home was enjoying Nowruz? I thought of Shirin every minute I was lying in that hospital bed, but there was no chance to get any information from her. A silent, pitch-black sea stood between me and her. I had no vessel to sail toward her, and even if I did, I didn't know in which way to go to find her.

Maman finally convinced the doctors to let me go home before my birthday. I had never been happier about being born during the Nowruz holiday. I always nagged and told Maman no one appreciated my birthday since everyone was busy celebrating Nowruz, but on the dawn of my thirteenth birthday, I took my words back. Maman told me they were preparing the main guest room upstairs for me.

Mar Mar opened the gate the moment Baba turned onto Sun Street. She was waiting for me, listening to every car engine that turned onto the cul-de-sac. As soon as Baba parked the car, she ran to the car door and pulled the handle. She hugged me before I even had a chance to get out of the Beetle, and her soft black hair enveloped my face and shoulders. I had missed the dimples in her cheeks when she smiled.

"Khosh oomadi," she whispered into my ears.

Mo jumped into the car as well, and the two of them knocked me down on the back seat. Maman appeared at the gate with the censer in her hand. The white smoke trailed her like a fluffy cloud as she walked toward the car. She took all three of us in her arms and swirled the incense burner around our heads. The crisp scent of espand brought back pleasant memories of the past—the prayers and pleas we made to heaven when a loved one left the house or came back. I never thought I would be the subject of one of those odes that ascended to the sky.

"Uncle Reza is here with his girls," Mar Mar said. "Sami and Somi are impatient for the cake."

The blankets had vanished from behind the windows in all the rooms. The Iraqis had stopped the air raids before Nowruz. The voile curtains glittered like pristine snow in the living room once again. Agha Joon had bought a new cream and turquoise paisley patterned rug for the living room, and its light blue hue gave a serene ambience to the room. Agha Joon and Azra were both sitting under the sunlight seeping through the voiles. I rushed toward them and embraced them before they attempted to stand. Azra had hennaed her hair, and the scent of the henna and coffee mix was still in her hair. Agha Joon had clipped his silver-thread kufi to his sparse, gray hair. He stroked my hair, pulled me close to his bosom and said, "Noore cheshmam, koja boodi? Where have you been, the light of my eyes? Your mom cried so much when you were in the hospital."

"Rang-o-root baz shode dokhtar," Azra said as she dabbed the skin over my cheeks.

Sami and Somi stormed into the room after Mar Mar. They were wearing matching red velvet frocks over long-sleeve white shirts. They both rushed up to me and clung to my manteau, which I hadn't taken off yet.

"Happy birthday, khaleh Moji. Are you thirteen now?" Somi asked.

"Azra, Maman is asking for the herbal teapot," Mar Mar asked.

"It's in the second-floor pantry," Azra answered.

I walked from the living room to the kitchen. Maman had peeled two fresh ginger roots and sliced them into thin pieces. She was about to place the water pot on the stove as I walked in.

"What are you making, Maman?" I asked.

"Ginger tea," she said. "It's good for your appetite."

"But I've never tasted it before. I don't like herbal teas," I said.

"I know. I'll add lime juice and honey to it. It'll give the sour-sweet flavor you like." She poured the thin slices of ginger root from the cutting board into the water. The blue flames under the pot spiked yellow blazes as tiny water drops spilled from the board.

Mar Mar came back to the kitchen with the herbal teapot. I remembered the time Azra made borage tea for Reza in that teapot. Mar Mar took off the lid and brought out the cotton tea infuser, which had turned purplish blue midway between the top and the bottom. Mar Mar smelled the infuser and said, "It doesn't smell like that yukky borage tea anymore."

Maman laughed out loud. "I don't need the infuser, Mar Mar. Leave it out. Just rinse the inside."

The water boiled in the pot. I had never smelled the aroma of the boiling ginger before. It had a pleasing scent. Maman lowered the flames and let the ginger simmer in the water. I stared at her while she stirred the wooden spoon in the brew. Fine pearls of sweat had emerged above her upper lip, and she had dark circles under her eyes.

"Thank you, Maman, for making this for me," I said.

She stole her eyes from the simmering ginger and glanced at me. "Baba has searched many grocery stores to find fresh ginger for you. Drink this. It's good for you."

––––––––––––

Late in the afternoon, we all gathered in the guest room. Since its lattice-framed door remained locked throughout the year, the guest room remained mysterious to all of Agha Joon's grandchildren. Mo and my cousins only went into that room when Azra opened it for Nowruz. They peeped at the guests who came to visit Agha Joon from the four windows facing the front garden. History was repeating itself—Mar Mar and I used to sneak a peek at the guests as they crossed the garden and walked up to that room. What made the room so elegant were two broken-mirror artworks facing each other on opposite walls. I loved to stand in front of the mirrors and try to count the infinite broken images of myself reflected on them.

Maman placed the *Tavalodet Mobarak* record on the gramophone Saba had taken out of her room after the Revolution. I didn't know how Maman had found that record. The gramophone worked better than the Phillips cassette player in the living room. The children danced to the song's joyful rhythm. Nastaran was wearing a light blue chador that day and wasn't holding the hems in a tight grip under her chin, and to everyone's surprise, Reza had shaved his beard. Neither Reza nor Saba objected to Maman's playing the prerevolutionary music. Baba brought the cake on a round silver tray, holding it carefully, trying not to drop the candles. The kids shrieked when they saw the cake with its cherry-mixed red jelly on top and thirteen spiral candles burning nice and bright. Everyone chanted along with the song and clapped for me to blow out the candles. The children helped me blow them all out in one long breath.

I don't remember what I received from everyone else as my birthday gift that night, but I do remember the moment Agha Joon came to the guest room wearing his pistachio robe and carrying his gift for me. It was his habit to bring a golden bangle or a small bracelet from the treasure box in his bedroom closet. He never wrapped his gifts or placed them in a gift box, but that night he came with a wrapped termeh that I recognized the moment I saw it under his arm. He sat beside me on the sofa and placed it on his lap. As he unwrapped the termeh, an old, bulky rectangular book with a brown leather cover appeared. Though its edges were soft, the spine seemed sturdy and stable.

The cover had no title on it, and the alluring picture of Shah-razad that had once been on the cover was no longer there. It was the same lithographic print book he used to read to me, albeit with a new cover. The papers were yellow and dog-eared on some pages, and they smelled of rose water, the scent of the books kept in old mosques.

"Do you remember the days I read this to you?" he asked.

How could I not remember? How could I not remember those bloody days of revolution when he used to read that book to me? Wrapped inside termeh, there lay every story I remembered from *One Thousand and One Nights*. As he flipped through the pages, the events of my uneasy past all came back to me. Every fragment of those fearful days was glued to the pages of the book. He found the page he was looking for and handed it to me.

"Can you read this sort of writing?"

It was a struggle for me to read the old text in a handwritten print, but I didn't want to say no to him. With a trembling voice I read:

> By Allah, O my father, how long shall this slaughter of women
> endure? Shall I tell thee what is in my mind in order to save
> both sides from destruction? "Say on, O my daughter," quoth
> he, and quoth she, "I wish thou wouldst give me in marriage
> to this King Shahryar; either I shall live or I shall be a ran-
> som for the virgin daughters of Moslems and the cause of their
> deliverance from his hands and thine."

"This book now belongs to you, Moji," Agha Joon said. He patted my back and kissed my forehead. "Pir shi dokhtar, I always wanted to give this book to you."

✳ ✳ ✳

Afterword

Every night Shahrazad came up with an inspiring new story to make her life last for one more day. Every night she spun a thrilling new yarn just to see one more sunrise from her window. I held my breath night after night, month after month, year after year, wondering how the story of one woman struggling to change her destiny would end. What conjurer of dreams or enchanter of magic must she become in order to outlive her dreadful situation? I wondered if she could pull through the thread of her life. I wondered if she could survive.

Decades have passed since the night I received *One Thousand and One Nights* as a gift. My Agha Joon is gone, and so is dear Azra and the house on Sun Street. The Islamic government seized my grandparents' house because of its vicinity to the prime minister's headquarters, and the street is now closed to the public for security reasons. I never saw Shirin after my thirteenth birthday. She left school to seek her life with her husband in Germany. Years later, when I graduated from high school, I heard from my friends that she'd returned to Iran with her two sons after her husband had finished his studies. She opened a vast new world in front of my eyes and introduced the principles of Islamic mysticism to me at a young age, but her love traumatized me for years to come. I dreaded falling in love again, thinking I would sink into that dark, loverless void that had tormented me. I was scared to lose a dear one once again because of the way she melted from my life like a snowball on an old charcoal stove.

I never sailed on a small vessel or traveled gravelly roads as my Agha Joon had traveled to Mecca, Baghdad, Cairo, and other ancient cities of the Middle East, but I kept Agha Joon's book on my journey from the motherland to America. He was the experienced, widely traveled man whom I was fortunate to know as a grandfather—the caring gardener who planted the seeds of storytelling in my mind by reading *One Thousand and One Nights* to me. I still keep his book bound in its old leather in a special place in my library. Every time the memories of the motherland conquer me, I take the book off its shelf, hold it close to my chest, and let the sweet scent of rose water emanating from its old pages fill my lungs. I touch its straw-colored papers and caress its dog-eared edges, the ones Agha Joon once touched. I close my eyes and picture us in his vast garden, on the divan where we used to sit—I hugging my dawn pillow and he with his sparse gray hair and white, glittering kufi—reading the love and betrayal stories of beautiful women and mighty kings. I would pluck a feather from my pillow and burn it to the shaft.

Agha Joon, I know! You'd always told me not to pluck my dearest companion, but who could resist the temptation to try to conjure up a magical ifrit? I am not scared of them anymore, but I'm still fascinated by their wondrous tales. If such creatures could exist, and if I could summon them at will, I would wait, dear Agha Joon, for the last flicker of the flame on the last barb of the feather to burn and for the ifrit's dreadful figure to appear. Once I felt the gravity of its presence around me, I would look for the images that appear in its belly. The ifrit would move, and its burning magma would melt the garden's terrazzo tiles. In the shapes of his blazing belly, I would spot myself as a middle-aged woman walking with a little boy on a wobbly, narrow bridge over the boiling magma. We're crossing over from east to west, and I'm carrying a book under my arm. Once, in a hurry to pass, the book drops on the bridge. Luckily the bridge's wooden slats are tight, and the book gets caught between them. I stop, free the book, and dust off the soot stuck to the cover. I lock the book to my chest with one arm and pull the little boy's hand with my other hand as we race to reach the edge of the creature's belly. There, on the monster's rocky liver, we sit side by side, our feet dangling from the cliff while the orange magma sizzles and gapes, seeking to devour us. But as I open the book, the inferno's frantic howl fades, and the soft sound of my voice reading overcomes the scene. The garden becomes quiet once again, and the sparkling Milky Way shines in the sky above. I read the thousandth-and-first night's story, when Shahrazad finishes the tale of Ma'aruf, the king. Shahrazad asks for a favor from King Shahriar, and when she is allowed to speak, she calls out to the nurse to bring her three children—one walking, one crawling, and one suckling. She says to Shahriar,

> O King of the age, these are thy children and I crave that thou release me from the doom of death, as a dole to these infants; for, an thou kill me, they will become motherless and will find none among women to rear them as they should be reared.

Shahriar calls the children to his bosom and grants her wish. He says in tears,

> Allah bless thee and thy father and thy mother and thy root and thy branch! I take the Almighty to witness against me that I exempt thee from aught that can harm thee.

I close the book and look sideways at the boy. He is looking at me with wide-open eyes, wanting to ask a question.

"Mommy, what saved Shahrazad from death? The stories or the kids?"

I pat his curly black hair. We have read these stories together for almost four years, from the time he hid his head under the pillow when he heard the name of the ifrit. Now he is old enough to embrace the beauty of mankind's imagination.

"What do you think, my dear?"

"The stories."